Dear Reader,

You probably think this book is about Cort Brannt, the brother of my heroine, Morie Brannt, in my mass-market Wyoming series called *Wyoming Tough*. Well, it's not. It's actually about the rooster who belongs to Cort's neighbor. A red rooster came into my yard several weeks ago. I tried to run him off, but he kept coming back. I discovered that roosters can fly, because he jumped a seven-foot high solid wooden fence to keep coming into my yard. I have lots of grass and a garden, which means bugs and worms and nice edibles. He wouldn't leave.

Over the weeks, people who work for me in the yard tried to catch him. Some of the neighbors got into the act. I especially wanted him gone because every time I went out to feed the birds or look at my garden, he would attack me. I was spurred three times, and I have the scars to prove it. So the rooster had to go. That presented a problem. I didn't want him killed or eaten, which left his fate up to me, since his owner apparently moved away and left him behind. (I don't blame him. If you knew this rooster, you wouldn't blame him, either!)

Our nice Mr. Martin, who looks after the koi and goldfish ponds for us, had a friend who knew how to catch chickens. He also kept chickens. So he just walked into the backyard, picked the rooster up and carried him off. My jaw is still dropping. Anyway, the rooster is very happy, has many hens to court and I am happy because I can walk to my pumpkin patch without being mauled on the way.

Cort Brannt is going to have the same problem. His nice little frumpy neighbor has a pet rooster named Pumpkin and she loves him. She loves Cort, too, but Cort loves Odalie Everett who wants to train as a soprano and sing in the great opera houses of the world. Ah, the eternal triangle. It will all end well, I promise. And Pumpkin will have a happy future. Just like my unwanted red rooster visitor.

Hope you like the book. It has roots in Branntville, Texas, and spins off from one of my first romance novels, *To Love and Cherish*. King Brannt is Cort's dad.

Your greatest fan,

Diana Palmer

DIANA PALMER

The prolific author of more than a hundred books, Diana Palmer got her start as a newspaper reporter. A multiple *New York Times* bestselling author and one of the top ten romance writers in America, she has a gift for telling the most sensual tales with charm and humor. Diana lives with her family in Cornelia, Georgia.

Visit her website at www.DianaPalmer.com.

DIANA PALMER

THE Rancher

&

HEART of STONE

HARLEQUIN®

entertain, enrich, inspire™

ISBN-13: 978-0-373-83785-4

THE RANCHER & HEART OF STONE

Copyright © 2010 by Harlequin Books S.A.

The publisher acknowledges the copyright holder
of the individual works as follows:

THE RANCHER
Copyright © 2012 by Diana Palmer

HEART OF STONE
Copyright © 2008 by Diana Palmer

Recycling programs
for this product may
not exist in your area.

www.Harlequin.com

Printed in U.S.A.

CONTENTS

The Rancher

CHAPTER ONE

Maddie Lane was worried. She was standing in her big yard, looking at her chickens, and all she saw was a mixture of hens. There were red ones and white ones and gray speckled ones. But they were all hens. Someone was missing: her big Rhode Island Red rooster, Pumpkin.

She knew where he likely was. It made her grind her teeth together. There was going to be trouble, again, and she was going to be on the receiving end of it.

She pushed back her short, wavy blond hair and grimaced. Her wide gray eyes searched the yard, hoping against hope that she was mistaken, that Pumpkin had only gone in search of bugs, not cowboys.

"Pumpkin?" she called loudly.

Great-Aunt Sadie came to the door. She was slight and a little dumpy, with short, thin gray hair, wearing glasses and a worried look.

"I saw him go over toward the Brannt place, Maddie," she said as she moved out onto the porch. "I'm sorry."

Maddie groaned aloud. "I'll have to go after him. Cort will kill me!"

"Well, he hasn't so far," Sadie replied gently. "And he could have shot Pumpkin, but he didn't…"

"Only because he missed!" Maddie huffed. She sighed and put her hands on her slim hips. She had a boyish figure. She wasn't tall or short, just sort of in the middle. But she was graceful, for all that. And she could work on a ranch, which she did. Her father had taught her how to raise cattle, how to market them, how to plan and how to budget. Her little ranch wasn't anything big or special, but she made a little money. Things had been going fine until she decided she wanted to branch out her organic egg-laying business and bought Pumpkin after her other rooster was killed by a coyote, along with several hens. But now things weren't so great financially.

Maddie had worried about getting a new rooster. Her other one wasn't really vicious, but she did have to carry a tree branch around with her to keep from getting spurred. She didn't want another aggressive one.

"Oh, he's gentle as a lamb," the former owner assured her. "Great bloodlines, good breeder, you'll get along just fine with him!"

Sure, she thought when she put him in the chicken yard and his first act was to jump on her foreman, old Ben Harrison, when he started to gather eggs.

"Better get rid of him now," Ben had warned as she doctored the cuts on his arms the rooster had made even through the fabric.

"He'll settle down, he's just excited about being in a new place," Maddie assured him.

Looking back at that conversation now, she laughed. Ben had been right. She should have sent the rooster back to the vendor in a shoebox. But she'd gotten attached to the feathered assassin. Sadly, Cort Brannt hadn't.

Cort Matthew Brannt was every woman's dream of the perfect man. He was tall, muscular without making it obvious, cultured, and he could play a guitar like a professional. He had jet-black hair with a slight wave, large dark brown eyes and a sensuous mouth that Maddie often dreamed of kissing.

The problem was that Cort was in love with their other neighbor, Odalie Everett. Odalie was the daughter of big-time rancher Cole Everett and his wife, Heather, who was a former singer and songwriter. She had two brothers, John and Tanner. John still lived at home, but Tanner lived in Europe. Nobody talked about him.

Odalie loved grand opera. She had her mother's clear, beautiful voice and she wanted to be a professional soprano. That meant specialized training.

Cort wanted to marry Odalie, who couldn't see him for dust. She'd gone off to Italy to study with some famous voice trainer. Cort was distraught and it didn't help that Maddie's rooster kept showing up in his yard and attacking him without warning.

"I can't understand why he wants to go all the way over there to attack Cort," Maddie said aloud. "I mean, we've got cowboys here!"

"Cort threw a rake at him the last time he came over here to look at one of your yearling bulls," Sadie reminded her.

"I throw things at him all the time," Maddie pointed out.

"Yes, but Cort chased him around the yard, picked him up by his feet, and carried him out to the hen yard to show him to the hens. Hurt his pride," Sadie continued. "He's getting even."

"You think so?"

"Roosters are unpredictable. That particular one," she added with a bite in her voice that was very out of character, "should have been chicken soup!"

"Great-Aunt Sadie!"

"Just telling you the way it is," Sadie huffed. "My brother—your granddaddy—would have killed him the first time he spurred you."

Maddie smiled. "I guess he would. I don't like killing things. Not even mean roosters."

"Cort would kill him for you if he could shoot straight," Sadie said with veiled contempt. "You load that .28 gauge shotgun in the closet for me, and I'll do it."

"Great-Aunt Sadie!"

She made a face. "Stupid thing. I wanted to pet the hens and he ran me all the way into the house. Pitiful, when a chicken can terrorize a whole ranch. You go ask Ben how he feels about that red rooster. I dare you. If you'd let him, he'd run a truck over it!"

Maddie sighed. "I guess Pumpkin is a terror. Well, maybe Cort will deal with him once and for all and I can go get us a nice rooster."

"In my experience, no such thing," the older woman said. "And about Cort dealing with him…" She nodded toward the highway.

Maddie grimaced. A big black ranch truck turned off the highway and came careening down the road toward the house. It was obviously being driven by a maniac.

The truck screeched to a stop at the front porch, sending chickens running for cover in the hen yard because of the noise.

"Great," Maddie muttered. "Now they'll stop laying for two days because he's terrified them!"

"Better worry about yourself," Great-Aunt Sadie said. "Hello, Cort! Nice to see you," she added with a wave and ran back into the house, almost at a run.

Maddie bit off what she was going to say about traitors. She braced herself as a tall, lean, furious cowboy in jeans, boots, a chambray shirt and a black Stetson cocked over one eye came straight toward her. She knew what the set of that hat meant. He was out for blood.

"I'm sorry!" she said at once, raising her hands, palms out. "I'll do something about him, I promise!"

"Andy landed in a cow patty," he raged in his deep voice. "That's nothing compared to what happened to the others while we were chasing him. I went headfirst into the dipping tray!"

She wouldn't laugh, she wouldn't laugh, she wouldn't...

"Oh, hell, stop that!" he raged while she bent over double at the mental image of big, handsome Cort lying facedown in the stinky stuff they dipped cattle in to prevent disease.

"I'm sorry. Really!" She forced herself to stop laughing. She wiped her wet eyes and tried to look serious. "Go ahead, keep yelling at me. Really. It's okay."

"Your stupid rooster is going to feed my ranch hands if you don't keep him at home!" he said angrily.

"Oh, my, chance would be a fine thing, wouldn't it?" she asked wistfully. "I mean, I guess I could hire an off-duty army unit to come out here and spend the next week trying to run him down." She gave him a droll look. "If you and your men can't catch him, how do you expect me to catch him?"

"I caught him the first day he was here," he reminded her.

"Yes, but that was three months ago," she pointed out. "And he'd just arrived. Now he's learned evasion techniques." She frowned. "I wonder if they've ever thought of using roosters as attack animals for the military? I should suggest it to someone."

"I'd suggest you find some way to keep him at home before I resort to the courts."

"You'd sue me over a chicken?" she exclaimed. "Wow, what a headline that would be. Rich, Successful Rancher Sues Starving, Female Small-Rancher for Rooster Attack. Wouldn't your dad love reading that headline in the local paper?" she asked with a bland smile.

His expression was growing so hard that his high cheekbones stood out. "One more flying red feather attack and I'll risk it. I'm not kidding."

"Oh, me, neither." She crossed her heart. "I'll have the vet prescribe some tranquilizers for Pumpkin to calm him down," she said facetiously. She frowned. "Ever thought about asking your family doctor for some? You look very stressed."

"I'm stressed because your damned rooster keeps attacking me! On my own damned ranch!" he raged.

"Well, I can see that it's a stressful situation to be in," she sympathized. "With him attacking you, and all." She knew it would make him furious, but she had to know. "I hear Odalie Everett went to Italy."

The anger grew. Now it was cold and threatening. "Since when is Odalie of interest to you?"

"Just passing on the latest gossip." She peered at him through her lashes. "Maybe you should study opera…"

"You venomous little snake," he said furiously. "As if you could sing a note that wasn't flat!"

She colored. "I could sing if I wanted to!"

He looked her up and down. "Sure. And get suddenly beautiful with it?"

The color left her face.

"You're too thin, too flat-chested, too plain and too untalented to ever appeal to me, just in case you wondered," he added with unconcealed distaste.

She drew herself up to her full height, which only brought the top of her head to his chin, and stared at him with ragged dignity. "Thank you. I was wondering why men don't come around. It's nice to know the reason."

Her damaged pride hit him soundly, and he felt small. He shifted from one big booted foot to the other. "I didn't mean it like that," he said after a minute.

She turned away. She wasn't going to cry in front of him.

Her sudden vulnerability hurt him. He started after her. "Listen, Madeline," he began.

She whirled on her booted heel. Her pale eyes shot fire at him. Her exquisite complexion went ruddy. Beside her thighs, her hands were clenched. "You think you're God's gift to women, don't you? Well, let me tell you a thing or two! You've traded on your good looks for years to get you what you want, but it didn't get you Odalie, did it?"

His face went stony. "Odalie is none of your damned business," he said in a soft, dangerous tone.

"Looks like she's none of yours, either," she said spitefully. "Or she'd never have left you."

He turned around and stomped back to his truck.

"And don't you dare roar out of my driveway and scare my hens again!"

He slammed the door, started the truck and deliberately gunned the engine as he roared out toward the main highway.

"Three days they won't lay, now," Maddie said to herself. She turned, miserable, and went up the porch steps. Her pride was never going to heal from that attack. She'd had secret feelings for Cort since she was sixteen. He'd never noticed her, of course, not even to tease her as men sometimes did. He simply ignored her existence most of the time, when her rooster wasn't attacking him. Now she knew why. Now she knew what he really thought of her.

Great-Aunt Sadie was waiting by the porch screen door. She was frowning. "No call for him to say that about you," she muttered. "Conceited man!"

Maddie fought tears and lost.

Great-Aunt Sadie wrapped her up tight and hugged her. "Don't you believe what he said. He was just mad and looking for a way to hurt you because you mentioned his precious Odalie. She's too good for any cowboy. At least, she thinks she is."

"She's beautiful and rich and talented. But so is Cort," Maddie choked out. "It really would have been a good match, to pair the Everett's Big Spur ranch with Skylance, the Brannt ranch. What a merger that would be."

"Except that Odalie doesn't love Cort and she probably never will."

"She may come home with changed feelings," Maddie replied, drawing away. "She might have a change of heart. He's always been around, sending her flowers, calling her. All that romantic stuff. The sudden stop might open her eyes to what a catch he is."

"You either love somebody or you don't," the older woman said quietly.

"You think?"

"I'll make you a nice pound cake. That will cheer you up."

"Thanks. That's sweet of you." She wiped her eyes.

"Well, at least I've lost all my illusions. Now I can just deal with my ranch and stop mooning over a man who thinks he's too good for me."

"No man is too good for you, sweetheart," Great-Aunt Sadie said gently. "You're pure gold. Don't you ever let anyone tell you different."

She smiled.

WHEN SHE WENT out late in the afternoon to put her hens in their henhouse to protect them from overnight predators, Pumpkin was right where he should be—back in the yard.

"You're going to get me sued, you red-feathered problem child," she muttered. She was carrying a small tree branch and a metal garbage can lid as she herded her hens into the large chicken house. Pumpkin lowered his head and charged her, but he bounced off the lid.

"Get in there, you fowl assassin," she said, evading and turning on him.

He ran into the henhouse. She closed the door behind him and latched it, leaned back against it with a sigh.

"Need to get rid of that rooster, Miss Maddie," Ben murmured as he walked by. "Be delicious with some dumplings."

"I'm not eating Pumpkin!"

He shrugged. "That's okay. I'll eat him for you."

"I'm not feeding him to you, either, Ben."

He made a face and kept walking.

She went inside to wash her hands and put antibiotic cream on the places where her knuckles were scraped from using the garbage can lid. She looked at her hands under the running water. They weren't elegant hands.

They had short nails and they were functional, not pretty. She remembered Odalie Everett's long, beautiful white fingers on the keyboard at church, because Odalie could play as well as she sang. The woman was gorgeous, except for her snobbish attitude. No wonder Cort was in love with her.

Maddie looked in the mirror on the medicine cabinet above the sink and winced. She really was plain, she thought. Of course, she never used makeup or perfume, because she worked from dawn to dusk on the ranch. Not that makeup would make her beautiful, or give her bigger breasts or anything like that. She was basically just pleasant to look at, and Cort wanted beauty, brains and talent.

"I guess you'll end up an old spinster with a rooster who terrorizes the countryside."

The thought made her laugh. She thought of photographing Pumpkin and making a giant Wanted poster, with the legend, Wanted: Dead or Alive. She could hardly contain herself at the image that presented itself if she offered some outlandish reward. Men would wander the land with shotguns, looking for a small red rooster.

"Now you're getting silly," she told her image, and went back to work.

CORT BRANNT SLAMMED out of his pickup truck and into the ranch house, flushed with anger and self-contempt.

His mother, beautiful Shelby Brannt, glanced up as he passed the living room.

"Wow," she murmured. "Cloudy and looking like rain."

He paused and glanced at her. He grimaced, retraced his steps, tossed his hat onto the sofa and sat down beside her. "Yeah."

"That rooster again, huh?" she teased.

His dark eyes widened. "How did you guess?"

She tried to suppress laughter and lost. "Your father came in here bent over double, laughing his head off. He said half the cowboys were ready to load rifles and go rooster-hunting about the time you drove off. He wondered if we might need to find legal representation for you…?"

"I didn't shoot her," he said. He shrugged his powerful shoulders and let out a long sigh, his hands dangling between his splayed legs as he stared at the carpet. "But I said some really terrible things to her."

Shelby put down the European fashion magazine she'd been reading. In her younger days, she had been a world-class model before she married King Brannt. "Want to talk about it, Matt?" she asked gently.

"Cort," he corrected with a grin.

She sighed. "Cort. Listen, your dad and I were calling you Matt until you were teenager, so it's hard…"

"Yes, well, you were calling Morie 'Dana,' too, weren't you?"

Shelby laughed. "It was an inside-joke. I'll tell it to you one day." She smiled. "Come on. Talk to me."

His mother could always take the weight off his shoulders. He'd never been able to speak so comfortably about personal things to his father, although he loved the older man dearly. He and his mother were on the same wavelength. She could almost read his mind.

"I was pretty mad," he confessed. "And she was cracking jokes about that stupid rooster. Then she made a crack about Odalie and I just, well, I just lost it."

Odalie, she knew, was a sore spot with her son.

"I'm sorry about the way things worked out, Cort," she said gently. "But there's always hope. Never lose sight of that."

"I sent her roses. Serenaded her. Called her just to talk. Listened to her problems." He looked up. "None of that mattered. That Italian voice trainer gave her an invitation and she got on the next plane to Rome."

"She wants to sing. You know that. You've always known it. Her mother has the voice of an angel, too."

"Yes, but Heather never wanted fame. She wanted Cole Everett," he pointed out with a faint smile.

"That was one hard case of a man," Shelby pointed out. "Like your father." She shook her head. "We had a very, very rocky road to the altar. And so did Heather and Cole."

She continued pensively. "You and Odalie's brother, John Everett, were good friends for a while. What happened there?"

"His sister happened," Cort replied. "She got tired of having me at their place all the time playing video games with John and was very vocal about it, so he stopped inviting me over. I invited him here, but he got into rodeo and then I never saw him much. We're still friends, in spite of everything."

"He's a good fellow."

"Yeah."

Shelby got up, ruffled his hair and grinned. "You're a good fellow, too."

He laughed softly. "Thanks."

"Try not to dwell so much on things," she advised. "Sit back and just let life happen for a while. You're so intense, Cort. Like your dad," she said affectionately, her dark eyes soft on his face. "One day Odalie may discover that you're the sun in her sky and come home.

But you have to let her try her wings. She's traveled, but only with her parents. This is her first real taste of freedom. Let her enjoy it."

"Even if she messes up her life with that Italian guy?"

"Even then. It's her life," she reminded him gently. "You don't like people telling you what to do, even if it's for your own good, right?"

He glowered at her. "If you're going to mention that time you told me not to climb up the barn roof and I didn't listen…"

"Your first broken arm," she recalled, and pursed her lips. "And I didn't even say I told you so," she reminded him.

"No. You didn't." He stared at his linked fingers. "Maddie Lane sets me off. But I should never have said she was ugly and no man would want her."

"You said that?" she exclaimed, wincing. "Cort…!"

"I know." He sighed. "Not my finest moment. She's not a bad person. It's just she gets these goofy notions about animals. That rooster is going to hurt somebody bad one day, maybe put an eye out, and she thinks it's funny."

"She doesn't realize he's dangerous," she replied.

"She doesn't want to realize it. She's in over her head with these expansion projects. Cage-free eggs. She hasn't got the capital to go into that sort of operation, and she's probably already breaking half a dozen laws by selling them to restaurants."

"She's hurting for money," Shelby reminded somberly. "Most ranchers are, even us. The drought is killing us. But Maddie only has a few head of cattle and she can't buy feed for them if her corn crop dies. She'll have to sell at a loss. Her breeding program is already losing money." She shook her head. "Her father was a fine rancher. He taught your father things about breeding bulls. But Maddie just doesn't have the experience. She jumped in at the deep end when her father died, but it was by necessity, not choice. I'm sure she'd much rather be drawing pictures than trying to produce calves."

"Drawing." He said it with contempt.

She stared at him. "Cort, haven't you ever noticed that?" She indicated a beautiful rendering in pastels of a fairy in a patch of daisies in an exquisite frame on the wall.

He glanced at it. "Not bad. Didn't you get that at an art show last year?"

"I got it from Maddie last year. She drew it."

He frowned. He actually got up and went to look at the piece. "She drew that?" he asked.

"Yes. She was selling two pastel drawings at the art show. This was one of them. She sculpts, too— beautiful little fairies—but she doesn't like to show those to people. I told her she should draw professionally, perhaps in graphic design or even illustration. She laughed. She doesn't think she's good enough." She sighed. "Maddie is insecure. She has one of the poorest self-images of anyone I know."

Cort knew that. His lips made a thin line. He felt even worse after what he'd said to her. "I should probably call and apologize," he murmured.

"That's not a bad idea, son," she agreed.

"And then I should drive over there, hide in the grass and shoot that damned red-feathered son of a...!"

"Cort!"

He let out a harsh breath. "Okay. I'll call her."

"Roosters don't live that long," she called after him. "He'll die of old age before too much longer."

"With my luck, he'll hit fifteen and keep going. Animals that nasty never die!" he called back.

HE WANTED TO apologize to Maddie. But when he turned on his cell phone, he realized that he didn't even know her phone number. He tried to look it up on the internet, but couldn't find a listing.

He went back downstairs. His mother was in the kitchen.

"Do you know the Lanes' phone number?" he asked.

She blinked. "Well, no. I don't think I've ever tried to call them, not since Pierce Lane died last year, anyway."

"No number listed, anywhere," he said.

"You might drive by there later in the week," she suggested gently. "It's not that far."

He hesitated. "She'd lock the doors and hide inside when I drove up," he predicted.

His mother didn't know what to say. He was probably right.

"I need to get away," he said after a minute. "I'm wired like a piano. I need to get away from the rooster and Odalie and…everything."

"Why don't you go to Wyoming and visit your sister?" she suggested.

He sighed. "She's not expecting me until Thursday."

She laughed. "She won't care. Go early. It would do both of you good."

"It might at that."

"It won't take you long to fly up there," she added. "You can use the corporate jet. I'm sure your father wouldn't mind. He misses Morie. So do I."

"Yeah, I miss her, too," he said. He hugged his mother. "I'll go pack a bag. If that rooster shows up looking for me, put him on a plane to France, would you? I hear they love chicken over there. Get him a business-class ticket. If someone can ship a lobster from Maine," he added with a laugh, referring to a joke that had gone the rounds years before, "I can ship a chicken to France."

"I'll take it under advisement," she promised.

HIS MOTHER WAS right, Cort thought that evening. He loved being with his sister. He and Morie were a lot alike, from their hot tempers to their very Puritan attitudes. They'd always been friends. When she was just five, she'd followed her big brother around everywhere, to the amusement of his friends. Cort was tolerant and he adored her. He never minded the kidding.

"I'm sorry about your rooster problems," Morie told him with a gentle laugh. "Believe me, we can understand. My poor sister-in-law has fits with ours."

"I like Bodie," he said, smiling. "Cane sure seems different these days."

"He is. He's back in therapy, he's stopped smashing bars and he seems to have settled down for good. Bodie's wonderful for him. She and Cane have had some problems, but they're mostly solved now," she said. She smiled secretly. "Actually, Bodie and I are going to have a lot more in common for the next few months."

Cort was quick. He glanced at her in the semidarkness of the front porch, with fireflies darting around. "A baby?"

She laughed with pure delight. "A baby," she said, and her voice was like velvet. "I only found out a little while ago. Bodie found out the day you showed up."

She sighed. "So much happiness. It's almost too much to bear. Mal's over the moon."

"Is it a boy or a girl? Do you know yet?"

She shook her head. "Too early to tell. But we're not going to ask. We want it to be a surprise, however old-fashioned that might be."

He chuckled. "I'm going to be an uncle. Wow. That's super. Have you told Mom and Dad?"

"Not yet. I'll call Mom tonight, though."

"She'll be so excited. Her first grandchild."

Morie glanced at him. "You ever going to get married?" she asked.

"Sure, if Odalie ever says yes." He sighed. "She was warming up to me there just for a while. Then that Italian fellow came along and offered her voice training. He's something of a legend among opera stars. And that's what she wants, to sing at the Met." He grimaced. "Just my luck, to fall in love with a woman who only wants a career."

"I believe her mother was the same way, wasn't she?" Morie asked gently. "And then she and Cole Everett got really close. She gave up being a professional singer to come home and have kids. Although she still composes. That Wyoming group, Desperado, had a major hit from a song she wrote for them some years ago."

"I think she still composes. But she likes living on a ranch. Odalie hates it. She says she's never going to marry a man who smells like cow droppings." He looked at one of his big boots, where his ankle was resting on his other knee in the rocking chair. "I'm a rancher, damn it," he muttered. "I can't learn another trade. Dad's counting on me to take over when he can't do the work anymore."

"Yes, I know," she said sadly. "What else could you do?"

"Teach, I guess," he replied. "I have a degree in animal husbandry." He made a face. "I'd rather be shot. I'd rather let that red-feathered assassin loose on my nose. I hate the whole idea of routine."

"Me, too," Morie confessed. "I love ranching. I guess the drought is giving Dad problems, too, huh?"

"It's been pretty bad," Cort agreed. "People in Oklahoma and the other plains states are having it worse, though. No rain. It's like the Dust Bowl in the thirties, people are saying. So many disaster declarations."

"How are you getting around it?"

"Wells, mostly," he said. "We've drilled new ones and filled the tanks to the top. Irrigating our grain crops. Of course, we'll still have to buy some feed through the winter. But we're in better shape than a lot of other cattle producers. Damn, I hate how it's going to impact small ranchers and farmers. Those huge combines will be standing in the shadows, just waiting to pounce when the foreclosures come."

"Family ranches are going to be obsolete one day, like family farms," Morie said sadly. "Except, maybe, for the big ones, like ours."

"True words. People don't realize how critical this really is."

She reached over and squeezed his hand. "That's why we have the National Cattleman's Association and the state organizations," she reminded him. "Now stop worrying. We're going fishing tomorrow!"

"Really?" he asked, delighted. "Trout?"

"Yes. The water's just cold enough, still. When it heats up too much, you can't eat them." She sighed. "This may be the last chance we'll get for a while, if this heat doesn't relent."

"Tell me about it. We hardly had winter at all in Texas. Spring was like summer, and it's gone downhill since. I'd love to stand in a trout stream, even if I don't catch a thing."

"Me, too."

"Does Bodie fish?"

"You know, I've never asked. We'll do that tomorrow. For now," she said, rising, "I'm for bed." She paused and hugged him. "It's nice to have you here for a while."

"For me, too, little sis." He hugged her back, and kissed her forehead. "See you in the morning."

CHAPTER TWO

MADDIE HADN'T THOUGHT about Cort for one whole hour. She laughed at herself while she fed her hens. Pumpkin was in the henhouse, locked in for the time being, so that she could feed the chickens without having to defend herself.

The laughter died away as she recalled the things Cort had said to her. She was ugly and flat-chested and he could never be attracted to her. She looked down at her slender body and frowned. She couldn't suddenly become beautiful. She didn't have the money to buy fancy clothes that flattered her, like Odalie did. In fact, her wardrobe was two years old.

When her father had been dying of cancer, every penny they had was tied up trying to keep up with doctor bills that the insurance didn't cover. Her father did carry life insurance, which was a lucky break because at his death, it was enough to pay back everybody.

But things were still hard. This year, they'd struggled to pay just the utility bills. It was going to come down to a hard choice, sell off cattle or sell off land. There was a developer who'd already been to see Maddie about selling the ranch. He wanted to build a huge hotel and amusement park complex. He was offering her over a million dollars, and he was persistent.

"You just run a few head of cattle here, don't you?" the tall man in the expensive suit said, but his smile didn't really reach his eyes. He was an opportunist, looking for a great deal. He thought Maddie would be a pushover once he pulled out a figure that would tempt a saint.

But Maddie's whole heritage was in that land. Her great-grandfather had started the ranch and suffered all sorts of deprivations to get it going. Her grandfather had taken over where he left off, improving both the cattle herd and the land. Her father had toiled for years to find just the right mix of grasses to pursue a purebred cattle breeding herd that was now the envy of several neighbors. All that would be gone. The cattle sold off, the productive grasslands torn up and paved for the complex, which would attract people passing by on the long, monotonous interstate highway that ran close to the border of the ranch.

"I'll have to think about it," she told him, nodding. Her smile didn't reach her eyes, either.

He pursed his lips. "You know, we're looking at other land in the area, too. You might get left out in the cold if we find someone who's more enthusiastic about the price we're offering."

Maddie didn't like threats. Even nice ones, that came with soft words and smiles.

"Whatever," she said. She smiled again. "I did say I'd have to think about it."

His smile faded, and his eyes narrowed. "You have a prime location here, only one close neighbor and a nearby interstate. I really want this place. I want it a lot."

"Listen, I hate being pressured…!"

He held up both hands. "Okay! But you think about it. You think hard." His expression became dangerous-looking. "We know how to deal with reluctant buyers. That's not a threat, it's just a statement. Here's my card."

She took it gingerly, as if she thought it had germs.

He made a huffing sound and climbed back into his fantastically expensive foreign car. He roared out of the driveway, scattering chickens.

She glared after it. No more eggs for two more days, she thought irritably. She'd rather starve than sell the ranch. But money was getting very tight. The drought was going to be a major hit to their poor finances, she thought dismally.

"Miss Maddie, you got that rooster locked up?" Ben called at the fence, interrupting her depressing reverie.

She turned. "Yes, Ben, he's restrained." She laughed.

"Thanks." He grimaced. "Going to feed the livestock and I'd just as soon not be mauled in the process."

"I know." She glanced at the wire door behind which Pumpkin was calling to the hens in that odd tone that roosters used when there was some special treat on the ground for them. It was actually a handful of mealworms that Maddie had tossed in the henhouse to keep him occupied while she locked him in.

Two of the hens went running to the door.

"He's lying," Maddie told them solemnly. "He's already eaten the mealworms, he just wants out."

"Cort left town, you hear?" Ben asked.

Her heart jumped. "Where did he go?" she asked miserably, waiting to hear that he'd flown to Italy to see Odalie.

"Wyoming, one of his cowboys said, to see his sister."

"Oh."

"Mooning over that Odalie girl, I guess," he muttered. "She said she hated men who smelled like cattle. I guess she hates her dad, then, because he made his fortune on the Big Spur raising cattle, and he still does!"

"She's just been spoiled," Maddie said quietly.

Ben glanced at her irritably. "She was mean to you when you were in school. Your dad actually went to the school to get it stopped. He went to see Cole Everett about it, too, didn't he?"

"Yes." She flushed. She didn't like remembering that situation, although Odalie had quickly stopped victimizing her after her father got involved.

"Had a nasty attitude, that one," Ben muttered. "Looked down her nose at every other girl and most of the boys. Thought she was too good to live in a hick town in Texas." His eyes narrowed. "She's going to come a cropper one day, you mark my words. What's that quote, 'pride goeth after a fall'? And she's got a lot farther to fall than some women."

"There's another quote, something about love your enemies?" she teased.

"Yes, well, she's given a lot of people reason to put that one into practice."

Maddie grimaced. "It must be nice, to have beauty and talent. I'd settle for one or the other myself." She laughed.

"You ought to be selling them little fairy statues you make," he advised. "Prettiest little things I ever saw. That one you sent my granddaughter for her birthday sits in the living room, because her mother loves to look at it. One of her friends has an art gallery in San Antonio. She said," he emphasized, "that you could make a fortune with those things."

Maddie flushed. "Wow."

"Not that those pretty drawings are bad, either. Sold one to Shelby Brannt, didn't you?"

"Yes." She'd loved the idea of Cort having to see her artwork every day, because she knew that Shelby had mounted it on a wall in the dining room of her home. But he probably never even looked at it. Though cultured, Cort had little use for art or sculpture. Unless it was a sculpture of one of the ranch's prize bulls. They had one done in bronze. It sat on the mantel in the living room of the Brannt home.

"Ought to paint that rooster while he's still alive," Ben said darkly.

"Ben!"

He held up both hands. "Didn't say I was going to hurt him."

"Okay."

"But somebody else might." He pursed his lips. "You know, he could be the victim of a terrible traffic accident one day. He loves to run down that dirt road in front of the house."

"You bite your tongue," she admonished.

"Spoilsport."

"That visitor who came the other day, that developer, you see him again?" Ben asked curiously.

"No, but he left his name." She pulled his business card out of her pocket and held it up. "He's from Las Vegas. He wants to build a hotel and amusement park complex right here." She looked around wistfully. "Offered me a million dollars. Gosh, what I could do with that!"

"You could sell and throw away everything your family worked for here?" Ben asked sadly. "My great-grandfather started working here with your great-grandfather. Our families have been together all that time." He sighed. "Guess I could learn to use a computer and make a killing with a dot-com business," he mused facetiously.

"Aw, Ben," she said gently. "I don't want to sell up. I was just thinking out loud." She smiled, and this time it was genuine. "I'd put a lot of people out of work, and God knows what I'd do with all the animals who live here."

"Especially them fancy breeding bulls and cows," he replied. "Cort Brannt would love to get his hands on them. He's always over here buying our calves."

"So he is."

Ben hesitated. "Heard something about that developer, that Archie Lawson fellow."

"You did? What?"

"Just gossip, mind."

"So? Tell me!" she prodded.

He made a face. "Well, he wanted a piece of land over around Cheyenne, on the interstate. The owner wouldn't sell. So cattle started dying of mysterious causes. So did the owner's dog, a big border collie he'd had for years. He hired a private investigator, and had the dog autopsied. It was poison. They could never prove it was Lawson, but they were pretty sure of it. See, he has a background in chemistry. Used to work at a big government lab, they say, before he started buying and selling land."

Her heart stopped. "Oh, dear." She bit her lip. "He said something about knowing how to force deals…"

"I'll get a couple of my pals to keep an eye on the cattle in the outer pastures," Ben said. "I'll tell them to shoot first and ask questions later if they see anybody prowling around here."

"Thanks, Ben," she said heavily. "Good heavens,

as if we don't already have enough trouble here with no rain, for God knows how long."

"Everybody's praying for it." He cocked his head. "I know a Cheyenne medicine man. Been friends for a couple of years. They say he can make rain."

"Well!" She hesitated. "What does he charge?"

"He doesn't. He says he has these abilities that God gave him, and if he ever takes money for it, he'll lose it. Seems to believe it, and I hear he's made rain at least twice in the area. If things go from bad to worse, maybe we should talk to him."

She grinned. "Let's talk to him."

He chuckled. "I'll give him a call later."

Her eyebrows arched. "He has a telephone?"

"Miss Maddie," he scoffed, "do you think Native American people still live in teepees and wear headdresses?"

She flushed. "Of course not," she lied.

"He lives in a house just like ours, he wears jeans and T-shirts mostly and he's got a degree in anthropology. When he's not fossicking, they say he goes overseas with a group of mercs from Texas for top secret operations."

She was fascinated. "Really!"

"He's something of a local celebrity on the rez. He lives there."

"Could you call him and ask him to come over when he has time?"

He laughed. "I'll do that tonight."

"Even if he can't make rain, I'd love to meet him," she said. "He sounds very interesting."

"Take my word for it, he is. Doesn't talk much, but when he does, it's worth hearing. Well, I'll get back to work."

"Thanks, Ben."

He smiled. "My pleasure. And don't let that developer bully you," he said firmly. "Maybe you need to talk to Cort's dad and tell him what's going on. He's not going to like that, about the development. It's too close to his barns. In these hard times, even the Brannts couldn't afford to build new ones with all that high tech they use."

"Got a point. I'll talk to him."

Maddie went back to the house. She put the feed basket absently on the kitchen counter, mentally reviewing all the things she had planned for the week. She missed Cort already. But at least it meant the rooster was likely to stay at home. He only went over to the Brannt ranch when Cort was in residence, to attack him.

"Better wash those eggs and put them in the refrigerator," Great-Aunt Sadie advised. "They're the ones for the restaurant, aren't they?"

"Yes. Old Mr. Bailey said his customers have been raving about the taste of his egg omelets lately." She laughed. "I'll have to give my girls a treat for that."

Great-Aunt Sadie was frowning. "Maddie, did you ever look up the law about selling raw products?"

Maddie shook her head. "I meant to. But I'm sure it's not illegal to sell eggs. My mother did it for years before she died...."

"That was a long time ago, honey. Don't you remember that raid a few years ago on those poor farmers who were selling raw milk?" She made a face. "What sort of country do we live in? Sending an armed raid team after helpless farmers for selling milk!"

Maddie felt uneasy. "I'd forgotten that."

"I hadn't. In my day we had homemade butter and

we could drink all the raw milk we wanted—didn't have all this fancy stuff a hundred years ago and it seems to me people were a whole lot healthier."

"You weren't here a hundred years ago," Maddie pointed out with a grin. "Anyway, the government's not going to come out here and attack me for selling a few eggs!"

She did look on the internet for the law pertaining to egg production and found that she was in compliance. In fact, there were even places in the country licensed to sell raw milk. She'd have to tell Great-Aunt Sadie about that, she mused. Apparently armed teams weren't raiding farms out west.

MEANWHILE, A DAY later, she did call King Brannt. She was hesitant about it. Not only was he Cort's father, he had a reputation in the county for being one tough customer, and difficult to get along with. He had a fiery temper that he wasn't shy about using. But the developer's determination to get the Lane ranch could have repercussions. A lot of them.

She picked up the phone and dialed the ranch.

The housekeeper answered.

"Could I speak to King Brannt, please?" she asked. "It's Maddie Lane."

There was a skirl of laughter. "Yes, you've got a rooster named Pumpkin."

Maddie laughed. "Is he famous?"

"He is around here," the woman said. "Cort isn't laughing, but the rest of us are. Imagine having a personal devil in the form of a little red rooster! We've been teasing Cort that he must have done something terrible that we don't know about."

Maddie sighed. "I'm afraid Pumpkin has it in for

Cort. See, he picked him up by the feet and showed him to my girls, my hens, I mean, and hurt his pride. That was when he started looking for Cort."

"Oh, I see. It's vengeance." She laughed again. "Nice talking to you, I'll go get Mr. Brannt. Take just a minute…"

Maddie held on. Her gaze fell on one of her little fairy statues. It was delicate and beautiful; the tiny face perfect, lovely, with sculpted long blond hair, sitting on a stone with a butterfly in its hand. It was a new piece, one she'd just finished with the plastic sculpture mix that was the best on the market. Her egg money paid for the materials. She loved the little things and could never bear to sell one. But she did wonder if there was a market for such a specialized piece.

"Brannt," a deep voice said curtly.

She almost jumped. "Mr. Brannt? It's… I mean I'm Maddie Lane. I live on the little ranch next door to yours," she faltered.

"Hi, Maddie," he said, and his voice lost its curt edge and was pleasant. "What can I do for you?"

"I've got sort of a situation over here. I wanted to tell you about it."

"What's wrong? Can we help?"

"That's so nice of you." She didn't add that she'd been told some very scary things about his temper. "It's this developer. He's from Las Vegas…"

"Yes. Archie Lawson. I had him investigated."

"He's trying to get me to sell my ranch to him. I don't want to. This ranch has been in my family for generations. But he's very pushy and he made some threats."

"He's carried them out in the past," King said, very curtly. "But you can be sure I'm not going to let him hurt you or your cattle herd. I'll put on extra patrols on the land boundary we share, and station men at the cabin out there. We use it for roundup, but it's been vacant for a week or so. I'll make sure someone's there at all times, and we'll hook up cameras around your cattle herd and monitor them constantly."

"You'd do that for me?" she faltered. "Cameras. It's so expensive." She knew, because in desperation she'd looked at them and been shocked at the prices for even a cheap system.

"I'd do that for you," he replied. "You have one of the finest breeding herds I know of, which is why we buy so many of your young bulls."

"Why, thank you."

"You're welcome. You see, it's looking out for our interests as well as yours. I can't have a complex so close to my barns, or my purebred herd. The noise of construction would be bad enough, but the constant traffic would injure production."

"Yes, I know what you mean."

"Besides that, Lawson is unscrupulous. He's got his fingers in lots of dirty pies. He's had several brushes with the law, too."

"I'm not surprised. He was a little scary."

"Don't you worry. If he comes back and makes any threat at all, you call over here. If you can't find me, talk to Cort. He'll take care of it."

She hesitated. "Actually Cort isn't speaking to me right now."

There was a pause. "Because of the rooster?" His voice was almost smiling.

"Actually because I made a nasty crack about Odalie Everett," she confessed heavily. "I didn't mean to. He made me mad. I guess he was justified to complain. Pumpkin is really mean to him."

"So I heard. That rooster has had brushes with several of our cowboys." She could tell that he was trying not to laugh.

"The man who sold him to me said he was real gentle and wouldn't hurt a fly. That's sort of true. I've never seen Pumpkin hurt a fly." She laughed. "Just people."

"You need a gentle rooster, especially if you're going to be selling eggs and baby chicks."

"The baby chick operation is down the road, but I'm doing well with my egg business."

"Glad to hear it. Our housekeeper wants to get on your customer list, by the way."

"I'll talk to her, and thanks!"

He chuckled. "My pleasure."

"If Mr. Lawson comes back, I'll let you know."

"Please do. The man is trouble."

"I know. Thanks again, Mr. Brannt. I feel better now."

"Your dad was a friend of mine," he said quietly. "I miss him. I know you do, too."

"I miss him a lot," she said. "But Great-Aunt Sadie and I are coping. It's just this ranching thing," she added miserably. "Dad was good at it, he had charts in the barn, he knew which traits to breed for, all that technical stuff. He taught me well, but I'm not as good as he was at it. Not at all. I like to paint and sculpt." She hesitated. "Creative people shouldn't have to breed cattle!" she burst out.

He laughed. "I hear you. Listen, suppose I send Cort over there to help you with the genetics? He's even better at it than I am. And I'm good. No conceit, just fact."

She laughed, too. "You really are. We read about your bulls in the cattle journals." She paused. "I don't think Cort would come."

"He'll come." He sounded certain of it. "He needs something to take his mind off that woman. She's a sweet girl, in her way, but she's got some serious growing up to do. She thinks the world revolves around her. It doesn't."

"She's just been a little spoiled, I think." She tried to be gracious.

"Rotten," he replied. "My kids never were."

"You and Mrs. Brannt did a great job with yours. And John Everett is a really nice man. So the Everetts did a great job there, too." She didn't mention the second Everett son, Tanner. The Everetts never spoke about him. Neither did anyone else. He was something of a mystery man. But gossip was that he and his dad didn't get along.

"They did a great job on John, for sure." He let out a breath. "I just wish Cort would wake up. Odalie is never going to settle in a small community. She's meant for high society and big cities. Cort would die in a high-rise apartment. He's got too much country in him, although he'd jump at the chance if Odalie would offer him one. Just between us," he added quietly, "I hope she doesn't. If she makes it in opera, and I think she can, what would Cort do with himself while she trained and performed? He'd be bored out of his mind. He doesn't even like opera. He likes country-western."

"He plays it very well," Maddie said softly. "I loved coming to the barbecue at your place during the spring sale and hearing him sing. It was nice of you to invite all of us. Even old Ben. He was over the moon."

He laughed. "You're all neighbors. I know you think

of Ben as more family than employee. His family has worked for your family for four generations."

"That's a long time," she agreed. "I'm not selling my place," she added firmly. "No matter what that fancy Las Vegas man does."

"Good for you. I'll help you make sure of that. I'll send Cort on over."

"He's back from visiting his sister?" she stammered.

"Yes. Got back yesterday. They went trout fishing."

She sighed. "I'd love to go trout fishing."

"Cort loves it. He said they did close the trout streams for fishing a couple of days after he and Dana—Morie, I mean, went. The heat makes it impossible. "

"That's true." She hesitated. "Why do you call Morie Dana?" she blurted out.

He laughed. "When Shelby was carrying them, we called them Matt and Dana. Those were the names we picked out. Except that two of our friends used those names for theirs and we had to change ours. It got to be a habit, though, until the kids were adolescents.

"Hey, Cort," she heard King call, his hand covering the receiver so his voice was a little muffled.

"Yes, Dad?" came the reply.

"I want you to go over to the Lane place and give Maddie some help with her breeding program."

"The hell I will!" Cort burst out.

The hand over the phone seemed to close, because the rest of it was muffled. Angry voices, followed by more discussion, followed like what seemed a string of horrible curses from Cort.

King came back on the line. "He said he'd be pleased to come over and help," he lied. "But he did ask if you'd shut your rooster up first." He chuckled.

"I'll put him in the chicken house right now." She tried not to sound as miserable as she felt. She knew Cort didn't want to help her. He hated her. "And thank you again."

"You're very welcome. Call us if you need help with Lawson. Okay?"

"Okay."

TRUE TO HIS father's words, Cort drove up in front of the house less than an hour later. He wasn't slamming doors or scattering chickens this time, either. He looked almost pleasant. Apparently his father had talked to him very firmly.

Maddie had combed her hair and washed her face. She still wasn't going to win any beauty contests. She had on her nicest jeans and a pink T-shirt that said La Vie en Rose.

It called attention, unfortunately, to breasts that were small and pert instead of big and tempting. But Cort was looking at her shirt with his lips pursed.

"The world through rose-colored glasses?" he mused.

"You speak French."

"Of course. French, Spanish and enough German to get me arrested in Munich. We do cattle deals all over the world," he added.

"Yes, I remember." She swallowed, hard, recalling the things he'd said at their last unfortunate meeting. "Your father said you could help me figure out Dad's breeding program."

"I think so. I helped him work up the new one before he passed away," he added quietly. "We were all shocked by how fast it happened."

"So were we," Maddie confessed. "Two months

from the time he was diagnosed until he passed on." She drew in a long breath. "He hated tests, you know. He wouldn't go to the doctor about anything unless he was already at death's door. I think the doctor suspected something, but Dad just passed right over the lecture about tests being necessary and walked out. By the time they diagnosed the cancer, it was too late for anything except radiation. And somebody said that they only did that to help contain the pain." Her pale eyes grew sad. "It was terrible, the pain. At the last, he was so sedated that he hardly knew me. It was the only way he could cope."

"I'm sorry," he said. "I haven't lost parents, but I lost both my grandparents. They were wonderful people. It was hard to let them go."

"Life goes on," she said quietly. "Everybody dies. It's just a matter of how and when."

"True."

She swallowed. "Dad kept his chalkboard in the barn, and his books in the library, along with his journals. I've read them all, but I can't make sense of what he was doing. I'm not college educated, and I don't really know much about animal husbandry. I know what I do from watching Dad."

"I can explain it to you."

She nodded. "Thanks."

She turned and led the way to the house.

"Where's that...rooster?" he asked.

"Shut up in the henhouse with a fan."

"A fan?" he exclaimed and burst out laughing.

"It really isn't funny," she said softly. "I lost two of my girls to the heat. Found them dead in the henhouse, trying to lay. I had Ben go and get us a fan and install it there. It does help with the heat, a little at least."

"My grandmother used to keep hens," he recalled. "But we only have one or two now. Foxes got the rest." He glanced at her. "Andie, our housekeeper, wants to get on your egg customer list for two dozen a week."

She nodded. "Your dad mentioned that. I can do that. I've got pullets that should start laying soon. My flock is growing by leaps and bounds." She indicated the large fenced chicken yard, dotted with all sorts of chickens. The henhouse was huge, enough to accommodate them all, complete with perches and ladders and egg boxes and, now, a fan.

"Nice operation."

"I'm going to expand it next year, if I do enough business."

"Did you check the law on egg production?"

She laughed. "Yes, I did. I'm in compliance. I don't have a middleman, or I could be in trouble. I sell directly to the customer, so it's all okay."

"Good." He shrugged, his hands in his jean pockets. "I'd hate to have to bail you out of jail."

"You wouldn't," she sighed.

He stopped and looked down at her. She seemed so dejected. "Yes, I would," he said, his deep voice quiet and almost tender as he studied her small frame, her short wavy blond hair, her wide, soft gray eyes. Her complexion was exquisite, not a blemish on it except for one small mole on her cheek. She had a pretty mouth, too. It looked tempting. Bow-shaped, soft, naturally pink…

"Cort?" she asked suddenly, her whole body tingling, her heart racing at the way he was staring at her mouth.

"What? Oh. Yes. The breeding books." He nodded. "We should get to it."

"Yes." She swallowed, tried to hide her blush and opened the front door.

CHAPTER THREE

MADDIE COULDN'T HELP but stare at Cort as he leaned over the desk to read the last page of her father's breeding journal. He was the handsomest man she'd ever seen. And that physique! He was long and lean, but also muscular. Broad-shouldered, narrow-hipped, and in the opening of his chambray shirt, thick curling black hair peeked out.

She'd never been overly interested in intimacy. Never having indulged, she had no idea how it felt, although she'd been reading romance novels since her early teens. She did know how things worked between men and women from health class. What she didn't know was why women gave in to men. She supposed it came naturally.

Cort felt her eyes on him and turned, so that he was looking directly into her wide, shocked gray eyes. His own dark ones narrowed. He knew that look, that expression. She was trying to hide it, but he wasn't fooled.

"Take a picture," he drawled, because her interest irritated him. She wasn't his type. Not at all.

Her reaction shamed him. She looked away, cleared her throat and went beet-red. "Sorry," she choked. "I was just thinking. You were sort of in the way. I was thinking about my fairies..."

He felt guilty. That made him even more irritable. "What fairies?"

She stumbled and had to catch herself as she went past him. She was so embarrassed she could hardly even walk.

She went to the shelf where she'd put the newest one. Taking it down very carefully, she carried it to the desk and put it in front of him.

He caught his breath. He picked it up, delicately for a man with such large, strong hands, and held it up to his eyes. He turned it. He was smiling. "This is really beautiful," he said, as if it surprised him. He glanced at her. "You did this by yourself?"

She moved uneasily. "Yes," she muttered. What did he think—that she had somebody come in and do the work so she could claim credit for it?

"I didn't mean it like that, Maddie," he said gently. The sound of her name on his lips made her tingle. She didn't dare look up, because her attraction to him would surely show. He knew a lot more about women than she knew about men. He could probably tell already that she liked him. It had made him mad. So she'd have to hide it.

"Okay," she said. But she still wouldn't look up.

He gave the beautiful little statuette another look before he put it down very gently on the desk. "You should be marketing those," he said firmly. "I've seen things half as lovely sell for thousands of dollars."

"Thousands?" she exclaimed.

"Yes. Sometimes five figures. I was staying at a hotel in Arizona during a cattlemen's conference and a doll show was exhibiting at the same hotel. I talked to some of the artists." He shook his head. "It's amazing how much collectors will pay for stuff like that."

He indicated the fairy with his head. "You should look into it."

She was stunned. "I never dreamed people would pay so much for a little sculpture."

"Your paintings are nice, too," he admitted. "My mother loves the drawing you did. She bought it at that art show last year. She said you should be selling the sculptures, too."

"I would. It's just that they're like my children," she confessed, and flushed because that sounded nutty. "I mean…well, it's hard to explain."

"Each one is unique and you put a lot of yourself into it," he guessed. "So it would be hard to sell one."

"Yes." She did look up then, surprised that he was so perceptive.

"You have the talent. All you need is the drive."

"Drive." She sighed. She smiled faintly. "How about imminent starvation? Does that work for drive?"

He laughed. "We wouldn't let you starve. Your bull calves are too valuable to us," he added, just when she thought he might actually care.

"Thanks," she said shyly. "In that journal of Dad's—" she changed the subject "—he talks about heritability traits for lean meat with marbling to produce cuts that health-conscious consumers will buy. Can you explain to me how I go about producing herd sires that carry the traits we breed for?"

He smiled. "It's complicated. Want to take notes?"

She sighed. "Just like going back to school." Then she remembered school, and the agonies she went through in her junior and senior years because of Odalie Everett, and her face clenched.

"What's wrong?" he asked, frowning.

She swallowed. She almost said what was wrong.

But she'd been down that road with him already, making comments she shouldn't have made about Odalie. She wasn't going to make him mad. Not now, when he was being pleasant and helpful.

"Nothing. Just a stray thought." She smiled. "I'll get some paper and a pencil."

AFTER A HALF hour she put down the pencil. "It's got to be like learning to speak Martian," she muttered.

He laughed out loud. "Listen, I didn't come into the world knowing how this stuff worked, either. I had to learn it, and if my dad hadn't been a patient man, I'd have jumped off a cliff."

"Your dad is patient?" she asked, and couldn't help sounding surprised.

"I know he's got a reputation for being just the opposite. But he really is patient. I had a hard time with algebra in high school. He'd take me into the office every night and go over problems with me until I understood how to do them. He never fussed, or yelled, or raised his voice. And I was a problem child." He shook his head. "I'm amazed I got through my childhood in one piece. I've broken half the bones in my body at some point, and I know my mother's gray hairs are all because of me. Morie was a little lady. She never caused anybody any trouble."

"I remember," Maddie said with a smile. "She was always kind to me. She was a couple of years ahead of me, but she was never snobby."

His dark eyes narrowed. "There's a hidden comment in there."

She flushed. "I didn't mention anybody else."

"You meant Odalie," he said. "She can't help being beautiful and rich and talented," he pointed out. "And it wasn't her fault that her parents put her in public school instead of private school, where she might have been better treated."

"Better treated." She glared at him. "Not one teacher or administrator ever had a bad word to say about her, even though she bullied younger girls mercilessly and spent most of her time bad-mouthing people she didn't like. One year she had a party for our whole class, at the ranch. She invited every single girl in the class— except me."

Cort's eyes narrowed. "I'm sure it wasn't intentional."

"My father went to see her father, that's how unintentional it was," she replied quietly. "When Cole Everett knew what she'd done to me, he grounded her for a month and took away her end-of-school trip as punishment."

"That seems extreme for not inviting someone to a party," he scoffed.

"I guess that's because you don't know about the other things she did to me," she replied.

"Let me guess—she didn't send you a Valentine's Day card, either," he drawled in a tone that dripped sarcasm.

She looked at him with open sadness. "Sure. That's it. I held a grudge because she didn't send me a holiday card and my father went to see the school principal and Odalie's father because he liked starting trouble."

Cort remembered her father. He was the mildest, most forgiving man anywhere around Branntville. He'd walk away from a fight if he could. The very fact that he got involved meant that he felt there was more than a slight problem.

But Cort loved Odalie, and here was this bad-tempered little frump making cracks about her, probably because she was jealous.

"I guess if you don't have a real talent and you aren't as pretty, it's hard to get along with someone who has it all," he commented.

Her face went beet-red. She stood up, took her father's journal, closed it and put it back in the desk drawer. She faced him across the width of the desk.

"Thank you for explaining the journal to me," she said in a formal tone. "I'll study the notes I took very carefully."

"Fine." He started to leave, hesitated. He turned and looked back at her. He could see an unusual brightness in her eyes. "Look, I didn't mean to hurt your feelings. It's just, well, you don't know Odalie. She's sweet and kind, she'd never hurt anybody on purpose."

"I don't have any talent, I'm ugly and I lie." She nodded. "Thanks."

"Hell, I never said you lied!"

She swallowed. Loud voices and curses made her nervous. She gripped the edge of the desk.

"Now what's wrong?" he asked angrily.

She shook her head. "Nothing," she said quickly.

He took a sudden, quick step toward her. She backed up, knocked over the desk chair and almost fell again getting it between him and herself. She was white in the face.

He stopped in his tracks. His lips fell open. In all his life, he'd never seen a woman react that way.

"What the hell is wrong with you?" he asked, but not in a loud or menacing tone.

She swallowed. "Nothing. Thanks for coming over."

He scowled. She looked scared to death.

Great-Aunt Sadie had heard a crash in the room. She

opened the door gingerly and looked in. She glanced from Maddie's white face to Cort's drawn one. "Maddie, you okay?" she asked hesitantly, her eyes flicking back and forth to Cort's as if she, too, was uneasy.

"I'm fine. I just…knocked the chair over." She laughed, but it was a nervous, quick laugh. "Cort was just leaving. He gave me lots of information."

"Nice of him," Sadie agreed. She moved closer to Maddie, as if prepared to act as a human shield if Cort took another step toward the younger woman. "Good night, Cort."

He wanted to know what was wrong. It was true he'd said some mean things, but the fear in Maddie's eyes, and the looks he was getting, really disturbed him. He moved to the door, hesitated. "If you need any more help…" he began.

"I'll call. Sure. Thanks for offering." Maddie's voice sounded tight. She was standing very still. He was reminded forcibly of deer's eyes in headlights.

"Well, I'll get on home. Good night."

"Night," Maddie choked out.

He glanced from one woman to the other, turned and pulled the door closed behind him.

Maddie almost collapsed into the chair. Tears were running down her cheeks. Great-Aunt Sadie knelt beside the chair and pulled her close, rocking her. "There, there, it's all right. He's gone. What happened?"

"I mentioned about Odalie not inviting me to the party and he said I was just jealous of her. I said something, I don't…remember what, and he started toward me, all mad and impatient…" She closed her eyes, shivering. "I can't forget. All those years ago, and I still can't forget!"

"Nobody ever told Cort just what Odalie did to you, did they?"

"Apparently not," Maddie said heavily. She wiped her eyes. "Her dad made her apologize, but I know she never regretted it." She drew in a breath. "I told her that one day somebody was going to pay her back for all the mean things she did." She looked up. "Cort thinks she's a saint. If he only knew what she's really like…"

"It wouldn't matter," the older woman said sadly. "Men get hooked on a pretty face and they'd believe white was black if the woman told them it was. He's infatuated, baby. No cure for that but time."

"I thought he was so sexy." Maddie laughed. She brushed at her eyes again. "Then he lost his temper like that. He scared me," she said on a nervous smile.

"It's all right. Nobody's going to hurt you here. I promise."

She hugged the older woman tight. "Thanks."

"At the time, that boy did apologize, and he meant it," Sadie reminded her. "He was as much a victim as you were."

"Yes, but he got in trouble and he should have. No man, even an angry young one with justification, should ever do what he did to a girl. He didn't have nightmares for a month, either, did he, or carry emotional scars that never go away? Sad thing about him," she added quietly, "he died overseas when a roadside bomb blew up when he was serving in the Middle East. With a temper like that, I often wondered what he might do to a woman if he got even more upset than he was at me that time."

"No telling. And just as well we don't have to find out." Her face hardened. "But you're right about that Odalie girl. Got a bad attitude and no compassion for anybody. One of these days, life is going to pay her out in her own coin. She'll be sorry for the things she's done, but it will be too late. God forgives," she added. "But there's a price."

"What's that old saying, 'God's mill grinds slowly, but relentlessly'?"

"Something like that. Come on. I'll make you a nice cup of hot coffee."

"Make that a nice cup of hot chocolate instead," Maddie said. "I've had a rough day and I want to go to bed."

"I don't blame you. Not one bit."

CORT WAS THOUGHTFUL at breakfast the next morning. He was usually animated with his parents while he ate. But now he was quiet and retrospective.

"Something wrong?" his dad asked.

Cort glanced at him. He managed a smile. "Yeah. Something." He sipped coffee. "I went over her dad's journal with Maddie. We had sort of an argument and I started toward her while I was mad." He hesitated. "She knocked over a chair getting away from me. White in the face, shaking all over. It was an extreme reaction. We've argued before, but that's the first time she's been afraid of me."

"And you don't understand why." His father's expression was troubled.

"I don't." Cort's eyes narrowed. "But you do, don't you?"

He nodded.

"King, should you tell him?" Shelby asked worriedly.

"I think I should, honey," he said gently, and his dark eyes smiled with affection. "Somebody needs to."

"Okay then." She got up with her coffee. "You men talk. I'm going to phone Morie and see how she's doing."

"Give her my love," King called after her.

"Mine, too," Cort added.

She waved a hand and closed the door behind her. "Tell me," Cort asked his dad.

King put down his coffee cup. "In her senior year, Maddie was Odalie's worst enemy. There was a boy, seemingly a nice boy, who liked Maddie. But Odalie liked him, and she was angry that Maddie, a younger girl who wasn't pretty or rich or talented, seemed to be winning in the affection sweepstakes."

"I told Maddie, Odalie's not like that," Cort began angrily.

King held up a hand. "Just hear me out. Don't interrupt."

Cort made a face, but he shut up.

"So Odalie and a girlfriend got on one of the social websites and started posting things that she said Maddie told her about the boy. She said Maddie thought he was a hick, that his mother was stupid, that both his parents couldn't even pass a basic IQ test."

"What? That's a lie…!"

"Sit down!" King's voice was soft, but the look in his eyes wasn't. Cort sat.

"The boy's mother was dying of cancer. He was outraged and furious at what Maddie had allegedly said about his family. His mother had just been taken to the hospital, not expected to live. She died that same day. He went to school just to find Maddie. She was in the library." He picked up his cup and sipped coffee. "He jerked her out of her chair, slapped her over a table and pulled her by her hair to the window. He was in the act of throwing her out—and it was on the second floor—when the librarian screamed for help and two big, stronger boys restrained him, in the nick of time."

Cort's face froze. "Maddie told you that?"

"Her father's lawyer told Cole Everett that," came the terse reply. "There were at least five witnesses. The boy was arrested for assault. It was hushed up, because that's what's done in small communities to protect the families. Odalie was implicated, because the attorney hired a private investigator to find the source of the allegations. They traced the posts to her computer."

Cort felt uneasy. He was certain Odalie couldn't have done such a thing. "Maybe somebody used her computer," he began.

"She confessed," King said curtly.

Cort was even more uneasy now.

"Cole Everett had his own attorney speak to the one Maddie's father had hired. They worked out a compromise that wouldn't involve a trial. But Odalie had to toe the line from that time forward. They put her on probation, you see. She had first-offender status, so her record was wiped when she stayed out of trouble for the next two years. She had a girlfriend who'd egged her on. The girlfriend left town shortly thereafter."

"Yes," Cort replied, relaxing. "I see now. The girlfriend forced her to do it."

King made a curt sound deep in his throat. "Son, nobody forced her to do a damned thing. She was jealous of Maddie. She was lucky the boy didn't kill Maddie, or she'd have been an accessory to murder." He watched Cort's face pale. "That's right. And I don't think even Cole Everett could have kept her out of jail if that had happened."

Cort leaned back in his chair. "Poor Odalie."

"Funny," King said. "I would have said, 'Poor Maddie.'"

Cort flushed. "It must have been terrible for both of them, I suppose."

King just shook his head. He got up. "Blind as a bat," he mused. "Just like me, when I was giving your mother hell twice a day for being engaged to my little brother. God, I hated him. Hated them both. Never would admit why."

"Uncle Danny?" Cort exclaimed. "He was engaged to Mom?"

"He was. It was a fake engagcment, however." He chuckled. "He was just trying to show me what my feelings for Shelby really were. I forgave him every minute's agony. She's the best thing that ever happened to me. I didn't realize how deeply a man could love a woman. All these years," he added in a soft tone, "and those feelings haven't lessened a bit. I hope you find that sort of happiness in your life. I wish it for you."

"Thanks," Cort said. He smiled. "If I can get Odalie to marry me, I promise you, I'll have it."

King started to speak, but thought better of it. "I've got some book work to do."

"I've got a new video game I'm dying to try." Cort chuckled. "It's been a long day."

"I appreciate you going over to talk to Maddie."

"No problem. She just needed a few pointers."

"She's no cattlewoman," King said worriedly. "She's swimming upstream. She doesn't even like cattle. She likes chickens."

"Don't say chickens," Cort pleaded with a groan.

"Your problem isn't with chickens, it's with a rooster."

"I'd dearly love to help him have a fatal heart attack," Cort said irritably.

"He'll die of old age one day." His dad laughed.

"Maddie said that developer had been putting pressure on her to sell," King added solemnly. "I've put on some extra help to keep an eye over that way, just to make sure her breeding stock doesn't start dying mysteriously."

"What?" Cort asked, shocked. "She didn't say anything about that."

"Probably wouldn't, to you. It smacks of weakness to mention such things to the enemy."

"I'm not the enemy."

King smiled. "Aren't you?"

He left his son sitting at the table, deep in thought.

MADDIE WAS WORKING in the yard when the developer drove up a week later. She leaned on the pitchfork she was using to put hay into a trough, and waited, miserable, for him to get out of his car and talk to her.

"I won't sell," she said when he came up to her. "And in case you feel like high pressure tactics, my neighbor has mounted cameras all over the ranch." She flushed at his fury.

"Well, how about that?" he drawled, and his eyes were blazing with anger. He forced a smile. "You did know that cameras can be disabled?" he asked.

"The cameras also have listening devices that can pick up a whisper."

He actually seemed to go pale. He looked at the poles that contained the outside lighting and mumbled a curse under his breath. There was some sort of electronic device up there.

"I'll come back again one day and ask you the same

question," he promised, but he smiled and his voice was pleasant. "Maybe you'll change your mind."

"We also have cowboys in the line cabins on the borders of this ranch. Mr. Brannt is very protective of me since my father died. He buys many of our young breeding bulls," she added for good measure.

He was very still. "King Brannt?"

"Yes. You've heard of him, I gather."

He didn't reply. He turned on his heel and marched back to his car. But this time he didn't spin his wheels.

Maddie almost fell over with relief.

Just as the developer left, another car drove up, a sleek Jaguar, black with silver trim. Maddie didn't recognize it. Oh, dear, didn't some hit men drive fancy cars…?

The door opened and big John Everett climbed out of the low-slung luxury car, holding on to his white Stetson so that it wouldn't be dislodged from his thick head of blond hair. Maddie almost laughed with relief.

John grinned as he approached her. He had pale blue eyes, almost silver-colored, like his dad's, and he was a real dish. He and Odalie both had their mother's blond fairness, instead of Cole Everett's dark hair and olive complexion.

"What the hell's wrong with you?" he drawled. "Black cars make you twitchy or something?"

"I think hit men drive them, is all."

He burst out laughing. "I've never shot one single person. A deer or two, maybe, in season." He moved toward her and stopped, towering over her. His pale eyes were dancing on her flushed face. "I ran into King Brannt at a cattlemen's association meeting last night. He said you were having some problems trying to work out your father's breeding program. He said Cort explained it to you."

"Uh, well, yes, sort of." It was hard to admit that even taking notes, she hadn't understood much of what Cort had told her.

"Cort tried to tutor me in biology in high school. I got a D on the test. He's good at genetics, lousy at trying to explain them." He shoved his hat back on his head and grinned. "So I thought, maybe I'll come over and have a try at helping you understand it."

"You're a nice guy, John," she said gently. And he was. At the height of his sister's intimidation, John had been on Maddie's side.

He shrugged. "I'm the flower of my family." His face hardened. "Even if she is my sister, Odalie makes me ashamed sometimes. I haven't forgotten the things she did to you."

"We all make mistakes when we're young," she faltered, trying to be fair.

"You have a gentle nature," he observed. "Like Cort's mother. And mine," he added with a smile. "Mom can't bear to see anything hurt. She cried for days when your father's lawyer came over and told her and Dad what Odalie had done to you."

"I know. She called me. Your dad did, too. They're good people."

"Odalie might be a better person if she had a few disadvantages," John said coldly. "As things stand, she'll give in to Cort's persuasion one day and marry him. He'll be in hell for the rest of his life. The only person she's ever really loved is herself."

"That's harsh, John," she chided gently.

"It's the truth, Maddie." He swung his pointing finger at her nose. "You're like my mother...she'd find one nice thing to say about the devil." He smiled. "I'm in the mood to do some tutoring today. But I require payment. Your great-aunt makes a mean cup of coffee, and I'm partial to French vanilla."

"That's my favorite."

He chuckled. "Mine, too." He went back to the car, opened the passenger seat, took out a big box and a bag. "So since I drink a lot of it, I brought my own."

She caught her breath. It was one of those European coffee machines that used pods. Maddie had always wanted one, but the price was prohibitive.

"Sad thing is it only brews one cup at a time, but we'll compensate." He grinned. "So lead the way to the kitchen and I'll show you how to use it."

Two cups of mouthwatering coffee later, they were sitting in Maddie's father's office, going over breeding charts. John found the blackboard her father had used to map out the genetics. He was able to explain it so simply that Maddie understood almost at once which herd sires to breed to which cows.

"You make it sound so simple!" she exclaimed. "You're a wonder, John!"

He laughed. "It's all a matter of simplification," he drawled. He leaned back in the chair and sketched Maddie's radiant face with narrowed pale blue eyes. "You sell yourself short. It's not that you can't understand. You just have to have things explained. Cort's too impatient."

She averted her eyes. Mention of Cort made her uneasy.

"Yes, he loses his temper," John said thoughtfully. "But he's not dangerous. Not like that boy."

She paled. "I can't talk about it."

"You can, and you should," he replied solemnly. "Your father was advised to get some counseling for you, but he didn't believe in such things. That boy had a record for domestic assault, did you ever know? He beat his grandmother almost to death one day. She refused to press charges, or he would have gone to jail. His parents jumped in and got a fancy lawyer and convinced the authorities that he wasn't dangerous. I believe they contributed to the reelection campaign of the man who was police chief at the time as well."

"That's a harsh accusation," she said, shocked.

"It's a harsh world, and politics is the dirtiest business in town. Corruption doesn't stop at criminals, you know. Rich people have a way of subverting justice from time to time."

"You're rich, and you don't do those types of things."

"Yes, I am rich," he replied honestly. "And I'm honest. I have my own business, but I didn't get where I am by depending on my dad to support me."

She searched his eyes curiously. "Is that a dig at Cort?"

"It is," he replied quietly. "He stays at home, works on the ranch and does what King tells him to do. I told him some time ago that he's hurting himself by doing no more than wait to inherit Skylance, but he just nods and walks off."

"Somebody will have to take over the ranch when King is too old to manage it," she pointed out reasonably. "There isn't anybody else."

John grimaced. "I suppose that's true. But it's the same with me. Can you really see Odalie running a ranch?" He burst out laughing. "God, she might chip a fingernail!"

She grinned from ear to ear.

"Anyway, I was a maverick. I wanted my own business. I have a farm-equipment business and I also specialize in marketing native grasses for pasture improvement."

"You're an entrepreneur," she said with a chuckle.

"Something like that, I guess." He cocked his head and studied her. "You know I don't date much."

"Yes. Sort of like me. I'm not modern enough for most men."

"I'm not modern enough for most women," he replied, and smiled. "Uh, there's going to be a dressy party over at the Hancock place to introduce a new rancher in the area. I wondered if you might like to go with me?"

"A party?" she asked. She did have one good dress. She'd bought it for a special occasion a while ago, and she couldn't really afford another one with the ranch having financial issues. But it was a nice dress. Her eyes brightened. "I haven't been to a party in a long time. I went with Dad to a conference in Denver before he got sick."

"I remember. You looked very nice."

"Well, I'd be wearing the same dress I had on then," she pointed out.

He laughed. "I don't follow the current fashions for women," he mused. "I'm inviting you, not the dress."

"In that case," she said with a pert smile, "I'd be delighted!"

CHAPTER FOUR

SOME MEN DRAGGED their feet around the room and called it dancing. John Everett could actually dance! He knew all the Latin dances and how to waltz, although he was uncomfortable with some of the newer ways to display on a dance floor. Fortunately the organizers of the party were older people and they liked older music.

Only a minute into an enthusiastic samba, John and Maddie found themselves in the middle of the dance floor with the other guests clapping as they marked the fast rhythm.

"We should take this show on the road." John chuckled as they danced.

"I'm game. I'll give up ranching and become a professional samba performer, if you'll come, too," she suggested.

"Maybe only part of the year," he mused. "We can't let our businesses go to pot."

"Spoilsport."

He grinned.

While the two were dancing, oblivious to the other guests, a tall, dark man in a suit walked in and found himself a flute of champagne. He tasted it, nodding to other guests. Everyone was gathered around the dance floor of the ballroom in the Victorian mansion. He wandered to the fringes and caught his breath. There, on the dance floor, was Maddie Lane.

She was wearing a dress, a sheath of black slinky material that dipped in front to display just a hint of the lovely curve of her breasts and display her long elegant neck and rounded arms. Her pale blond hair shone like gold in the light from the chandeliers. She was wearing makeup, just enough to enhance what seemed to be a rather pretty face, and the pretty calves of her legs were displayed to their best advantage from the arch of her spiked high-heel shoes. He'd rarely seen her dressed up. Not that he'd been interested in her or anything.

But there she was, decked out like a Christmas tree, dancing with his best friend. John didn't date anybody. Until now.

Cort Brannt felt irritation rise in him like bile. He scowled at the display they were making of themselves. Had they no modesty at all? And people were clapping like idiots.

He glared at Maddie. He remembered the last time he'd seen her. She backed away from Cort, but she was dancing with John as if she really liked him. Her face was radiant. She was smiling. Cort had rarely seen her smile at all. Of course, usually he was yelling at her or making hurtful remarks. Not much incentive for smiles.

He sipped champagne. Someone spoke to him. He just nodded. He was intent on the dancing couple, focused and furious.

Suddenly he noticed that the flute was empty. He turned and went back to the hors d'oeuvres table and had them refill it. But he didn't go back to the dance floor. Instead he found a fellow cattleman to talk to about the drought and selling off cattle.

A few minutes later he was aware of two people helping themselves to punch and cake.

"Oh, hi, Cort," John greeted him with a smile. "I didn't think you were coming."

"Hadn't planned to," Cort said in a cool tone. "My dad had an emergency on the ranch, so I'm filling in. One of the officers of the cattlemen's association is here." He indicated the man with a nod of his head. "Dad wanted me to ask him about any pending legislation that might help us through the drought. We've heard rumors, but nothing substantial."

"My dad was wondering the same." John frowned. "You okay?"

"I'm fine," Cort said, making sure that he enunciated as plainly as possible. He stood taller, although he still wasn't as tall, or as big, as his friend. "Why do you ask?"

"Because that's your second glass of champagne and you don't drink," John said flatly.

Cort held the flute up and looked at it. It was empty. "Where did that go?" he murmured.

"Just a guess, but maybe you drank it?" John replied.

Cort set the flute on the spotless white tablecloth and looked down at Maddie. "You're keeping expensive company these days."

She was shocked at the implication.

"Hold it right there," John said, and his deep tone was menacing. "I invited her."

"Got plans, have you?" Cort replied coldly.

"Why shouldn't I?" came the droll reply. "Oh, by the way, Odalie says her Italian voice teacher is an idiot. He doesn't know beans about how to sing, and he isn't teaching her anything. So she thinks she may come home soon."

Maddie felt her heart sink. Cort's expression lightened. "You think she might?"

"It's possible. You should lay off that stuff."

Cort glanced at the flute. "I suppose so."

"Hey, John, can I talk to you for a minute?" a man called to him. "I need a new combine!"

"I need a new sale," John teased. He glanced at Maddie. "I won't be a minute, okay?"

"Okay," she said. But she was clutching her small evening bag as if she was afraid that it might escape. She started looking around for someone, anyone, to talk to besides Cort Brannt.

While she was thinking about running, he slid his big hand into her small one and pulled her onto the dance floor. He didn't even ask. He folded her into his arms and led her to the lazy, slow rhythm.

He smelled of spicy, rich cologne. He was much taller than she was, so her she couldn't see his face. She felt his cheek against the big wave of blond hair at her temple and her body began to do odd things. She felt uneasy, nervous. She felt…safe, excited.

"Your hand is like ice," he murmured as he danced with her around the room.

"They get cold all the time," she lied.

He laughed deep in his throat. "Really."

She wondered why he was doing this. Surely he should be pleased about Odalie's imminent reappearance in his life. He hated Maddie. Why was he dancing with her?

"I've never raised my hand to a woman," he said at her ear. "I never would, no matter how angry I was."

She swallowed and stopped dancing. She didn't want to talk about that.

He coaxed her eyes up. His were dark, narrow, intent. He was remembering what his father had told him, about the boy who tried to throw Maddie out a second-story window because of Odalie's lies. He didn't want to believe that Odalie had meant that to happen. Surely her female visitor had talked her into putting those nasty things about the boy and his family on the internet. But however it had happened, the thought of someone manhandling Maddie made him angry. It upset him.

He didn't really understand why. He'd never thought of her in any romantic way. She was just Pierce Lane's daughter. He'd known her since she was a child, watched her follow her dad around the ranch. She was always petting a calf or a dog, or carrying chickens around because she liked the sounds they made.

"Why are you watching me like that?" she faltered.

"You love animals, don't you?" he asked, and there was an odd, soft glow about his dark eyes. "I remember you carrying Mom's chickens around like cuddly toys when you'd come over to the ranch with your dad. You were very small then. I had to rescue you from one of the herding dogs. You tried to pet him, and he wasn't a pet."

"His name was Rowdy," she recalled. "He was so pretty."

"We never let anybody touch those dogs except the man who trains and uses them. They have to be focused. You didn't know." He smiled. "You were a cute little kid. Always asking questions, always curious about everything."

She shifted uncomfortably. He wasn't dancing and they were drawing attention.

He looked around, cocked an eyebrow and moved her back around the room in his arms. "Sorry."

She didn't know what to think. She was tingling all over. She wanted him to hold her so close that she could feel every inch of his powerful frame against her. She wanted him to bend his head and kiss her so hard that her lips would sting. She wanted…something. Something more. She didn't understand these new and unexpected longings. It was getting hard to breathe and her heartbeat was almost shaking her. She couldn't bear it if he noticed.

He did notice. She was like melting ice in his arms. He felt her shiver when he drew her even closer, so that her soft, pert little breasts were hard against his chest through the thin suit jacket he was wearing. He liked the way she smelled, of wildflowers in the sun.

He drank in that scent. It made his head swim. His arm contracted. He was feeling sensations that he'd almost forgotten. Odalie didn't like him close to her, so his longing for her had been stifled. But Maddie was soft and warm and receptive. Too receptive.

His mouth touched her ear. "You make me hungry," he whispered roughly.

"Ex-excuse me?" she stammered.

"I want to lay you down on the carpet and kiss your breasts until my body stops hurting."

She caught her breath and stopped dancing. She pushed back from him, her eyes blazing, her face red with embarrassment. She wanted to kick him in the shin, but that would cause more problems.

She turned away from him, almost shivering with the emotions he'd kindled in her, shocked at the things he'd said to her. She almost ran toward John, who was walking toward her, frowning.

"What is it?" he asked suddenly, putting his arm around her.

She hid her face against him.

He glared at Cort, who was approaching them with more conflicting emotions than he'd ever felt in his life.

"You need to go home," John told Cort in a patient tone that was belied by his expression. "You've had too much to drink and you're going to make a spectacle of yourself and us if you keep this up."

"I want to dance with her," Cort muttered stubbornly.

"Well, it's pretty obvious that she doesn't want to dance with you." John leaned closer. "I can pick you up over my shoulder and carry you out of here, and I will."

"I'd like to see you try it," Cort replied, and his eyes blazed with anger.

Another cattleman, seeing a confrontation building, came strolling over and deliberately got between the two men.

"Hey, Cort," he said pleasantly, "I need to ask you about those new calves your dad's going to put up at the fall production sale. Can I ride home with you and see them?"

Cort blinked. "It's the middle of the night."

"The barn doesn't have lights?" the older man asked, raising an eyebrow.

Cort was torn. He knew the man. He was from up around the Frio river. He had a huge ranch, and Cort's dad was hungry for new customers.

"The barn has lights. I guess we could…go look at the calves." He was feeling very light-headed. He wasn't used to alcohol. Not at all.

"I'll drive you home," the rancher said gently. "You can have one of your cowboys fetch your car, can't you?"

"Yeah. I guess so."

"Thanks," John told the man.

He shrugged and smiled. "No problem."

He indicated the door. Cort hesitated for just a minute. He looked back at Maddie with dark, stormy eyes, long enough that she dropped her own like hot bricks. He gave John a smug glance and followed the visiting cattleman out the door.

"Oh, boy," John said to himself. "Now we get to the complications."

"Complications?" Maddie was only half listening. Her eyes were on Cort's long, elegant back. She couldn't remember ever being so confused.

AFTER THE PARTY was over, John drove her to her front door and cut off the engine.

"What happened?" he asked her gently, because she was still visibly upset.

"Cort was out of line," she murmured without lifting her eyes.

"Not surprising. He doesn't drink. I can't imagine what got him started."

"I guess he's missing your sister," she replied with a sigh. She looked up at him. "She's really coming home?"

"She says she is," he told her. He made a face. "That's Odalie. She always knows more than anybody else about any subject. My parents let her get away with being sassy because she was pretty and talented." He laughed shortly. "My dad let me have it if I was ever rude or impolite or spoke out of turn. My brother had it even rougher."

She cocked her head. "You never talk about Tanner."

He grimaced. "I can't. It's a family thing. Maybe I'll tell you one day. Anyway, Dad pulled me up short if I didn't toe the line at home." He shook his head. "You wouldn't believe how many times I had to clean the horse stalls when I made him mad."

"Odalie is beautiful," Maddie conceded, but in a subdued tone.

"Only a very few people know what she did to you," John said quietly. "It shamed the family. Odalie was only sorry she got caught. I think she finally realized how tragic the results could have been, though."

"How so?"

"For one thing, she never spoke again to the girl-friend who put her up to it," he said. "After she got out of school, she stopped posting on her social page and threw herself into studying music."

"The girlfriend moved away, didn't she, though?"

"She moved because threats were made. Legal ones," John confided. "My dad sent his attorneys after her. He was pretty sure that Odalie didn't know how to link internet sites and post simultaneously, which is what was done about you." He touched her short hair gently. "Odalie is spoiled and snobbish and she thinks she's the center of the universe. But she isn't cruel."

"Isn't she?"

"Well, not anymore," he added. "Not since the law-yers got involved. You weren't the only girl she victim-ized. Several others came forward and talked to my dad when they heard about what happened to you in the library. He was absolutely dumbfounded. So was my mother." He shook his head. "Odalie never got over what they said to her. She started making a real effort to consider the feelings of other people. Years too late, of course, and she's still got that bad attitude."

"It's a shame she isn't more like your mother," Maddie said gently, and she smiled. "Mrs. Everett is a sweet woman."

"Yes. Mom has an amazing voice and is not conceited. She was offered a career in opera but she turned it down. She liked singing the blues, she said. Now, she just plays and sings for us, and composes. There's still the occasional journalist who shows up at the door when one of her songs is a big hit, like Desperado's."

"Do they still perform...I mean Desperado?" she qualified.

"Yes, but not so much. They've all got kids now. It makes it tough to go on the road, except during summer holidays."

She laughed. "I love their music."

"Me, too." He studied her. "Odd."

"What is?"

"You're so easy to talk to. I don't get along with most women. I'm strung up and nervous and the aggressive ones make me uncomfortable. I sort of gave up dating after my last bad experience." He laughed. "I don't like women making crude remarks to me."

"Isn't it funny how things have changed?" she wondered aloud. "Not that I'm making fun of you. It's just that women used to get hassled. They still do, but it's turned around somewhat—now men get it, too."

"Yes, life is much more complicated now."

"I really enjoyed the party. Especially the dancing."

"Me, too. We might do that again one day."

She raised both eyebrows. "We might?"

He chuckled. "I'll call you."

"That would be nice."

He smiled, got out, went around and opened the door for her. He seemed to be debating whether or not to kiss her. She liked that lack of aggression in him. She smiled, went on tiptoe and kissed him right beside his chiseled mouth.

"Thanks again," she said. "See you!"

She went up the steps and into the house. John Everett stood looking after her wistfully. She thought he was nice. She liked him. But when she'd come off the dance floor trailing Cort Brannt, she'd been radiating like a furnace. Whether she knew it or not, she was in love with Cort. Shame, he thought as he drove off. She was just the sort of woman he'd like to settle down with. Not much chance of that, now.

Maddie didn't sleep at all. She stared at the ceiling. Her body tingled from the long contact with Cort's. She could feel his breath on her forehead, his lips in her hair. She could hear what he'd whispered.

She flushed at the memory. It had evoked incredible hunger. She didn't understand why she had these feelings now, when she hadn't had them for that boy who'd tried to hurt her so badly. She'd really thought she was crazy about him. But it was nothing like this.

Since her bad experience, she hadn't dated much. She'd seen her father get mad, but it was always quick and never physical. She hadn't been exposed to men who hit women. Now she knew they existed. It had been a worrying discovery.

Cort had frightened her when he'd lost his temper so violently in her father's office. She didn't think he'd attack her. But she'd been wary of him, until they danced together. Even if he was drunk, it had been the experience of a lifetime. She thought she could live on it forever, even if Odalie came home and Cort married her. He was never going to be happy with her, though. Odalie loved herself so much that there was no room in her life for a man.

If only the other woman had fallen in love with the Italian voice trainer and married him. Then Cort would have to let go of his unrequited feelings for Odalie, and maybe look in another direction. Maybe look in Maddie's direction.

On the other hand, he'd only been teasing at the dance. He wasn't himself.

Cold sober, he'd never have anything to do with Maddie. Probably, he'd just been missing Odalie and wanted a warm body to hold. Yes. That was probably it.

JUST BEFORE DAWN she fell asleep, but all too soon it was time to get up and start doing the chores around the ranch.

She went to feed her flock of hens, clutching the metal garbage can lid and the leafy limb to fend off Pumpkin. Somewhere in the back of her mind, she realized that it was going to come down to a hard decision one day. Pumpkin protected her hens, yes; he would be the bane of predators everywhere. But he was equally dangerous to people. What if he flew up and got one of her cowboys in the eye? She'd been reading up on rooster behavior, and she'd read some horror stories.

There had been all sorts of helpful advice, like giving him special treats and being nice to him. That had resulted in more gouges on her legs, even through her slacks, where his spurs had landed. Then there was the advice about having his spurs trimmed. Good advice, but who was going to catch and hold him while someone did that? None of her cowboys were lining up to volunteer.

"You problem child," she told Pumpkin as he chased her toward the gate. "One day, I'll have to do something about you!"

She got through the gate in the nick of time and shut it, hard. At least he wasn't going to get out of there, she told herself. She'd had Ben go around the perimeter of the large fenced area that surrounded the henhouse and plug any openings where that sneaky feathered fiend could possibly get out. If she kept him shut up, he couldn't hurt anybody, and the fence was seven feet high. No way he was jumping that!

She said so to Ben as she made her way to the barn to check on a calf they were nursing; it had dropped late and its mother had been killed by predators. They found it far on the outskirts of the ranch. They couldn't figure how it had wandered so far, but then, cattle did that. It was why you brought pregnant cows up close to the barn, so that you'd know when they were calving. It was especially important to do that in winter, just before the spring calves were due.

She looked over the gate at the little calf in the stall and smiled. "Pretty boy," she teased.

He was a purebred Santa Gertrudis bull. Some were culled and castrated and became steers, if they had poor conformation or were less than robust. But the best ones were treated like cattle royalty, spoiled rotten and watched over. This little guy would one day bring a handsome price as a breeding bull.

She heard a car door slam and turned just as Cort came into the barn.

She felt her heartbeat shoot off like a rocket.

He tilted his hat back and moved to the stall, peering over it. "That's a nice young one," he remarked.

"His mother was killed, so we're nursing him," she faltered.

He frowned. "Killed?"

"Predators, we think," she replied. "She was pretty torn up. We found her almost at the highway, out near your line cabin. Odd, that she wandered so far."

"Very odd," he agreed.

Ben came walking in with a bottle. "'Day, Cort," he said pleasantly.

"How's it going, Ben?" the younger man replied.

"So far so good."

Maddie smiled as Ben settled down in the hay and fed the bottle to the hungry calf.

"Poor little guy," Maddie said.

"He'll make it," Ben promised, smiling up at her.

"Well, I'll leave you to it," Maddie said. She was reluctant to be alone with Cort after the night before, but she couldn't see any way around it.

"You're up early," she said, fishing for a safe topic.

"I didn't sleep." He stuck his hands into his pockets as he strolled along with her toward the house.

"Oh?"

He stopped, so that she had to. His eyes were bloodshot and they had dark circles under them. "I drank too much," he said. "I wanted to apologize for the way I behaved with you."

"Oh." She looked around for anything more than one syllable that she could reply with. "That's...that's okay."

He stared down at her with curiously intent eyes. "You're incredibly naive."

She averted her eyes and her jaw clenched. "Yes,

well, with my background, you'd probably be the same way. I haven't been anxious to repeat the mistakes of the past with some other man who wasn't what he seemed to be."

"I'm sorry. About what happened to you."

"Everybody was sorry," she replied heavily. "But nobody else has to live with the emotional baggage I'm carrying around."

"How did you end up at the party with John?"

She blinked. "Well, he came over to show me some things about animal husbandry, and he asked me to go with him. It was sort of surprising, really. He doesn't date anybody."

"He's had a few bad experiences with women. So have I."

She'd heard about Cort's, but she wasn't opening that topic with him. "Would you like coffee?" she asked. "Great-Aunt Sadie went shopping, but she left a nice coffee cake baking in the oven. It should be about ready."

"Thanks. I could use a second cup," he added with a smile.

But the smile faded when he saw the fancy European coffee machine on the counter. "Where the hell did you buy that?" he asked.

She flushed. "I didn't. John likes European coffee, so he brought the machine and the pods over with him."

He lifted his chin. "Did he, now? I gather he thinks he'll be having coffee here often, then?"

She frowned. "He didn't say anything about that."

He made a huffing sound in his throat, just as the stove timer rang. Maddie went to take the coffee cake out of the oven. She was feeling so rattled, it was a good thing she'd remembered that it was baking. She placed it on a trivet. It smelled of cinnamon and butter.

"My great-aunt can really cook," she remarked as she took off the oven mitts she'd used to lift it out.

"She can, can't she?"

She turned and walked right into Cort. She hadn't realized he was so close. He caught her small waist in his big hands and lifted her right onto the counter next to the coffee cake, so that she was even with his dark, probing eyes.

"You looked lovely last night," he said in a strange, deep tone. "I've never really seen you dressed up before."

"I…I don't dress up," she stammered. He was tracing her collarbone and the sensations it aroused were delicious and unsettling. "Just occasionally."

"I didn't know you could do those complicated Latin dances, either," he continued.

"I learned them from watching television," she said.

His head was lower now. She could feel his breath on her lips; feel the heat from his body as he moved closer, in between her legs so that he was right up against her.

"I'm not in John Everett's class as a dancer," he drawled, tilting her chin up. "But, then, he's not in my class…at this…"

His mouth slowly covered hers, teasing gently, so that he didn't startle her. He tilted her head just a little more, so that her mouth was at just the right angle. His firm lips pushed hers apart, easing them back, so that he had access to the soft, warm depths of her mouth.

He kissed her with muted hunger, so slowly that she didn't realize until too late how much a trap it was. He grew insistent then, one lean hand at the back of her head, holding it still, as his mouth devoured her soft lips.

"Sweet," he whispered huskily. "You taste like honey...."

His arms went under hers and around her, lifting her, so that her breasts were flattened against his broad, strong chest.

Involuntarily her cold hands snaked around his neck. She'd never felt hunger like this. She hadn't known it was possible. She let him open her mouth with his, let him grind her breasts against him. She moaned softly as sensations she'd never experienced left her helpless, vulnerable.

She felt his hand in her hair, tangling in it, while he kissed her in the soft silence of the kitchen. It was a moment out of time when she wished it could never end, that she could go on kissing him forever.

But just when he lifted his head, and looked into her eyes, and started to speak...

A car pulled up at the front porch and a door slammed.

Maddie looked into Cort's eyes with shock. He seemed almost as unsettled as she did. He moved back, helping her off the counter and onto her feet. He backed up just as Great-Aunt Sadie walked in with two bags of groceries.

"Didn't even have fresh mushrooms, can you believe it?" she was moaning, her mind on the door that was trying to close in her face rather than the two dazed people in the kitchen.

"Here, let me have those," Cort said politely, and he took the bags and put them on the counter. "Are there more in the car?" he asked.

"No, but thank you, Cort," Sadie said with a warm smile.

He grinned. "No problem." He glanced at Maddie, who still looked rattled. "I have to go. Thanks for the offer of coffee. Rain check?" he added, and his eyes were almost black with feeling.

"Oh, yes," Maddie managed breathlessly. "Rain check."

He smiled at her and left her standing there, vibrating with new hope.

CHAPTER FIVE

MADDIE STILL COULDN'T believe what had happened right there in her kitchen. Cort had kissed her, and as if he really did feel something for her. Besides that, he was very obviously jealous of John Everett. She felt as if she could actually walk on air.

"You look happier than I've seen you in years, sweetie," Great-Aunt Sadie said with a smile.

"I am."

Sadie grinned. "It's that John Everett, isn't it?" she teased. She indicated the coffeemaker. "Thought he was pretty interested. I mean, those things cost the earth. Not every man would start out courting a girl with a present like that!"

"Oh. Well, of course, I like John," Maddie stammered. And then she realized that she couldn't very well tell her great-aunt what was going on. Sadie might start gossiping. Maddie's ranch hands had friends who worked for the Brannts. She didn't want Cort to think she was telling tales about him, even in an innocent way. After all, it might have been a fluke. He could be missing Odalie and just reacted to Maddie in unexpected ways.

"He's a dish," Sadie continued as she peeled potatoes in the kitchen. "Handsome young man, just like his dad." She grimaced. "I'm not too fond of his sister, but, then, no family is perfect."

"No." She hesitated. "Sadie, do you know why no-body talks about the oldest brother, Tanner?"

Sadie smiled. "Just gossip. They said he and his dad had a major falling out over his choice of careers and he packed up and went to Europe. That was when he was in his late teens. As far as I know, he's never contacted the family since. It's a sore spot with the Everetts, so they don't talk about him anymore. Too painful, I expect."

"That's sad."

"Yes, it is. There was a rumor that he was hanging out with some dangerous people as well. But you know what rumors are."

"Yes," Maddie said.

"What was Cort doing over here earlier in the week?" Sadie asked suddenly.

"Oh, he was just…giving me some more pointers on dad's breeding program," Maddie lied.

"Scared you to death, too," Sadie said irritably. "I don't think he'd hurt you, but he's got a bad temper, sweetie."

Maddie had forgotten that, in the new relationship she seemed to be building with Cort. "People say his father was like that, when he was young. But Shelby married him and tamed him," she added with a se-cret smile.

Sadie glanced at her curiously. "I guess that can happen. A good woman can be the salvation of a man. But just…be careful."

"I will," she promised. "Cort isn't a mean person."

Sadie gave her a careful look. "So that's how it is."

Maddie flushed. "I don't know what you mean."

"John likes you, a lot," she replied.

Maddie sighed. "John's got a barracuda for a sister, too," she reminded the older woman. "No way in the world am I having her for a sister-in-law, no matter how nice John is."

Sadie grimaced. "Should have thought of that, shouldn't I?"

"I did."

She laughed. "I guess so. But just a suggestion, if you stick your neck out with Cort," she added very seriously. "Make him mad. Make him really mad, someplace where you can get help if you need to. Don't wait and find out when it's too late if he can't control his temper."

"I remember that boy in high school," Maddie reminded her. "He didn't stop. Cort frightened me, yes, but when he saw I was afraid, he started apologizing. If he couldn't control his temper, he'd never have been able to stop."

Sadie looked calmer. "No. I don't think he would."

"He's still apologizing for it, in fact," Maddie added.

Sadie smiled and her eyes were kind. "All right, then. I won't harp on it. He's a lot like his father, and his dad is a good man."

"They're all nice people. Morie was wonderful to me in school. She stuck up for me when Odalie and her girlfriend were making my life a daily purgatory."

"Pity Odalie never really gets paid back for the things she does," Sadie muttered."

Maddie hugged her. "That mill grinds slowly but relentlessly," she reminded her. She grinned. "One day…"

Sadie laughed. "One day."

Maddie let her go with a sigh. "I hope I can learn enough of this stuff not to sink dad's cattle operation," she moaned. "I wasn't really faced with having to deal with the breeding aspect until now, with roundup ahead and fall breeding standing on the line in front of me. Which bull do I put on which cows? Gosh! It's enough to drive you nuts!"

"Getting a lot of help in that, though, aren't you?" Sadie teased. "Did you tell Cort that John had been coaching you, too?"

"Yes." She sighed. "Cort wasn't overjoyed about it, either. But John makes it understandable." She threw up her hands. "I'm just slow. I don't understand cattle. I love to paint and sculpt. But Dad never expected to go so soon and have to leave me in charge of things. We're going in the hole because I don't know what I'm doing." She glanced at the older woman. "In about two years, we're going to start losing customers. It terrifies me. I don't want to lose the ranch, but it's going to go downhill without dad to run it." She toyed with a bag on the counter. "I've been thinking about that developer..."

"Don't you dare," Sadie said firmly. "Darlin', do you realize what he'd do to this place if he got his hands on it?" she exclaimed. "He'd sell off all the livestock to anybody who wanted it, even for slaughter, and he'd rip the land to pieces. All that prime farmland, gone, all the native grasses your dad planted and nurtured, gone. This house—" she indicated it "—where your father and your grandfather and I were born! Gone!"

Maddie felt sick. "Oh, dear."

"You're not going to run the ranch into the ground. Not when you have people, like King Brannt, who want to help you get it going again," she said firmly. "If you ever want to sell up, you talk to him. I'll bet he'd offer for it and put in a manager. We could probably even stay on and pay rent."

"With what?" Maddie asked reasonably. "Your social security check and my egg money?" She sighed. "I can't sell enough paintings or enough eggs to pay for lunch in town," she added miserably. "I should have gone to school and learned a trade or something." She grimaced. "I don't know what to do."

"Give it a little time," the older woman said gently. "I know it's overwhelming, but you can learn. Ask John to make you a chart and have Ben in on the conversation. Your dad trusted Ben with everything, even the finances. I daresay he knows as much as you do about things."

"That's an idea." She smiled sadly. "I don't really want to sell that developer anything. He's got a shady look about him."

"You're telling me."

"I guess I'll wait a bit."

"Meanwhile, you might look in that bag I brought home yesterday."

"Isn't it groceries…dry goods?"

"Look."

She peered in the big brown bag and caught her breath. "Sculpting material. Paint! Great-Aunt Sadie!" she exclaimed, and ran and hugged the other woman. "That's so sweet of you!"

"Looking out for you, darling," she teased. "I want you to be famous so those big TV people will want to interview me on account of we're related!" She stood up and struck a pose. "Don't you think I'd be a hit?"

Maddie hugged her even tighter. "I think you're already a hit. Okay. I can take a hint. I'll get to work right now!"

Sadie chortled as she rushed from the room.

CORT CAME IN several days later while she was retouching one of the four new fairies she'd created, working where the light was best, in a corner of her father's old office. She looked up, startled, when Great-Aunt Sadie let him in.

She froze. "Pumpkin came after you again?" she asked, worried.

"What?" He looked around, as if expecting the big red rooster to appear. "Oh, Pumpkin." He chuckled. "No. He was in the hen yard giving me mean looks, but he seems to be well contained."

"Thank goodness!"

He moved to the table and looked at her handiwork. "What a group," he mused, smiling. "They're all beautiful."

"Thanks." She wished she didn't sound so breathless, and that she didn't have paint dabbed all over her face from her days' efforts. She probably looked like a painting herself.

"Going to sell them?"

"Oh, I couldn't," she said hesitantly. "I mean, I... well, I just couldn't."

"Can't you imagine what joy they'd bring to other people?" he asked, thinking out loud. "Why do you think doll collectors pay so much for one-of-a-kind creations like those? They build special cabinets for them, take them out and talk to them..."

"You're kidding!" she exclaimed, laughing. "Really?"

"This one guy I met at the conference said he had about ten really rare dolls. He sat them around the dining room table every night and talked to them while he ate. He was very rich and very eccentric, but you get the idea. He loved his dolls. He goes to all the doll collector conventions. In fact, there's one coming up in Denver, where they're holding a cattlemen's workshop." He smiled. "Anyway, your fairies wouldn't be sitting on a shelf collecting dust on the shelf of a collector like that. They'd be loved."

"Wow." She looked back at the little statuettes. "I never thought of it like that."

"Maybe you should."

She managed a shy smile. He looked delicious in a pair of beige slacks and a yellow, very expensive pullover shirt with an emblem on the pocket. Thick black hair peeked out where the top buttons were undone. She wondered how his bare chest would feel against her hands. She blushed. "What can I do for you?" she asked quickly, trying to hide her interest.

Her reaction to him was amusing. He found it really touching. Flattering. He hadn't been able to get her out of his mind since he'd kissed her so hungrily in her kitchen. He'd wanted to come back sooner than this, but business had overwhelmed him.

"I have to drive down to Jacobsville, Texas, to see a rancher about some livestock," he said. "I thought you might like to ride with me."

She stared at him as if she'd won the lottery. "Me?"

"You." He smiled. "I'll buy you lunch on the way. I know this little tearoom off the beaten path. We can have high tea and buttermilk pie."

She caught her breath. "I used to hear my mother talk about that one. I've never had high tea. I'm not even sure what it is, exactly."

"Come with me and find out."

She grinned. "Okay! Just let me wash up first."

"Take your time. I'm not in any hurry."

"I'll just be a few minutes."

She almost ran up the staircase to her room.

Cort picked up one of the delicate little fairies and

stared at it with utter fascination. It was ethereal, beautiful, stunning. He'd seen such things before, but never anything so small with such personality. The little fairy had short blond hair, like Maddie's, and pale eyes. It amused him that she could paint something so tiny. He noted the magnifying glass standing on the table, and realized that she must use it for the more detailed work. Still, it was like magic, making something so small look so realistic.

He put it down, very carefully, and went into the kitchen to talk to Sadie while he waited for Maddie to get ready.

"Those little fairies she makes are amazing," he commented, lounging against the counter.

Sadie smiled at him. "They really are. I don't know how she does all that tiny detailed work without going blind. The little faces are so realistic. She has a gift."

"She does. I wish she'd do something with it."

"Me, too," Sadie replied. "But she doesn't want to sell her babies, as she calls them."

"She's sitting on a gold mine here." Cort sighed. "You know, breeding herd sires is hard work, even for people who've done it for generations and love it."

She glanced at him and she looked worried. "I know. She doesn't really want to do it. My nephew had to toss her in at the deep end when he knew his cancer was fatal." She shook her head. "I hate it for her. You shouldn't be locked into a job you don't want to do. But she's had no training. She really can't do anything else."

"She can paint. And she can sculpt."

"Yes, but there's still the ranch," Sadie emphasized. "Any problem has a solution. It's just a question of finding it." He sighed. "Ben said you'd had another cow go missing."

"Yes." She frowned. "Odd thing, too, she was in a pasture with several other cows, all of them healthier than her. I can't think somebody would steal her."

"I know what you mean. They do wander off. It's just that it looks suspicious, having two go missing in the same month."

"Could it be that developer man?"

Cort shook his head. "I wouldn't think so. We've got armed patrols and cameras mounted everywhere. If anything like that was going on, we'd see it."

"I suppose so."

There was the clatter of footsteps almost leaping down the staircase.

"Okay, I'm ready," Maddie said, breathless. She was wearing jeans and boots and a pretty pink button-up blouse. She looked radiant.

"Where are you off to?" Sadie asked, laughing.

"I'm going to Jacobsville with Cort to look at livestock."

"Oh." Sadie forced a smile. "Well, have fun, then."

Cort started the sleek two-seater Jaguar. He glanced at Maddie, who was looking at everything with utter fascination.

"Not quite like your little Volkswagen, huh?" he teased.

"No! It's like a spaceship or something."

"Watch this."

As he started the car, the air vents suddenly opened up and the Jaguar symbol lit up on a touch screen between the steering wheel and the glove compartment. At the same time, the gearshift rose up from the console, where it had been lying flat.

"Oh, gosh!" she exclaimed. "That's amazing!"

He chuckled. "I like high-tech gadgets."

"John has one of these," she recalled.

His eyes narrowed. "So he does. I rode him around in mine and he found a dealership the next day. His is more sedate."

"I just think they're incredible."

He smiled. "Fasten your seat belt."

"Oops, sorry, wasn't thinking." She reached up and drew it between her breasts, to fasten it beside her hip.

"I always wear my seat belt," he said. "Dad refused to drive the car until we were all strapped in. He was in a wreck once. He said he never forgot that he'd be dead except for the seat belt."

"My dad wasn't in a wreck, but he was always careful about them, too." She put her strappy purse on the floorboard. "Did Odalie come home?" she asked, trying not to sound too interested.

"Not yet," he said. He had to hide a smile, because the question lacked any subtlety.

"Oh."

He was beginning to realize that Odalie had been a major infatuation for him. Someone unreachable that he'd dreamed about, much as young boys dreamed about movie stars. He knew somewhere in the back of his mind that he and Odalie were as different as night and day. She wanted an operatic career and wasn't interested in fitting him into that picture. Would he be forever hanging around opera houses where she performed, carrying bags and organizing fans? Or would he be in Texas, waiting for her rare visits? She couldn't have a family and be a performer, not in the early stages of her career, maybe never. Cort wanted a family. He wanted children.

Funny, he'd never thought of himself as a parent before. But when he'd listened to Maddie talk about her little fairy sculptures and spoke of them as her children, he'd pictured her with a baby in her arms. It had shocked him how much he wanted to see that for real.

"You like kids, don't you?" he asked suddenly.

"What brought that on?" She laughed.

"What you said, about your little fairy sculptures. They're beautiful kids."

"Thanks." She looked out the window at the dry, parched grasslands they were passing through. "Yes, I love kids. Oh, Cort, look at the poor corn crops! That's old Mr. Raines's land, isn't it?" she added. "He's already holding on to his place by his fingernails I guess he'll have to sell if it doesn't rain."

"My sister said they're having the same issues up in Wyoming." He glanced at her. "Her husband knows a medicine man from one of the plains tribes. She said that he actually did make it rain a few times. Nobody understands how, and most people think it's fake, but I wonder."

"Ben was talking about a Cheyenne medicine man who can make rain. He's friends with him. I've known people who could douse for water," she said.

"Now, there's a rare talent indeed," he commented. He pursed his lips. "Can't Ben do that?"

"Shh," she said, laughing. "He doesn't want people to think he's odd, so he doesn't want us to tell anybody."

"Still, you might ask him to go see if he could find water. If he does, we could send a well-borer over to do the job for him."

She looked at him with new eyes. "That's really nice of you."

He shrugged. "I'm nice enough. From time to time."
He glanced at her pointedly. "When women aren't driving me to drink."

"What? I didn't drive you to drink!"

"The hell you didn't," he mused, his eyes on the road so that he missed her blush. "Dancing with John Everett. Fancy dancing. Latin dancing." He sighed. "I can't even do a waltz."

"Oh, but that doesn't matter," she faltered, trying to deal with the fact that he was jealous. Was he? That was how it sounded! "I mean, I think you dance very nicely."

"I said some crude things to you," he said heavily. "I'm really sorry. I don't drink, you see. When I do…" He let the sentence trail off. "Anyway, I apologize."

"You already apologized."

"Yes, but it weighs on my conscience." He stopped at a traffic light. He glanced at her with dark, soft eyes. "John's my friend. I think a lot of him. But I don't like him taking you out on dates and hanging around you."

She went beet-red. She didn't even know what to say.

"I thought it might come as a shock," he said softly. He reached a big hand across the console and caught hers in it. He linked her fingers with his and looked into her eyes while he waited for the lights to change. "I thought we might take in a movie Friday night. There's that new Batman one."

"There's that new Ice Age one," she said at the same time.

He gave her a long, amused look. "You like cartoon movies?"

She flushed. "Well…"

He burst out laughing. "So do I. Dad thinks I'm nuts."

"Oh, I don't!"

His fingers contracted around hers. "Well, in that case, we'll see the Ice Age one."

"Great!"

The light changed and he drove on. But he didn't let go of her hand.

High tea was amazing! There were several kinds of tea, china cups and saucers to contain it, and little cucumber sandwiches, chicken salad sandwiches, little cakes and other nibbles. Maddie had never seen anything like it. The tearoom was full, too, with tourists almost overflowing out of the building, which also housed an antique shop.

"This is awesome!" she exclaimed as she sampled one thing after another.

"Why, thank you." The owner laughed, pausing by their table. "We hoped it would be a success." She shook her head. "Everybody thought we were crazy. We're from Charleston, South Carolina. We came out here when my husband was stationed in the air force base at San Antonio, and stayed. We'd seen another tearoom, way north, almost in Dallas, and we were so impressed with it that we thought we might try one of our own. Neither of us knew a thing about restaurants, but we learned, with help from our staff." She shook her head. "Never dreamed we'd have this kind of success," she added, looking around. "It's quite a dream come true."

"That cameo," Maddie said hesitantly, nodding toward a display case close by. "Does it have a story?"

"A sad one. The lady who owned it said it was handed down in her family for five generations. Finally there was nobody to leave it to. She fell on hard times and asked me to sell it for her." She sighed. "She died a month ago." She opened the case with a key and pulled out the cameo, handing it to Maddie. It was black lacquer with a beautiful black-haired Spanish lady painted on it. She had laughing black eyes and a sweet smile. "She was so beautiful."

"It was the great-great-grandmother of the owner. They said a visiting artist made it and gave it to her. She and her husband owned a huge ranch, from one of those Spanish land grants. Pity there's nobody to keep the legend going."

"Oh, but there is." Cort took it from the woman and handed it to Maddie. "Put it on the tab, if you will," he told the owner. "I can't think of anyone who'll take better care of her."

"No, you can't," Maddie protested, because she saw the price tag.

"I can," Cort said firmly. "It was a family legacy. It still is." His dark eyes stared meaningfully into hers. "It can be handed down, to your own children. You might have a daughter who'd love it one day."

Maddie's heart ran wild. She looked into Cort's dark eyes and couldn't turn away.

"I'll put the ticket with lunch," the owner said with a soft laugh. "I'm glad she'll have a home," she added gently.

"Can you write down the woman's name who sold it to you?" Maddie asked. "I want to remember her, too."

"That I can. How about some buttermilk pie? It's the house specialty," she added with a grin.

"I'd love some."

"Me, too," Cort said.

Maddie touched the beautiful cheek of the cameo's subject. "I should sculpt a fairy who looks like her."

"Yes, you should," Cort agreed at once. "And show it with the cameo."

She nodded. "How sad," she said, "to be the last of your family."

"I can almost guarantee that you won't be the last of yours," he said in a breathlessly tender tone.

She looked up into his face and her whole heart was in her eyes.

He had to fight his first impulse, which was to drag her across the table into his arms and kiss the breath out of her.

She saw that hunger in him and was fascinated that she seemed to have inspired it. He'd said that she was plain and uninteresting. But he was looking at her as if he thought her the most beautiful woman on earth.

"Dangerous," he teased softly, "looking at me like that in a public place."

"Huh?" She caught her breath as she realized what he was saying. She laughed nervously, put the beautiful cameo beside her plate and smiled at him. "Thank you, for the cameo."

"My pleasure. Eat up. We've still got a long drive ahead of us!"

Jacobsville, Texas, was a place Maddie had heard of all her life, but she'd never seen it before. In the town square, there was a towering statue of Big John Jacobs, the founder of Jacobsville, for whom Jacobs County was named. Legend had it that he came to Texas from Georgia after the Civil War, with a wagonload of black sharecroppers. He also had a couple of Comanche men who helped him on the ranch. It was a fascinating story, how he'd married the spunky but not so pretty daughter of a multimillionaire and started a dynasty in Texas.

Maddie shared the history with Cort as they drove down a long dirt road to the ranch, which was owned by Cy Parks. He was an odd sort of person, very reticent, with jet-black hair sprinkled with silver and piercing green eyes. He favored one of his arms, and Maddie could tell that it had been badly burned at some point. His wife was a plain little blonde woman who wore glasses and obviously adored her husband. The feeling seemed to be mutual. They had two sons who were in school, Lisa explained shyly. She was sorry she couldn't introduce them to the visitors.

Cy Parks showed them around his ranch in a huge SUV. He stopped at one pasture and then another, grimacing at the dry grass.

"We're having to use up our winter hay to feed them," he said with a sigh. "It's going to make it a very hard winter if we have to buy extra feed to carry us through." He glanced at Cort and laughed. "You'll make my situation a bit easier if you want to carry a couple of my young bulls home with you."

Cort grinned, too. "I think I might manage that. Although we're in the same situation you are. Even my sister's husband, who runs purebred cattle in Wyoming, is having it rough. This drought is out of anybody's experience. People are likening it to the famous Dust Bowl of the thirties."

"There was another bad drought in the fifties," Parks added. "When we live on the land, we always have issues with weather, even in good years. This one has been a disaster, though. It will put a lot of the family farms and ranches out of business." He made a face. "They'll be bought up by those damned great combines, corporate ranching, I call it. Animals pumped up with drugs, genetically altered—damned shame. Pardon the language," he added, smiling apologetically at Maddie.

"She's lived around cattlemen all her life," Cort said affectionately, smiling over the back of the seat at her.

"Yes, I have." Maddie laughed. She looked into Cort's dark eyes and blushed. He grinned.

They stopped at the big barn on the way back and Cy led them through it to a stall in the rear. It connected to a huge paddock with plenty of feed and fresh water.

"Now this is my pride and joy," he said, indicating a sleek, exquisite young Santa Gertrudis bull.

"That is some conformation," Cort said, whistling. "He's out of Red Irony, isn't he?" he added.

Cy chuckled. "So you read the cattle journals, do you?"

"All of them. Your ranch has some of the best breeding stock in Texas. In the country, in fact."

"So does Skylance," Parks replied. "I've bought your own bulls over the years. And your father's," he added to Maddie. "Good stock."

"Thanks," she said.

"Same here," Cort replied. He drew in a breath. "Well, if this little fellow's up for bids, I'll put ours in."

"No bids. He's yours if you want him." He named a price that made Maddie feel faint, but Cort just smiled.

"Done," he said, and they shook hands.

On the way back home, Maddie was still astonished at the price. "That's a fortune," she exclaimed.

"Worth every penny, though," Cort assured her. "Healthy genetics make healthy progeny. We have to put new bulls on our cows every couple of years to avoid any defects. Too much inbreeding can be dangerous to the cattle and disastrous for us."

"I guess so. Mr. Parks seems like a very nice man," she mused.

He chuckled. "You don't know his history, do you? He led one of the most respected groups of mercenaries in the world into small wars overseas. His friend Eb Scott still runs a world-class counterterrorism school on his ranch. He was part of the merc group, along with a couple of other citizens of Jacobsville."

"I didn't know!"

"He's a good guy. Dad's known him for years."

"What a dangerous way to make a living, though."

"No more dangerous than dealing with livestock," Cort returned.

That was true. There were many pitfalls of working with cattle, the least of which was broken bones. Concussions could be, and sometimes were, fatal. You could drown in a river or be trampled…the list went on and on.

"You're very thoughtful," Cort remarked.

She smiled. "I was just thinking."

"Me, too." He turned off onto a side road that led to a park. "I want to stretch my legs for a bit. You game?"

"Of course."

He pulled into the car park and led the way down a small bank to the nearby river. The water level was down, but flowing beautifully over mossy rocks, with mesquite trees drooping a little in the heat, but still pretty enough to catch the eye.

"It's lovely here."

"Yes." He turned and pulled her into his arms, looking down into her wide eyes. "It's very lovely here." He bent his head and kissed her.

CHAPTER SIX

MADDIE'S HEAD WAS swimming. She felt the blood rush to her heart as Cort riveted her to his long, hard body and kissed her as if he might never see her again. She pressed closer, wrapping her arms around him, holding on for dear life.

His mouth tasted of coffee. It was warm and hard, insistent as it ground into hers. She thought if she died now, it would be all right. She'd never been so happy.

She heard a soft groan from his mouth. One lean hand swept down her back and pressed her hips firmly into his. She stiffened a little. She didn't know much about men, but she was a great reader. The contours of his body had changed quite suddenly.

"Nothing to worry about," he whispered into her mouth. "Just relax…"

She did. It was intoxicating. His free hand went under her blouse and expertly unclasped her bra to give free rein to his searching fingers. They found her breast and teased the nipple until it went hard. He groaned and bent his head, putting his mouth right over it, over the cloth. She arched up to him, so entranced that she couldn't even find means to protest.

"Yes," he groaned. "Yes, yes…!"

Her hands tangled in his thick black hair, tugging it closer. She arched backward, held by his strong arms as he fed on the softness of her breast under his demanding mouth. His hand at her back was more insistent now, grinding her against the growing hardness of his body.

She was melting, dying, starving to death. She wanted him to take off her clothes; she wanted to lie down with him and she wanted something, anything that would ease the terrible ache in her young body.

And just when she was certain that it would happen, that he wasn't going to stop, a noisy car pulled into the car park above and a car door slammed.

She jerked back from him, tugging down her blouse, shivering at the interruption. His eyes were almost black with hunger. He cursed under his breath, biting his lip as he fought down the need that almost bent him over double.

From above there were children's voices, laughing and calling to each other. Maddie stood with her back to him, her arms wrapped around her body, while she struggled with wild excitement, embarrassment and confusion. He didn't like her. He thought she was ugly. But he'd kissed her as if he were dying for her mouth. It was one big puzzle...

She felt his big, warm hands on her shoulders. "Don't sweat it," he said in a deep, soft tone. "Things happen."

She swallowed and forced a smile. "Right."

He turned her around, tipping her red face up to his eyes. He searched them in a silence punctuated with the screams and laughter of children. She was very pretty like that, her mouth swollen from his kisses, her face shy, timid. He was used to women who demanded. Aggressive women. Even Odalie, when he'd kissed her once, had been very outspoken about what she liked and didn't like. Maddie simply...accepted.

"Don't be embarrassed," he said softly. "Everything's all right. But we should probably go now. It's getting late."

She nodded. He took her small hand in his, curled his fingers into hers and drew her with him along the dirt path that led back up to the parking lot.

Two bedraggled parents were trying to put out food in plastic containers on a picnic table, fighting the wind, which was blowing like crazy in the sweltering heat. They glanced at the couple and grinned.

Cort grinned back. There were three children, all under school age, one in his father's arms. They looked happy, even though they were driving a car that looked as if it wouldn't make it out of the parking lot.

"Nice day for a picnic," Cort remarked.

The father made a face. "Not so much, but we've got a long drive ahead of us and it's hard to sit in a fast-food joint with this company." He indicated the leaping, running toddlers. He laughed. "Tomorrow, they'll be hijacking my car," he added with an ear-to-ear smile, "so we're enjoying it while we can."

"Nothing like kids to make a home a home," the mother commented.

"Nice looking kids, too," Cort said.

"Very nice," Maddie said, finally finding her voice.

"Thanks," the mother said. "They're a handful, but we don't mind."

She went back to her food containers, and the father went running after the toddlers, who were about to climb down the bank.

"Nice family," Cort remarked as they reached his car.

"Yes. They seemed so happy."

He glanced down at her as he stopped to open the

passenger door. He was thoughtful. He didn't say anything, but his eyes were soft and full of secrets. "In you go."

She got in, fastened her seat belt without any prompting and smiled all the way back home.

Things were going great, until they got out of the car in front of Maddie's house. Pumpkin had found a way out of the hen enclosure. He spotted Cort and broke into a halting run, with his head down and his feathers ruffled.

"No!" Maddie yelled. "Pumpkin, no!"

She tried to head him off, but he jumped at her and she turned away just in time to avoid spurs in her face. "Cort, run! It's okay, just run!" she called when he hesitated.

He threw his hands up and darted toward his car. "You have to do something about that damned rooster, Maddie!" he called back.

"I know," she wailed. "I will, honest! I had fun. Thanks so much!"

He threw up his hands and dived into the car. He started it and drove off just before Pumpkin reached him.

"You stupid chicken! I'm going to let Ben eat you, I swear I am!" she raged.

But when he started toward her, she ran up the steps, into the house and slammed the door.

She opened her cell phone and called her foreman.

"Ben, can you please get Pumpkin back into the hen lot and try to see where he got out? Be sure to wear your chaps and carry a shield," she added.

"Need to eat that rooster, Maddie," he drawled.

"I know." She groaned. "Please?"

There was a long sigh. "All right. One more time…"
He hung up.

Great-Aunt Sadie gave her a long look. "Pumpkin
got out again?"

"Yes. There must be a hole in the fence or something," she moaned. "I don't know how in the world
he does it!"

"Ben will find a way to shut him in, don't worry.
But you are going to have to do something, you know.
He's dangerous."

"I love him," Maddie said miserably.

"Well, sometimes things we love don't love us back
and should be made into chicken and dumplings,"
Sadie mused with pursed lips.

Maddie made a face at her. She opened her shoulder
bag and pulled out a box. "I want to show you something. Cort bought it for me."

"Cort's buying you presents?" Sadie exclaimed.

"It's some present, too," Maddie said with a flushed
smile.

She opened the box. There, inside, was the hand-
painted cameo of the little Spanish lady, with a card
that gave all the information about the woman, now
deceased, who left it with the antiques dealer.

"She's lovely," Sadie said, tracing the face with a
forefinger very gently.

"Read the card." Maddie showed it to her.

When Sadie finished reading it, she was almost in
tears. "How sad, to be the last one in your family."

"Yes. But this will be handed down someday." She
was remembering the family at the picnic tables and
Cort's strange smile, holding hands with him, kissing
him. "Someday," she said again, and she sounded as
breathless as she felt.

Sadie didn't ask any questions. But she didn't have to. Maddie's bemused expression told her everything she needed to know. Apparently Maddie and Cort were getting along very well, all of a sudden.

CORT WALKED INTO the house muttering about the rooster.

"Trouble again?" Shelby asked. She was curled up on the sofa watching the news, but she turned off the television when she saw her son. She smiled, dark-eyed and still beautiful.

"The rooster," he sighed. He tossed his hat into a chair and dropped down into his father's big recliner. "I bought us a bull. He's very nice."

"From Cy Parks?"

He nodded. "He's quite a character."

"So I've heard."

"I bought Maddie a cameo," he added. "In that tearoom halfway between here and Jacobsville. It's got an antiques store in with it." He shook his head. "Beautiful thing. It's hand-painted…a pretty Spanish lady with a fan, enameled. She had a fit over it. The seller died recently and had no family."

"Sad. But it was nice of you to buy it for Maddie."

He pursed his lips. "When you met Dad, you said you didn't get along."

She shivered dramatically. "That's putting it mildly. He hated me. Or he seemed to. But when my mother, your grandmother, died, I was alone in a media circus. They think she committed suicide and she was a big-name movie star, you see. So there was a lot of publicity. I was almost in hysterics when your father showed up out of nowhere and managed everything."

"Well!"

"I was shocked. He'd sent me home, told me he had a girlfriend and broke me up with Danny. Not that I needed breaking-up, Danny was only pretending to be engaged to me to make King face how he really felt. But it was fireworks from the start." She peered at him through her thick black eyelashes. "Sort of the way it was with you and Maddie, I think."

"It's fireworks, now, too. But of a different sort," he added very slowly.

"Oh?" She didn't want to pry, but she was curious.

"I'm confused. Maddie isn't pretty. She can't sing or play anything. But she can paint and sculpt and she's sharp about people." He grimaced. "Odalie is beautiful, like the rising sun, and she can play any instrument and sing like an angel."

"Accomplishments and education don't matter as much as personality and character," his mother replied quietly. "I'm not an educated person, although I've taken online courses. I made my living modeling. Do you think I'm less valuable to your father than a woman with a college degree and greater beauty?"

"Goodness, no!" he exclaimed at once.

She smiled gently. "See what I mean?"

"I think I'm beginning to." He leaned back. "It was a good day."

"I'm glad."

"Except for that damned rooster," he muttered. "One of these days…!"

She laughed.

He was about to call Maddie, just to talk, when his cell phone rang.

He didn't recognize the number. He put it up to his ear. "Hello?"

"Hello, Cort," Odalie's voice purred in his ear.

"Guess what, I'm home! Want to come over for supper tonight?"

He hesitated. Things had just gotten complicated.

MADDIE HALF EXPECTED Cort to phone her, after their lovely day together, but he didn't. The next morning, she heard a car pull up in the driveway and went running out. But it wasn't Cort. It was John Everett.

She tried not to let her disappointment show. "Hi!" she said. "Would you like a cup of very nice European coffee from a fancy European coffeemaker?" she added, grinning.

He burst out laughing. "I would. Thanks. It's been a hectic day and night."

"Has it? Why?" she asked as they walked up the steps.

"I had to drive up to Dallas-Fort Worth airport to pick up Odalie yesterday."

Her heart did a nosedive. She'd hoped against hope that the other woman would stay in Italy, marry her voice teacher, get a job at the opera house, anything but come home, and especially right now! She and Cort were only just beginning to get to know each other. It wasn't fair!

"How is she?" she asked, her heart shattering.

"Good," he said heavily. "She and the voice teacher disagreed, so she's going to find someone in this country to take over from him." He grimaced. "I don't know who. Since she knows more than the voice trainers do, I don't really see the point in it. She can't take criticism."

She swallowed, hard, as she went to work at the coffee machine. "Has Cort seen her?"

"Oh, yes," he said, sitting down at the little kitchen table. "He came over for supper last night. They went driving."

She froze at the counter. She didn't let him see her face, but her stiff back was a good indication of how she'd received the news.

"I'm really sorry," he said gently. "But I thought you should know before you heard gossip."

She nodded. Tears were stinging her eyes, but she hid them. "Thanks, John."

He drew in a long breath. "She doesn't love him," he said. "He's just a habit she can't give up. I don't think he loves her, either, really. It's like those crushes we get on movie stars. Odalie is an image, not someone real who wants to settle down and have kids and live on a ranch. She can't stand cattle!"

She started the coffee machine, collected herself, smiled and turned around. "Good thing your parents don't mind them," she said.

"And I've told her so. Repeatedly." He studied her through narrowed eyes. His thick blond hair shone like pale yellow diamonds in the overhead light. He was so good-looking, she thought. She wished she could feel for him what she felt for Cort.

"People can't help being who they are," she replied quietly.

"You're wise for your years," he teased.

She laughed. "Not so wise, or I'd get out of the cattle business." She chuckled. "After we have coffee, want to have another go at explaining genetics to me? I'm a lost cause, but we can try."

"You're not a lost cause, and I'd love to try."

ODALIE WAS IRRITABLE and not trying to hide it. "What's the matter with you?" she snapped at Cort. "You haven't heard a word I've said."

He glanced at her and grimaced. "Sorry. We've got a new bull coming. I'm distracted."

Her pale blue eyes narrowed. "More than distracted, I think. What's this I hear about you taking that Lane girl with you to buy the new bull?"

He gave her a long look and didn't reply.

She cleared her throat. Cort was usually running after her, doing everything he could to make her happy, make her smile. She'd come home to find a stranger, a man she didn't know. Her beauty hadn't interested the voice trainer; her voice hadn't really impressed him. She'd come home with a damaged ego and wanted Cort to fix it by catering to her. That hadn't happened. She'd invited him over today for lunch and he'd eaten it in a fog. He actually seemed to not want to be with her, and that was new and scary.

"Well, she's plain as toast," Odalie said haughtily. "She has no talent and she's not educated."

He cocked his head. "And you think those are the most important character traits?"

She didn't like the way he was looking at her. "None of my friends had anything to do with her in school," she muttered.

"You had plenty to do with that, didn't you?" Cort asked with a cold smile. "I believe attorneys were involved…?"

"Cort!" She went flaming red. She turned her head. "That was a terrible misunderstanding. And it was Millie who put me up to it. That's the truth. I didn't like Maddie, but I'd never have done it if I'd realized what that boy might do." She bit her lip. She'd thought about that a lot in recent weeks, she didn't know why. "He could have killed her. I'd have had it on my conscience forever," she added in a strange, absent tone.

Cort was not impressed. This was the first time he'd heard Odalie say anything about the other woman that didn't have a barb in it, and even this comment was self-centered. Though it was small, he still took her words as a sign that maybe she was changing and becoming more tolerant...

"Deep thoughts," he told her.

She glanced at him and smiled. "Yes. I've become introspective. Enjoy it while it lasts." She laughed, and she was so beautiful that he was really confused.

"I love your car," she said, glancing out the window. "Would you let me drive it?"

He hesitated. She was the worst driver he'd ever known. "As long as I'm in it," he said firmly.

She laughed. "I didn't mean I wanted to go alone," she teased.

She knew where she wanted to drive it, too. Right past Maddie Lane's house, so that she'd see Odalie with Cort. So she'd know that he was no longer available. Odalie seemed to have lost her chance at a career in opera, but here was Cort, who'd always loved her. Maybe she'd settle down, maybe she wouldn't, but Cort was hers. She wanted Maddie to know it.

She'd never driven a Jaguar before. This was a very fast, very powerful, very expensive two-seater. Cort handed her the key.

She clicked it to open the door. She frowned. "Where's the key?" she asked.

"You don't need a key. It's a smart key. You just keep it in your pocket or lay it in the cup holder."

"Oh."

She climbed into the car and put the smart key in the cup holder.

"Seat belt," he emphasized.

She glared at him. "It will wrinkle my dress," she said fussily, because it was delicate silk, pink and very pretty.

"Seat belt or the car doesn't move," he repeated.

She sighed. He was very forceful. She liked that. She smiled at him prettily. "Okay."

She put it on, grimacing as it wrinkled the delicate fabric. Oh, well, the dry cleaners could fix it. She didn't want to make Cort mad. She pushed the button Cort showed her, the button that would start the car, but nothing happened.

"Brake," he said.

She glared at him. "I'm not going fast enough to brake!"

"You have to put your foot on the brake or it won't start," he explained patiently.

"Oh."

She put her foot on the brake and it started. The air vents opened and the touch screen came on. "It's like something out of a science-fiction movie," she said, impressed.

"Isn't it, though?" He chuckled.

She glanced at him, her face radiant. "I have got to have Daddy get me one of these!" she exclaimed.

Cort hoped her father wouldn't murder him when he saw what they cost.

Odalie pulled the car out of the driveway in short jerks. She grimaced. "I haven't driven in a while, but it will come back to me, honest."

"Okay. I'm not worried." He was petrified, but he wasn't showing it. He hoped he could grab the wheel if he had to.

She smoothed out the motions when she got onto the highway. "There, better?" she teased, looking at him.

"Eyes on the road," he cautioned.

She sighed. "Cort, you're no fun."

"It's a powerful machine. You have to respect it. That means keeping your eyes on the road and paying attention to your surroundings."

"I'm doing that," she argued, looking at him again.

He prayed silently that they'd get home again.

She pulled off on a side road and he began to worry.

"Why are we going this way?" he asked suspiciously.

"Isn't this the way to Catelow?" she asked in all innocence.

"No, it's not," he said. "It's the road that leads to the Lane ranch."

"Oh, dear, I don't want to go there. But there's no place to turn off," she worried. "Anyway, the ranch is just ahead, I'll turn around there."

Cort had to bite his lip to keep from saying something.

Maddie was out in the yard with her garbage can lid. This time Pumpkin had gotten out of the pen when she was looking. He'd jumped a seven-foot-high fence. If she hadn't seen it with her own eyes, she'd never have believed it.

"Pumpkin, you fool!" she yelled at him. "Why can't you stay where I put you? Get back in there!"

But he ran around her. This time he wasn't even trying to spur her. He ran toward the road. It was his favorite place, for some reason, despite the heat that made the ribbon of black asphalt hotter than a frying pan.

"You come back here!" she yelled.

Just as she started after him, Odalie's foot hit the accelerator pedal too hard, Cort called out, Odalie looked at him instead of the road…

MADDIE HEARD SCREAMING. She was numb. She opened her eyes and there was Cort, his face contorted with horror. Beside him, Odalie was screaming and crying.

"Just lie still," Cort said hoarsely. "The ambulance is on the way. Just lie still, baby."

"I hit her, I hit her!" Odalie screamed. "I didn't see her until it was too late! I hit her!"

"Odalie, you have to calm down. You're not helping!" Cort snapped at her. "Find something to cover her. Hurry!"

"Yes…there's a blanket…in the backseat, isn't there…?"

Odalie fetched it with cold, shaking hands. She drew it over Maddie's prone body. There was blood. So much blood. She felt as if she were going to faint, or throw up. Then she saw Maddie's face and tears ran down her cheeks. "Oh, Maddie," she sobbed, "I'm so sorry!"

"Find something to prop her head, in case her spine is injured," Cort gritted. He was terrified. He brushed back Maddie's blond hair, listened to her ragged breathing, saw her face go even paler. "Please hurry!" he groaned.

There wasn't anything. Odalie put her beautiful white leather purse on one side of Maddie's head without a single word, knowing it would ruin the leather and not caring at all. She put her knit overblouse on the other, crumpled up. She knelt in the dirt road beside Maddie and sat down, tears in her eyes. She touched Maddie's arm. "Help is coming," she whispered brokenly. "You hold on, Maddie. Hold on!"

Maddie couldn't believe it. Her worst enemy was

sitting beside her in a vision of a horrifically expensive pink silk dress that was going to be absolutely ruined, and apparently didn't mind at all.

She tried to speak. "Pum…Pumpkin?" she rasped.

Cort looked past her and grimaced. He didn't say anything. He didn't have to.

Maddie started to cry, great heaving sobs.

"We'll get you another rooster," Cort said at once. "I'll train him to attack me. Anything. You just have to…hold on, baby," he pleaded. "Hold on!"

She couldn't breathe. "Hurts," she whispered as sensation rushed back in and she began to shudder.

Cort was in hell. There was no other word that would express what he felt as he saw her lying there in bloody clothing, maybe dying, and he couldn't do one damned thing to help her. He was sick to his soul.

He brushed back her hair, trying to remember anything else, anything that would help her until the ambulance arrived.

"Call them again!" Odalie said firmly.

He did. The operator assured them that the ambulance was almost there. She began asking questions, which Cort did his best to answer.

"Where's your great-aunt?" he asked Maddie softly.

"Store," she choked out.

"It's okay, I'll call her," he said when she looked upset.

Odalie had come out of her stupor and she was checking for injuries while Cort talked to the 911 operator. "I don't see anything that looks dangerous, but I'm afraid to move her," she said, ignoring the blood in her efforts to give aid. "There are some abrasions, pretty raw ones. Maddie, can you move your arms and legs?" she asked in a voice so tender that Maddie thought maybe she really was just dreaming all this.

She moved. "Yes," she said. "But…it hurts…"

"Move your ankles."

"Okay."

Odalie looked at Cort with horror.

"I moved…them," Maddie said, wincing. "Hurts!"

"Please, ask them to hurry," Cort groaned into the phone.

"No need," Odalie said, noting the red-and-white vehicle that was speeding toward them.

"No sirens?" Cort asked blankly.

"They don't run the sirens or lights unless they have to," the operator explained kindly. "It scares people to death and can cause wrecks. They'll use them to get the victim to the hospital, though, you bet," she reassured him.

"Thanks so much," Cort said.

"I hope she does well."

"Me, too," he replied huskily and hung up.

Odalie took one of the EMTs aside. "She can't move her feet," she whispered.

He nodded. "We won't let her know."

They went to the patient.

MADDIE WASN'T AWARE of anything after they loaded her into the ambulance on a backboard. They talked to someone on the radio and stuck a needle into her arm. She slept.

When she woke again, she was in a hospital bed with two people hovering. Cort and Odalie. Odalie's dress was dirty and bloodstained.

"Your…beautiful dress," Maddie whispered, wincing.

Odalie went to the bed. She felt very strange. Her

whole life she'd lived as if there was nobody else around. She'd never been in the position of nursing anybody—her parents and brother had never even sprained a hand. She'd been petted, spoiled, praised, but never depended upon.

Now here was this woman, this enemy, whom her actions had placed almost at death's door. And suddenly she was needed. Really needed.

Maddie's great-aunt had been called. She was in the waiting room, but in no condition to be let near the patient. The hospital staff had to calm her down, she was so terrified.

They hadn't told Maddie yet. When Sadie was calmer, they'd let her in to see the injured woman.

"Your great-aunt is here, too," Odalie said gently. "You're going to be fine."

"Fine." Maddie felt tears run down her cheeks. "So much...to be done at the ranch, and I'm stove up...!"

"I'll handle it," Cort said firmly. "No worries there."

"Pumpkin," she sobbed. "He was horrible. Just horrible. But I loved him." She cried harder.

Odalie leaned down and kissed her unkempt hair. "We'll find you another horrible rooster. Honest."

Maddie sobbed. "You hate me."

"No," Odalie said softly. "No, I don't. And I'm so sorry that I put you in here. I was driving." She bit her lip. "I wasn't watching the road," she said stiffly. "God, I'm sorry!"

Maddie reached out a lacerated hand and touched Odalie's. "I ran into the road after Pumpkin...I wasn't looking. Not your fault. My fault."

Odalie was crying, too. "Okay. Both our faults. Now we have to get you well."

"Both of us," Cort agreed, touching Maddie's bruised cheek.

Maddie swallowed, hard. She wanted to say something else, but they'd given her drugs to make her comfortable, apparently. She opened her mouth to speak and went right to sleep.

CHAPTER SEVEN

"IS SHE GOING to be all right?" Great-Aunt Sadie asked when Odalie and Cort dropped into chairs in the waiting room while Maddie was sleeping.

"Yes, but it's going to be a long recovery," Cort said heavily.

"You can't tell her," Odalie said gently, "but there seems to be some paralysis in her legs. No, it's all right," she interrupted when Sadie looked as if she might start crying. "We've called one of the foremost orthopedic surgeons in the country at the Mayo Clinic. We're flying him down here to see her. We'll go from there, once he's examined her."

"But the expense," Sadie exclaimed.

"No expense. None. This is my fault and I'm paying for it," Odalie said firmly.

"It's my car, I'm helping," Cort added.

She started crying again. "It's so nice of you, both of you."

Odalie hugged her. "I'm so sorry," she said sadly. "I didn't mean to hit her. I wasn't looking, and I should have been."

Sadie hugged her back. "Accidents happen," she sobbed. "It was that stupid rooster, wasn't it?"

"It was." Cort sighed. "He ran right into the road and Maddie ran after him. The road was clear and then, seconds later, she was in the middle of it."

Odalie couldn't confess that she'd gone that way deliberately to show Maddie she was with Cort. She was too ashamed. "She'll be all right," she promised.

"Oh, my poor little girl," Sadie said miserably. "She'll give up, if she knows she might not be able to walk again. She won't fight!"

"She will. Because we'll make her," Odalie said quietly.

Sadie looked at her with new eyes. Her gaze fell to Odalie's dress. "Oh, your dress," she exclaimed.

Odalie just smiled. "I can get another dress. It's Maddie I'm worried about." It sounded like a glib reply, but it wasn't. In the past few hours, Odalie's outlook had totally shifted from herself to someone who needed her. She knew that her life would never be the same again.

A sheriff's deputy came into the waiting room, spotted Odalie and Cort and approached them, shaking his head.

"I know," Odalie said. "It's my fault. I was driving his car—" she indicated Cort "—and not looking where I was going. Maddie ran out into the road after her stupid rooster, trying to save him. She's like that."

The deputy smiled. "We know all that from the recreation of the scene that we did," he said. "It's very scientific," he added. "How is she?"

"Bad," Odalie said heavily. "They think she may lose the use of her legs. But we've called in a world-famous surgeon. If anything can be done, it will be. We're going to take care of her."

The deputy looked at the beautiful woman, at her bloodstained, dirty, expensive dress, with kind eyes. "I know some women who would be much more concerned with the state of their clothing than the state of the victim. Your parents must be very proud of you, young lady. If you were my daughter, I would be."

Odalie flushed and smiled. "I feel pretty guilty right now. So thanks for making me feel better."

"You going to charge her?" Cort asked.

The deputy shook his head. "Probably not, as long as she survives. In the law, everything is intent. You didn't mean to do it, and the young lady ran into the road by her own admission." He didn't add that having to watch the results of the accident day after day would probably be a worse punishment than anything the law could prescribe. But he was thinking it.

"That doesn't preclude the young lady pressing charges, however," the deputy added.

Odalie smiled wanly. "I wouldn't blame her if she did."

He smiled back. "I hope she does well."

"So do we," Odalie agreed. "Thanks."

He nodded and went back out again.

"Tell me what the doctor said about her legs," Sadie said sadly, leaning toward them.

Odalie took a long breath. She was very tired and she had no plans to go home that night. She'd have to call her family and tell them what was happening here. She hadn't had time to do that yet, nor had Cort.

"He said that there's a great deal of bruising, with inflammation and swelling. That can cause partial paralysis, apparently. He's started her on anti-inflammatories and when she's able, he'll have her in rehab to help get her moving," she added gently.

"But she was in so much pain…surely they won't make her get up!" Sadie was astonished.

"The longer she stays there, the stronger the possibility that she won't ever get up, Sadie," Odalie said gently. She patted the other woman's hands, which were resting clenched in her lap. "He's a very good doctor."

"Yes," Sadie said absently. "He treated my nephew when he had cancer. Sent him to some of the best oncologists in Texas." She looked up. "So maybe it isn't going to be permanent?"

"A good chance. So you stop worrying. We all have to be strong so that we can make her look ahead instead of behind, so that we can keep her from brooding." She bit her lower lip. "It's going to be very depressing for her, and it's going to be a long haul, even if it has a good result."

"I don't care. I'm just so happy she's still alive," the older woman cried.

"Oh, so am I," Odalie said heavily. "I can't remember ever feeling quite so bad in all my life. I took my eyes off the road, just for a minute." Her eyes closed and she shuddered. "I'll be able to hear that horrible sound when I'm an old lady…"

Cort put his arm around her. "Stop that. I shouldn't have let you drive the car until you were familiar with it. My fault, too. I feel as bad as you do. But we're going to get Maddie back on her feet."

"Yes," Odalie agreed, forcing a smile. "Yes, we are."

Sadie wiped her eyes and looked from one young determined face to the other. Funny how things worked out, she was thinking. Here was Odalie, Maddie's worst enemy, being protective of her, and Cort just as determined to make her walk again when he'd been yelling at her only a week or so earlier. What odd companions they were going to be for her young great-niece. But what a blessing.

She considered how it could have worked out, if

Maddie had chased that stupid red rooster out into the road and been hit by someone else, maybe someone who ran and left her there to die. It did happen. The newspapers were full of such cases.

"What are you thinking so hard about?" Cort asked with a faint smile.

Sadie laughed self-consciously. "That if she had to get run over, it was by such nice people who stopped and rendered aid."

"I know what you mean," Cort replied. "A man was killed just a couple of weeks ago by a hit-and-run driver who was drunk and took off. The pedestrian died. I wondered at the time if his life might have been spared, if the man had just stopped to call an ambulance before he ran." He shook his head. "So many cases like that."

"Well, you didn't run, either of you." Sadie smiled. "Thanks, for saving my baby."

Odalie hugged her again, impulsively. "For the foreseeable future, she's my baby, too," she said with a laugh. "Now, how about some coffee? I don't know about you, but I'm about to go to sleep out here and I have no intention of leaving the hospital."

"Nor do I," Cort agreed. He stood up. "Let's go down to the cafeteria and see what we can find to eat, too. I just realized I'm starving."

The women smiled, as they were meant to.

MADDIE CAME AROUND a long time later, or so it seemed. A dignified man with black wavy hair was standing over her with a nurse. He was wearing a white lab coat with a stethoscope draped around his neck.

"Miss Lane?" the nurse asked gently. She smiled. "This is Dr. Parker from the Mayo Clinic. He's an orthopedic specialist, and we'd like him to have a look at your back. If you don't mind."

Maddie cleared her throat. She didn't seem to be in pain, which was odd. She felt very drowsy. "Of course," she said, puzzled as to why they would have such a famous man at such a small rural hospital.

"Just a few questions first," he said in a deep, pleasant tone, "and then I'll examine you." He smiled down at her.

"Okay."

The pain came back as the examination progressed, but he said it was a good sign. Especially the pain she felt in one leg. He pressed and poked and asked questions while he did it. After a few minutes she was allowed to lie down in the bed, which she did with a grimace of pure relief.

"There's a great deal of edema—swelling," he translated quietly. "Bruising of the spinal column, inflammation, all to be expected from the trauma you experienced."

"I can't feel my legs. I can't move them," Maddie said with anguish in her wan face.

He dropped down elegantly into the chair by her bed, crossed his legs and picked up her chart. "Yes, I know. But you mustn't give up hope. I have every confidence that you'll start to regain feeling in a couple of weeks, three at the outside. You have to believe that as well." He made notations and read what her attending physician had written in the forms on the clipboard, very intent on every word. "He's started you on anti-inflammatories," he murmured. "Good, good, just what I would have advised. Getting fluids into you intravenously, antibiotics…" He stopped and made another notation. "And then, physical therapy."

"Physical therapy." She laughed and almost cried. "I can't stand up!"

"It's much more than just exercise," he said and smiled gently. "Heat, massage, gentle movements, you'll see. You've never had physical therapy I see."

She shook her head. "I've never really had an injury that required it."

"You're very lucky, then," he said.

"You think I'll walk again?" she prompted, her eyes wide and full of fear.

"I think so," he said. "I won't lie to you, there's a possibility that the injury may result in permanent disability." He held up a hand when she seemed distraught. "If that happens, you have a wonderful support group here. Your family. They'll make sure you have everything you need. You'll cope. You'll learn how to adapt. I've seen some miraculous things in my career, Miss Lane," he added. "One of my newest patients lost a leg overseas in a bombing. We repaired the damage, got him a prosthesis and now he's playing basketball."

She caught her breath. "Basketball?"

He grinned, looking much younger. "You'd be amazed at the advances science has made in such things. Right now, they're working on an interface that will allow quadriplegics to use a computer with just thought. Sounds like science fiction, doesn't it? But it's real. I watched a video of a researcher who linked a man's mind electronically to a computer screen, and he was able to move a curser just with the power of his thoughts." He shook his head. "Give those guys ten years and they'll build something that can read minds."

"Truly fascinating," she agreed.

"But right now, what I want from you is a promise that you'll do what your doctor tells you and work hard at getting back on your feet," he said. "No brooding. No pessimism. You have to believe you'll walk again."

She swallowed. She was bruised and broken and miserable. She drew in a breath. "I'll try," she said.

He stood up and handed the chart to the nurse with a smile. "I'll settle for that, as long as it's your very best try," he promised. He shook hands with her. "I'm going to stay in touch with your doctor and be available for consultation. If I'm needed, I can fly back down here. Your friends out there sent a private jet for me." He chuckled. "I felt like a rock star."

She laughed, then, for the first time since her ordeal had begun.

"That's more like it," he said. "Ninety-nine percent of recovery is in the mind. You remember that."

"I'll remember," she promised. "Thanks for coming all this way."

He threw up a hand. "Don't apologize for that. It got me out of a board meeting," he said. "I hate board meetings."

She grinned.

LATER, AFTER SHE'D been given her medicines and fed, Odalie and Cort came into the private room she'd been moved to.

"Dr. Parker is very nice," she told them. "He came all the way from the Mayo Clinic, though…!"

"Whatever it takes is what you'll get," Odalie said with a smile.

Maddie grimaced as she looked at Odalie's beautiful pink dress, creased and stained with blood and dirt. "Your dress," she moaned.

"I've got a dozen pretty much just like it," Odalie

told her. "I won't even miss it." She sighed. "But I really should go home and change."

"Go home and go to bed," Maddie said softly. "You've done more than I ever expected already..."

"No," Odalie replied. "I'm staying with you. I got permission."

"But there's no bed," Maddie exclaimed. "You can't sleep in a chair...!"

"There's a rollaway bed. They're bringing it in." She glanced at Cort with a wicked smile. "Cort gets to sleep in the chair."

He made a face. "Don't rub it in."

"But you don't have to stay," Maddie tried to reason with them. "I have nurses. I'll be fine, honest I will."

Odalie moved to the bed and brushed Maddie's unkempt hair away from her wan face. "You'll brood if we leave you alone," she said reasonably. "It's not as if I've got a full social calendar these days, and I'm not much for cocktail parties. I'd just as soon be here with you. We can talk about art. I majored in it at college."

"I remember," Maddie said slowly. "I don't go to college," she began.

"I'll wager you know more about it than I do," Odalie returned. "You had to learn something of anatomy to make those sculptures so accurate."

"Well, yes, I did," Maddie faltered. "I went on the internet and read everything I could find."

"I have all sorts of books on medieval legends and romances, I'll bring them over for you to read when they let you go home. Right now you have to rest," Odalie said.

Maddie flushed. "That would be so nice of you."

Odalie's eyes were sad. "I've been not so nice to you for most of the time we've known one another," she replied. "You can't imagine how I felt, after what happened because I let an idiot girl talk me into telling lies about you online. I've had to live with that, just as you have. I never even said I was sorry for it. But I am," she added.

Maddie drew in a breath. She was feeling drowsy. "Thanks," she said. "It means a lot."

"Don't you worry about a thing," Odalie added. "I'll take care of you."

Maddie flushed. She'd never even really had a girlfriend, and here was Odalie turning out to be one.

Odalie smiled. "Now go to sleep. Things will look brighter tomorrow. Sometimes a day can make all the difference in how we look at life."

"I'll try."

"Good girl." She glanced at Cort. "Can you drive me home and bring me back?"

"Sure," he said. "I need a change of clothes, too. I'll drop you off at Big Spur, go home and clean up and we'll both come back. We need to tell our parents what's going on, too."

"John will be beside himself," Odalie said without thinking. "All I've heard since I got home is how sweet Maddie is," she added with a smile.

She didn't see Cort's expression, and she couldn't understand why Maddie suddenly looked so miserable at the mention of her brother's name.

"Well, don't worry about that right now," Odalie said quickly. "But I'm sure he'll be in to see you as soon as he knows what happened."

Maddie nodded.

"I'll be right out," Cort said, smiling at Odalie.

"Sure. Sleep tight," she told Maddie. She hesitated.

"I'm sorry about your rooster, too. Really sorry," she stammered, and left quickly.

Maddie felt tears running down her cheeks.

Cort picked a tissue out of the box by the bed, bent down and dabbed at both her eyes. "Stop that," he said softly. "They'll think I'm pinching you and throw me out."

She smiled sadly. "Nobody would ever think you were mean."

"Don't you believe it."

"You and Odalie…you've both been so kind," she said hesitantly. "Thank you."

"We feel terrible," he replied, resting his hand beside her tousled hair on the pillow. "It could have been a worse tragedy than it is. And Pumpkin…" He grimaced and dabbed at more tears on her face. "As much as I hated him, I really am sorry. I know you loved him."

She sniffed, and he dabbed at her nose, too. "He was so mean," she choked out. "But I really did love him."

"We'll get you a new rooster. I'll train him to attack me," he promised.

She laughed through her tears.

"That's better. The way you looked just now was breaking my heart."

She searched his eyes. He wasn't joking. He meant it.

He brushed back her hair. "God, I don't know what I would have done if you'd died," he whispered hoarsely. He bent and crushed his mouth down over hers, ground into it with helpless need. After a few seconds, he forced himself to pull back. "Sorry," he said huskily. "Couldn't help myself. I was terrified when I saw you lying there so still."

"You were?" She looked fascinated.

He shook his head and forced a smile. "Clueless," he murmured. "I guess that's not such a bad thing. Not for the moment anyway." He bent and brushed his mouth tenderly over hers. "I'll be back. Don't go anywhere."

"If I tried to, three nurses would tackle me, and a doctor would sit on me while they sent for a gurney," she assured him, her eyes twinkling.

He wrinkled his nose and kissed her again. "Okay. He stood up. "Anything you want me to bring you?"

"A steak dinner, two strawberry milkshakes, a large order of fries…"

"For that, they'd drag me out the front door and pin me to a wall with scalpels," he assured her.

She sighed. "Oh, well. It was worth a try. They fed me green gelatin." She made a face.

"When we get you out of here, I'll buy you the tastiest steak in Texas, and that's a promise. With fries."

"Ooooh," she murmured.

He grinned. "Incentive to get better. Yes?"

She nodded. "Yes." The smile faded. "You don't have to come back. Odalie, either. I'll be okay."

"We're coming back, just the same. We'll drop Great-Aunt Sadie off at the house, but she can stay at Skylance if she's nervous about being there alone. She's been a real trooper, but she's very upset."

"Can I see her?"

"For just a minute. I'll bring her in. You be good."

She nodded.

Great-Aunt Sadie was still crying when she went to the bed and very carefully bent down to hug Maddie. "I'm so glad you're going to be all right," she sobbed.

Maddie touched her gray hair gently. "Can't kill a weed." She laughed.

"You're no weed, my baby." She smoothed back her hair. "You keep getting better. I'll bring your gown and robe and slippers and some cash when I come back. Here. This is for the machines if you want them to get you anything…"

"Put that back," Cort said, "Maddie won't need cash."

"Oh, but—" Sadie started to argue.

"It won't do any good," Cort interrupted with a grin. "Ask my dad."

"He's right," Maddie said drowsily. "I heard one of his cowboys say that it's easier to argue with a signpost, and you'll get further."

"Stop bad-mouthing me. Bad girl," he teased.

She grinned sleepily.

"You go to sleep," he told her. "Odalie and I will be back later, and we'll bring Sadie in the morning."

"You're a nice boy, Cort," Sadie said tearfully.

He hugged her. "You're a nice girl," he teased. "Good night, honey," he told Maddie, and didn't miss the faint blush in her cheeks as she registered the endearment.

"Good night," she replied.

She drifted off to sleep before they got out of the hospital. In her mind, she could still hear that soft, deep voice drawling "honey."

The next morning, Maddie opened her eyes when she heard a commotion.

"I can't bathe her with you sitting there," the nurse was saying reasonably.

Cort frowned as he stood up. "I know, I know. Sorry. I only fell asleep about four," he added with a sheepish smile.

The nurse smiled back. "It's all right. A lot of patients don't have anybody who even cares if they live or die. Your friend's very fortunate that the two of you care so much."

"She's a sweet girl," Odalie said gently.

"So are you," Cort said, and smiled warmly at her. She flushed a little.

Maddie, watching, felt her heart sink. They'd both been so caring and attentive that she'd actually forgotten how Cort felt about Odalie. And now it seemed that Odalie was seeing him with new eyes.

Cort turned, but Maddie closed her eyes. She couldn't deal with this. Not now.

"Tell her we went to have breakfast and we'll be back," Cort said, studying Maddie's relaxed face.

"I will," the nurse promised.

Cort let Odalie go out before him and closed the door as he left.

"Time to wake up, sweetie," the nurse told Maddie. "I'm going to give you your bath and then you can have breakfast."

"Oh, is it morning?" Maddie asked, and pretended to yawn. "I slept very well."

"Good. Your friends went to have breakfast. That handsome man said they'd be back," she added with a laugh. "And that woman. What I wouldn't give to be that beautiful!"

"She sings like an angel, too," Maddie said.

"My, my, as handsome as he is, can you imagine what beautiful children they'd have?" the nurse murmured as she got her things together to bathe Maddie.

"Yes, wouldn't they?" Maddie echoed.

Something in her tone made the other woman look at her curiously.

But Maddie just smiled wanly. "They've both been very kind," she said. "They're my neighbors."

"I see."

No, she didn't, but Maddie changed the subject to a popular television series that she watched. The nurse watched it, too, which gave them a talking point.

LATER, SADIE CAME in with a small overnight bag.

"I brought all your stuff," she told Maddie. "You look better," she lied, because Maddie was pale and lethargic and obviously fighting pain.

"It's a little worse today," she replied heavily. "You know what they say about injuries, they're worse until the third day and then they start getting better."

"Who said that?" Sadie wondered.

"Beats me, but I've heard it all my life. Did you bring me anything to read?" she added curiously.

"I didn't. But somebody else did." She glanced at the door. Odalie came in with three beautifully illustrated fairy-tale books. After breakfast, both Odalie and Cort had gone home to change, and then picked up Great-Aunt Sadie when returning to the hospital.

"I bought these while I was in college," Odalie said, handing one to Maddie. "I thought they had some of the most exquisite plates I'd ever seen."

And by plates, she meant paintings. Maddie caught her breath as she opened the book and saw fairies, like the ones she made, depicted in a fantasy forest with a shimmering lake.

"Oh, this is…it's beyond words," she exclaimed, breathlessly turning pages.

"Yes. I thought you'd like them." She beamed. "These are updated versions of the ones I have. I bought these for you."

"For me?" Maddie looked as if she'd won the lottery. "You mean it?"

"I mean it. I'm so glad you like them."

"They're beautiful," she whispered reverently. She traced one of the fairies. "I have my own ideas about faces and expressions, but these are absolutely inspiring!"

"Fantasy art is my favorite."

"Mine, too." She looked up, flushing a little. "How can I ever thank you enough?"

"You can get better so that my conscience will stop killing me," Odalie said gently.

Maddie smiled. "Okay. I promise to try."

"I'll settle for that."

"I put your best gowns and slippers in the bag," Sadie told her. "And Cort brought you something, too."

"Cort?"

She looked toward the door. He was smiling and nodding at the nurses, backing into the room. Behind his back was a strange, bottom-heavy bear with a big grin and bushy eyebrows.

He turned into the room and handed it to Maddie. "I don't know if they'll let you keep it, but if they won't, I'll let Sadie take him home and put him in your room. His name's Bubba."

"Bubba?" She burst out laughing as she took the bear from him. It was the cutest stuffed bear she'd ever seen. "Oh, he's so cute!"

"I'm glad you like him. I wanted to smuggle in a steak, but they'd have smelled it at the door."

"Thanks for the thought," she said shyly.

"You're welcome."

"Bears and books." She sighed. "I feel spoiled."

"I should hope so," Odalie said with a grin. "We're doing our best."

"When we get you out of here, we're taking you up to Dallas and we'll hit all the major museums and art galleries," Cort said, dropping into a chair. "Culture. Might give you some new ideas for your paintings and sculptures."

"Plus we bought out an art supply store for you," Odalie said with twinkling eyes. "You'll have enough to make all sorts of creations when you get home."

"Home." Maddie looked from one of them to the other. "When? When can I go home?"

"In a few days." Cort spoke for the others. "First they have to get you stabilized. Then you'll be on a regimen of medicine and physical therapy. We'll go from there."

Maddie drew in a long breath. It sounded like an ordeal. She wasn't looking forward to it. And afterward, what if she could never walk again? What if…?

"No pessimistic thoughts." Odalie spoke for the visitors. "You're going to get well. You're going to walk. Period."

"Absolutely," Sadie said.

"Amen," Cort added.

Maddie managed a sheepish smile. With a cheering section like that, she thought, perhaps she could, after all.

CHAPTER EIGHT

THE THIRD DAY was definitely the worst. Maddie was in incredible pain from all the bruising. It was agony to move at all, and her legs were still numb. They kept her sedated most of the day. And at night, as usual, Cort and Odalie stayed with her.

"How are you getting away with this?" Maddie asked Odalie when Cort left to get them both a cup of coffee.

"With this?" Odalie asked gently.

"Staying in the room with me," she replied drowsily. "I thought hospitals made people leave at eight-thirty."

"Well, they mostly do," Odalie said sheepishly. "But, you see, Cort's Dad endowed the new pediatric unit, and mine paid for the equipment in the physical therapy unit. So, they sort of made an exception for us."

Maddie laughed in spite of the pain. "Oh, my."

"As my dad explained it, you can do a lot of good for other people and help defray your own taxes, all at once. But, just between us, my dad would give away money even if it didn't help his tax bill. So would Cort's. It's just the sort of people they are."

"It's very nice of them." She shifted and grimaced. "How are things at my ranch, do you know?" she asked worriedly.

"Great. Not that the boys don't miss you. But Cort's been over there every day getting roundup organized and deciding on your breeding program. I hope you don't mind."

"Are you kidding? I make fairies…I don't know anything about creating bloodlines." She sighed. "My dad knew all that stuff. He was great at it. But he should have had a boy who'd have loved running a ranch. I just got stuck with it because there was nobody else he could leave it to."

"Your father must have known that you'd do the best you could to keep it going," Odalie said gently.

"I am. It's just I have no aptitude for it, that's all."

"I think…"

"Finally!" John Everett said as he walked in, frowning at his sister. "There was such a conspiracy of silence. I couldn't get Cort to tell me where you were. I called every hospital in Dallas…"

"I left you seven emails and ten text messages!" Odalie gasped. "Don't tell me you never read them?"

He glowered at her. "I don't read my personal email because it's always advertisements, and I hate text messages. I disabled them from coming to my phone. You couldn't have called me in Denver and told me what happened?"

Odalie would have told him that Cort talked her out of it, but he was mad, and John in a temper would discourage most people from confessing that.

"Sorry," she said instead.

He turned his attention to Maddie and grimaced. The bruises were visible around the short-sleeved gown she was wearing. "Poor little thing," he said gently. "I brought you flowers."

He opened the door and nodded to a lady standing outside with a huge square vase full of every flower known to man—or so it seemed. "Right over there looks like a good place," he said, indicating a side table.

The lady, probably from the gift shop, smiled at Maddie and placed the flowers on the table. "I hope you feel better soon," she told her.

"The flowers are just lovely," Maddie exclaimed.

"Thanks," the lady replied, smiled at John and left them to it.

"Oh, how beautiful. Thanks, John!" she exclaimed.

Odalie looked very uncomfortable. John didn't even look at her. He went to the bedside, removed his Stetson and sat down in the chair by the bed, grasping one of Maddie's hands in his. "I've been beside myself since I knew what happened. I wanted to fly right home, but I was in the middle of negotiations for Dad and I couldn't. I did try to call your house, but nobody answered, and I didn't have your cell phone number." He glared at his sister again. "Nobody would even tell me which hospital you were in!"

"I sent you emails," Odalie said again.

"The telephone has a voice mode," he drawled sarcastically.

Odalie swallowed hard and got to her feet. "Maybe I should help Cort carry the coffee," she said. "Do you want some?"

"Don't be mean to her," Maddie said firmly. "She's been wonderful to me."

John blinked. He glanced at Odalie with wide-eyed surprise. "Her?"

"Yes, her," Maddie replied. "She hasn't left me since I've been in here. She brought me books..."

"Her?" John exclaimed again.

Odalie glared at him. "I am not totally beyond redemption," she said haughtily.

"Maybe I have a fever," John mused, touching his forehead as he looked back down into Maddie's eyes. "I thought you said she stayed with you in the hospital. She hates hospitals."

"She's been here all night every night," Maddie said softly. She smiled at Odalie. "She's been amazing."

Odalie went beet-red. She didn't know how to handle the compliment. She'd had so many, all her life, about her beauty and her talent. But nobody had ever said she was amazing for exhibiting compassion. It felt really good.

"It was my fault, what happened," Odalie said quietly. "I was driving."

"Who the hell let you drive a car?" John exclaimed.

"I did," Cort said heavily as he joined them. He looked at John's hand holding Maddie's and his dark eyes began to burn with irritation. "Don't hold her hand, it's bruised," he blurted out before he thought.

John's blue eyes twinkled suddenly. "It is?" He turned it over and looked at it. "Doesn't look bruised. That hurt?" he asked Maddie.

"Well, no," she answered. The way Cort was looking at John was very odd.

"Yes, he let me drive because I badgered him into it," Odalie broke in. "Poor Maddie tried to save her rooster and ran out into the road. I didn't see her until it was too late."

"Oh, no," John said, concerned. "Will you be all right?" he asked Maddie.

"I'm going to be fine," she assured him with more confidence than she really felt.

"Yes, she is," Odalie said, smiling. "We're all going to make sure of it."

"What about Pumpkin?" John asked.

Odalie tried to stop him from asking, but she was too late.

"It's all right," Maddie said gently. "I'm getting used to it. Pumpkin…didn't make it."

Sadie had told her that Ben had buried the awful rooster under a mesquite tree and even made a little headstone to go on the grave. Considering how many scars Ben had, it was quite a feat of compassion.

"I'll get you a new rooster," John said firmly.

"Already taken care of," Cort replied. "You're in my seat, bro."

John gave him a strange look. "Excuse me?"

"That's my seat. I've got it just the way I like it, from sleeping in it for two nights."

John was getting the picture. He laughed inside. Amazing how determined Cort was to get him away from Maddie. He glanced at his sister, who should be fuming. But she wasn't. Her eyes were smiling. She didn't even seem to be jealous.

Maddie was so out of it that she barely noticed the byplay. The sedative was working on her. She could barely keep her eyes open.

As she drifted off, Cort was saying something about a rooster with feathers on his feet.…

A WEEK AFTER the accident, Maddie began to feel her back again. It was agonizing pain. Dr. Brooks came in to examine her, his face impassive as he had her grip his fingers. He used a pin on the bottom of her feet, and actually grinned when she flinched.

"I'm not going to be paralyzed?" she asked, excited and hopeful.

"We can't say that for sure," Dr. Brooks said gently. "Once the swelling and edema are reduced, there may be additional injuries that become apparent. But I will say it's a good sign."

She let out a breath. "I'd have coped," she assured him. "But I'm hoping I won't have to."

He smiled and patted her on the shoulder. "One step at a time, young lady. Recovery first, then rehabilitation with physiotherapy. Meanwhile I'm going to consult with your orthopedic surgeon and put in a call to a friend of mine, a neurologist. We want to cover all our bases."

"You're being very cautious," she murmured.

"I have to be. The fact that you got excellent immediate care at the scene is greatly in your favor, however. Cort knew exactly what to do, and the paramedics followed up in textbook perfection. However," he added with a smile, "my personal opinion is your condition comes from bad bruising and it is not a permanent injury. We saw nothing on the tests that indicated a tearing of the spinal cord or critical damage to any of your lumbar vertebrae."

"You didn't say," she replied.

"Until the swelling goes down, we can't be absolutely sure of anything, which is why I'm reluctant to go all bright-eyed over a cheery prognosis," he explained. "But on the evidence of what I see, I think you're going to make a complete recovery."

She beamed. "Thank you!"

He held up a hand. "We'll still wait and see."

"When can I go home?" she asked.

"Ask me next week."

She made a face. "I'm tired of colored gelatin," she complained. "They're force feeding me water and stuff with fiber in it."

"To keep your kidney and bowel function within acceptable levels," he said. "Don't fuss. Do what they tell you."

She sighed. "Okay. Thanks for letting Cort and Odalie stay with me at night. One of the nurses said you spoke to the administrator himself."

He shrugged. "He and I were at med school together. I beat him at chess regularly."

She laughed. "Can you thank him for me? You don't know what it meant, that they wanted to stay."

"Yes, I do," he replied solemnly. "I've never seen anybody do a greater turnaround than your friend Odalie." He was the doctor who'd treated Maddie after the boy tried to throw her out of the window at school. He'd given a statement to the attorneys who went to see Cole Everett, as well. He shook his head. "I've known your families since you were children. I know more about Odalie than most people do. I must say, she's impressed me. And I'm hard to impress."

Maddie smiled. "She's impressed me, too. I never expected her to be so compassionate. Of course, it could be guilt," she said hesitantly. She didn't add that Odalie could be trying to win back Cort. She made a face. "I'm ashamed that I said that."

"Don't be. It's natural to be suspicious of someone who's been nothing short of an enemy. But this time, I believe her motives are quite sincere."

"Thanks. That helps."

He smiled. "You keep improving. I'll be back to see you from time to time. But I'm pleased with the progress I see."

"Thanks more for that."

He chuckled. "I love my job," he said at the door.

LATE AT NIGHT, Maddie was prey to her secret fears of losing the use of her legs. Despite Dr. Brooks's assurances, she knew that the prognosis could change. The traumatic nature of her injury made it unpredictable.

"Hey," Cort said softly, holding her hand when she moved restlessly in bed. "Don't think about tomorrow. Just get through one day at a time."

She rolled her head on the pillow and looked at him with tormented eyes. Odalie was sound asleep on the rollaway bed nearby, oblivious. But last night, it had been the other woman who'd been awake while Cort slept, to make sure Maddie had anything she needed.

"It's hard not to think about it," she said worriedly. "I'm letting everybody at the ranch down...."

"Baloney," he mused, smiling. "I've got Ben and the others organized. We're making progress on your breeding program." He made a face. "John went over there today to oversee things while I was here with you."

"John's your best friend," she reminded him.

He didn't want to tell her that he was jealous of his friend. He'd wanted to thump John when he walked in and found him holding Maddie's hand. But he was trying to be reasonable. He couldn't be here and at the ranch. And John was talented with breeding livestock. He'd learned from Cole Everett, whose skills were at least equal with King Brannt's and, some people said, just a tad more scientific.

"That's nice of John," she remarked.

He forced a smile. "Yeah. He's a good guy."

She searched his eyes.

"Oh, hell," he muttered, "he's got an honors degree in animal husbandry. I've got an associate's."

She brightened. "Doesn't experience count for something?" she teased lightly.

He chuckled deep in his throat. "Nice of you, to

make me feel better, when I've landed you in that hospital bed," he added with guilt in his eyes.

She squeezed his hand. "My dad used to say," she said softly, "that God sends people into our lives at various times, sometimes to help, sometimes as instruments to test us. He said that you should never blame people who cause things to happen to you, because that might be a test to teach you something you needed to know." She glanced at Odalie. "I can't be the only person who's noticed how much she's changed," she added in a low tone. "She's been my rock through all this. You have, too, but…"

"I understand." He squeezed her hand back, turning it over to look at the neat, clean fingernails tipping her small, capable fingers. "I've been very proud of her."

"Me, too," Maddie confessed. "Honestly this whole experience has changed the way I look at the world, at people."

"Your dad," he replied, "was a very smart man. And not just with cattle."

She smiled. "I always thought so. I do miss him."

He nodded. "I know you do."

He put her hand back on the bed. "You try to go back to sleep. Want me to call the nurse and see if she can give you something else for pain?"

She laughed softly and indicated the patch on her arm. "It's automatic. Isn't science incredible?"

"Gets more incredible every day," he agreed. He got up. "I'm going for more coffee. I won't be long."

"Thanks. For all you're doing," she said seriously.

He stared down at her with quiet, guilty eyes. "It will never be enough to make up for what happened."

"That's not true," she began.

"I'll be back in a bit." He left her brooding.

"YOU HAVE TO try to make Cort stop blaming himself," Maddie told Odalie the next day after she'd had breakfast and Cort had gone to the ranch for a shower and change of clothes. Odalie would go when he returned, they'd decided.

"That's going to be a tall order," the other woman said with a gentle smile.

"If there was a fault, it was Pumpkin's and mine," Maddie said doggedly. "He ran out into the road and I chased after him without paying any attention to traffic."

Odalie sat down in the seat beside the bed, her face covered in guilt. "I have a confession," she said heavily. "You're going to hate me when you hear it."

"I couldn't hate you after all you've done," came the soft reply. "It isn't possible."

Odalie flushed. "Thanks," she said in a subdued tone. She drew in a deep breath. "I drove by your place deliberately. Cort had been talking about you when I got home. I was jealous. I wanted you to see me with him." She averted her eyes. "I swear to God, if I'd had any idea what misery and grief I was going to cause, I'd never have gotten in the car at all!"

"Oh, goodness," Maddie said unsteadily. But she was much more unsettled by Odalie's jealousy than she was of her actions. It meant that Odalie cared for Cort. And everybody knew how he felt about her; he'd never made any secret of it.

But Maddie had been hurt, and Cort felt responsible. So he was paying attention to Maddie instead of Odalie out of guilt.

Everything became clear. Maddie felt her heart break. But it wasn't Odalie's fault. She couldn't force Cort not to care about her.

Odalie's clear blue eyes lifted and looked into Maddie's gray ones. "You care for him, don't you?" she asked heavily. "I'm so sorry!"

Maddie reached out a hand and touched hers. "One thing I've learned in my life is that you can't make people love you," she said softly. She drew in a long breath and stared at the ceiling. "Life just doesn't work that way."

"So it seems..." Odalie said, and her voice trailed away. "But you see the accident really was my fault."

Maddie shook her head. She wasn't vindictive. She smiled. "It was Pumpkin's."

Odalie felt tears streaming down her cheeks. "All this time, all I could think about is the things I did to you when we were in school. I'm so ashamed, Maddie."

Maddie was stunned.

"I put on a great act for the adults. I was shy and sweet and everybody's idea of the perfect child. But when they weren't looking, I was horrible. My parents didn't know how horrible until your father came to the house with an attorney, and laid it out for them." She grimaced. "I didn't know what happened to you. There was gossip, but it was hushed up. And gossip is usually exaggerated, you know." She picked at her fingernail, her head lowered. "I pretended that I didn't care. But I did." She looked up. "It wasn't until the accident that I really faced up to the person I'd become." She shook her own head. "I didn't like what I saw."

Maddie didn't speak. She just listened.

Odalie smiled sadly. "You know, I've spent my life listening to people rave about how pretty I was, how talented I was. But until now, nobody ever liked me because I was kind to someone." She flushed red. "You

needed me. That's new, having somebody need me."
She grinned. "I really like it."

Maddie burst out laughing.

Odalie laughed, too, wiping at tears. "Anyway, I
apologize wholeheartedly for all the misery I've caused
you, and I'm going to work really hard at being the
person I hope I can be."

"I don't know what I would have done without you,"
Maddie said with genuine feeling. "Nobody could have
been kinder."

"Some of that was guilt. But I really like you," she
said, and laughed again sheepishly. "I never knew what
beautiful little creatures you could create from clay
and paint."

"My hobby." She laughed.

"It's going to be a life-changing hobby. You wait."

Maddie only smiled. She didn't really believe that.
But she wanted to.

CORT CAME BACK later and Odalie went home to freshen
up.

Cort dropped into the chair beside Maddie's bed
with a sigh. "I saw your doctor outside, doing rounds.
He thinks you're progressing nicely."

She smiled. "Yes, he told me so. He said I might be
able to go home in a few days. I'll still have to have
physical therapy, though."

"Odalie and I will take turns bringing you here for
it," he said, answering one of her fears that her car
wouldn't stand up to the demands of daily trips, much
less her gas budget.

"But, Cort," she protested automatically.

He held up a hand. "It won't do any good," he assured her.

She sighed. "Okay. Thanks, then." She studied his worn face. "Odalie's been amazing, hasn't she?"

He laughed. "Oh, I could think of better words. She really shocked me. I wouldn't have believed her capable of it."

"I know."

"I'm very proud of her," he said, smiling wistfully. He was thinking what a blessing it was that Odalie hadn't shown that side of herself to him when he thought he was in love with her. Because with hindsight, he realized that it was only an infatuation. He'd had a crush on Odalie that he'd mistaken for true love.

Maddie couldn't hear his thoughts. She saw that wistful smile and thought he was seeing Odalie as he'd always hoped she could be, and that he was more in love with her than ever before.

"So am I," she replied.

He noted the odd look in her eyes and started to question it when his mother came in with Heather Everett. Both women had been visiting every day. This time they had something with them. It was a beautiful arrangement of orchids.

"We worked on it together," Heather said, smiling. She was Odalie, aged, still beautiful with blue eyes and platinum blond hair. A knockout, like dark-eyed, dark-haired Shelby Brannt, even with a sprinkle of gray hairs.

"Yes, and we're not florists, but we wanted to do something personal," Shelby added.

Heather put it on the far table, by the window, where it caught the light and looked exotic and lush.

"It's so beautiful! Thank you both," Maddie enthused.

"How are you feeling, sweetheart?" Shelby asked, hovering.

"The pain is easing, and I have feeling in my legs," she said, the excitement in her gray eyes. "The doctor thinks I'll walk again."

"That's wonderful news," Shelby said heavily. "We've been so worried."

"All of us," Heather agreed. She smiled. "It's worse for us, because Odalie was driving."

"Odalie has been my rock in a storm," Maddie said gently. "She hasn't left me, except to freshen up, since they brought me in here. I honestly don't know how I would have made it without her. Or without Cort," she added, smiling at him. "They've stopped me from brooding, cheered me up, cheered me on…they've been wonderful."

Shelby hugged her tall son. "Well, of course, I think so." She laughed. "Still, it's been hard on all three families," she added quietly. "It could have been even more of a tragedy if—"

"I'm going to be fine," Maddie interrupted her.

"Yes, she is," Cort agreed. He smiled at Maddie. His dark eyes were like velvet. There was an expression in them that she'd never noticed before. Affection. Real affection.

She smiled back, shyly, and averted her eyes.

"Odalie wants you to talk to one of our friends, who has an art gallery in Dallas," Heather said. "She thinks your talent is quite incredible."

"It's not, but she's nice to say so…" Maddie began.

"They're her kids," Cort explained to the women, and Maddie's eyes widened. "Don't deny it, you told me so," he added, making a face at her. "She puts so much of herself into them that she can't bear to think of selling one."

"Well, I know it sounds odd, but it's like that with me and the songs I compose," Heather confessed, and flushed a little when they stared at her. "I really do put my whole heart into them. And I hesitate to share that with other people."

"Desperado owes you a lot for those wonderful songs." Shelby chuckled. "And not just money. They've made an international reputation with them."

"Thanks," Heather said. "I don't know where they come from. It's a gift. Truly a gift."

"Like Odalie's voice," Maddie replied. "She really does sing like an angel."

Heather smiled. "Thank you. I've always thought so. I wanted her to realize her dream, to sing at the Met, at the Italian opera houses." She looked introspective. "But it doesn't look like she's going to do that at all."

"Why not?" Shelby asked, curious.

Heather smiled. "I think she's hungry for a home of her own and a family. She's been talking about children lately."

"Has she?" Cort asked, amused.

He didn't seem to realize that Maddie immediately connected Heather's statement with Odalie's changed nature and Cort's pride in her. She added those facts together and came up with Cort and Odalie getting married.

It was so depressing that she had to force herself to smile and pretend that she didn't care.

"Can you imagine what beautiful children she'll have?" Maddie asked with a wistful smile.

"Well, yours aren't going to be ugly," Cort retorted. Then he remembered that he'd called Maddie that, during one of their arguments, and his face paled with shame.

Maddie averted her eyes and tried not to show what she was feeling. "Not like Odalie's," she said. "Is she thinking about getting married?" she asked Heather.

"She says she is," she replied. "I don't know if she's really given it enough thought, though," she added with sadness in her tone. "Very often, we mistake infatuation for the real thing."

"You didn't," Shelby teased before anyone could react to Heather's statement. "You knew you wanted to marry Cole before you were even an adult."

Heather saw Maddie's curious glance. "Cole's mother married my father," she explained. "There was some terrible gossip spread, to the effect that we were related by blood. It broke my heart. I gave up on life. And then the truth came out, and I realized that Cole didn't hate me at all. He'd only been shoving me out of his life because he thought I was totally off-limits, and his pride wouldn't let him admit how thoroughly he'd accepted the gossip for truth."

"You made a good match." Shelby smiled.

"So did you, my friend." Heather laughed. "Your road to the altar was even more precarious than mine."

Shelby beamed. "Yes, but it was worth every tear." She hugged her son. "Look at my consolation prize!"

BUT WHEN THE women left, and Cort walked them out to the parking lot, Maddie was left with her fears and insecurities.

Odalie wanted to marry and raise a family. She'd seen how mature and caring Cort was, and she wanted to drive him by Maddie's house because she was jealous of her. She'd wanted Maddie to see her with Cort.

She could have cried. Once, Odalie's feelings wouldn't have mattered. But since she'd been in the hospital, Maddie had learned things about the other woman. She genuinely liked her. She was like the sister Maddie had never had.

What was she going to do? Cort seemed to like Maddie now, but she'd been hurt and it was his car that had hit her. Certainly he felt guilty. And nobody could deny how much he'd loved Odalie. He'd grieved for weeks after she left for Italy.

Surely his love for her hadn't died just because Maddie had been in an accident. He'd told Maddie that she was ugly and that she didn't appeal to him as a man, long before the wreck. That had been honest; she'd seen it in his dark eyes.

Now he was trying to make up for what had happened. He was trying to sacrifice himself to Maddie in a vain attempt to atone for her injuries. He was denying himself Odalie out of guilt.

Maddie closed her eyes. She couldn't have that. She wanted him to be happy. In fact, she wanted Odalie to be happy. Cort would be miserable if he forced himself into a relationship with Maddie that he didn't feel.

So that wasn't going to be allowed to happen. Maddie was going to make sure of it.

CHAPTER NINE

BY THE END of the second week after the accident, Maddie was back home, with a high-tech wheelchair to get around the house in.

Odalie and Cort had insisted on buying her one to use while she was recuperating, because she still couldn't walk, even though the feeling had come back into her legs. She was exhilarated with the doctor's cautious prognosis that she would probably heal completely after several months.

But she'd made her friends promise to get her an inexpensive manual wheelchair. Of course, they'd said, smiling.

Then they walked in with a salesman who asked questions, measured her and asked about her choice of colors. Oh, bright yellow, she'd teased, because she was sure they didn't make a bright yellow wheelchair. The only ones she'd seen were black and ugly and plain, and they all looked alike. She'd dreaded the thought of having to sit in one.

A few days later, the wheelchair was delivered. It came from Europe. It was the most advanced wheelchair of its type, fully motorized, able to turn in its own circumference, able to lift the user up to eye level with other people, and all-terrain. Oh, and also, bright yellow in color.

"This must have cost a fortune!" Maddie almost

screamed when she saw it. "I said something inexpensive!"

Cort gave her a patient smile. "You said inexpensive. This is inexpensive," he added, glancing at Odalie.

"Cheap," the blonde girl nodded. She grinned unrepentantly. "When you get out of it, you can donate it to someone in need."

"Oh. Well." The thought that she would get out of it eventually sustained her. "I can donate it?"

Odalie nodded. She smiled.

Cort smiled, too.

"Barracudas," she concluded, looking from one to the other. "I can't get around either one of you!"

They both grinned.

She laughed. "Okay. Thanks. Really. Thanks."

"You might try it out," Odalie coaxed.

"Yes, in the direction of the hen yard," Cort added.

She looked from one of them to the other. They had very suspicious expressions. "Okay."

She was still learning to drive it, but the controls were straightforward, and it didn't take long to learn them. The salesman had come out with it, to further explain its operation.

It had big tires, and it went down steps. That was a revelation. It didn't even bump very much. She followed Cort and Odalie over the sandy yard to the huge enclosure where her hens lived. It was grassy, despite the tendency of chickens to scratch and eat the grass, with trees on one side. The other contained multiple feeders and hanging waterers. The enormous henhouse had individual nests and cowboys cleaned it out daily. There was almost no odor, and the hens were clean and beautiful.

"My girls look very happy," Maddie said, laughing.

"They have a good reason to be happy." Cort went into the enclosure, and a minute later, he came back out, carrying a large red rooster with a big comb and immaculate feathers.

He brought him to Maddie. The rooster looked sort of like Pumpkin, but he was much bigger. He didn't seem at all bothered to be carried under someone's arm. He handed the rooster to Maddie.

She perched him on her jean-clad lap and stared at him. He cocked his head and looked at her and made a sort of purring sound.

She was aghast. She looked up at Cort wide-eyed.

"His name's Percival," Cort told her with a chuckle. "He has impeccable bloodlines."

She looked at the feathery pet again. "I've never seen a rooster this tame," she remarked.

"That's from those impeccable bloodlines." Odalie giggled. "All their roosters are like this. They're even guaranteed to be tame, or your money back. So he's sort of returnable. But you won't need to return him. He's been here for a week and he hasn't attacked anybody yet. Considering his age, he's not likely to do it."

"His age?" Maddie prompted.

"He's two," Cort said. "Never attacked anybody on the farm for all that time. The owners' kids carry the roosters around with them all the time. They're gentled. But they're also bred for temperament. They have exceptions from time to time. But Percy's no exception. He's just sweet."

"Yes, he is." She hugged the big rooster, careful not to hug him too closely, because chickens have no diaphragm and they can be smothered if their chests are compressed for too long. "Percy, you're gorgeous!"

He made that purring sound again. Almost as if he

were laughing. She handed him back to Cort. "You've got him separate from the girls?"

He nodded. "If you want biddies, we can put him with them in time for spring chicks. But they know he's nearby, and so will predators. He likes people. He hates predators. The owner says there's a fox who'll never trouble a henhouse again after the drubbing Percy gave him."

Maddie laughed with pure joy. "It will be such a relief not to have to carry a limb with me to gather eggs," she said. The smile faded. "I'll always miss Pumpkin," she said softly, "but even I knew that something had to give eventually. He was dangerous. I just didn't have the heart to do anything about him."

"Providence did that for you," Cort replied. He smiled warmly. Maddie smiled back but she avoided his eyes.

That bothered him. He put Percy back in the enclosure in his own fenced area, very thoughtful. Maddie was polite, but she'd been backing away from him for days now. He felt insecure. He wanted to ask her what was wrong. Probably, he was going to have to do that pretty soon.

MADDIE WENT TO work on her sculptures with a vengeance, now that she had enough materials to produce anything she liked.

Her first work, though, was a tribute to her new friend. She made a fairy who looked just like Odalie, perched on a lily pad, holding a firefly. She kept it hidden when Cort and Odalie came to see her, which was pretty much every single day. It was her secret project.

She was so thrilled with it that at first she didn't even want to share it with them. Of all the pieces she'd done, this was her best effort. It had been costly, too. Sitting in one position for a long time, even in her cushy imported wheelchair, was uncomfortable and took a toll on her back.

"You mustn't stress your back muscles like this," the therapist fussed when she went in for therapy, which she did every other day. "It's too much strain so early in your recovery."

She smiled while the woman used a heat lamp and massage on her taut back. "I know. I like to sculpt things. I got overenthusiastic."

"Take frequent breaks," the therapist advised.

"I'll do that. I promise."

SHE WAS WALKING now, just a little at a time, but steadily. Cort had bought a unit for her bathtub that created a Jacuzzi-like effect in the water. It felt wonderful on her sore and bruised back. He'd had a bar installed, too, so that she could ease herself up out of the water and not have to worry about slipping.

Odalie brought her exotic cheeses and crackers to eat them with, having found out that cheese was pretty much Maddie's favorite food. She brought more art books, and classical music that Maddie loved.

Cort brought his guitar and sang to her. That was the hardest thing to bear. Because Maddie knew he was only doing it because he thought Maddie had feelings for him. It was humiliating that she couldn't hide them, especially since she knew that he loved Odalie and always would.

But she couldn't help but be entranced by it. She loved his deep, rich voice, loved the sound of the guitar, with its mix of nylon and steel strings. It was a classical guitar. He'd ordered it from Spain. He played as wonderfully as he sang.

When he'd played *"Recuerdos de la Alhambra"* for her, one of the most beautiful classical guitar compositions ever conceived, she wept like a baby.

"It is beautiful, isn't it?" he asked, drying her tears with a handkerchief. "It was composed by a Spaniard, Francisco Tárrega, in 1896." He smiled. "It's my favorite piece."

"Mine, too," she said. "I had a recording of guitar solos on my iPod with it. But you play it just as beautifully as that performer did. Even better than he did."

"Thanks." He put the guitar back into its case, very carefully. "From the time I was ten, there was never any other instrument I wanted to play. I worried my folks to death until they bought me one. And Morie used to go sit outside while I practiced, with earplugs in." He chuckled, referring to his sister.

"Poor Morie," she teased.

"She loves to hear me play, now. She said it was worth the pain while I learned."

She grinned. "You know, you could sing professionally."

He waved that thought away. "I'm a cattleman," he replied. "Never wanted to be anything else. The guitar is a nice hobby. But I don't think I'd enjoy playing and singing as much if I had to do it all the time."

"Good point."

"How's that sculpture coming along?"

Her eyes twinkled. "Come see."

She turned on the wheelchair and motored herself into the makeshift studio they'd furnished for her in her father's old bedroom. It had just the right airy, lighted accommodation that made it a great place to work. Besides that, she could almost feel her father's presence when she was in it.

"Don't tell her," she cautioned as she uncovered a mound on her worktable. "It's going to be a surprise."

"I promise."

She pulled off the handkerchief she'd used to conceal the little fairy sculpture. The paint was dry and the glossy finish she'd used over it gave the beautiful creature an ethereal glow.

"It looks just like her!" Cort exclaimed as he gently picked it up.

She grinned. "Do you think so? I did, but I'm too close to my work to be objective about it."

"It's the most beautiful thing you've done yet, and that's saying something." He looked down at her with an odd expression. "You really have the talent."

She flushed. "Thanks, Cort."

He put the sculpture down and bent, brushing his mouth tenderly over hers. "I have to be so careful with you," he whispered at her lips. "It's frustrating, in more ways than one."

She caught her breath. She couldn't resist him. But it was tearing her apart, to think that he might be caught in a web of deception laced by guilt. She looked up into his eyes with real pain.

He traced her lips with his forefinger. "When you're back on your feet," he whispered, "we have to talk."

She managed a smile. "Okay." Because she knew that, by then, she'd find a way to ease his guilt, and Odalie's, and step out of the picture. She wasn't going to let them sacrifice their happiness for her. That was far too much.

He kissed her again and stood up, smiling. "So when are you going to give it to her?"

"Tomorrow," she decided.

"I'll make sure she comes over."

"Thanks."

He shrugged and then smiled. "She's going to be over the moon when she sees it."

THAT WAS AN understatement. Odalie cried. She turned the little fairy around and around in her elegant hands, gasping at the level of detail in the features that were so exactly like her own.

"It's the most beautiful gift I've ever been given."

She put it down, very gently, and hugged Maddie as carefully as she could. "You sweetie!" she exclaimed. "I'll never be able to thank you. It looks just like me!"

Maddie chuckled. "I'm glad you like it."

"You have to let me talk to my friend at the art gallery," Odalie said.

Maddie hesitated. "Maybe someday," she faltered. "Maybe."

"But you have so much talent, Maddie. It's such a gift."

Maddie flushed. "Thanks."

Odalie kept trying, but she couldn't move the other girl. Not at all.

"Okay," she relented. "You know your own mind. Oh, goodness, what is that?" she exclaimed, indicating a cameo lying beside another fairy, a black-haired one sitting on a riverbank holding a book.

Maddie told her the story of the antique dealer and the cameo that had no family to inherit.

"What an incredible story," Odalie said, impressed. "She's quite beautiful. You can do that, from a picture?"

Maddie laughed. "I did yours from the one in our

school yearbook," she said, and this time she didn't flinch remembering the past.

Odalie looked uncomfortable, but she didn't refer to it. Perhaps in time she and Maddie could both let go of that terrible memory. "Maddie, could you do one of my great-grandmother if I brought you a picture of her? It's a commission, now…"

Maddie held up a hand. "No. I'd love to do it. It's just a hobby, you know, not a job. Just bring me a picture."

Odalie's eyes were unusually bright. "Okay. I'll bring it tomorrow!"

Maddie laughed at her enthusiasm. "I'll get started as soon as I have it."

THE PICTURE WAS surprising. "This is your grand-mother?" Maddie asked, because it didn't look any-thing like Odalie. The subject of the painting had red hair and pale green eyes.

"My great-grandmother," Odalie assured her, but she averted her eyes to another sculpture while she said it.

"Oh. That explains it. Yes, I can do it."

"That's so sweet of you, Maddie."

"It's nothing at all."

IT TOOK TWO weeks. Maddie still had periods of discom-fort that kept her in bed, but she made sure she walked and moved around, as the therapist and her doctor had told her to do. It was amazing that, considering the impact of the car, she hadn't suffered a permanent disability. The swelling and inflammation had been pretty bad, as was the bruising, but she wasn't going to lose the use of her legs. The doctor was still being cautious about that prognosis. But Maddie could tell from the way she was healing that she was going to be all right. She'd never been more certain of anything.

She finished the little fairy sculpture on a Friday. She was very pleased with the result. It looked just like the photograph, but with exquisite detail. This fairy was sitting on a tree stump, with a small green frog perched on her palm. She was laughing. Maddie loved the way it had turned out. But now it was going to be hard to part with it. She did put part of herself into her sculptures. It was like giving herself away with the art.

She'd promised Odalie, though, so she had to come to terms with it.

Odalie was overwhelmed with the result. She stared at it and just shook her head. "I can't believe how skilled you are," she said, smiling at Maddie. "This is so beautiful. She'll, I mean my mother, will love it!"

"Oh, it's her grandmother," Maddie recalled.

"Yes." Odalie still wouldn't meet her eyes, but she laughed. "What a treat this is going to be! Can I take it with me?" she asked.

Maddie only hesitated for a second. She smiled. "Of course you can."

"Wonderful!"

She bent and hugged Maddie gently. "Still doing okay?" she asked worriedly.

Maddie nodded. "Getting better all the time, thanks to a small pharmacy of meds on my bedside table," she quipped.

"I'm so glad. I mean that," she said solemnly. "The day you can walk to your car and drive it, I'll dance in the yard."

Maddie laughed. "Okay. I'll hold you to that!"

Odalie just grinned.

CORT CAME OVER every day. Saturday morning he went
to the barn to study the charts he and John Everett
had made. John had just come over to bring Maddie
flowers. She was sitting on the porch with Great-Aunt
Sadie. As soon as John arrived, Cort came back from
the barn and joined the group on the porch. The way
Cort glared at him was surprising.

"They'll give her allergies," Cort muttered.

John gave him a stunned look, and waved around
the yard at the blooming crepe myrtle and jasmine and
sunflowers and sultanas and zinnias. "Are you nuts?"
he asked, wide-eyed. "Look around you! Who do you
think planted all these?"

Cort's dark eyes narrowed. He jammed his hands
into his jean pockets. "Well, they're not in the house,
are they?" he persisted.

John just laughed. He handed the pot of flowers to
Great-Aunt Sadie, who was trying not to laugh. "Can
you put those inside?" he asked her with a smile. "I
want to check the board in the barn and see how the
breeding program needs to go."

"I sure can," Sadie replied, and she went into the
house.

Maddie was still staring at John with mixed feelings. "Uh, thanks for the flowers," she said haltingly.
Cort was looking irritated.

"You're very welcome," John said. He studied her
for a long moment. "You look better."

"I feel a lot better," she said. "In fact, I think I might
try to walk to the barn."

"In your dreams, honey," Cort said softly. He picked
her up, tenderly, and cradled her against his chest. "But
I'll walk you there."

John stared at him intently. "Should you be picking her up like that?" he asked.

Cort wasn't listening. His dark eyes were probing Maddie's gray ones with deep tenderness. Neither of them was looking at John, who suddenly seemed to understand what was going on around him.

"Darn, I left my notes in the car," he said, hiding a smile. "I'll be right back."

He strode off. Cort bent his head. "I thought he'd never leave," he whispered, and brought his mouth down, hard, on Maddie's.

"Cort..."

"Shh," he whispered against her lips. "Don't fuss. Open your mouth...!"

The kiss grew hotter by the second. Maddie was clinging to his neck for dear life while he crushed her breasts into the softness of his blue-checked shirt and devoured her soft lips.

He groaned harshly, but suddenly he remembered where they were. He lifted his head, grateful that his back was to the house, and John's car. He drew in a long breath.

"I wish you weren't so fragile," he whispered. He kissed her shocked eyes shut. "I'm starving."

Her fingers teased the hair at the back of his head. "I could feed you a biscuit," she whispered.

He smiled. "I don't want biscuits." He looked at her mouth. "I want you."

Her face flamed with a combination of embarrassment and sheer delight.

"But we can talk about that later, after I've disposed of John's body," he added, turning to watch the other man approach, his eyes buried in a black notebook.

"Wh-h-hat?" she stammered, and burst out laughing at his expression.

He sighed. "I suppose no war is ever won without a few uncomfortable battles," he said under his breath.

"I found them," John said with a grin, waving the notebook. "Let's have a look at the breeding strategy you've mapped out, then."

"I put it all on the board," Cort replied. He carried Maddie into the barn and set her on her feet very carefully, so as not to jar her spine. "It's right there," he told John, nodding toward the large board where he'd indicated which bulls were to be bred to which heifers and cows.

John studied it for a long moment. He turned and looked at Cort curiously. "This is remarkable," he said. "I would have gone a different way, but yours is better."

Cort seemed surprised. "You've got a four-year degree in animal husbandry," he said. "Mine is only an associate's degree."

"Yes, but you've got a lifetime of watching your father do this." He indicated the board. "I've been busy studying and traveling. I haven't really spent that much time observing. It's rather like an internship, and I don't have the experience, even if I have the education."

"Thanks," Cort said. He was touchy about his two-year degree. He smiled. "Took courses in diplomacy, too, did you?" he teased.

John bumped shoulders with him. "You're my best friend," he murmured. "I'd never be the one to try to put you down."

Cort punched his shoulder gently. "Same here."

Maddie had both hands on her slender hips as she stared at the breeding chart. "Would either of you like to try to translate this for me?" She waved one hand at the blackboard. "Because it looks like Martian to me!"

Both men burst out laughing.

Cort had to go out of town. He was worried when he called Maddie to tell her, apologizing for his absence.

"Mom and Dad will look out for you while I'm gone," he promised. "If you need anything, you call them. I'll phone you when I get to Denver."

Her heart raced. "Okay."

"Will you miss me?" he teased.

She drew in a breath. "Of course," she said.

There was a pause. "I'll miss you more," he said quietly. His deep voice was like velvet. "What do you want me to bring you from Denver?"

"Yourself."

There was a soft chuckle. "That's a deal. Talk to you later."

"Have a safe trip."

He sighed. "At least Dad isn't flying me. He flies like he drives. But we'll get there."

The plural went right over her head. She laughed. She'd heard stories about King Brannt's driving. "It's safer than driving, everybody says so."

"In my dad's case, it's actually true. He flies a lot better than he drives."

"I heard that!" came a deep voice from beside him.

"Sorry, Dad," Cort replied. "See you, Maddie."

He hung up. She held the cell phone to her ear for an extra minute, just drinking in the sound of his voice promising to miss her.

WHILE CORT WAS away, Odalie didn't come, either. But even though she called, Maddie missed her daily visits. She apologized over the phone. She was actually out of town, but her mother had volunteered to do any run-ning-around that Maddie needed if Sadie couldn't go.

Maddie thanked her warmly. But when she hung up she couldn't help but wonder at the fact that Cort and Odalie were out of town at the same time. Had Odalie gone to Denver with Cort and they didn't want to tell her? It was worrying.

She rode her wheelchair out to the hen enclosure. Ben was just coming out of it with the first of many egg baskets. There were a lot of hens, and her cus-tomer list for her fresh eggs was growing by the week.

"That's a lot of eggs," she ventured.

He chuckled. "Ya, and I still have to wash 'em and check 'em for cracks."

"I like Percy," she remarked.

"I love Percy," Ben replied. "Never saw such a gen-tle rooster."

"Thanks. For what you did for Pumpkin's grave," she said, averting her eyes. She still cried easily when she talked about him.

"It was no problem at all, Miss Maddie," he said gently.

She looked over her hens with proud eyes. "My girls look good."

"They do, don't they?" he agreed, then added, "Well, I should get to work."

"Ben, do you know where Odalie went?" she asked suddenly.

He bit his lip.

"Come on," she prodded. "Tell me."

He looked sad. "She went to Denver, Miss Maddie. Heard it from her dad when I went to pick up feed in town."

Maddie's heart fell to her feet. But she smiled. "She

and Cort make a beautiful couple," she remarked, and tried to hide the fact that she was dying inside.

"Guess they do," he said. He tried to say something else, but he couldn't get the words to come out right. "I'll just go get these eggs cleaned."

She nodded. The eyes he couldn't see were wet with tears.

IT SEEMED THAT disaster followed disaster. While Cort and Odalie were away, bills flooded the mailbox. Maddie almost passed out when she saw the hospital bill. Even the minimum payment was more than she had in the bank.

"What are we going to do?" she wailed.

Sadie winced at her expression. "Well, we'll just manage," she said firmly. "There's got to be something we can sell that will help pay those bills." She didn't add that Cort and Odalie had promised they were taking care of all that. But they were out of town, and Sadie knew that Maddie's pride would stand in the way of asking them for money. She'd never do it.

"There is something," Maddie said heavily. She looked up at Sadie.

"No," Sadie said shortly. "No, you can't!"

"Look at these bills, Sadie," she replied, and spread them out on the table. "There's nothing I can hock, nothing I can do that will make enough money fast enough to cover all this. There just isn't anything else to do."

"You aren't going to talk to that developer fellow?"

"Heavens, no!" Maddie assured her. "I'll call a real estate agent in town."

"I think that's…"

Just as she spoke, a car pulled up in the yard.

"Well, speak of the devil," Maddie muttered.

The developer climbed out of his car, looked around and started for the front porch.

"Do you suppose we could lock the door and pretend to be gone?" Sadie wondered aloud.

"No. We're not hiding. Let him in," Maddie said firmly.

"Don't you give in to his fancy talk," Sadie advised.

"Never in a million years. Let him in."

The developer, Arthur Lawson, came in the door with a smug look on his face. "Miss Lane," he greeted. He smiled like a crocodile. "Bad news does travel fast. I heard you were in an accident and that your bills are piling up. I believe I can help you."

Maddie looked at Sadie. Her expression was eloquent.

Archie Lawson grinned like the barracuda he was.

"I heard that your neighbors have gone away together," he said with mock sympathy. "Just left you with all those medical bills to pay, did they?"

Maddie felt terrible. She didn't want to say anything unkind about Odalie and Cort. They'd done more than most people could have expected of them. But Maddie was left with the bills, and she had no money to pay them with. She'd read about people who didn't pay their hospital bill on time and had to deal with collectors' agencies. She was terrified.

"They don't say I have to pay them at once," Maddie began.

"Yes, but the longer you wait, the higher the interest they charge," he pointed out.

"Interest?"

"It's such and such a percent," he continued. He sat down without being asked in her father's old easy chair. "Let me spell it out for you. I can write you a check that will cover all those medical bills, the hospital bill, everything. All you have to do is sign over the property to me. I'll even take care of the livestock. I'll make sure they're sold to people who will take good care of them."

"I don't know," Maddie faltered. She was torn. It was so quick…

"Maddie, can I talk to you for a minute?" Sadie asked tersely. "It's about supper," she lied.

"Okay."

She excused herself and followed Sadie into the kitchen.

Sadie closed the door. "Listen to me, don't you do that until you talk to Mr. Brannt," Sadie said firmly. "Don't you dare!"

"But, Sadie," she said in anguish, "we can't pay the bills, and we can't expect the Brannts and the Everetts to keep paying them forever!"

"Cort said he'd take care of the hospital bill, at least," Sadie reminded her.

"Miss Lane?" Lawson called. "I have to leave soon!"

"Don't let him push you into this," Sadie cautioned. "Make him wait. Tell him you have to make sure the estate's not entailed before you can sell, you'll have to talk to your lawyer!"

Maddie bit her lower lip.

"Tell him!" Sadie said, gesturing her toward the porch.

Maddie took a deep breath and Sadie opened the door for her to motor through.

"Sadie was reminding me that we had a couple of outstanding liens on the property after Dad died," Maddie lied. "I'll have to talk to our attorney and make sure they've been lifted before I can legally sell it to you."

"Oh." He stood up. "Well." He glared. "You didn't mention that earlier."

"I didn't think you thought I was going to sell the ranch today," Maddie said, and with a bland smile. "That's all. You wouldn't want to find out later that you didn't actually own it…?"

"No. Of course not." He made a face. "All right, I'll be back in, say, two days? Will that give you enough time?"

"Yes," Maddie said.

He picked up his briefcase and looked around the living room. "This house will have to be torn down. But if you want some pictures and stuff, I can let you have it after we wrap up the sale. The furniture's no loss." He laughed coldly. "I'll be in touch. And if your answer is no—well, don't be surprised if your cattle suddenly come down with unusual diseases. Anthrax always comes to mind… And if federal agencies have to be called in, your operation will be closed down immediately."

He left and Maddie had to bite back curses. "The furniture's no loss," she muttered. "These are antiques! And anthrax! What kind of horrible person would infect defenseless animals! Maddie went inside, a chill settling in her heart.

"NASTY MAN. YOU can't let him have our house!" Sadie glared out the window as the developer drove off.

Maddie leaned back in her chair. "I wish I didn't," she said heavily. "But I don't know what else to do." She felt sick to her soul at the man's threats. "Cort is going to marry Odalie, you know."

Sadie wanted to argue, but she didn't know how to. It seemed pretty obvious that if he hadn't told Maddie he was leaving with Odalie, he had a guilty conscience and was trying to shield her from the truth.

"Should have just told you, instead of sneaking off together," Sadie muttered.

"They didn't want to hurt me," Maddie said heavily. "It's pretty obvious how I feel about Cort, you know."

"Still…"

Maddie looked at the bills lying open on the table. She leaned forward with her face in her hands. Her heart was breaking. At least she might be able to walk eventually. But that still left the problem of how she was going to walk herself out of this financial mess. The ranch was all she had left for collateral.

Collateral! She turned to Sadie. "We can take out a mortgage, can't we?" she asked Sadie.

Sadie frowned. "I don't know. Best you should call the lawyer and find out."

"I'll do that right now!"

She did at least have hope that there were options. A few options, at least.

BUT THE LIE she'd told Lawson turned out to be the truth.

"I'm really sorry, Maddie," Burt Davies told her. "But your dad did take out a lien on the property when he bought that last seed bull. I've been keeping up the payments out of the ranch revenues when I did the bills for you the past few months."

"You mean, I can't sell or even borrow on the ranch."

"You could sell," he admitted. "If you got enough for it that would pay off the lien… But, Maddie, that land's been in your family for generations. You can't mean to sell it."

She swallowed. "Burt, I've got medical bills I can't begin to pay."

"Odalie and Cort are taking care of those," he reminded her. "Legally, even if not morally, they're obligated to."

"Yes, but, they're getting married, don't you see?" she burst out. "I can't tie them up with my bills."

"You can and you will, if I have to go to court for you," Burt said firmly. "The accident wasn't your fault."

"Yes, it was," she said in a wan tone. "I ran out in the road to save my stupid rooster, who died anyway. As for guilt, Odalie and Cort have done everything humanly possible for me since the wreck. Nobody could fault them for that."

"I know, but..."

"If I sell the ranch," she argued gently, "I can pay off all my debts and I won't owe anyone anything."

"That's bad legal advice. You should never try to act as your own attorney."

She laughed. "Yes, I know. Okay, I'll think about it for a couple of days," she said.

"You think about it hard," he replied. "No sense in letting yourself be forced into a decision you don't want to make."

"All right. Thanks, Burt."

She hung up. "Life," she told the room at large, "is just not fair."

THE NEXT DAY, Ben came walking in with a sad expression. "Got bad news," he said.

"What now?" Maddie asked with a faint smile.

"Lost two more purebred cows. They wandered off."

"All right, that's more than coincidence," she muttered. She moved to the phone, picked it up and called King Brannt.

"How many cows does that make?" King asked, aghast.

"Four, in the past few weeks," she said. "Something's not right."

"I agree. I'll get our computer expert to check those recordings and see if he can find anything."

"Thanks, Mr. Brannt."

He hesitated. "How are things over there?"

She hesitated, too. "Just fine," she lied. "Fine."

"Cort's coming home day after tomorrow," he added.

"I hope he and Odalie have had a good time," she said, and tried not to sound as hurt as she felt. "They've both been very kind to me. I owe them a lot."

"Maddie," he began slowly, "about that trip they took—"

"They're my friends," she interrupted. "I want them to be happy. Look I have to go, okay? But if you find out anything about my cows, can you call me?"

"Sure."

"Thanks, Mr. Brannt."

She hung up. She didn't think she'd ever felt so miserable in her whole young life. She loved Cort. But he was never going to be hers. She realized now that he'd been pretending, to keep her spirits up so that she wouldn't despair. But he'd always loved Odalie, and she'd always known it. She couldn't expect him to give up everything he loved just to placate an injured woman, out of guilt. She wasn't going to let him do it.

And Odalie might have been her enemy once, but

that was certainly no longer the case. Odalie had become a friend. She couldn't have hard feelings toward her....

Oh, what a bunch of bull, she told herself angrily. Of course she had hard feelings. She loved Cort. She wanted him! But he loved Odalie and that was never going to change. How would it feel, to let a man hang around just because he felt guilty that you'd been hurt? Knowing every day that he was smiling and pretending to care, when he really wanted that beautiful golden girl, Odalie Everett, and always would?

No. That would cheat all three of them. She had to let him go. He belonged to Odalie, and Maddie had always known it. She was going to sell the ranch to that terrible developer and make herself homeless out of pride, because she didn't want her friends to sacrifice any more than they already had for her.

That developer, could he have been responsible for her lost cows? But why would he hurt the livestock when he was hoping to buy the ranch? No. It made no sense. None at all.

LATER, WITH HER door closed, she cried herself to sleep. She couldn't stop thinking about Cort, about how tender he'd been to her, how kind. Surely he hadn't been able to pretend the passion she felt in his long, hard, insistent kisses? Could men pretend to want a woman?

She wished she knew. She wanted to believe that his hints at a shared future had been honest and real. But she didn't dare trust her instincts. Not when Cort had taken Odalie with him to Denver and hidden it from Maddie.

He hadn't wanted her to know. That meant he knew

it would hurt her feelings and he couldn't bear to do it, not after all she'd been through.

She wiped her eyes. Crying wasn't going to solve anything. After all, what did she have to be sad about? There was a good chance that she would be able to walk normally again, when she was through recuperating. She'd still have Great-Aunt Sadie, and the developer said that he'd let her have her odds and ends out of the house.

The developer. She hated him. He was willing to set her up, to let her whole herd of cattle be destroyed, her breeding stock, just to get his hands on the ranch. She could tell someone, Mr. Brannt, maybe. But it would be her word against Lawson's. She had so much to lose. What if he could actually infect her cattle? Better to let her cattle be sold at auction to someone than risk having them destroyed. She couldn't bear to step on a spider, much less watch her prize cattle, her father's prize cattle, be exterminated.

No, she really didn't have a choice. She was going to lose the ranch one way or another, to the developer or to bill collectors.

She got up and went to the kitchen to make coffee. It was two in the morning, but it didn't matter. She was never going to sleep anyway.

She heard a sound out in the yard. She wished she kept a dog. She'd had one, but it had died not long after her father did. There was nothing to alert her to an intruder's presence anymore. She turned out the lights and motored to the window, hoping the sound of the wheelchair wouldn't be heard outside.

She saw something shadowy near the barn. That was where the surveillance equipment was set up.

She turned on all the outside lights, opened the door

and yelled, "Who's out there?!" The best defense was offense, she told herself.

There was startled movement, a dark blur going out behind the barn. Without a second thought, she got her cell phone and called the sheriff.

THE SHERIFF'S DEPARTMENT came, and so did King Brannt. He climbed out of his ranch pickup with another man about two steps behind the tall deputy.

Maddie rolled onto the porch. She'd been afraid to go outside until help arrived. She was no match, even with two good legs, for someone bent upon mischief.

"Miss Lane?" the deputy asked.

"Yes, sir," she said. "Someone was out here. I turned on the outside lights and yelled. Whoever it was ran."

The deputy's lips made a thin line.

"Yes, I know," she said heavily. "Stupid thing to do, opening the door. But I didn't go outside, and the screen was latched."

He didn't mention that any intruder could have gone through that latched screen like it was tissue paper.

"Miss Lane's had some threats," King commented. "This is Blair, my computer expert. We set up surveillance cameras on the ranch at cross fences to see if we could head off trouble." He smiled. "Looks like we might have succeeded."

"Have you noticed anything suspicious?" the deputy asked.

She grimaced. "Well, I've had a couple of cows found dead. Predators," she said, averting her eyes.

"Anyone prowling around the house, any break-ins?" he persisted.

"No, sir."

The deputy turned to King. "Mr. Brannt, I'd like

to see what those cameras of yours picked up, if any-thing."

"Sure. Come on, Blair." He turned to Maddie. "You should go back inside, honey," he said gently. "Just in case."

"Okay." She went very quickly. She didn't want any of the men to ask her more questions. She was afraid of what Lawson might do if he was backed into a cor-ner. She didn't want the government to come over and shut her cattle operation down, even if it meant giving away the ranch.

LATER, THE DEPUTY came inside, asked more questions and had her write out a report for him in her own words. He took that, and statements from King and Blair and told Maddie to call if she heard anything else.

"Did you find anything?" she asked worriedly.

"No," the deputy said. "But my guess is that some-one meant to disable that surveillance equipment."

"Mine, too," King replied. "Which is why I've just sent several of my cowboys out to ride fence lines and watch for anything suspicious."

"That's very nice of you," she commented.

He shrugged. "We're neighbors and I like your breeding bulls," he told her.

"Well, thanks, just the same."

"If you think of anything else that would help us, please get in touch with me," the deputy said, hand-ing her a card.

"I'll do that," she promised. "And thanks again."

King didn't leave when the deputy did. Sadie was making coffee in the kitchen, her face lined with worry.

"It will be all right," she assured the older woman.

"No, it won't," Sadie muttered. She glanced at Maddie. "You should tell him the truth. He's the one person who could help you!"

"Sadie!" Maddie groaned.

King pulled Blair aside, spoke to him in whispers, and sent him off. He moved into the kitchen, straddled a chair at the table and perched his Stetson on a free chair.

"Okay," he said. "No witnesses. Let's have it."

Maddie went pale.

King laughed softly. "I'm not an ogre. If you want my word that I won't tell anyone what you say, you have it."

Maddie bit her lower lip. "That developer," she said after a minute. "He said that he could bring in a federal agency and prove that my cattle had anthrax."

"Only if he put it there to begin with," King said, his dark eyes flashing with anger.

"That's what I think he means to do," she said. "I don't know what to do. The bills are just burying me..."

He held up a hand. "Cort and Odalie are taking care of those," he said.

"Yes, but they've done too much already, I'm not a charity case!" she burst out.

"It was an accident that they caused, Maddie," he said gently.

"I caused it, by running into the road," she said miserably.

"Accidents are things that don't happen on purpose," he said with a faint grin. "Now, listen, whatever trouble you're in, that developer has no right to make threats to do harm to your cattle."

"It would be my word against his," she sighed.

"I'd take your word against anyone else's, in a heartbeat," he replied. "You let me handle this. I know how to deal with people like Lawson. "

"He's really vindictive."

"He won't get a chance to be vindictive. I promise." He got up. "I won't stay for coffee, Sadie, I've got a lot of phone calls to make."

"Thanks, Mr. Brannt," Maddie said gently. "Thanks a lot."

He put a hand on her shoulder. "We take care of our own," he said. "Cort will be back day after tomorrow."

"So will that developer," she said worriedly. So many complications, she was thinking. Poor Cort, he'd feel even more guilty.

"He won't stay long," King drawled, and he grinned. "Cort will make sure of that, believe me."

CHAPTER TEN

MADDIE WAS ON pins and needles Saturday morning. It was worrying enough to know that Cort and Odalie were coming back. She'd have to smile and pretend to be happy for them, even though her heart was breaking.

But also she was going to have to face the developer. She didn't know what King Brannt had in mind to save her from him. She might have to go through with signing the contracts to ensure that her poor cattle weren't infected. She hadn't slept a wink.

She and Sadie had coffee and then Maddie wandered around the house in her wheelchair, making ruts.

"Will you relax?" Sadie said. "I know it's going to be all right. You have to trust that Mr. Brannt knows what to do."

"I hope so. My poor cattle!"

"Is that a car?"

Even as she spoke a car drove up in front of the house and stopped. "Mr. Lawson, no doubt. I hope he's wearing body armor," she muttered, and she wheeled her chair to the front porch.

But it wasn't the developer. It was Odalie and Cort. They were grinning from ear to ear as they climbed out of his Jaguar and came to the porch.

Just what I need right now, Maddie thought miserably. But she put on a happy face. "You're both home again. And I guess you have news?" she added. "I'm so happy for you."

"For us?" Cort looked at Odalie and back at Maddie blankly. "Why?"

They followed her into the house. She turned the chair around and swallowed. "Well," she began uneasily.

Odalie knew at once what she thought. She came forward. "No, it's not like that," she said quickly. "There was a doll collectors' convention at the hotel where the cattlemen were meeting. I want you to see this." She pulled a check out of her purse and handed it to Maddie.

It was a good thing she was sitting down. The check was for five figures. Five high figures. She looked at Odalie blankly.

"The fairy," she said, smiling. "I'm sorry I wasn't honest with you. It wasn't my great-grandmother's picture. It was a collector's. He wanted a fairy who looked like her to add to his collection, and I said I knew someone who would do the perfect one. So I flew to Denver to take him the one you made from the photograph." Odalie's blue eyes were soft. "He cried. He said the old lady was the light of his life... She was the only person in his family who didn't laugh and disown him when he said he wanted to go into the business of doll collecting. She encouraged him to follow his dream. He's worth millions now and all because he followed his dream." She nodded at the check. "He owns a doll boutique in Los Angeles. He ships all over the world. He said he'd pay that—" she indicated the check again "—for every fairy you made for him. And he wants to discuss licensing and branding. He thinks you can make a fortune with these. He said so."

Maddie couldn't even find words. The check would pay her medical bills, buy feed and pay taxes. It would save the ranch. She was sobbing and she didn't even realize it until Odalie took the check back and motioned to Cort.

Cort lifted her out of the wheelchair and cradled her against him. "You'll blot the ink off the check with those tears, sweetheart." He chuckled, and kissed them away. "And just for the record, Odalie and I aren't getting married."

"You aren't?" she asked with wet eyes.

"We aren't." Odalie giggled. "He's my friend. I love him. But not like that," she added softly.

"And she's my friend," Cort added. He smiled down at Maddie. "I went a little goofy over her, but, then, I got over it."

"Gee, thanks," Odalie said with amused sarcasm.

"You know what I mean." He laughed. "You're beautiful and talented."

"Not as talented as *our* friend over there." She indicated Maddie, with a warm smile. "She has magic in her hands."

"And other places," Cort mused, looking pointedly at her mouth.

She hid her face against him. He cuddled her close.

"Oh, dear," Sadie said from the doorway. "Maddie, he's back! What are you going to tell him?"

"Tell who?" Cort asked. He turned. His face grew hard. "Oh. Him. My dad gave me an earful about him when I got home."

He put Maddie gently back down into the wheelchair.

"You didn't encourage him?" he asked her.

She grimaced. "The medical bills and doctor bills

and feed bills all came in at once," she began miserably. "I couldn't even pay taxes. He offered me a fortune…"

"We're paying the medical bills," Odalie told her firmly. "We even said so."

"It's not right to ask you," Maddie said stubbornly.

"That's okay. You're not asking. We're telling." Odalie said.

"Exactly." Cort was looking more dangerous by the second as the developer got out of his car with a briefcase. "My dad said you've had more cows killed over here, too."

"Yes." She was so miserable she could hardly talk.

"Dad found out a lot more than that about him. He was arrested up in Billings, Montana, on charges of intimidation and poisoning in another land deal," Cort added. "He's out on bond, but apparently it didn't teach him a thing."

"Well, he threatened to plant anthrax in my herd and have the feds come out and destroy them," she said sadly. "He says if I don't sell to him, he'll do it. I think he will."

"He might have," Cort said mysteriously. "Good thing my dad has a real suspicious nature and watches a lot of spy films."

"Excuse me?" Maddie inquired.

He grinned. "Wait and see, honey." He bent and kissed the tip of her nose.

Odalie laughed softly. "One fried developer, coming right up," she teased, and it was obvious that she wasn't jealous of Maddie at all.

THERE WAS A tap at the door and the developer walked right in. He was so intent on his contracts that he must not have noticed the other car in the driveway. "Miss Lane, I've brought the paper...work—" He stopped dead when he saw her companions.

"You can take your paperwork and shove it," Cort said pleasantly. He tilted his Stetson over one eye and put both hands on his narrow hips. "Or you can argue. Personally, I'd love it if you argued."

"She said she wanted to sell," the developer shot back. But he didn't move a step closer.

"She changed her mind," Cort replied.

"You changed it for her," the developer snarled. "Well, she can just change it right back. Things happen sometimes when people don't make the right decisions."

"You mean diseases can be planted in cattle?" Odalie asked sweetly.

The older man gave her a wary look. "What do you mean?"

"Maddie told us how you threatened her," Cort said evenly.

Lawson hesitated. "You can't prove that."

Cort smiled. "I don't have to." He pulled out a DVD in a plastic sleeve and held it up. "You're very trusting, Lawson. I mean, you knew there was surveillance equipment all over the ranch, but you didn't guess the house and porch were wired as well?"

Lawson looked a lot less confident. "You're bluffing."

Cort didn't look like he was bluffing. "My dad has a call in to the district attorney up in Billings, Montana. I believe you're facing indictment there for the destruction of a purebred herd of Herefords because of suspected anthrax?"

"They can't prove that!"

"I'm afraid they can," Cort replied. "There are two witnesses, one of whom used to work with you," he added easily. "He's willing to testify to save his butt." He held up the DVD. "This may not be admissible in court, but it will certainly help to encourage charges against you here for the loss of Miss Lane's purebred stock."

"You wouldn't dare!" the developer said harshly.

"I would dare," Cort replied.

The developer gripped his briefcase tighter. "On second thought," he said, looking around with disdain, "I've decided I don't want this property. It's not good enough for the sort of development I have in mind, and the location is terrible for business. Sorry," he spat at Maddie. "I guess you'll have to manage some other way to pay your medical bills."

"Speaking of medical bills," Cort said angrily, and stepped forward.

"Now, Cort," Maddie exclaimed.

The developer turned and almost ran out of the house to his car. He fumbled to start it and managed to get it in gear just before Cort got to him. He sped out the driveway, fishtailing all the way.

Cort was almost bent over double laughing when he went back into the house. He stopped when three wide-eyed females gaped at him worriedly.

"Oh, I wasn't going to kill him," he said, still laughing. "But I didn't mind letting him think I might. What do you want to bet that he's out of town by tonight and can't be reached by telephone?"

"I wouldn't bet against that," Odalie agreed.

"Me, neither," Sadie said.

"Dad said that Lawson's in more trouble than he can

manage up in Billings already. I don't expect he'll wait around for more charges to be filed here."

"Are you going to turn that DVD over to the district attorney?" she asked, nodding toward the jacketed disc.

He glanced at her. "And give up my best performance of 'Recuerdos de la Alhambra?' he exclaimed. "I'll never get this good a recording again!"

Maddie's eyes brightened. "You were bluffing!"

"For all I was worth." He chuckled.

"Cort, you're wonderful!"

He pursed his lips. "Am I, now?"

"We could take a vote," Odalie suggested. "You've got mine."

"And mine!" Sadie agreed. "Oh, Maddie, you'll have a way to make a living now," she exclaimed, indicating the little fairy. "You won't have to sell our ranch!"

"No, but we still have the problem of running it," Maddie said heavily. "If I'm going to be spending my life sculpting, and thanks to you two, I probably will—" she grinned "—who's going to manage the ranch?"

"I think we can work something out about that," Cort told her, and his dark eyes were flashing with amusement. "We'll talk about it later."

"Okay," she said. "Maybe Ben could manage it?"

Cort nodded. "He's a good man, with a good business head. We'll see."

We'll see? She stared at him as if she'd never seen him before. It was an odd statement. But before she could question it, Sadie went into the kitchen.

"Who wants chocolate pound cake?" she asked.

Three hands went up, and all discussion about the ranch went away.

MADDIE WANTED TO know all about the doll collector. He was a man in his fifties, very distinguished and he had a collection that was famous all over the world.

"There are magazines devoted to collectors," Odalie said excitedly. "They showcased his collection last year. I met him when we were at the Met last year during opera season. We spoke and he said that he loved small, very intricate work. When I saw your sculptures, I remembered him. I looked him up on his website and phoned him. He said he was always looking for new talent, but he wanted to see what you could do. So I asked him for a photo of someone he'd like made into a sculpture and he faxed me the one I gave you."

"I will never be able to repay you for this," Maddie said fervently.

"Maddie, you already have, over and over," Odalie said softly. "Most especially with that little fairy statue that looks just like me." She shook her head. "I've never owned anything so beautiful."

"Thanks."

"Besides, you're my best friend," Odalie said with a gamine grin. "I have to take care of you."

Maddie felt all warm inside. "I'll take care of you, if you ever need me to," she promised.

Odalie flushed. "Thanks."

"This is great cake," Cort murmured. "Can you cook?" he asked Maddie.

"Yes, but not so much right now." She indicated the wheelchair with a grimace.

"Give it time," he said gently. He smiled, and his whole face grew radiant as he looked at her. "You'll be out of that thing before you know it."

"You think so?" she asked.

He nodded. "Yes, I do."

She smiled. He smiled back. Odalie smiled into her cake and pretended not to notice that they couldn't take their eyes off each other.

ODALIE SAID HER goodbyes and gave Maddie the collector's telephone number so that she could thank him personally for giving her fairy a good home. But Cort lingered.

He bent over the wheelchair, his hands on the arms, and looked into Maddie's eyes. "Later we'll talk about going behind my back to do business with a crook."

"I was scared. And not just that he might poison my cattle. There were so many bills!"

He brushed his mouth over her lips. "I told you I'd take care of all those bills."

"But they all came due, and you've done so much… I couldn't ask…"

He was kissing her. It made talking hard.

She reached up with cold, nervous hands and framed his face in them. She looked into his eyes and saw secrets revealed there. Her breath caught. "It isn't Odalie," she stammered. "It's me."

He nodded. And he didn't smile. "It was always you. I just didn't know it until there was a good chance that I was going to lose you." He smiled tightly then. "Couldn't do that. Couldn't live, if you didn't."

She bit her lip, fighting tears.

He kissed them away. "I don't have a life without you," he whispered at her nose. "So we have to make plans."

"When?" she asked, bursting with happiness.

"When you're out of that wheelchair," he said. He gave her a wicked smile. "Because when we start talking, things are apt to get, well, physical." He wiggled his eyebrows.

She laughed.

He laughed.

He kissed her affectionately and stood back up. "I'll drive Odalie home. I'll call you later. And I'll see you tomorrow. And the day after. And the day after. And the day after that…"

"And the day after that?" she prompted.

"Don't get pushy," he teased.

He threw up a hand and went out to the car. This time, when he drove off with Odalie, Maddie didn't go through pangs of jealousy. The look in his eyes had been as sweet as a promise.

EPILOGUE

PHYSICAL THERAPY SEEMED to go on forever. The days turned to weeks, the leaves began to fall. The cows grew big with calves. Rain had come in time for some of the grain crops to come to harvest, and there would be enough hay, hopefully, to get them through the winter.

Maddie's legs were growing stronger. Little by little, she made progress.

Odalie and Cort were still around, prodding her, keeping her spirits up during the long mending process. She didn't let herself get discouraged. She created new fairies and Odalie shipped them off, carefully packed, to a man named Angus Moore, who acted as Maddie's agent and sold her dainty little creations for what amounted to a small fortune for the artist.

The developer, sure enough, left town and left no forwarding address. Gossip was that the authorities wanted to talk to him about several cases of dead cattle on properties he'd tried to buy in several states. Maddie hoped they caught up with him one day.

MEANWHILE, CORT CAME over every night for supper. He brought his guitar most nights, and serenaded Maddie on the porch until the nights got too cold for that. Then he serenaded her in the living room, by the fireplace with its leaping flames while she curled up under a blanket on the sofa.

From time to time, when Sadie was occupied in the kitchen, he curled up under the blanket with her.

She loved his big hands smoothing her bare skin under her shirt, the warmth and strength of them arousing sensations that grew sweeter by the day. He was familiar to her now. She had no fear of his temper. He didn't lose it with her, although he'd been volatile about a man who left a gate open and cattle poured through it onto the highway. At least none of the cattle was injured, and no cars were wrecked.

"He was just a kid," Cort murmured against her collarbone. "He works for us after school. Usually does a pretty good job, too, cleaning out the stables."

She arched her back and winced.

"Damn." He lifted his head and his hands stilled on her body. "Too soon."

She looked miserable.

He laughed. He peered toward the doorway before he slid the hem of her T-shirt up under her chin and looked at the pert little breasts he'd uncovered. "Buried treasure," he whispered, "and I'm a pirate…"

She moaned.

"Stop that. She'll hear you."

She bit her lip and gave him an anguished look. He grinned before he bent his head again, producing even more eloquent sounds that were, thankfully, soon muffled by his mouth.

But things between them were heating up more every day. She had his shirt unbuttoned just before he eased over her. Her hard-tipped breasts nestled into the thick hair on his muscular chest and one long, powerful leg eased between both of hers. He levered himself down very gently while he was kissing her, but she felt the quick, hard swell of him as he began to move helplessly on her, grinding his hips into hers.

"Oh, God," he bit off. He jerked himself back and up, to sit beside her on the sofa with his head bent, shuddering.

"I'm sorry," she whispered shakily.

He drew in short, harsh breaths while his hands worked at buttoning up the shirt. "Well, I'm not," he murmured, glancing down at her. He groaned. "Honey, you have to cover those up or we're going to be back at first base all over again!"

She looked down and flushed a little as she pulled her shirt down and fumbled behind her to do up the bra again. "First base."

He laughed softly. "First base."

She beamed at him. "I'm getting better every day. It won't be long."

"It had better not be," he sighed. "I think I'll die of it pretty soon."

"No!"

"Just kidding." He turned on the sofa and looked down at her with warm, dark, possessive eyes. "I talked to a minister."

"You did? What did he have to say?"

He traced her nose. "We have to have a marriage license first."

Her heart jumped. They'd been kissing and petting for quite a long time, and he'd insinuated, but he'd never actually asked.

"I thought we might get one with flowers and stuff. You know. So it would look nice framed on the wall."

"Framed."

He nodded. His eyes were steady on her face. "Madeline Edith Lane, will you do me the honor of becoming my wife?" he asked softly.

She fought tears. "Yes," she whispered. "Yes!"

He brushed the tears away, his eyes so dark they seemed black. "I'll love you all my life," he whispered. "I'll love you until the sun burns out."

"I'll love you longer," she whispered back, and it was all there, in her eyes and his.

He smiled slowly. "And we'll have beautiful kids," he said softly. He pushed back her hair. "Absolutely beautiful. Like you."

Now she was really bawling.

He pulled her gently into his arms and across his lap, and rocked her and kissed away the tears.

Sadie came walking in with coffee and stopped dead. "Oh, goodness, what's wrong?"

"I told her we were going to have beautiful kids," he said with a chuckle. "She's very emotional."

"Beautiful kids? You're going to get married?" Sadie exclaimed.

"Yes." Maddie smiled.

"Whoopee!"

"Oh, dear!" Maddie exclaimed.

Sadie looked down at the remains of the glass coffeepot and two ceramic mugs. "Oh, dear," she echoed.

Cort just laughed. But then, like the gentleman he was, he went to help Sadie clean up the mess.

THEY WERE MARRIED at Christmas. Maddie was able to wear an exquisite designer gown that Odalie had insisted on buying for her, as her "something new." It was an A-line gown of white satin with cap sleeves and a lacy bodice that went up to encase her throat like a high-necked Victorian dress.

There was a train, also of delicate white lace, and a fingertip veil with lace and appliquéd roses. She wore lace gloves and carried a bouquet of white roses. There was a single red rose in the center of the bouquet. One red rose for true love, Cort had insisted, and white ones for purity because in a modern age of easy virtue, Maddie was a throwback to Victorian times. She went to her marriage a virgin, and never apologized once for not following the crowd.

She walked down the aisle on the arm of Cole Everett, who had volunteered to give her away. Odalie was her maid of honor. Heather Everett and Shelby Brannt were her matrons of honor. Four local girls she'd known all her life were bridesmaids, and John Everett was Cort's best man.

At an altar with pots of white and red roses they were married in the local Methodist church, where all three families were members. The minister had preached the funeral of most of their deceased kin. He was elderly and kind, and beloved of the community.

When he pronounced Cort and Maddie man and wife, Cort lifted the veil, ignoring the flash from the professional photographer's camera, and closed in to kiss his new bride.

Nobody heard him when he bent, very low, and whispered, "First base."

Nobody heard the soft, mischievous laughter the comment provoked from the bride. There was a huge reception. John Everett stopped by the table where Cort and Maddie were cutting the wedding cake.

"So, tell me, Cort," John said when the photographer finished shooting the cake-eating segment, "if I'm really the best man, why are you married to my girl?"

"Now, a remark like that could get you punched," Cort teased, catching the other man around the neck, "even at a wedding."

John chuckled, embracing him in a bear hug. "I was just kidding. No doubt in my mind from the beginning where her heart was." He indicated a beaming Maddie.

Cort glanced at her and smiled. "What an idiot I was," he said, shaking his head. "I almost lost her."

"Crazy, the way things turn out," John mused, his eyes on Odalie as she paused to speak to Maddie. "My sister, Attila the Hun, is ending up as Maddie's best friend. Go figure."

"I wouldn't have believed it myself. Odalie's quite a girl."

John smiled. "I thought it would be you and Odalie, eventually."

Cort shook his head. "We're too different. Neither of us would fit in the other's world. It took me a long time to realize that. But I saw my future in Maddie's eyes. I always will. I hope Odalie finds someone who can make her half as happy as I am today. She deserves it."

John nodded. "I'm very proud of her. She's matured a lot in the past few months." He turned back to Cort. "Christmas is next week. You guys coming home for it or not?"

"Oh, we have to…my folks would kill us, to say nothing of Sadie." He indicated the older woman in her pretty blue dress talking to some other people. "Maddie's like the daughter she never had. They can't have Christmas without us," he stated. "We're just going down to Panama City for a couple of days. Maybe later I can take Maddie to Europe and show her the sights. Right now, even a short plane trip is going to make her uncomfortable, much less a long one to some-where exotic."

"I don't think Maddie will mind where you go, as long as she's with you," John said. "I wish you all the best. You know that."

"Thanks, bro."

"And when you come home, maybe we can crack open some new video games, now that my sister won't complain about my having you over," he added with a sigh.

Cort just grinned.

THE HOTEL WAS right on the beach. It was cold in Pan-ama City, but not so cold that they couldn't sit on the patio beyond the glass sliding doors and look at the cold moonlight on the ocean.

Predictably, they'd barely made it into the hotel room when all the months of pent-up anguished de-sire were taken off the bridle for the first time.

He tried to be gentle, he really did, but his body was shivering with need long before he could do what he wanted to do: to show his love for Maddie.

Not that she noticed. She was with him every step of the way, even when the first encounter stung and made her cry out.

"This is part of it," he gritted, trying to slow down. "I'm so sorry!"

"Don't…sweat it," she panted, moving up to meet the furious downward motion of his hips. "You can hang out…the bedsheet in the morning…to prove I was a virgin…!"

"Wha-a-at?" he yelped, and burst out laughing even as his body shuddered with the beginning of ecstasy.

"First…base," she choked out, and bit him.

It was the most glorious high he'd ever experienced. He groaned and groaned as his body shuddered over hers. The pleasure was exquisite. He felt it in every cell of his body, with every beat of his heart. He could hear his own heartbeat, the passion was so violent.

Under him, her soft body was rising and falling like a pistol as she kept pace with his need, encouraged it, fanned the flames and, finally, glued itself to his in an absolute epiphany of satisfaction that convulsed both of them as they almost passed out from the climax.

She clung to him, shivering with pleasure in the aftermath. Neither of them could stop moving, savoring the dregs of passion until they drained the cup dry.

"Wow," she whispered as she looked into his eyes.

"Wow," he whispered back. He looked down their bodies to where they were joined. They hadn't even thought of turning out the lights. He was glad. Looking at her, like this, was a joy he hadn't expected.

"Beautiful," he breathed.

She smiled slowly. "And to think I was nervous about the first time," she said.

"Obviously unnecessary, since I have skills far beyond those of most mortal men...*oof!*"

She'd hit him. She grinned, though. And then she wiggled her eyebrows and moved her hips ever so slowly. Despite the sting, and the discomfort, pleasure welled up like water above a dam in a flood.

"Oh, yes," she whispered as he began to move, looking straight into her eyes. "Yes. Do that."

He smiled. "This," he murmured, "is going to be indescribable."

And it was.

WHEN THEY GOT back, in time for the Christmas celebrations at Skylance, nobody could understand why, when Cort whispered, "first base," Maddie almost fell down laughing. But that was one secret neither one of them ever shared with another living soul.

* * * * *

Heart of Stone

CHAPTER ONE

KEELY WELSH FELT his presence before she looked up and saw him. It had been that way from the day she met Boone Sinclair, her best friend's eldest brother. The man wasn't movie-star handsome or gregarious. He was a recluse, a loner who hardly ever smiled, who intimidated people simply by walking into a room. For some unknown reason, Keely always knew when he was around, even if she didn't see him.

He was tall and slender, but he had powerful legs and big hands and feet. There were rumors about him that grew more exaggerated with the telling. He'd been in Special Forces overseas five years earlier. He'd saved his unit from certain destruction. He'd won medals. He'd had lunch with the president at the White House. He'd taken a cruise with a world-famous author. He'd almost married a European princess. And on and on and on.

Nobody knew the truth. Well, maybe Winona and Clark Sinclair did. Winnie and Clark and Boone were closer than brothers and sisters usually were. But Winnie didn't talk about her brother's private life, not even to Keely.

There hadn't been a day since she was thirteen when Keely hadn't loved Boone Sinclair. She watched him from a distance, her green eyes soft and covetous. Her hands would shake when she happened on him unexpectedly. They were shaking now. He was standing at the counter, signing in. He had an appointment for his dog's routine shots. He made one every year. He loved the old tan-and-black German shepherd, whose name was Bailey. People said it was the only thing on earth that he did love. Maybe he was fond of his siblings, but it didn't show. His affection for Bailey did.

One of the other vet techs came out with a pad and called in Bailey, with a grin at Boone. It wasn't returned. He led the old dog into one of the examination rooms. He walked right past Keely. He never looked at her. He didn't speak to her. As far as he was concerned, she was invisible.

She sighed as the door closed behind him and his dog. It was that way anyplace in town that he saw her. In fact, it was like that at his huge ranch near Comanche Wells, west of Jacobsville, Texas. He never told Winnie that she couldn't have Keely over for lunch or an occasional horseback ride. But he ignored her, just the same.

"It's funny, you know," Winnie had remarked one day when they were out riding. "I mean, Boone never makes any comment about you, but he does make a point of pretending he doesn't see you. I wonder why." She looked at Keely then, with her dark eyes mischievous in their frame of blond hair. "You wouldn't know, I guess?"

Keely only smiled. "I haven't got a clue," she said. It was the truth.

"It's only you, too," her friend continued thoughtfully. "He's very polite to our brother Clark's occasional date—even to that waitress that Clark brought home one night for dinner, and you know what a snob Boone can be. But he pretends you don't exist."

"I may remind him of somebody he doesn't like," Keely replied.

"There was that girl he was engaged to," Winnie said out of the blue.

Keely's heart jumped. "Yes, I remember when he was engaged," she replied. It had been when she was fourteen, almost fifteen years old, just before he came back from overseas. Keely's young heart had been broken.

"It was just before you came back here to live with your mom," Winnie continued as if she'd read Keely's mind. "In fact, it was just about the time she started drinking so much more…" She hesitated. Keely's mother was an alcoholic and it was a sensitive subject to her friend. "Anyway, Boone was mustering out of the Army at the time. His fiancée rushed to Germany where he'd been taken when he was airlifted out of combat, wounded, and then…poof. She was gone, Boone came home, and he never mentioned her name again. None of us could find out what happened."

"Somebody said she was European royalty," Keely ventured shyly.

"She was distantly related to some man who was knighted in England," came the sarcastic reply. "Anyway, she ran out on Boone and he was bitter for a long time. So three weeks ago the phone rings and he gets a call from her. She's been living with her father, who owns a private detective agency in San Antonio. She told Boone she'd made a terrible mistake and wanted to make up."

Keely's heart fell. A rival who had a history with Boone. It made her miserable just to think about it, despite the fact that she would never get close enough to Boone to give the other woman any competition.

"Boone doesn't forgive people," she said, thinking aloud.

"That's right," Winnie replied, smiling. "But he's mellowed a bit. He takes her out on dates occasionally now. In fact, they're going to a Desperado concert next week."

Keely frowned. "He likes hard rock?" she asked, surprised. He looked so staid and dignified that she couldn't picture him at a rock concert. She said so.

Winnie laughed. "I can," she said. "He's not the conservative, quiet man he seems to be. Especially when he loses his temper or gets in an argument."

"Boone doesn't argue," Keely mused aloud.

He didn't. If he was angry enough, he punched. Never women, of course, but his men knew not to push him, especially if he was broody. One horse handler had found out the hard way that nobody made jokes at the boss's expense. Boone had been kicked by a horse, which the handler thought was hilarious. Boone roped the man, tied him to a post and anointed him with a bucket of recycled hay. All without saying a word.

Keely laughed out loud.

"What?" Winnie asked.

"I was remembering that horse wrangler...."

Winnie laughed, too. "He couldn't believe it, he said, even when it was happening. Boone really does look so straitlaced, as if he'd never stoop to dirty his hands. His cowboys used to underestimate him. Not anymore."

"The rattlesnake episode is noteworthy, as well," came the amused reply.

"That cook was so shocked!" Winnie blurted out. "He was a really rotten cook, but he threatened to sue Boone if he fired him, so it looked as if we were stuck with him. He'd threatened to cook Boone a rattler if he made any more remarks about the food. He added a few spicy comments about why Boone's fiancée took a powder. Then one morning he looks in his Dutch oven to see if it's clean enough to cook in, and a rattlesnake jumps up right into his face!"

"Lucky for the cook it didn't have any fangs."

"The cook didn't know that!" Winnie laughed. "He didn't know who did it, either. He resigned on the spot. The men actually cheered as he drove off. The next cook was talented, and the soul of politeness to my brother."

"I am not surprised."

She shook her head. "Boone does have these little quirks," his sister murmured. "Like never turning on the heat in his bedroom, even in icy weather, and always going around with his shirts buttoned to the neck."

"I've never seen him with his shirt off," Keely remarked. It was unusual, because most of the cowboys worked topless in summer heat when they were branding or doctoring cattle. But Boone never did.

"He used to be less prudish," Winnie said.

"Boone, prudish?" Keely sounded shocked.

Winnie glanced at her and chuckled. "Well, I guess that really doesn't fit at all."

"No, it doesn't."

Winnie pursed her lips. "Come to think of it, he's not the only prude around here. I've never even seen you in a T-shirt, Keely. You always wear long sleeves and high necklines."

Keely had a good reason for that, one she'd never shared with anyone. It was the reason she didn't date.

It was a terrible secret. She would have died rather than
tell Winnie, who might tell Boone....

"I was raised very strictly," Keely said quietly. And
she had been; for all their odd tendencies, both her parents had insisted that Keely go to Sunday School and
church every single Sunday. "My father didn't approve
of clothing that was too flashy or revealing."

Probably because Keely's mother propositioned
any man she fancied when she drank. She'd even tried
to seduce Boone. Keely didn't know that, and Winnie didn't know how to tell her. It was one reason for
Boone's antagonism toward Keely.

Things would have been better if Keely knew where
her father was. She'd told people she thought he was
dead, because it was easier than admitting that he was
an alcoholic, just like her mother, and linked up with
a bunch of dangerous men. She'd missed her father
at first. But she'd have been in more danger if she'd
stayed with him.

She still loved him, in her way, despite what had
happened to her.

"Come to think of it, Keely, you don't even date."

Keely shrugged. "I'm a vet tech. I have a busy life.
I work on call, you know. If there's an emergency at
midnight on a weekend, I still go to the office."

"That's a lot of hogwash," Winnie said gently as
they paused to let the horses drink from one of the
crystal-clear streams on the wooded property where
they were riding. "I've even tried to set you up with
nice men I know from work. You freeze when a man
comes near you."

"That's because you work with the police, Winnie,
and you bring cops home as prospective dates for me,"
Keely said mischievously. It was true. Winnie worked

as a clerk in the Jacobsville Police Department's office during the day, and now she was doing a stint two nights a week as a dispatcher for the 911 center. In fact, she was hoping that job would work into something permanent, because being around Officer Kilraven all day when he was on the day shift was killing her.

"Policemen make me nervous," Keely was saying. "For all you know, I might have a criminal past."

Winnie wasn't smiling. She shook her head. "You're hiding something."

"Nothing major. Honest." What she suspected about her father, if true, would have shamed her. If Boone ever found out, she'd really die of shame. But she hadn't heard from her father since she was thirteen, so it wasn't likely that he'd just turn up someday with his new outlaw friends. She prayed that he wouldn't. Her mother's behavior was hard enough to live down as it was.

"There's this really handsome policeman who's been working with us for a few weeks. He's just your type."

"Kilraven," Keely guessed.

"Yes! How did you know?"

"Because you talk about him all the time," Keely returned. She pursed her lips. "Are you sure you aren't interested in him? I mean, you're single and eligible yourself."

Winnie flushed. "He's not my type."

"Why not?"

Winnie shifted in the saddle uneasily. "He told me he wasn't my type. He said I was too young to be mooning over a used-up lobo wolf like him and not to do it anymore."

Keely gasped out loud. "He didn't!"

The older girl nodded sadly. "He did. I didn't realize that I was so obvious with it. I mean, he's drop-dead gorgeous, most women look at him. He just noticed more when I did it. Because I'm who I am, I guess," she added darkly. "Boone might have said something to him. He's very protective of me. He thinks I'm too naive to be let loose on the world."

"In his defense, you have led a sheltered life," Keely said gently. "Kilraven is street smart. And he's dangerous."

"I know," Winnie muttered. "There have been times that he's been in situations where I sweat blood until he walks back into the station. He's noticed that, too. He didn't like it and he said so." She took a long, sad breath and looked at Keely. "So you can know all about my private agony, but you won't share yours? It's no use, Keely. I know."

Keely laughed nervously. "Know what? I don't keep secrets."

"Your whole life is a secret. But your biggest one is that you're in love with my brother."

Keely looked as if she'd been slapped.

"I would never tell him," Winnie said quietly. "That's the truth. I'm sorry for the way he treats you. I know how much it hurts."

Keely shifted her eyes, embarrassed.

"Don't be like that," Winnie said, her voice gentle. "I won't tell. Ever. Honest."

Keely relaxed. She drew in a breath, watching the creek bubble over rocks. "It doesn't hurt anything, what I feel. He'll never know. And it helps me to understand what it might be like to love a man—even if that love is never returned. It's a taste of something I can never have, that's all."

Winnie frowned. "What do you mean? Of course you'll be loved one day! Keely, you're only nineteen. Your whole life is ahead of you!"

Keely looked at her friend, and her dark eyes were soft and sad. "Not that way, it isn't. I won't ever marry."

"But one day…"

She shook her head. "No."

Winnie bit her lower lip. "When you're a little older, it might be different," she began. "Keely, you're nineteen. Boone is thirty. That's a big age difference, and he thinks about things like that. His fiancée was only a year younger than he was. He said that people should never marry unless they're the same age."

"Why?"

Winnie sighed. "I've never talked about it much, but our mother was twelve years younger than Dad. He died a broken man because she ran away with his younger brother. He always said he made a major mistake by marrying someone from another generation. It was just too many years between them. They had nothing in common."

Keely felt heartsick for the family. "Is your mother still alive?"

She bit her lip. "We…don't know," she said. "We've never tried to find her or our uncle. They married, after the divorce, and moved to Montana. Neither one of them ever tried to contact us again."

"That's so sad."

"It made Boone bitter. Well, that and then his fiancée cutting out on him. He doesn't have a high opinion of women."

"You can't blame him, really," Keely had to admit. She patted her horse's neck. "It's sad, isn't it, that we're both too young for the men we care about?"

"Only in their minds," Winnie returned. "But we can always change their opinions. We just have to find an angle. One that works."

Keely laughed. "Doesn't that sound easy?"

Winnie grimaced. "Not really." She tugged on the reins, backing her horse out of the creek. Keely followed suit. "Let's talk about something more cheerful," Winnie said on the way back to the ranch. "Are you coming to the big charity dance?"

Keely shook her head. "I'd like to, even without a date, but both my junior bosses are going, and so is our senior tech. I have to be on call."

"That's awful!"

"It's fair, though. I was off last year."

"I remember. Last year you stayed home."

Keely studied the pommel as the leather squeaked under the steady motion of the horse's body. "Nobody asked me to go with them."

"You don't encourage men," Winnie pointed out.

Keely smiled sadly. "What for?" she asked. "Any man who asked me would have been second best. I don't want to get involved with anyone."

Winnie had always been curious about Keely's odd private life. She wondered what had happened to the other woman to leave her so alone. "It's just a dance," she pointed out. "You don't have to agree to marry the man when he takes you home."

Keely burst out laughing. "You're terrible!" she choked.

"Just pointing out an obvious fact," came the amused reply.

"Anyway, I'll be working. You go and have enough fun for both of us."

"Any man who took me would be second choice,

too," she reminded her friend. "The difference is, I want to go so I can rub my date in Kilraven's face."

"He won't go," Keely murmured.

"What makes you think so?"

"Just a guess. He keeps to himself. He reminds me of Cash Grier, the way he was before he married Tippy Moore. Grier was a bona fide woman hater. I think Kilraven is, too."

Winnie hesitated. "I wonder."

Keely didn't follow up on the remark. She felt sorry for Winnie. She felt sorry for herself, too. Men were such a headache....

She came back to the present in time to see Boone coming out of the examination room with Bailey on a leash. He walked right past Keely without looking at her or saying a word to her. She stared after him with her heart breaking right inside her chest. Then she turned and went back to work, putting on a happy face for the benefit of her coworkers.

KEELY HATED BOONE'S ex-fiancée on sight. Misty Harris's father ran a private detective agency in San Antonio, and she was wealthy. She was pretty, she was very intelligent and she looked down on other women. Boone, Winnie had told Keely, liked a woman with a good mind and an independent spirit. She also thought that the woman probably was good in bed, which made Keely uncomfortable.

The woman had a poisonous tongue, and she didn't like Keely. It was obvious when she arrived for a date with Boone the next Friday night and found Keely sitting in the living room with Winnie.

"No dates?" she chided the other women, looking sleek in a black cocktail dress with her long black hair flowing over her shoulders. Her deep blue eyes were twinkling with malicious amusement. "Too bad. Boone's taking me to the Desperado concert. He's going to introduce me to the lead singer. We've had tickets for two months. It's going to be a great evening!"

"I love Desperado," Winnie had to agree.

"I wouldn't miss this concert for anything," the brunette purred.

There was a noise at the side door, scratching and howling.

"Oh, it's that dog," the brunette muttered. "He's filthy. For God's sake, Winnie, you aren't going to let him in? The Persian rugs are priceless! He'll get mud all over them!"

"Bailey is a member of the family," Winnie said icily as she opened the door and pulled a towel from a shelf nearby. "Hello, old fellow!" she greeted the old German shepherd. "Did you get wet?"

She started toweling him dry and wiping his paws. He was panting and whining. His tongue was purple. He shuddered. His stomach was swollen.

With a practiced eye, Keely observed him. Something was wrong. She got up and joined Winnie at the sliding glass door, going down on one knee. Her hands touched the dog's distended belly.

She clenched her teeth. "He's got bloat," she told Winnie.

"What was that?" Boone asked, taking the steps two at a time.

Keely looked up at him, trying not to betray her pleasure at just the sight of him. "Bailey's got bloat. He needs to be seen by a vet right now."

"Don't be absurd," Boone shot back. "Dogs don't get bloat."

"Big dogs do," Keely said urgently. "You must have seen the condition in cattle at one time or another. Here. Feel!"

She grabbed his hand and carried it to the dog's belly.

He felt it and scowled.

"Look at the color of his tongue," Keely persisted. "He isn't getting enough oxygen. If you don't get him to the vet soon, he'll be dead."

"Oh, that's ridiculous," the brunette spat. "He's just eaten too much. Put him in his kennel. He'll be fine by morning."

"He'll be dead," Keely repeated flatly.

"Listen, you, I'm not missing that concert for a stupid old dog with an upset stomach!" the brunette raged. "You're just trying to get Boone to notice you by telling him something's wrong with that dog! He knows what a crush you have on him. This is a pathetic act!"

Boone looked at Keely, who was pale and sick at heart to have her innermost secret spoken aloud for Boone to hear.

He ran his hand over Bailey's stomach one last time. "It's not bloat," he pronounced. "He's just had too much to eat and he's got gas." He got to his feet, patting the old dog on the head, smiling. "You'll be fine, won't you, old man?"

Keely glared at him. The dog was still panting and now he was whimpering loudly.

"He's not your dog," Boone shot at her. "Misty's right. This is a bid for attention, just like old Bailey whining so that I'll pet him. But it won't work. I'm taking Misty to the concert."

Keely was so infuriated that she wouldn't even look at him. Bailey was dying.

"Let's go," Boone told Misty.

He didn't speak to Keely again, or to Winnie. He and his date walked back to the garage. Minutes later, his car roared out down the driveway.

"What are we going to do?" Winnie asked, because she believed her best friend.

"We can let him die or take him to the vet," Keely said curtly.

"Who's driving?" was all the other woman asked.

THE OLDEST OF the three vets, Bentley Rydel, and the owner of the clinic, was on call. He was the best surgeon of the group. At thirty-two, he was the only unmarried one. People said it was because he was so antagonistic that no woman could get near him. It was probably the truth.

He helped Keely get Bailey into the X-ray room and onto the table. She held him while the X-rays were taken, petting him and talking soothingly to him. For a man who resembled nothing more than a human pit viper with other members of his own species, he was the soul of compassion with animals.

He and Winnie were back in ten minutes with the X-rays. He looked somber as he showed them the proof that Bailey's stomach had turned over. "It's a complicated and expensive procedure, and I can't promise you that it will succeed. If I don't operate, the necrosis will spread and he'll die. He may die anyway. You have to make a decision."

"He's my brother's dog," Winnie said uneasily, petting the whimpering old animal.

"Your brother will have to give consent."

"He won't," Keely said miserably. "He doesn't think it's bloat."

Bentley's eyebrows arched. "And what veterinary school did he graduate from?"

Winnie's phone playing the theme from *Star Wars* interrupted the conversation. She answered it nervously. She'd recognized Boone's number on the caller ID screen.

"It's Boone!" she whispered with her hand over the phone. She grimaced. "Hello?" she said hesitantly.

"Where the hell is my dog?" he demanded.

Winnie took a deep breath. "Boone, we brought Bailey here to the vet…"

"*We?* Keely's mixed up in this, isn't she?" he demanded, outraged.

The vet, seeing Winnie's pained expression, held out his hand for the phone. Winnie gave it to him gladly.

"This animal," the vet began firmly, "has a severe case of bloat. I can show you on the X-rays where necrosis of tissue has already begun. If I don't operate, he will be dead in an hour. The decision is yours, but I urge you to make it quickly."

Boone hesitated. "Will he live?"

"I can't promise you that," Bentley said curtly. "He should have been brought in when the symptoms first presented. The delay has complicated the procedure. This conversation," he added acidly, "is another delay."

The curse was audible two feet from the cell phone. "Do it," Boone said. "I'll give you permission. My sister can be your witness. Do what you can. Please."

"Certainly I will." He handed the phone to Winnie. "Keely, we need to prep him for surgery."

"Yes, sir." Keely was smiling. Her boss was a great

negotiator. Now, at least Bailey had a chance, no thanks to the heartless woman who'd have sacrificed his life for a concert ticket.

THE OPERATION TOOK two hours. Keely stood gowned beside the vet, administering anesthetic to the dog and checking his vital signs constantly. There was only a small amount of dead tissue, luckily, and she watched Bentley's skillful hands cut it away efficiently.

"What was the delay?" he asked her.

She clenched her teeth. "Concert tickets for Desperado. Boone's date didn't want to miss it."

"So she decided that Bailey should die."

She grimaced. "I'm not sure she was being deliberately coldhearted."

"You'd be surprised at how many people consider animals inanimate objects with no feelings. Old-timers come in sometimes and tell me in all seriousness that no animal feels pain."

"Baloney," she muttered.

He laughed shortly. "My opinion exactly."

"How's he doing?" she asked.

He nodded as he worked. "All right. There are no complications to worry about. I operated on Tom Walker's Shiloh shepherd for this about two months ago, remember, and he had a tumor the size of my fist. We lost him despite the timely intervention."

"We aren't going to lose Bailey?" she asked worriedly.

"Not a chance. He's old, but he's a fighter."

She smiled. Even if Boone gave her hell, it would be worth it. She was fond of the old dog, too, even if Boone felt she was using his pet. It made her furious that Boone believed that heartless brunette. Keely wasn't stupid enough to think that such a play would work on a man with a head like a steel block. Boone wouldn't care if she was Helen of Troy, he'd walk right by her without looking. She knew better than to try to chase him. She was amazed that he didn't realize that.

"Done," Bentley announced finally when the last suture was in place. Keely took away the anesthetic and waited while the vet examined the old dog. "I think he'll do, but don't quote me. We'll know in the morning."

"Yes, sir."

"I'll carry him in for you," he volunteered, because the dog was very heavy and Keely had problems carrying weight.

"You don't have to," she began self-consciously.

His pale blue eyes were kind as they met hers. "You've had some sort of injury to your left shoulder. I don't have to see it to know it's there. It won't let you bear weight."

She grimaced. "I didn't realize it was so obvious."

"I won't give you away," he said with a smile. "But I won't make you carry loads too heavy, either."

"Thanks, boss," she said, smiling back.

He shrugged. "You're the hardest worker I've got." He seemed self-conscious after he said that, and he made a big production of lifting Bailey, very carefully, to one of the recovery cages where he'd be kept and monitored until he came out from under the anesthetic.

"I can stay and watch him," she began.

He shook his head. "I had a call on my cell phone while we were prepping Bailey," he reminded her. "There's a heifer calving over at Cy Parks's place. She's having a hard time. It's one of his purebred herd and he wants me there to make sure the calf is born alive."

"So you have to go out there."

He nodded. "I'll check on Bailey when I get back. It's Friday night," he added with a faint smile. "Usually we get emergency cases all night, you know."

"Want me to stay and answer the phone?" she asked.

He studied her quizzically. "It's Friday night," he repeated. "Why don't you have a date?"

She shrugged. "Men hate me. If you don't believe that, just ask Boone Sinclair."

He looked over her shoulder and his eyebrows lifted as a door opened. "Speak of the devil," he said in a voice that didn't carry over Winnie's greeting to her brother.

CHAPTER TWO

BOONE STALKED INTO the room where Keely and Bentley were standing together beside the recovery cage, which contained Bailey. He didn't look very belligerent now, and his concern for the old dog was evident as he knelt beside the cage and touched the head of the sleeping animal gently with his fingertips.

"Will he live?" he asked without looking up.

"We'll know that in the morning," Bentley said curtly. "He came through the surgery very well, and I didn't find anything that would complicate his recovery. For an animal his age, he's in excellent shape."

Boone stood up, facing the vet. "Thank you."

"Thank Keely," came the short reply. "She ignored your suggestion to leave the animal alone until morning. At which time," the vet added with a glitter in his eyes, "you'd have found him dead."

Boone's own eyes flashed. "I thought he was trying to get attention. Like Keely," he added with icy sarcasm.

Bentley's eyebrows lifted. "Do you really think Keely needs to beg any man for attention?" he asked, as if the remark was incredible to him.

Boone stiffened. "Her social life is not my concern. I'm grateful to you for saving Bailey."

"We'll know how successful I was in the morning,"

Bentley replied. "Keely, can you get my medical bag for me, please?"

"Yes, sir." She left the room, glad for something that would take her out of Boone's immediate presence.

Boone glanced again at the cage. "He and I have been through some hard times together," he told the vet. "If I'd realized how dangerous his condition was, I'd never have left him." He looked at Bentley. "I didn't know that dogs got bloat."

"Now you do," the vet replied. "Most large dogs are at risk for it."

"What causes it?"

Bentley shook his head. "We don't know. There are half a dozen theories, but no definite answers."

"What did you do?"

"I excised the dead tissue and tacked his stomach to his backbone," Bentley replied quietly. "I'll prescribe a special diet for him. For the next couple of days, of course, he'll get fluids."

"You'll let me know?" Boone added slowly.

Bentley recognized the worry in those dark eyes. "Of course."

Boone turned to Winnie. His eyes were accusing.

She grimaced. "Now, listen, Keely knows what she's doing, whatever you think," she began defensively. "I agreed with her and I'll take full responsibility for bringing Bailey over here."

"I'm not complaining," he said. His stern expression lightened. He bent and brushed an affectionate kiss onto Winnie's forehead. "Thanks."

She smiled, relieved that he wasn't angry. "I love old Bailey, too."

Keely came back with the medical bag and handed it to Bentley. She was holding his old raincoat, as well.

"I hate raincoats," he began angrily.

She just held it up. He grimaced, but he slid his long arms into it and pulled it up. "Worrywart," he muttered.

"You got pneumonia the last time you went out into a cold rain," she reminded him.

He turned and smiled down at her; actually, it was more of a faint turning up of one side of his mouth. Bentley Rydel never smiled. "Go home," he said.

She shook her head. "I won't leave Bailey until I'm sure he's out from under the anesthesia," she said, and she didn't look at Boone. "Besides, you're sure to have at least one emergency call waiting for you when you get back."

"I don't pay you enough for all this overtime," he pointed out.

She shrugged. "So I'll never get rich." She grinned.

He sighed. "Okay. I'm on my cell phone, if you need me."

"Drive carefully."

He made a face at her. But his expression was staid and impassive as he nodded to the Sinclairs on his way out.

Boone was glaring at Keely. She averted her eyes and went back to Bailey's cage to check on him.

"We should go," Winnie told her brother. "See you later, Keely."

Keely nodded. She didn't look at them.

Boone hesitated uncharacteristically, but he didn't speak. He took Winnie's arm and led her out the door.

"You couldn't even say thanks to Keely for saving Bailey's life?" she chided as they paused beside their respective vehicles.

He looked down at her coldly in the misty rain. "I

could sue her for bringing Bailey here without permission."

Winnie was shocked. "She saved his life!"

He avoided her gaze. "That's beside the point. Let's go. We're getting wet."

"What about your concert?" Winnie asked, and there was a faint bite in her tone.

"It's not over. I'm going back."

She wanted to say that his ex-fiancée wasn't going to be pleased that he'd deserted her, even for a few minutes. But she didn't say it. He was obviously out of humor, and it was never wise to push him.

KEELY STAYED WITH Bailey until he came to and Bentley returned from his call. There was a new emergency, a woman whose champion English springer spaniel was whelping and one of the puppies wouldn't emerge. Once again, they had to do an emergency surgery to save mother and child.

It was two in the morning before they finished and Keely cleaned up. "Now go home," Bentley said gently.

"I'll have to." She laughed. "I can't keep my eyes open."

"No matter what Boone Sinclair says," he told her, "you did the right thing." He glanced at Bailey, who was now sleeping peacefully thanks to a painkiller. "I think he'll do."

She smiled. Even though Boone had been a pain in the neck, he did love the old dog. She was glad that he wouldn't have to give up his companion just yet.

She went home, tiptoeing past her mother's room, and went to bed.

THE NEXT DAY, she worked until noon and then went home to do all the housework that her mother never bothered with. She finished just in time to start supper. By then, her mother was finishing the second whiskey highball and her best friend, Carly, had shown up for supper. Keely, who'd prepared enough just for her mother and herself, had to add potatoes and carrots to her stew to stretch it out. The grocery budget was meager. It took second place to the liquor budget.

It was the same every Saturday night that she was home, Keely thought miserably, hiding her discomfort while she served up a light supper in the dining room. Her mother, Ella, already drunk, was making fun of Keely's conservative clothing while her best friend, Carly, added her own sarcastic comments to the mix. Both women were in their forties, and highly unconventional. Carly was no beauty, but Ella was. Ella had a lovely face and a good figure, and she used both to good advantage. A list of her past lovers, despite her substance abuse problem, would fill a small notebook. The mischief she caused was one of her favorite sources of amusement. Next to ridiculing Keely, that was. She and Carly considered virtue obsolete. No man, they emphasized, wanted an innocent woman these days. Virginity was a liability to a single woman.

"All you need is a man, Keely." Carly Blair giggled, hoisting a potent Turkish cigarette to her too-red lips. "A few nights in the sack with an experienced man would take that prudish pout out of your lips."

"You need to wear makeup," her mother added, in between sips of her third whiskey highball. "And buy some clothes that don't look like they came out of a mission thrift shop."

Keely would have reminded them that she worked with animals in a veterinary clinic, not in an exclusive boutique, and that men were thin on the ground. But it only amused them more if she fought back. She'd learned to keep her head down when she was under fire.

The beef stew she'd had cooking all day in her Crock-Pot was fragrant and thick. She'd made yeast rolls to go with it, and a simple pound cake for dessert. Her efforts were unappreciated. The women hardly noticed what they were eating as they gossiped about a woman they knew in town who was having an affair. Their comments were earthy and embarrassing to Keely.

They knew that, of course; it was why they did it. What the two women didn't know was that Keely couldn't sustain a relationship with a boyfriend, much less a lover. She had a secret that she'd never shared with anyone except the doctor who had treated her. It would keep her alone for the rest of her life. She'd made sure that her mother didn't know what she was hiding. The older woman was bitter and miserable and she loved making a victim of her daughter. Keely's secret would have been more fodder for her attacks. So Keely kept a good distance between herself and her coldhearted parent.

She wondered often what had become of her father. She'd loved him very much, and she'd thought that he loved her. But he hadn't been the same since he'd lost his game park. He'd turned to alcohol and then drugs to numb the pain and disappointment. He'd had no way to support himself, much less an adolescent daughter. He'd had to leave her with her mother. She'd done her best to make him let her stay, offering to get a job after school, anything! But he'd said that she needed security while she was growing up, and he could no longer provide it. Her mother wasn't such a bad person, he'd said. Keely knew better, but she couldn't change her father's mind, so she rationalized that he'd probably forgotten what a cruel woman Ella could be. Besides that, she was terrified of his new friends; especially one of them, who'd slapped her around.

Ella owned land that she'd inherited, along with a sizable amount of money from her late parents. She'd loaned her husband the money for his game park to get him out of her life, Ella said. She'd quickly gone through the money she'd inherited, spending it on luxurious vacations, fancy cars and a mansion while Keely was living in meager circumstances with her father. But her mother's wealth or lack of it was no concern to Keely. As soon as she was settled comfortably in her job, she was going to get another part-time job so that she could afford to move into a boardinghouse. She'd had all she could take of living here.

Her father had just left her on Ella's front porch, crying and still pleading to go with him. Ella hadn't been happy to find the adolescent back in her life, but she took her in, at least. At the age of thirteen, Keely had settled down slowly with the mother she barely remembered from childhood, who proceeded to make her life a misery.

"Boone Sinclair is dating that ex-fiancée of his who threw him over when he got out of the Army," Carly Blair drawled, with a quick glance at Keely.

"Is he?" Ella looked at Keely, too. "Have you seen her?" she asked, because she knew that her daughter was friendly with Clark and Winnie Sinclair. "What does the woman look like?"

"She's very pretty," Keely replied calmly between bites of stew. "Long black hair and dark blue eyes."

"Very pretty." Ella laughed. "Nothing like you,

Keely, right? You look like your father. I wanted a beautiful little girl who looked like me." She wrinkled her nose. "What a disappointment you turned out to be."

"We can't all be beautiful, Mother," Keely replied. "I'd rather be smart."

"If you were smart, you'd go to college and get a better job," Ella retorted. "Working as a technician for a veterinarian," she added haughtily. "What a vulgar sort of job."

"The senior veterinarian where Keely works is very good-looking," Carly interrupted, shifting in her chair. She chuckled. "I tried to get him to take me out, but he gave me an icy glare and went back into his office." She shrugged. "I guess he's got a girlfriend somewhere."

Keely was surprised at the remark. Carly was in her mid-forties and Bentley Rydel was only thirty-two years old. Bentley had mentioned, only once, that he couldn't stand Carly. He probably didn't like Keely's mother, either, but he was too polite to say so. Not that they had pets that would need his services. Ella hated animals.

"Keely's boss is a cold fish, like Boone Sinclair," Ella said. She leaned back in her chair and studied her daughter with a cold expression. "You'll never get anywhere with that man, you know," she added in a slow drawl. "He may take his ex-fiancée around with him, but he's no passionate lover."

"How would you know?" Keely returned, stung by the comment and the way her mother aimed it at her.

Ella smiled mockingly. "Because I tried to seduce him myself, on more than one occasion," she said, enjoying the look of horror on her daughter's face. "He's ice-cold. He doesn't respond normally to women, not even when they come on to him physically. No matter what people say about his hot relationship with his ex-fiancée, I can assure you that he isn't all that responsive to women."

"Maybe he just doesn't like older women," Keely muttered icily, her eyes sparkling with temper as she pictured her mother using her wiles on Boone.

A cruel look passed over Ella's face. "Well, he certainly doesn't like you," she retorted with deliberate sarcasm. "I told him you're hot for your veterinarian boss and sleeping with him on the side."

Keely was horrified. "What!" she burst out. "But, why?"

Ella laughed at her expression. "I wanted to see what he'd say," she mused. "It was a disappointment. He didn't react at all. So I asked him if he hadn't noticed what a nice figure you've got, even if you aren't pretty, and he said he didn't feel attracted to children."

Children. Keely was nineteen. That wasn't childish. She didn't think of herself as a child. But Boone did...

"Then I said that you might look like a child, but you knew what to do with a man, and he just walked away," Ella continued. She saw Keely's stricken expression. "So I suppose your little fantasy of love isn't going to be fulfilled." Her face took on a wicked cast. "I did mention in the course of conversation, before he left so rudely, that you had a crush on him and he could probably cut you out with your boss if he tried. He said that you were the last woman on earth he'd want."

Keely wanted to sink through the floor. Some of Boone's antagonistic behavior began to make sense. Her mother was feeding him lies about Keely, and he was swallowing them whole. She wondered how long

Ella had been doing it, and if it was revenge because Boone wouldn't touch her. Maybe she saw Keely as a rival and wanted to make sure there was no chance that Boone would weaken toward her daughter. Either way, it was devastating to the younger woman. She left the rest of her food untouched. She couldn't choke down another bite.

"You might get somewhere with him if you stopped dressing out of thrift shops and wore a little makeup," Ella chided.

"On my salary, all I can afford are clothes from thrift shops," Keely said.

There was a hot silence. "Is that a dig at me?" Ella demanded, eyes flashing. "Because I give you a roof over your head and food to eat," she added curtly. "You only have to do a little cooking and housework from time to time to earn your keep. That's more than fair. I'm not obligated to dress you, as well!"

"I never said you were, Mother," Keely replied.

"Don't call me 'Mother'!" Ella shot back, weaving a little in her chair. "I never wanted you in the first place. Your father was hot to have a son. He was disappointed when you turned out to be a girl, and I refused to get pregnant again. It ruined my waistline! It took me years to get my figure back!

"I wanted to give you up for adoption when you were eleven and your father divorced me, but he said he'd take you if I'd loan him enough money to open that game park. So I loaned him the money—which he never repaid, by the way—and he took you off my hands. He didn't want you, either, Keely," she added with a drunken smile. "Nobody wanted you. And nobody wants you now."

"Ella," Carly interrupted uneasily, "that's harsh." Keely's face was as white as flour.

Ella blinked, as if she wasn't quite aware of what she was saying. She stared blankly at Carly. "What's harsh?"

Carly winced as Keely got to her feet and began clearing the table without saying a word.

She carried empty plates into the kitchen, trying desperately not to let the women see her cry. Behind her, she heard murmuring, which grew louder, and then her mother's voice arguing. She went out into the cold night air in her shirtsleeves, tears pouring down her cheeks. She wrapped her arms around herself and walked to the front yard, stopping at the railing that looked out over Comanche Wells, at the rolling pastureland and little oasis of deciduous trees that shaded the fenced land where purebred cattle grazed. It was a beautiful sight, with the air crisp and the moon shining on the leaves on the big oak tree that stood in the front yard, making it look as if the leaves had been painted silver. But Keely was blind to the beauty of it. She was sick to her stomach.

She heard the phone ring in the house, but she ignored it. First Boone's fierce antagonism and the argument over Bailey and the ex-fiancée's taunts the night before, and then her mother's horrible assertions tonight. It was the worst two days of Keely's recent life. She didn't want to go back in. She wanted to stay out in the cold until she froze to death and the pain stopped.

"Keely?" Carly called from the back door. "It's Clark Sinclair. He wants to speak to you."

Keely hesitated for a moment. She turned and went back inside without meeting Carly's eyes or looking toward the dining room where her mother sat finishing her drink.

She picked up the phone and said "Hello?" in a subdued tone.

"The old girl's giving you hell, is she?" Clark mused. "How about going out? I know it's late notice, but I just got in from Jacksonville and I want to talk to somebody. Winnie's working late at dispatch, and God knows where Boone's off to. How about it?"

"Oh, I'd really like that," Keely said fervently.

"Need an escape plan, do we? I'll be there in ten minutes."

"I'll be ready. I'll wait for you on the front porch."

"God, it must be bad over there tonight!" he exclaimed. "I'll hurry, so you don't catch cold." He hung up. So did Keely.

"Got a date?" Ella drawled, coming to the doorway in a zigzag with her highball glass still in her hands. It was empty now. "Who's taking you someplace?"

Keely didn't answer her. She went down the hall to her room and closed and locked the door behind her.

"I TOLD YOU it was a mistake to tell her that," Carly said plaintively. "You'll be sorry tomorrow when you sober up."

"Mistake to tell her what?" Ella muttered. "I need another drink."

"No. You need to go to bed and sleep it off. Come on." Carly led her down the hall to her own bedroom, pushed her inside and closed the door behind them. "How could you tell her that, Ella?" she asked softly as she helped her friend down onto the big double bed with its expensive pink comforter.

"I don't care," Ella said defiantly. "She's in my way. I don't want her here. I never did."

"She does all the housework and all the cooking," Carly said in one of her rare moments of compassion. "She works all day and sometimes half the night for her boss, and then she comes home and works like a housekeeper. You don't appreciate how much she does for you."

"I could hire somebody to do all that." Ella waved the idea away.

"Could you afford to pay them?" Carly retorted.

Ella frowned. She was hard put just to pay utilities and buy groceries. But she didn't reply.

Carly eyed her quietly. "If you push her, she'll leave. Then what will you do?"

"I'll do my own housework and cooking," Ella said grandly.

Carly shook her head. "Okay. It's your life. But you're missing out."

"On what?" Ella muttered.

"On the only family you have," Carly replied in a subdued tone. "I don't have anybody," she added. "My parents are dead. I had no siblings. I was married, but I was never able to have a child. My husband is dead, too. You have a child, and you don't want her. I'd have given anything to have a child of my own."

"You can have Keely," Ella said, laughing. "I'll give her to you."

Carly moved toward the door. "You can't give people away, Ella." She looked back. "You don't really have anybody, either."

"I have men." Ella laughed coldly. "I can have any man I want."

"For a night," her friend agreed. "Old age is coming up fast, for both of us. Do you really want to drive your only child away? She'll marry someday and have children of her own. You won't even be allowed to see your grandchildren."

"I'm not having grandchildren," Ella shot back. "I'm not going to be old. I'm only in my late thirties!"

Carly laughed. "You're heading toward fifty, Ella," she reminded her friend. "All the beauty treatments in the world aren't going to change that."

"I'll have a face-lift," the other woman returned. "I'll sell more land to pay for it."

That was unwise. Ella had already sold most of the land her family had left her. If she sold the rest, she was going to be hard-pressed just to pay bills. But Carly could see that it did no good to argue with her.

"Good night," she told Ella.

Ella made a face at her, collapsed on the pillow and was asleep in seconds. Carly didn't say anything else. She just closed the door.

KEELY PUT ON a pair of brown corduroy slacks and a beige turtleneck sweater and ran a brush through her thick, straight blond hair. She hoped Clark didn't have an expensive date in mind. She couldn't dress for it. She threw an old beige Berber coat over her clothes and grabbed her purse.

True to his word, Clark pulled up in the yard in exactly ten minutes, driving his sports car.

Carly came out of Ella's bedroom just as Keely was leaving.

"Is she asleep?" Keely asked dully.

"Yes." Carly was worried, and it showed. "She should never have said that to you," she added. "She loved you when you were a baby. You wouldn't remember, you were too little, but I do. She was so happy…"

"So happy that she now treats me this way?" Keely asked, hurt.

Carly sighed. "She was different after your father left. She started drinking then, and it's just gotten worse year after year." She saw that she wasn't getting through to the younger woman. "There are things you don't know about your parents, Keely," she said gently.

"Such as?"

Carly shook her head. "That's not my place to tell you." She turned away. "I'm going home. She'll sleep until morning."

"Lock the door when you leave, please," Keely said.

"I'm leaving now. You can lock it." Carly got her purse and stopped just as the door closed behind the two women.

"I'm as bad as she is, sometimes," the older woman confessed quietly. "I shouldn't make fun of the way you are, and neither should she. But you don't fight back, Keely. You must learn to do that. You're nineteen. Don't spend the rest of your life knuckling under, just to keep peace."

Keely frowned. "I don't."

"You do, baby," Carly said softly. She sighed. "Ella and I are a bad influence on you. What you need to do is get an apartment of your own and live your own life."

Keely searched the other woman's eyes. "I've thought about that…."

"Do it," Carly advised. "Get out while you can."

Keely frowned. "What do you mean?"

Carly hesitated. "I've said too much already. Enjoy your date. Good night."

CARLY WALKED OFF to her small import car. Keely watched her for a minute before she went down the steps to where Clark was waiting in his sleek Lincoln. He leaned across and opened the door for her.

He grinned. "I'd come around and open it, but I'm too lazy," he teased.

She smiled back. He was like a kinder version of Boone. Clark had the same black hair and dark eyes, but he was a little shorter than his brother, and his hair was wavy—unlike Boone's, which was straight.

"Neither one of you resemble your sister," she remarked.

He shrugged. "Winnie got our mother's coloring. She doesn't like that. We hated our mother."

"So Winnie said."

He glanced at her as they pulled out of her mother's yard. "We share the feeling, don't we, Keely?" he probed. "Your mother is a walking headache."

She nodded. "She was in high form tonight," she said wearily. "Drunk and vicious."

"What was Carly saying to you?"

"That I have to learn to stand up to her," she said. "Surprising, isn't it, coming from Mother's best friend? The two of them make fun of me all the time."

Clark glanced at her, and he didn't smile. "She's right about that. You need to stand up to my brother, too. Boone walks all over people who won't fight back."

She shivered. "I'm not taking on your brother," she said. "He's scary."

"Scary? Boone?"

She averted her gaze to the window. "Can't we talk about something else?"

He was disconcerted by her remark, but he pulled

himself together quickly. "Sure! I just heard that the Chinese are launching another probe toward the moon."

She gave him a wry look.

"You don't like astronautics," he murmured. "Okay. Politics?"

She groaned out loud. "I'm so sick of presidential candidates that I'm thinking of moving to someplace where nobody runs for public office."

"The Amazon jungle comes to mind."

Her eyes narrowed. "If I went far enough in, I might escape television and the internet."

"I can see the headlines now," he said with mock horror. "Local vet technician eaten by jaguar in darkest jungles of South America!"

"No self-respecting jaguar would want to eat a human being," she retorted. "Especially one who eats anchovies on pizza."

"I didn't know you liked anchovies."

She sighed. "I don't. But when I was little, I discovered that if I ordered them, my dad would let me have more than two slices of pizza."

He laughed. "Your father must have been a card."

"He was." She smiled reminiscently. "Animals loved him. I've seen him feed tigers right out of his hand without ever being bitten. Even snakes liked him."

"That animal park must have been something else."

"It was wonderful," she replied. "We all loved it. But there was a tragic accident, and Dad lost everything."

"Somebody got eaten?"

"Almost," she replied, unwilling to say more. "There was a lawsuit."

"And he lost," he guessed.

She didn't correct him. "It destroyed him."

He frowned. "Did he commit suicide?"

She hesitated. This was Clark. He was her friend. She knew that he'd never tell Boone or even Winnie without asking her first. "He's not dead," she said quietly. "I don't know where he is or what he's doing. He developed a…a drinking problem." She couldn't tell him the whole truth. She glanced at him worriedly. "You won't tell anybody?"

"Of course not."

She studied her purse in her lap, turning it restlessly in her hands. "He left me with Mother and took off. That was six years ago, and I haven't heard a word from him. For all I know, he could be dead."

"You loved him."

She nodded. "Very much." She moved restlessly.

"What is it?"

She felt the pain of her mother's words go right through her. "My mother said that she never wanted me. I ruined her figure," she added with a hollow laugh.

"Good God! And I thought our mother was bad!" He stopped at a traffic light heading into Jacobsville and looked toward her. "Isn't it a hell of a shame that we can't choose our parents?"

"Yes, it is," she agreed. "I was just sick when she said it. I should have guessed. She didn't like me when I left, and she liked me even less when Dad dumped me on her, and now I think she hates me. I've tried to please her, keeping house and cooking and cleaning, but she doesn't appreciate it. She grudges me the very food I eat." She turned toward him. "I've got to get out of that house," she said desperately. "I can't take it anymore."

"Mrs. Brown runs a very respectable boarding-house," he began.

She grimaced. "Yes, and charges a respectable price for rooms. I can't afford it on my salary."

"Hit Bentley up for a raise," he suggested.

"Oh, right, I'll do that first thing tomorrow," she drawled.

"You're scared of Bentley. You're scared of Boone." He pulled out into traffic. "You're even scared of your mother. You have to step up and claim your own life, Keely."

"What do you mean?"

"You can't go through life being afraid of people. Especially people like my brother and Bentley Rydel. Do you know why they're scary?" he persisted. "It's because it's hard work to talk to them. They're both basically introverts who find it difficult to relate to other people. Consequently they're quiet and somber and they don't go out of their way to join in activities. They're loners."

She sighed. "I'm a loner, too, in my own way. But I don't stand on the sidelines and glare at people all the time—or, worse, pretend they're not there."

"Is that Boone's latest tactic?" he mused, chuckling. "He ignores you, does he?"

"He did until I argued about Bailey's condition."

"Thank God you did," he said fervently. "Bailey belongs to Boone, but we all love the old fellow. I'll never understand why Boone didn't realize what had happened to him. He's a cattleman—he's seen bloat before."

"His girlfriend convinced him that I was trying to get attention, using Bailey to lure Boone to my place of work."

"Oh, for heaven's sake!" he burst out. "Boone's not that stupid!"

"Well, apparently my mother's been telling him that I have a crush on him, and now he thinks everything I do or say is an attempt to worm my way into his life," she said bitterly.

"Ella told him that?" he exclaimed.

"Yes. And she told him that I'm sleeping with Bentley."

"Does Bentley know that you're sleeping with him?" he asked innocently.

She laughed. "I don't know. I'll ask him."

He burst out laughing, too. "That's more like it, kid," he said. "You have to learn to roll with the punches and not take life so seriously."

"It feels pretty serious to me lately," she replied. "I feel like I've hit a wall tonight."

"You should push your mother into one," he told her. "Or better yet, tell her what a lousy mother she's been."

"She doesn't listen when she's drunk, and she's mostly away from home when she's sober." She pursed her lips. "I work for veterinarians. I've been professionally taught to let sleeping dogs lie."

He smiled. "Have you, now?"

"Where are you taking me?" she asked when he took a state highway instead of the Jacobsville road. "I thought we were going to a movie."

"I'm not in the mood for a movie. I thought we might go to San Antonio for shrimp," he replied. "I'm in the mood for some. What do you think?"

"We'll be very late getting back," she reminded him worriedly.

"What the hell," he scoffed. "You can tell your mother you're sleeping with me now instead of Bentley and she can mind her own business about when you come home."

Her eyes almost popped.

He saw that and grinned. "Which brings to mind a matter I need a little help with. I think," he added, "that you and I can be the solution for each others' problems. If you're game."

All the way to San Antonio, she wondered what he meant, and how she would fit into his "solution."

CHAPTER THREE

THE RESTAURANT CLARK took Keely to was one of the most exclusive in town, famous for its seafood. Keely was worried that she was dressed too casually for such a grand place, but she saw people dressed up and dressed down for the evening out. She relaxed and followed Clark and the hostess to a corner table. They were seated and provided with menus. Keely had to bite her tongue at the prices. Any one of these dishes would have equaled a day's salary. But Clark just gave her a grin and told her to order what she wanted. They were celebrating. She wondered what they were celebrating, but he wouldn't say.

Keely had eaten earlier, so she just had a very light meal. After she'd finished, she wondered if it was really the food that drew him here. He couldn't take his eyes off the waitress who took their orders. And the waitress blushed prettily when he stared at her.

"Do you know her?" Keely asked softly when the waitress went to turn in their orders.

"Yes," he said, grimacing. "I'm in love with her."

Immediately Keely recalled Boone's attitude toward his siblings becoming involved with someone from a lower economic class. He'd been vocal about it in the past. The look on Clark's face was painful to see. She knew without asking that he was seeing the hopelessness of his own situation vividly.

"Is she the one you took to supper at the ranch?" she asked, remembering something she'd heard from Winnie.

He nodded. "Boone was polite to her, but later he asked me if I was out of my mind. He sees all working women as gold diggers who can't wait to marry me and then divorce me for a big settlement."

"Not all women want money," she pointed out.

"Tell Boone. He doesn't know."

"That woman he goes out with seems to be obsessed with it," Keely muttered.

"She doesn't count, because she's rich in her own right."

"Yes. She's beautiful, too," she added with more bitterness than she realized.

He studied her across the white tablecloth with its fresh flowers, candles and silverware. "Think about it—would a man like Boone stick his head into the same noose he escaped once? That woman walked away from him when he was lying in a hospital with shrapnel wounds that could have killed him. She didn't like hospitals. She thought he might be crippled, so she gave him back his ring. Now she's in San Antonio and wants to go back to where they started. How do you think Boone feels about that?"

For the first time, she felt a glimmer of hope. "Your brother doesn't forgive people," she said softly. It was what she'd said once to Winnie.

"Exactly. Much less people who stick pins in his pride."

"Then why is he taking her around with him?" Keely wanted to know.

He shrugged. "She's beautiful and she has polished manners. Maybe he's just lonely and he wants a showpiece on his arm. Or," he added slowly, "maybe he has something in mind that she isn't expecting. She wants to marry him again. But I don't think he wants to marry her. And I think he's got a good reason for going out with her at all."

"God knows what it is," Keely murmured.

"God does know. He probably doesn't like it, either."

"You think Boone is working on revenge?"

"Could be. He doesn't often share his innermost thoughts with Winnie or me. Boone plays his hand close to his chest. He doesn't give away anything."

"What was he like before he came home wounded?" she wanted to know.

"He was less somber," he told her. "He played practical jokes. He laughed. He enjoyed parties, and he loved to dance. Now, he's the total opposite of the man he used to be. He's bitter and edgy, and he won't say why. He's never talked to any of us about what happened to him over there."

"You think whatever it was is what changed him so much?"

He nodded. "I miss the brother I had. I can't get close to the man he's become. He avoids me like the plague. More so, since I brought Nellie home with me for supper. He gave me a long lecture on the dangers of encouraging hired help. He was eloquent."

"So you're uneasy about taking her out on a date."

"I'm uneasy about Boone finding out that I'm dating her," he confessed. "Which brings me," he added with a glance, "to the solution I need your help with."

She gave him a wary look. "Why do I get the feeling that I shouldn't have agreed to come here with you?"

"I can't imagine." He leaned toward her, smiling.

"But if you'll just cooperate in my little project, I'll return the favor one day."

She noticed that Nellie, waiting on another table, was sending pained looks toward Clark, who was oblivious to her interest. "This is upsetting Nellie," she pointed out.

"Not for long. I'll speak with her before we leave. Listen, you're my best friend. I need you to be a friend and help me divert Boone from guessing how involved I am with Nellie. We're going to pretend to get involved, if you're game."

"Involved?" Keely squeaked. "Listen here, Boone already thinks I'm sleeping with Bentley, thanks to my mother. He won't believe I'm turning my attention to you. He hates me!" she exclaimed. "He'll go out of his mind if he thinks you're serious about me, and he'll stop it any way he can. I'll lose my job and have to stay at home, my mother will drive me crazy—"

"Your mother will be thrilled if you go out with me, because I'm rich," Clark said sardonically. "She won't cause trouble. And Boone will spend his time trying to think up ways to get you out of my life, unaware of what's really going on."

"Boone isn't stupid," she worried. "He's going to wonder what you see in me. I'm poor, I work at a menial job…"

"I'll take care of all that," he said, smoothing it over. "All you have to do is pretend to find me fascinating." He grinned. "Actually I *am* fascinating," he added. "Not to mention highly eligible and charming."

She made a face at him.

"But my brother can't know it's not for real," Clark added seriously. "He's got control of all my money until I turn twenty-seven. Then I can get to my trust.

That's next year. I can't afford to tick him off just yet.
But I'm not giving up Nellie." He glanced toward the
young waitress, who blushed again at his interest and
almost overturned a tray looking at him. "You have
to help us," he told her. "You helped Bailey and he's
just a dog. I'm a kind, thoughtful man who treats you
like a little sister."

"That's it, play on my heartstrings," Keely muttered.

He grinned. "Come on. It will drive Boone nuts,
you know it will. You'll love it!"

Thinking of the way Boone had treated her, she
had to admit that the deception would pay dividends
in the form of revenge. But Boone was a formidable
enemy and Keely was uncertain about making one
of him. That was funny, considering his hostile and
condescending attitude toward her. He was her enemy
already.

"I'll save you if it gets too rough," he promised.

She knew it was a bad idea. She was going to regret
giving in. "If I agree to do it, I have to tell Winnie the
truth," she began.

"No," he said immediately. "Winnie can't keep a
secret, and she's afraid of Boone, too. If he puts on
the pressure, she'll tell him everything she knows."

Keely grimaced. "I just know this is going to end
badly."

"But you'll do it, won't you?" he asked with a ca-
joling smile.

She sighed. She grimaced. Clark had been her
friend as long as Winnie had. He'd helped her out of
half a dozen scrapes involving her mother. "Okay,"
she said at last.

He grinned from ear to ear. "Okay! Now. How about
dessert?"

BEFORE THEY LEFT the restaurant, he introduced her to Nellie and explained to the waitress who Keely was and what her place was in his life. Nellie brightened at once. She was glowing when Clark added that Keely was going to be the red herring so that he and Nellie could go on dates without Boone knowing.

Keely noticed that the other woman was very demure and meek, and Clark seemed to love that attitude. But Keely noticed something that he didn't; there was a faint glint in Nellie's eyes that didn't go with a meek demeanor. She couldn't help but be apprehensive. Maybe Nellie's allure for him was Boone's disapproval; in many ways, he'd only just started to try the boundaries of his big brother's control. And Nellie had to know that the family was rich. She was a working girl, like Keely. If she turned out to be a gold digger, Keely stood to be burned at the stake by Clark's older brother for her part in this. She wished she'd refused. She really did.

THEY WERE VERY late getting home. It was one o'clock in the morning when Clark drove up at Keely's front door.

Until that moment, she hadn't remembered her mother's vicious words. They came back with cruel force when she saw the living-room light still on. She didn't want to go inside. If she'd had anywhere else to go, she wouldn't set foot in the place.

But her choices, like her salary, were limited. She had to live with her mother until she could make better arrangements.

Clark was watching her with open sympathy. "She probably doesn't even remember saying it," he murmured. "Drunks aren't big on memory."

She glanced at him, curious. "How would you know that?"

He hesitated, but only for a minute. "After Boone's fiancée threw him over, he went on a two-week bender. He didn't remember a lot of the things he said to me, but I've never forgotten any of them. The crowning jewel," he added with taut features, "was that I'd never measure up to him and that I wasn't fit to run a ranch."

"Oh, Clark," she sympathized. She could only imagine being a man and having Boone as a big brother to try to live up to. Those were very big shoes to have to fill.

"He sobered up and didn't remember anything he'd said to me. But words hurt."

"Tell me about it," Keely sympathized.

He turned to her. "We're both in the same boat, aren't we? We're people who don't measure up to the expectations of the people we live with."

"Winnie and I think you're great just the way you are," she replied doggedly.

He laughed, surprised. "Really?"

"Really. You've got a wonderful sense of humor, you're never moody or sarcastic and you've got a big heart." Her eyes narrowed. "If I'd told you that Bailey needed emergency care immediately, you'd have packed him into the car and taken him right to the vet."

He sighed. "Yes, I guess I would have."

"Boone thought it was a pitiful plea for attention on my part," she added sadly. "I guess my mother's said a lot of things to him about me."

"Apparently. She doesn't like you, does she?"

"The feeling is mutual. We're sort of stuck together until I can get a raise or a second job."

"How would you manage a second job?" he asked.

"Getting away from my mother's constant abuse would make me manage. I can't imagine living in a place where nobody makes fun of me."

"You could work for me," he suggested.

She shook her head. "Thanks, but no thanks. I want to be completely independent."

"I figured that, but it didn't hurt to ask."

She smiled. "You really are a nice man."

"I'll pick you up next Saturday morning. We can go riding at the ranch. We might as well make a start at getting on Boone's nerves," he added with a dry chuckle.

"Take all his bullets away before I get there," she pleaded.

"He's not so bad," he told her.

She shivered. "Sure he isn't."

The front door opened and Keely's mother came out onto the porch. "Who's that out there?" she drawled, hanging on to one of the supporting posts. She was wearing floral silk slacks with a fluffy pink robe. Her hair was disheveled and she looked sleepy.

"Don't pay her any attention," Keely advised Clark with a sad little sigh. "She doesn't even know what she's saying. I'll see you next Saturday."

"Thanks, Keely," he told her with sincere affection.

She shrugged. "You'd do it for me," she said, and smiled. "Good night."

"Good night."

She got out of the car and walked up to the porch, shaking inside, dreading another confrontation with her parent. She tried to walk past Ella, but the older woman stopped her.

"Where have you been?" she demanded.

Keely looked at her. For the first time she didn't

back down, even though her knees were shaking. "Out," she replied tersely.

The older woman's face tautened. "Don't talk to me like that. You live in my house, in case you've forgotten!"

"Not for much longer," Keely gritted. "I'm moving out as soon as I can get a night job to go with my day job. I don't care if I have to live in my car, it will be worth it! I'm not staying here any longer."

She brushed past her mother and went into the house, down the hall, into her room. She locked the door behind her. She was shaking. It was the first time in memory that she'd stood up to her abusive parent.

Ella came to her door and knocked. Keely ignored her.

She knocked again, with the same result.

ELLA WAS SOBERING up quickly. It had just dawned on her that if Keely left, she'd have nobody to do the chores. She couldn't even cook. She'd been able to afford help until the past two or three years. But she was facing a drastic reduction in her capital, due to her bad business decisions. And there was something else, something more worrying, that she didn't dare think about right now.

"I didn't mean what I said!" she called through the door. "I'm sorry!"

"You're always sorry," Keely replied tightly.

"No. This time I'm really sorry!"

There was a hesitation. Keely started to weaken. Then she remembered her mother's track record and kept quiet.

"I can't cook!" Ella yelled through the door a minute later. "I'll starve to death if you leave!"

"Buy a restaurant," was Keely's dry retort.

With what, Ella was thinking, but Keely's light went off. She stood there, weaving, her mind dimmed, her heart racing. A long, long time ago, she'd cuddled Keely in her arms and sung lullabies to her. She'd loved her. What had happened to that soft, warm feeling? Had it died, all those years ago, when she learned the truth about her husband? So many secrets, she thought. So much pain. And it was still here. Nothing stopped it.

She needed another drink. She turned back down the hall toward her own room. She could plead her case with Keely tomorrow. There was plenty of time. The girl couldn't leave. She had no place to go, and no money. As for getting a second job, how would Keely manage that when she worked all hours for that vet? She relaxed. Keely would stay. Ella was sure of it.

SATURDAY MORNING, CLARK came to pick her up to go riding with him at the ranch.

She'd done that several times with Winnie. But she'd never done it with Clark. Winnie and Boone were usually both home on the weekend, but Winnie's red VW Beetle was nowhere in sight when Clark drove up in front of the stables with Keely beside him.

He got out and opened the door for her with a flourish. Boone, who was saddling a horse of his own in the barn, stopped with the saddle in midair to glare at them.

"Oh, dear," Keely muttered under her breath.

"He's just a man," Clark reminded her. "He can kill you, but he can't eat you."

"Are you sure?"

Boone had put the saddle back on the ground at the gate that kept his favorite gelding from leaving his stall. He stalked down the brick aisle toward Clark and Keely, who actually moved back a step as he approached with that measured, quick, dangerous tread.

He loomed over them, taller even than Clark, and looked intimidating. "I thought you were flying to Dallas today," he told Clark.

Clark was intimidated by his older sibling and couldn't hide it. He tried to look defiant, but he only looked guilty. "I'm going Monday," he said, and it sounded like an apology. "I brought Keely. She's going riding with me."

Boone looked down at Keely, who was staring at her feet and mentally kicking herself for ever agreeing to Clark's harebrained scheme.

"Is she, now?" Boone mused coldly. He glanced at Clark. "Fetch me a blanket for Tank from the tack room, will you? You can ask Billy to saddle two horses for you on the way."

Clark brightened. His brother sounded almost friendly. "Sure!"

He grinned at Keely and moved quickly down the aisle of the barn toward the tack room, leaving Keely stranded with Boone, who looked oddly like a lion confronted by a thick, juicy steak.

"Tell Clark you don't want to go riding, Keely," he said slowly. "And ask him to take you home. Right now."

First her mother, now Boone. She was so tired of people telling her what to do. She looked up at him with wide, dark green eyes. "Why do you care if I go riding with Clark?" she asked quietly. "I go riding with Winnie all the time."

"There's a difference."

She felt threatened. Then she felt insulted. She met

his dark, piercing stare with resignation. "It's because my people aren't rich or socially important, isn't it?" she asked. "It's because I'm poor."

"And uneducated," he added tauntingly.

Her face colored. "I have a diploma for the work I do," she stammered.

"You're a glorified groomer, Keely," he said flatly. "You hold dogs and cats while the vet treats them."

Her whole body tautened. "That isn't true. I give anesthesia and shots…"

He held up a hand. "Spare me the minute details," he said, sounding bored.

"We can't all go to Harvard, you know," she muttered.

"And some of us can't even face community college," he shot back. "You had a scholarship and you threw it away."

She felt sick. "A scholarship that paid just for textbooks," she corrected. "And only half of that. How in the world do you think I could afford to pay tuition and go to classes and hold down a full-time job, all at once?"

"You could give up the job."

She laughed hollowly. "My mother would love that. Then she wouldn't even have groceries."

His dark eyes narrowed. "Do you pay rent?"

Her big, soft green eyes met his. "I do all the housework and all the cooking and cleaning and shopping. That's my rent."

"Who buys her liquor?" he asked with a cold smile. "And her see-through negligees?"

Keely's face went scarlet. He was insinuating something. Her stare asked the question without words.

He stuck his hands in the pockets of his jeans, pulling the thick fabric taut over the hard, powerful muscles of his legs. "I dropped by your house to thank you, belatedly, for getting Bailey to the vet in time to save him," he said curtly. "You weren't home, but she was. She answered the door in a see-through negligee and invited me inside."

The shame was overpowering. She averted her face.

"Embarrassed?" he scoffed. "Why? Like mother, like daughter. I'm sure you wear similar things for Bentley," he added with honey-dripping sarcasm.

She couldn't manage a reply. His opinion of her was painful. She'd loved him secretly for years, and he could treat her like this. He wouldn't even give her the benefit of the doubt.

Her lack of response made him angry. Why it should also make him feel guilty was a question he couldn't answer. "You keep away from Clark," he said shortly. "I don't want you going out with him. Do you hear me, Keely?"

"It's just for a ride...."

"I don't give a damn what it's for!" he snapped, watching her body tense, her eyes grow frightened. That made him even angrier. He stepped toward her and was infuriated when she backed up. "Get out of Clark's life. Today!" he told her in a goaded undertone.

She felt her knees go weak. He was intimidating. She couldn't even force her eyes back up to his. She was so tired of being afraid of everybody; especially of Boone.

Before he could say anything else, Clark came up with a blanket. He was grinning. "Billy's got the horses saddled. He's bringing them right up!"

Boone glared down at Keely. "I think Keely wants to go home," he said.

"You do?" Clark exclaimed, surprised.

Keely drew in a quick breath and stepped close to Clark. "I'd like to go riding," she replied.

Clark glanced at Boone, whose eyes were black as jet. "What's going on?" he asked his brother. He frowned. "Do you really mind if I just take Keely riding?"

Boone glared at Keely as if he'd like to roast her on a spit. He glared at his brother, too. His lips made a thin line. "Oh, hell!" Boone bit off. "Do what you damned well please!"

He turned and strode out of the barn, apparently oblivious to the blanket Clark was holding out and the saddle he'd left sitting at the stall gate. His long, quick strides were audible on the paved floor, echoing down the aisle.

Clark ground his teeth together as he watched Boone's departure. "I hope he doesn't run into any of his men on the way to wherever he's going," he said with visible misgivings.

"Why?" Keely asked, relieved that Boone hadn't said anything more.

Suddenly there was a distant voice, a sharp curse and the sound of water being splashed.

"Oh, boy," Clark said heavily.

Keely stared down the aisle. A tall, dripping wet cowboy came into the barn, sloshing water as he walked. He was wringing out his felt hat, muttering. He looked up and saw Keely and Clark and grimaced.

"What happened to you, Riley?" Clark exclaimed.

The cowboy glowered at him. "I just made a comment about how good you and Miss Keely looked together," he said defensively. "Boone picked me up and tossed me into the watering trough!"

Clark exchanged a glance with Keely. She had to bite her lip to keep from laughing as the cowboy passed on down the aisle, muttering about his freshly laundered clothing having to go right back into the washing machine. He headed out the back door of the barn toward the bunkhouse beyond.

"Poor guy," Keely said. She looked up. "Your brother has a very nasty temper."

"Yes." He drew in a breath. "Well, it wasn't as bad as I expected it to be," he added, smiling. "Let's go for a nice ride and pretend that my brother likes you and can't wait to welcome you into our family!"

"Optimist," Keely said and grinned.

BOONE WAS GONE when they came back from the lazy ride around the ranch, but Winnie was just putting her car into the garage. She drove a cute little red Volkswagen Beetle, her pride and joy because she was paying for it herself.

She came out of the garage frowning. She didn't even notice Clark and Keely at first, not until she'd passed right by the barn.

"What's wrong with you?" Clark called to her.

She stopped, glanced at them and looked blank. "What?"

"I said, what's wrong with you?" Clark repeated as he and Keely joined his sister near the corral.

"Bad day at work?" Keely asked sympathetically.

Winnie was tight-mouthed. "I had a little upset with Kilraven," she muttered.

Keely's eyebrows arched. "What sort of upset?"

Winnie grimaced. "I didn't mention the ten-thirty-two involved in a ten-sixteen physical," she said, describing a possible weapon involved in a domestic dispute. "The caller said her husband was drunk, had beaten her up in front of the kids and was holding a pistol to her head. The phone went dead and I dispatched Kilraven. I'd just managed to get the caller back on the phone and I was listening to her while I gave him the information, and the caller was hysterical, so I got rattled and didn't tell him about the gun. When he got to the address I gave him, he had a .45 caliber Colt automatic shoved into his face."

Keely gasped. "Was he shot?"

"No thanks to me, he wasn't," Winnie said miserably. "I was also supposed to put out a ten-three, ten-thirty-three, calling for radio silence while he went into the house. I messed up everything. It was my first shift working all alone without my instructor, and I just blew it! My supervisor said I could have gotten someone killed, and she was right." She burst into tears. "Kilraven called for backup and talked the man out of the gun, God knows how. After the man was in custody on the way to the detention center, Kilraven called me on his cell phone and said that if I ever sent him on a call again and left out vital details of the disturbance, he'd have me fired."

Keely hugged her, muttering sympathetic things, while Clark patted her on the shoulder and said that it would all blow over.

Winnie blew her nose and wiped her eyes. "I'm going to put in my resignation at the police station and at 911 dispatch and come home," she sobbed. "I'm a menace! Kilraven said I was taking up jobs that some other woman needed desperately, anyway. He said rich women who got bored should find some other way to entertain themselves!"

"That's harsh," Clark muttered. "I'll have a talk with him."

Winnie looked up at her sweet brother through tear-filled eyes. "Are you kidding? Kilraven makes Boone look civilized!"

"Well, we could ask Boone to speak to him," Clark compromised.

Just as Winnie was starting to answer him, a Jacobsville police car came flying up the long driveway and skidded to a halt in front of the barn. A tall, black-haired, powerful-looking policeman got out and stalked toward them.

"Uh-oh," Winnie whispered, going pale.

"Who is that?" Clark asked.

Winnie took a breath. "Kilraven," she said heavily.

CHAPTER FOUR

WINNIE LOOKED LIKE a professional mourner. Her long, wavy blond hair was ruffled by the wind and her dark eyes were red from crying.

"It's all right," she said, trying to deflect trouble as Kilraven came to a stop, towering over her. "You didn't need to come all the way out here to tell me I'm fired. I'm going to put in my resignation first thing tomorrow morning."

He propped his hand on his holstered gun and stared down at her with glittering silver eyes. "Who asked you to quit?"

"You said I should," she accused, and dabbed at new tears. "You said I needed to leave law enforcement to people who were qualified to work in it."

The tall man grimaced. The tears were real. He'd been browbeaten into coming out here by his boss, Jacobsville Police Chief Cash Grier, protesting all the way because he thought Winnie was putting on an act for sympathy. But this was no act. His rage dissolved like tears on hot pavement.

"I could have gotten you killed," Winnie told him, red-eyed, and started crying all over again. "That man held a pistol to your head!"

Kilraven's perfect teeth clenched. "It wasn't loaded."

Winnie stared at him through a mist. "What?"

"It wasn't loaded," Kilraven repeated. "He was too drunk to realize the clip was missing."

"Wouldn't there still be one bullet chambered?" Winnie asked.

Kilraven shrugged. "Didn't matter."

Winnie frowned. "It didn't matter? Why?"

He drew in a long breath. "He couldn't remember how to get the safety off."

Winnie was just looking at him now, not saying anything.

"But it could have ended in tragedy," Kilraven continued quietly. "I mean, if he'd managed to actually fire the damned thing…" He left the rest unsaid.

Winnie blew her nose and wiped her eyes again. "I know."

"They stuck you in that dispatch job with no real training," he muttered. "Any big city 911 staff goes through a training program. Well, Jacobs County has one, too," he conceded. "But the director thought you were just playing around, that you weren't really serious about working in the 911 center since you worked full-time for us in the police department. So he just stuck you in as an assistant to one of the regulars and let you get on with it. He thought you'd fold after a few days, that you only took the job because you were bored with being at home, and that you thought working for the police and emergency dispatch was entertainment. I had a long talk with the director before I came here."

"You did?" Winnie was fascinated. She hesitated. "You didn't…hit him or anything?"

"I do not hit people," the tall officer replied haughtily.

"That's not what Harley Fowler says," Keely murmured under her breath.

Kilraven glared at her. "That guy pulled a knife on me and threatened to cut off my…well, never mind what he threatened, he was lunging at me with it. It was hit him or shoot him."

"How many pins did they have to put in his jaw?" Keely wondered aloud.

"It was better than having to have a bullet dug out," Kilraven protested. "And I should know. I've had three bullets dug out, over the years, along with various bits of shrapnel, and I'm wearing two steel pins, as well. The pins hurt less."

Winnie was studying him curiously.

"I'm not telling you where they are," Kilraven said. "And shame on you for what you're thinking!"

Winnie flushed. "You don't know!"

"The hell I don't," he huffed. "My great-grandfather was a full-fledged shaman who could read minds."

"That's not what Harley Fowler says he was," Keely interrupted.

He gave her an exasperated glance. "What does Harley Fowler know about me? I've never even met the man!"

"He doesn't know you, but he plays poker with Garon Grier, who works with Jon Blackhawk, who's your half brother," Keely explained.

"Damn the FBI!" Kilraven cursed.

"Harley doesn't belong to the FBI," Winnie pointed out.

"Garon and my brother do," Kilraven said. "And they can stop telling people lies about me and my family."

"Jon *is* your family," Winnie replied. "And Harley

didn't tell lies, he said your great-grandfather got mad at a local sheriff and smeared him with fresh meat and shoved him headfirst into a wolf den."

"Well, the wolf den was empty at the time," Kilraven defended his ancestor.

"Yes, but your great-grandfather didn't know that." Keely laughed.

Kilraven made a face at her. "You didn't get that from Harley Fowler, you got it from Bentley Rydel."

Keely blushed.

Kilraven threw up his hands. "You take your dog to a vet and expect him to stick to medicine, instead of which he pumps you for personal information and then tells the whole community!"

"You don't get to join the family unless we know everything about you," Clark pointed out.

Kilraven scowled. "What family?" he asked suspiciously, and glanced at Winnie, who blushed as warmly as Keely had.

"The Jacobsville family," Clark returned. "We're not a town. We're a big extended family."

"You don't live in Jacobsville, you live in Comanche Wells," Kilraven retorted.

"It's an extension of Jacobsville, and you're avoiding the issue," Clark said with a grin.

Kilraven's wide, sexy mouth pulled up into a faint snarl. "I'm leaving. I don't want to be part of a family."

"With that attitude, I wouldn't worry about it," Winnie said under her breath.

He paused to look down at her. "Your director will talk to you in the morning about some more training. He's going to do it personally. I don't want you fired. Neither do any of the other law enforcement and rescue personnel. You've got a real knack for the job."

Kilraven turned on his heel and stalked off back to his patrol car. He got in under the wheel, coaxed the engine into a roar and shot out of the driveway without a glance, a wave or anything else.

"Well, he's sort of nice," Clark had to admit.

"He's sort of scary, too," Keely said, watching Winnie.

Winnie was smiling through her tears. "Maybe I'm not a lost cause, after all."

Keely hugged her. "Definitely not a lost cause," she laughed.

"Well, I guess I'll go inside and find something to eat…" She stopped, her gaze moving from Clark to Keely. "What are you two doing together?"

"Driving Boone mad," Clark said, and he grinned.

"Would you like to explain how?" his sister asked.

"I invited Keely over to ride horses with me, and Boone was in the barn when we drove up together."

"So that's why," Winnie began thoughtfully.

"Why, what?" Keely wanted to know.

"Why my brother was sitting on the shoulder of the road in his car with a Texas Department of Public Safety car flashing its lights behind him, with a trooper sitting inside running wants and warrants."

"How do you know what he was doing?" Keely asked.

"Because I run tags all the time at work for the troopers and the local police," she replied.

"What was Boone doing?" Clark asked hesitantly.

Winnie chuckled. "Teaching the trooper new words, from the look of it. I didn't dare stop to ask."

"Oh, dear," Keely said, glancing at Clark.

"Stop that," Clark said firmly. "It's none of Boone's

business if I want to ask you over here to go riding with me."

"It shouldn't be," Winnie told her brother. "But he'll make it his business. He thinks Keely's too young to go out with men. Any men."

Clark's eyes popped. "She's almost twenty years old!"

"Well, of course she is," Winnie said gently. "But not to Boone. To him, she's still in pigtails trying to teach her dog how to fetch newspapers."

"Don't dig that up," Keely moaned.

"That was when your folks rented that place down the road while your house was being remodeled. You'd have been about eleven. That dog was very good at fetching newspapers," Winnie replied. "It was just that it was easier for him to bring you Boone's paper from our front porch than it was to fetch yours out of the paper box at the end of your driveway."

"Boone yelled at me," Keely recalled with a shudder.

"Boone yells at everybody," Winnie reminded her.

"Almost everybody," Clark qualified.

Keely's eyebrows arched. "Almost?"

"It didn't work when he yelled at Bentley Rydel, did it?" He chuckled. "Winnie told me," he added when Keely looked puzzled.

"Bentley isn't afraid of anybody," Keely agreed, smiling. "He's been good to me."

"I'd think he had a crush on you, except for his age," Clark said. "He's even older than Boone."

"I guess he is, at that," Keely said.

"Want some lunch?" Winnie asked them after a moment of silence. "We'll have to get it ourselves, because our Mrs. Johnston is off today, but I can make a salad and Keely can make real bread."

"I'd love homemade bread." Clark sighed. "The lunchroom ladies used to make it at school when I was a kid."

"Would you mind?" Winnie asked her best friend.

Keely smiled. "Not at all. I love to cook."

It would also give her an excuse not to have to go home for a while. Her mother would be getting up pretty soon, hungover as usual and driving Keely nuts. With a little luck, maybe Carly would come over and take Ella out partying, since it was Saturday. It would give Keely a lovely quiet night at home alone if she didn't get called out; something she rarely experienced.

THE THREE OF them worked in a companionable silence while they whipped together a light lunch. Keely took a little of the dough she was using for rolls and added real butter, pecans, cinnamon and sugar and made cinnamon buns for dessert.

Winnie's pasta salad had time to chill while the dough sat rising. Within an hour, Keely had fresh bread on the table and cinnamon buns cooking in the oven while they ate their way through pasta and fresh fruit.

In the middle of the impromptu feast, Boone walked in. He stopped in the doorway, his nostrils flaring.

"I smell fresh bread," he remarked, scowling. "Where the hell did you get fresh bread? Is there a bakery in town that I don't know about?"

"Keely made it," Clark mumbled, working his way through a third yeast roll liberally spread with butter. "Mmmm!" he added, closing his eyes and groaning at the delicious taste.

"Did you get a ticket?" Winnie asked, trying to divert him from the penetrating glance he was aiming at Keely, who squirmed in her chair.

"Ticket for what?" Boone asked, digging in the china cabinet for a plate.

"Speeding," she replied.

He put his plate on the table and fetched silverware and a napkin. He poured himself a cup of coffee from the pot and sat down with the other three. Keely's heart was already doing overtime, and she had to work at acting normal while Boone was so close.

"I got a warning," he said tautly.

"My friend Nora is the county deputy clerk of court," she reminded him. "If you get a speeding ticket, it will go through her office and she'll tell me."

His mouth twitched. "I got a small ticket."

"There's only one size," she said.

He ignored her. He reached for a roll, buttered it and took a bite. He wore the same expression that was dominating Clark's face. Fresh rolls were a treat. Their cook, Mrs. Johnston, couldn't make bread, although she was a great cook otherwise.

"There's some salad left," Winnie commented, pushing the bowl toward him.

"Where did you learn to make rolls?" he asked Keely, and seemed really interested in her answer.

"When I lived with my father, he ran a big game park. One of his temporary workers had been in the military and traveled all over the world," she recalled. "He was a gourmet chef. He taught me to make bread and French pastries when I was twelve years old."

"What sort of animals did your father have?" Boone persisted.

"The usual ones," she said, without meeting his eyes. "Giraffe, lions, monkeys and one elephant."

"African lions?"

She nodded. "And one mountain lion," she added.

No one noticed that her fingers, holding her fork, went white.

"They have mean tempers," Boone said. "One of my ranch hands had to track one down and kill it when he worked over in Arizona some years ago. It was bringing down cattle. He said it killed one of his tracking dogs before he could get a clear shot at it."

"They tend to be vicious, like most wild animals," she agreed. "They're not malicious, you know. They're just wild animals. They do what they do."

"What was your job at a wild game park?" Boone murmured.

"I fed the animals and watered them and made sure the gates were locked at night so they couldn't get out," she said.

He finished his roll and followed it with sips of black coffee. "Not a smart job for a twelve-year-old kid," he remarked.

"It was just Dad and me," she said, "except for old Barney, and he was crippled. He'd hunted a lion who became a man-killer in Africa and it fought back. He lost an arm and a foot to it."

"Did he keep the pelt when he killed it?" Boone asked.

She smiled faintly. "He made a rug out of it and slept on it every night. When he left us, he was still carrying it around."

"The rolls were good," Boone said unexpectedly.

"Thanks," Keely replied shyly.

"You could get a job cooking," he pointed out.

She frowned. "Why would I want to give up working for Bentley?"

His pleasant expression went into eclipse. "God knows."

Winnie gave her brother a piercing look. He ignored it. He studied her face and frowned. "You've been crying," he said abruptly. "Why?"

She paled. She didn't want to talk about it.

She knew it was useless to try to hide it from him. Someone would tell him, anyway.

"I almost got Kilraven killed," she confessed, putting down her fork.

"I got rattled and forgot to warn him that the man involved in a domestic dispute was armed," she said quietly. "Luckily for Kilraven, the clip was missing and the man couldn't figure out how to get the safety off."

"Luckily for the man," Clark elaborated dryly. "If he'd shot Kilraven, he'd be awaiting trial in the hospital."

"That would depend on where he shot him," Winnie replied.

"Kilraven's steel right through," Keely teased. "No bullet could get through that hard shell."

"She's right." Clark chuckled. "They'd have to hit him with a bomb to make a dent in him."

None of them noticed that Boone was sitting rigidly, with his eyes staring blindly into space. There was a look in them that any combat veteran would have recognized immediately. But nobody in his family had ever been in the military, except for himself.

Keely did notice. She knew that Boone had been in the war, that he'd been a front line, Special Forces soldier. She knew that he was reliving some terrible memory. Keely knew about those, because she had her own. Without saying a word, her eyes communicated that knowledge to the taciturn man across from her. He frowned and averted his eyes.

He finished his coffee and got to his feet. "I've got to make a few phone calls," he murmured.

"Keely made cinnamon buns," Winnie said. "Don't you want one?"

He hesitated uncharacteristically. "Bring me one in the office, with a second cup of coffee, will you?" he asked.

"Sure," Winnie said.

"No." His dark eyes slid to Keely. "You bring it," he said.

Before she could answer him, he strode out of the room.

"Well!" Clark said, surprised.

"He's in a mood to bite somebody," Winnie said solemnly. "Boone's a horror when there's no audience to slow him down. If he disapproves of you dating Clark, he'll make your life hell. I'll take his dessert to him."

"No," Clark said. He looked at Keely. "You have to stop being afraid of him and stand up to him," he told her. "This is a good time to start."

Keely became pale. She hesitated and looked to Winnie to save her.

But Winnie hesitated, too. She frowned. "Maybe Clark's right," she said after a minute. "You're afraid of Boone. He knows it, and uses it against you."

Keely bit her lower lip. "I suppose you're right. I'm a wimp."

"You're not," her best friend replied, smiling. "Here's your chance to prove it."

"With your shield or on it," Clark intoned dramatically.

Keely glowered at him. "I am not a Spartan."

"An Amazon, then," Clark compromised, and grinned. "Go get him!"

"We'll be right here," Winnie promised. "You can yell for help and we'll come running."

Keely had her doubts about that. Winnie and Clark loved Boone, but neither of them had ever been a match for his temper. If she yelled for help, they'd assume that Boone was bristling and ready for a fight, and they'd be under heavy pieces of furniture trying not to get noticed. Still, they had a point. She was almost twenty years old. It was time she learned to fight back.

She poured a cup of black coffee from the pot and took the cinnamon buns out of the oven. She put two of them on a saucer and added a napkin to her burdens. She glanced at her audience.

Clark flapped his hand at her.

Winnie mouthed, "Go on!"

She would have made a smart remark, but her heart was in her throat. It bothered her that Boone had asked her to bring dessert to him. Considering his reaction to her friendship with Clark, he had to be up to something.

She tapped nervously on the door.

"Come in," he called curtly.

She balanced the saucer holding the cinnamon buns on the cup of coffee and gingerly opened his office door, closing it with her back once she was inside.

It was a small, intimate room, with ceiling-to-floor bookcases on two walls, French windows opening onto a small patio and a fireplace with gas logs. The carpet was deep beige, the curtains echoing the earth tones. But the furniture was red leather, as if the very sedateness of the room commanded a touch of color.

Boone looked right at home in a big red leather-up-holstered chair behind his enormous solid oak desk. Over the mantel was a painting of Boone's father. It was a prophecy of what Boone would look like in old age—with silver hair and a distinguished, command-ing expression.

"You look like him," Keely mused as she put the coffee and its accompanying dessert gently in a bare spot on the paper-littered desktop. Her hands were cold and shaking and the cup rattled in the saucer. She hoped he hadn't noticed.

"Do I?" He glanced at the portrait. "He was a head shorter than I am."

"You can't see height in a painting," she pointed out.

She didn't want to argue. She started toward the door.

"Come back here," he said curtly. It wasn't a request.

It was now or never. She took a steadying breath and turned. "Winnie's waiting for me."

"Winnie?" he asked with a cynical smile. "Or Clark?"

She swallowed. Her hands began to shake again. She clasped them at her waist to still them. "Both of them," she compromised.

He leaned back in the chair, ignoring the buns and the coffee. "You and Clark have been like siblings for years. Why the sudden passion?"

"Passion?" she parroted.

"He's dating you. Didn't you notice?" he asked sar-castically.

"We went horseback riding," she pointed out. "There are a lot of things you can't do on a horse!"

His eyebrows made arches. "Really? What sort of things?"

He was baiting her. She glared at him. "You said you wanted cinnamon buns and coffee. There it is."

She started toward the door again.

Incredible, how fast he could move, she thought dazedly when he was already at the door before she reached it. She had to stop suddenly to keep from running right into his tall, powerful body.

He turned so that her back was against the door. His dark eyes narrowed as he looked down at her. She felt like a small, delicious and decidedly alarmed bunny.

He knew it. He smiled slowly and his eyes began to glitter. "You're afraid of me," he said in a slow, deep tone.

Her hands spread behind her against the door and she tried to melt into it. He was very close. She could feel the heat from his tall, powerful body, smell the clean, spicy scent of him as he leaned closer.

Now he had an advantage, and he knew it. She'd done a stupid thing, trying to run.

"You aren't afraid of Clark or Bentley, though, are you?" he persisted.

"They're nice people."

He made a short, rough sound deep in his throat. "And I'm not?"

She dragged in a ragged breath. Her eyes would only go as high as his top shirt button, which was unfastened. Thick, black curling hair peeked out from under it. She wondered if there was more across his broad, muscular chest under the fabric. He never took his shirt off, or even opened it past that top button. She was curious. Her thoughts surprised her. She hadn't thought that way about a man in a long time.

He recognized her fear for what it was. One lean hand came up to her cheek and brushed back strands of soft blond hair, the gesture sensuous enough to make her shiver. She couldn't hide her reaction to him. She didn't have the experience.

Pressing his advantage, he bent and brushed his nose lazily against hers in an odd, intimate little caress that made her breath stop in her throat.

"You smell of lilacs," he whispered. "It's a scent I never connect with any other woman."

"It's only shampoo," she blurted out. She was shy and nervous. She didn't understand what he was doing. Was this a pass? She couldn't remember a man ever treating her like this.

"Is it?" He shifted, just a little, but enough to bring his long legs in contact with hers, in an intimacy she'd never shared with a man.

Instinctively her small hands went to his chest and pushed once, jerkily.

He pulled back from her with a rough word. His eyes were blazing when he looked down at her. "Did you think I was making a pass at you?" he challenged tightly. "You'd be lucky! I don't waste my time on children."

She was shivering. His whole posture was threatening, and he looked murderous.

"Hell!" he burst out, furious at his own weakness and her cold reaction to it. She was just a little icicle.

Her lower lip trembled. He was scary like that. She still connected anger with physical violence, thanks to a friend of her father's. She cringed involuntarily when he lifted his hand.

Her blatant fear put a quick cap on his temper. He stopped for a moment, puzzled. What he was learning about her, without a word being spoken, fascinated him. She really *was* afraid of him. Not only of his ardor, but his temper, as well. She thought he was raising his hand to strike her. Which posed a worrying question. Had some man hit her in the past?

"I was going to open the door, Keely," he said in a totally different tone, the one he used with children. "I don't hit women. That's a coward's way."

She forced her eyes up to his. She couldn't tell him. She kept so many secrets. There were nightmares in her past.

He frowned. His fingers went to her cheek and drew down it with an odd tenderness. They moved to her soft mouth and traced it, and then lifted to smooth back her hair.

"What happened to you?" he asked in the softest tone he'd ever used with her.

She met his eyes evenly. "What happened to *you?*" she countered in a voice that was barely louder than a whisper to divert him.

"Me?"

She nodded. "When Clark was talking about bombs, you got all quiet and your eyes were terrible."

The expression on his face went from tender to indifferent, in seconds. He was shutting her out. "You'd better go back to the others," he said. He opened the door for her and stood aside, waiting for her to leave.

She went through it hesitantly, as though there was something unfinished between them.

"Thanks for the coffee and dessert," he said tautly, and closed the door before she could say another word.

CHAPTER FIVE

Boone came out of the office an hour later and left without saying a word. Keely and Winnie and Clark watched a new movie on pay-per-view and then shared a pizza before Clark drove Keely home. Boone still hadn't come back.

Keely didn't often get premonitions, but she had one now. It was getting dark and when they drove up at the Welsh house, two things registered at once. There were no lights on in the house and a Jacobs County Deputy Sheriff's car was sitting in the driveway.

"Oh, dear," Keely murmured fearfully, grabbing at the door handle.

Clark, concerned, got out of his car and walked with her to the deputy, who got out of his car when Keely approached.

"Sorry, ma'am," he told her with a quiet demeanor, "but we couldn't contact you by phone and there's, well, there's sort of an emergency."

"Something's happened to my mother?" Keely asked nervously.

"Not exactly." The deputy, a kind man, grimaced. "She's over at Shea's Roadhouse," he added, naming a sometimes notorious bar on the Victoria road. "She's very drunk, she's breaking bottles and she refuses to leave. We'd like you to come with us and see if you can get her to go home before we're forced to arrest her."

He, like most of Jacobs County, knew that Ella's fortunes had dwindled, even if Keely didn't. Keely likely wouldn't have enough money to bail Ella out of jail.

"I'll come right now," Keely agreed.

"I'll drive you and help you get her home," Clark said at once without being asked.

She smiled at the deputy. "Thanks."

He shrugged. "I used to have to drag my old man out of bars," he said. "It's why I went into law enforcement when I grew up. I'll follow you out there, in case there's any more trouble."

"Thanks."

"It goes with the job, but you're welcome."

WHEN THEY GOT to Shea's, Ella was screaming bloody murder and holding an empty whiskey bottle over her head while the bartender crouched in a corner.

"For goodness' sake!" Keely exclaimed, walking up to her mother with Clark and the deputy close behind. "What are you doing?"

Ella recognized her daughter and slowly put the bottle on the bar. She shivered. "Keely." In a rare show of emotion, she caught her daughter around the neck, hugged her and held on for dear life. "What will we do?" she sobbed. "Oh, Keely, what will we do?"

"About what?" Keely asked, shocked at the older woman's behavior. She was never affectionate.

"All my fault," Ella mumbled. "All my fault. If I'd told what I knew…"

Before she could elaborate on that cryptic remark, she began to collapse.

"Help!" Keely called.

The deputy and Clark got on both sides of the older woman and held her up.

"Do you want to press charges?" the deputy asked the bartender.

The man looked torn. But Keely's face decided him. "Not if she'll agree to pay for the damages."

"Of course we will," Keely replied, unaware of her mother's financial status.

"Where in the world is Tiny?" the deputy asked the bartender, because their bouncer usually prevented trouble like this.

"He's having knee replacement surgery," he confided. "One of our more volatile customers kicked him in the leg and put him out of commission. We usually have a relief bouncer, but we can't find one. Nobody except Tiny wants the job."

"If you get in trouble, all you have to do is call us," the deputy told him.

"I know that. Thanks." The bartender hesitated, frowning, as if he wanted to say more, but he glanced worriedly at Keely.

The deputy was a veteran of law enforcement. He knew the man wanted to tell him something. "I'll help them get Mrs. Welsh to the car, then I'll come back and get a list of the damages," he promised, and saw the bartender relax a little.

"Okay," he said.

KEELY FOLLOWED THE deputy and Clark, with her mother, out to Clark's car.

"Do you have a blanket or something, in case she gets sick?" Keely asked worriedly. It would be terrible if her mother threw up in that luxurious backseat.

Clark popped the trunk lid and pulled out a big comforter, throwing it over the backseat. "I keep it in case

I have to carry Bailey somewhere," he confessed. "He doesn't like to ride in the car."

They got Ella down on the seat and closed the door. After a couple of words with the deputy, they went back to the Welsh place and bundled Ella into the house and onto her bed. Keely was careful to use her right arm in the process. The left one was too weak and fragile for lifting.

"It's like deadweight," Clark commented when they'd placed her.

"She usually is," Keely replied, breathless. She frowned at the prone sight of her mother, who was still wearing slacks and a blouse and sweater and shoes. She'd take those off later, when Clark left. "I just wonder what set her off? She doesn't ever go to bars except with Carly, and she doesn't usually get this drunk even then."

"No telling," Clark said. "Well, I'll get home," he added, smiling. "Thanks for everything, Keely."

She smiled. "Thank you."

"I'll call you."

She waved as he drove away. It was already dark. She went back inside, still puzzled about Ella's condition.

BUT THERE WERE more puzzles to come. She'd tugged off her mother's shoes and thrown a coverlet over her. Undressing an unconscious person was heavy work and Keely's shoulder was already aching.

She was watching the news on their small color TV while doing a load of clothes when there was a knock at the door.

Most Saturday nights, there was an emergency at work and she was called in to assist. But the phone hadn't rung. There weren't even any messages, except for an odd call with nothing but static and then a click. She wondered if Bentley had driven over to collect her for an emergency.

When she opened the door, it was another surprise. Sheriff Hayes Carson was standing on her front porch. He wasn't smiling.

"Hi, Keely," he said. "Mind if I come in?"

"Of course not." She held the door wide so that he could enter. He was a head taller than Keely, with brown-streaked blond hair that had a stubborn wave right over his left eyebrow. He had dark eyes that seemed to see right through people. In his mid-thirties, he was still a confirmed bachelor, and considered quite a catch. But Keely knew he hadn't come calling in the middle of the night because he found her irresistible.

She went to turn the television down, and motioned him into a chair. She perched on the edge of the sofa.

"If it's about the bar tonight," she began worriedly.

"No," he said gently. "Not quite. Keely, have you heard from your father lately?"

She was stunned. It wasn't the question she'd anticipated. "No," she stammered. "I haven't heard a word from him since he dropped me off here when I was about thirteen," she added. "Why?"

He seemed to be considering his options. He leaned forward. "You knew he'd fallen into some bad company before you left?"

"Yes," she said, and shuddered. "One of his new friends slapped me around and left bruises," she recalled. She'd never told that to anyone else. "I think it was the main reason he brought me back to my mother."

Hayes's sensuous mouth made a thin line. "Pity he

wasn't living in Jacobs County at the time," he muttered.

Keely knew what he meant. She'd heard that Hayes was hell on woman-beaters. "It is, isn't it?" she agreed. "Is my father in some sort of trouble?"

"We think he needs money. He may get in touch with you or your mother. This is important, Keely. If he does, you need to call me right away." He was solemn as he spoke. "You could both be in terrible danger."

"From my own father?" she asked, agape.

He was hesitant. "He's not the father you remember. Not anymore."

He never had been the father she'd wanted, she recalled, even if she'd tried to give him the love a father was due from his daughter. She could remember times when she was sick and her father left her alone, going out at odd hours and staying gone, sometimes for two days at a time, while Keely and the hired help kept the game park going. At the last, his drinking and his violent friends worried Keely more than she'd ever admitted.

"Is he mixed up in something illegal, Sheriff Carson?" she asked worriedly.

His face was a closed book, revealing nothing. "He's got friends who are," he said, sharing with a little of the truth. "They're pushing him for money that he doesn't have, and they want it very badly. We think he may have tried to contact your mother."

"Why would you think that?" she asked slowly.

He sighed. "The bartender at Shea's said she was yelling that her husband was going to kill her if she didn't buy him off, and she was broke."

Her heart skipped. "Broke? She said she was

broke?" she exclaimed. "But she owns property, she gets rent—"

He hated being the one who had to tell her this. He ground his teeth. "She's sold all the property, Keely, probably to pay her bar bills," he said heavily. "One of the Realtors who was at the bar at the time mentioned it to me. There's nothing left. She's probably drained her savings, as well."

Keely felt sick. She sank down into the sofa and felt wounded all over again. No wonder Ella didn't want her to leave. Her mother couldn't afford to hire someone to replace her for domestic work.

"I'm sorry," Hayes said genuinely.

"No, it's all right," she replied, forcing a smile. "I did wonder. She let things slip from time to time." Her green eyes were troubled. Her own small salary barely allowed her to own an ancient used car and buy gas to get to work, much less pay for utilities and upkeep. What Hayes had told her was terrifying. "What do you want me to do?" she asked, surmising why he'd come.

"I want you to tell me if you hear anything from or about your father," he said gently. "There's a lot at stake here. I wish I could tell you what I know, but I can't."

Keely recalled that her father's friend had a police record. He'd bragged when he slapped her that he'd killed a woman for less than Keely had done, talking back to him.

She frowned. "Just before I came to Jacobsville," she recalled, "Dad's friend, Jock, said he'd killed a woman."

"Jock?" He drew out a PDA and pulled up a screen. "Jock Hardin?"

Her heart flipped. "Yes. He was the one who hit me."

He frowned. "Why did he hit you?"

She drew in a long breath. "I burned the rolls."

Hayes cursed roundly and then apologized. He leaned forward and stared right into her eyes. "Did he do anything more than hit you?" he asked.

"He wanted to." She couldn't say more. Jock had gotten her shirt halfway off and then pushed her away, revolted. Her pride wouldn't let her admit that to Hayes.

"He was prevented?"

She nodded. Her green eyes looked into his. "Do you know where he is? I mean, he isn't going to come here and make trouble for Mama and me, is he?"

"I don't know, Keely. He's on the run from a new charge, one he shares with your father. Don't ask. I can't tell you," he added when she started to speak. "Suffice it to say that we can put him away for life if we can catch him."

"And my father?" she prodded gently.

He bit his full lower lip. "He'll probably get the same sentence. I'm sorry. He's done some bad things since he left you here. Some very bad things. People have died."

Her heart sank right into her shoes. She remembered her father laughing, buying her a puppy and taking her around with him in the game park, teasing her about her affection for the big mountain lion, Hilton. He hadn't been a bad man in those days, and he'd been affectionate with her, and always kind. The man she remembered at the last had been very different, with violent mood swings. Jock had taken over his life. And Keely's. She'd realized, belatedly, that her father had probably saved her life by bringing her back to Jacobsville.

"He wasn't a bad man when we had the game park," she told Hayes. "He had a nice girlfriend who took me to church and he never teased me about it. She was also our bookkeeper. In those days, he was religious, in his own way. He loved the animals. They loved him, too. He could walk right in with the tiger and the mountain lion and pet them." She laughed, remembering. "They purred…" Her face fell. "What if Jock comes here?" she asked, and she was really afraid. The man had terrified her for weeks. Her father had been so far out of reality that he hadn't even intervened.

Hayes's face hardened. "I'll lock him up so tight he'll never get out," he promised.

She relaxed a little. "He was vicious to me."

"You were lucky he didn't kill you."

She nodded.

"We'll all keep a watch on you," he promised, rising to his feet. "I've worked it out with my deputies, and the Jacobsville police will increase patrols by your office at night when you work late. Call dispatch when you start home and let them know you're on the road. We'll watch your back."

"I will. Thanks, Sheriff Hayes," she added when they were at the front door.

"I'm sorry about the way things worked out for your father," he told her abruptly. "I know how it is. My only brother was an addict. He died of an overdose."

She did know. Everybody did. "I'm sorry, for you, too."

"Keep your doors locked."

"I will."

"Good night."

"Good night."

She watched him drive away. Then she locked the door and sat down, heavily, giving way to tears.

HER MOTHER SOBERED up the next day and became very quiet. Keely cooked and cleaned, equally silent. Neither of them mentioned the financial situation. Her mother was very watchful and she locked doors. But when Keely asked why, she would not reply.

Carly came over the next Friday night to take Ella out bar crawling, but Ella was sober and didn't want to go.

They were in the next room, talking softly, but Keely was listening and could hear them above the soft noise of the dishwasher.

"Are you going to tell Keely?" Carly was asking.

"I suppose I'll have to," Ella said tautly. "I hoped it would never come to this," she added brokenly. "I thought it was all over. I prayed he'd die, that he'd stay away forever."

"I know how you feel," Carly said. "But it's too late for that. You talked to the sheriff, didn't you?"

"Yes. I told him everything I know. He said he'd told Keely that she and I might be in danger and that she had to tell him if she heard from her father." She hesitated. "She loved her father. I know she still does, in spite of everything. She might not tell anybody if he called."

"He isn't the man she loved," Carly said tightly. "He'd kill her in a heartbeat if she got in his way. And that Jock man, he'd kill anybody without a reason. He's heartless."

"Yes," Ella said, and shuddered. "He came with Brent to bring Keely here. He wouldn't let Brent out of his sight for a second, and they didn't stay long."

"I remember," Carly replied. "He was the scariest man I ever met. He made my skin crawl when he looked at me."

"They can't come back here," Ella said forcefully.

"I don't care how much trouble they're in. I can't give them money I don't have!" She coughed. "He wanted me to sell the house!"

"It's all you've got left, you can't do that!"

"I'm not going to," Ella said. "But he threatened—"

"You told Sheriff Carson. They'll all watch out for Keely."

Keely felt her heart stop. Had one of the men threatened her? Surely not her father!

"Jock was in the military," Ella said dully. "Brent said he'd been in some top secret pacification program. He knows how to torture people and he likes it. Brent said he still had a yen for Keely, despite what happened to her."

"What did he mean, what happened to her?" Carly wondered aloud.

"I don't know. He wouldn't tell me." There was a long pause. "So many secrets. I've kept them from Keely and Brent's kept them from me. Apparently Keely's keeping some of her own. So many secrets. Oh God, I need a drink!"

"We can't go out," Carly said at once. "Not now."

"I had a little whiskey left," Ella said wistfully. "I don't know where it is."

"You're better off without it," Carly said. "You have to think of the consequences. Now, of all times, you need to think clearly!"

There was another pause. "Yes. I suppose I do."

Keely, her head full of what they were saying, felt numb. She didn't say a word. She only smiled at Carly when she left, and avoided being alone with her mother, who was as quiet as a church. It was so uncharacteristic that Keely felt chilled, as if she'd stepped over her own grave.

SHE DID TRY, once, to get her mother to open up about her father. Ella changed the subject and went to watch the news on television. She'd started doing that every day, as if she were waiting for some story to break. It made Keely nervous.

Clark came the next night, Saturday, to get her for one of their dates, and he was glum when they drove away from her mother's house.

"What's wrong with you?" Keely asked.

He glanced at her. "I wanted to drive us over to San Antonio for dinner and to take in a play. Boone said we couldn't go." He frowned, glancing at her. "He says you're in some sort of trouble, and you aren't supposed to go out of the county."

Her breath stopped in her throat. How had Boone known? What did he know? Then she remembered. Hayes Carson was his best friend. They went out together every week to play poker with Garon Grier and Jon Blackhawk, Officer Kilraven's half brother.

"What's going on, Keely?" Clark asked. "What does Boone know that I don't?"

She ground her teeth together. She didn't want to talk about it, but it would be nice to get some of her worries off her chest. "My father is in some sort of trouble and Sheriff Carson thinks Mama and I might be in danger. He wants money. Apparently he called my mother and threatened her. She won't tell me what he said."

"Good Lord!" Clark exclaimed. He glanced in the rearview mirror. "Would that have anything to do with why we're being followed?"

"Followed?"

"Yes. By a sheriff's car when I picked you up, and

by a Jacobsville police car now that we're here in town."

Keely remembered what Hayes had told her. She clutched her purse in her lap. "Sheriff Carson said they'd look out for me," she confessed. "They think I might be in danger if I go out at night."

"With me?"

"You could be in the line of fire, too, Clark," she said, just realizing it. "Maybe we should stop seeing each other...."

"No." His voice was firm. "I'm not giving up Nellie. This is a good plan. We'll work around your father. After all, a threat is just a threat. How is he going to hurt you when we're surrounded by uniforms?" he asked, grinning.

"I don't know."

"We'll be perfectly safe," he said. "When Boone said I couldn't take you to San Antonio, I called Nellie and had her drive down here. I'll leave you at the local library. It stays open until nine o'clock. That will give me a little time with her, if you're game. You'll be safe at the library," he added.

She knew that. The police would be able to watch her through the many glass windows if she sat at a table. "Okay," she agreed.

He grinned at her. "You're the nicest girl I know."

"Thanks, Clark."

"I mean it." He hesitated. "You don't think your own father would really hurt you?" he added, worried.

"Of course not," she lied.

"That makes me feel better."

"Will Nellie be safe, driving down here from San Antonio and back, alone at night?" she added, and she was concerned.

"She drives one of those huge SUVs," he said. "A tank couldn't dent it. And she has a cell phone that I pay for. She can call for help if she has to."

"She seems very nice," she replied.

"She's the best thing that's ever happened to me," he murmured, smiling wistfully. "She's just dynamite in bed, and when I give her presents, she embarrasses me with the gratitude. The diamond earrings made her cry."

She wondered if Clark realized what he was admitting. The woman was trading sex for expensive gifts, and he thought it was love. She didn't. She'd seen the greed in Nellie's eyes when Clark had talked to her at the restaurant. Men were so dim, she thought sadly. Even Boone, going out with that traitorous woman who'd left him in the lurch when he was wounded overseas. He'd taken her back in a heartbeat.

"You're very quiet," Clark remarked. "Sorry. I shouldn't have made that remark about Nellie being hot. I guess you think of sex outside marriage as a sin."

"I do," she confessed.

"Our dad never thought of it like that," he returned. "He enjoyed women. He never remarried, but he sure played the field. Winnie, though, didn't approve of his lifestyle. She's a lot like you." He glanced at her. "She didn't like Nellie at all." He grimaced. "I guess Nellie doesn't appeal to women," he added. "She has a lot of trouble at work. Her coworkers think she gets too many tips. They say she plays on men's vanity just so they'll leave her big tips. Ridiculous!"

It wasn't, but Keely wasn't going to say so. With any luck, when Clark spent enough time with his pretty girlfriend, he'd learn the truth for himself. If Winnie didn't like the girl, it meant something. Winnie loved people, and she wasn't possessive about her brothers.

"You don't mind staying here alone?" he asked when he pulled up in front of the library. He'd called Nellie on the way there.

She smiled. "Of course not. Go have fun."

He bent and kissed her on the cheek. "You're sweet. I'll make it up to you. How about some emerald earrings? I know you love emeralds…"

She frowned. "I don't want anything from you, Clark," she said, puzzled. "You're my friend!"

He looked as if she'd knocked him in the head. "But you love emeralds," he persisted.

She reached up and kissed his cheek. "If I want any, I'll buy them. One day," she added, laughing. "Isn't that Nellie?" she asked, indicating a big green SUV that had just pulled up next to them in the parking lot. The woman inside was openly glaring at them.

"Uh-oh." Clark laughed. "She saw you kiss me. She's terribly jealous. I'll have to sweeten her up." He pulled a jeweler's box out of his pocket, opened it and showed it to Keely. It was a diamond necklace. A real, glittery, very expensive diamond necklace. "I asked her what she'd really like, and she said one of these. Think she'll like it?"

Keely had to bite her tongue. "Sure!"

He closed the box. "It will put her in a good mood." He chuckled. "I'll be back in a little while."

"Okay."

She got out of the car. Nellie came around the SUV, locking it with her remote. She gave Keely, who was wearing corduroy slacks with a cotton blouse and Berber coat, a superior sort of look. Nellie was wearing a designer dress and expensive shoes with a coat that would cost Keely a year's salary—probably another gift from Clark. She looked expensive and greedy and very jealous.

"Why did you kiss him?" she asked Keely, keeping her back to Clark. "I don't want you touching him, do you hear? He's all mine."

"I noticed," Keely said, indicating the coat and dress. "Bought and paid for?"

"How dare you!" Nellie snapped.

Keely smiled sweetly. "One day he'll get a look at this side of you," she whispered. "And you'll be out on your ear."

"Think I care?" Nellie drawled. "There's always another one, a richer one. Besides, men are stupid."

She bypassed Keely and went rushing into Clark's outstretched arms. "Oh, darling, I missed you so!" she exclaimed, and kissed him hungrily. Clark was eating it up.

Keely shook her head. She walked into the library, thinking that P. T. Barnum was right. A sucker actually was born every minute. She wished she could tell Clark the truth. A man that much in love wouldn't hear her, or believe her, and it would ruin their friendship. But worse was to come, she knew. She wished she and Boone weren't enemies, so she could tell him what was going on. She knew that she was going to end up, inevitably, right in the middle of all the trouble.

CHAPTER SIX

THE LIBRARY WAS one of Keely's favorite places. She didn't get much time to spend there, because she was usually on call on the weekends. But this weekend, the senior vet tech had unexpectedly offered to take Keely's place. Her husband was in the military, and his unit had been called up for overseas deployment. She was blue about it and didn't want to spend so much time alone. Keely sympathized with her, but was glad to have the time off. Or she had been, until her life suddenly became complicated.

She was reading a thick biology text on canine anatomy when a shadow fell over her. She looked up, straight into Boone Sinclair's dark eyes. Her heart raced. She fumbled with the book and it fell onto the floor.

He picked it up and, glancing at the title with an odd smile, put it back on the table. He pulled up a chair and sat down next to her. Here, in the reading area, she was alone. The librarian was in the back cataloging, so they had the room to themselves.

"I thought you and Clark had a date," he murmured suspiciously.

She couldn't think. He was leaning toward her, and she could smell the minty scent of his breath on her face. She bit her lower lip nervously.

"I wanted to look up something," she stammered

inventively. She flushed. She wasn't good at lying. "He went to get gas. He's coming back for me." She forced a glare. "We were going up to San Antonio to the theater when you told him we couldn't go."

"San Antonio is too big and we don't know many police officers there," he said, unexpectedly somber. "You don't need to be out of sight of the police. It's easier to watch you here."

"You've been talking to Sheriff Hayes," she accused.

He nodded. "Hayes is pretty laid-back most of the time. When he worries, there's good reason." His eyes narrowed on hers. "Your mother hasn't been seen out at Shea's for a week?" It was a question.

She needed so desperately to talk to someone. Her face was drawn with worry. Clark was sweet, but he was too concerned with Nellie to pay more than a little attention to Keely's problems. Not that he didn't care about her. He just cared more about Nellie.

Incredibly Boone's big hand smoothed over hers where it lay on the book cover. He linked his warm, strong fingers into hers. "Talk to me," he said quietly.

She actually shivered. It had been years since a man had touched her. Not even a man, really, just a boy she dated. She hadn't been held, kissed, caressed. She was a woman with a woman's feelings, and she couldn't, didn't dare, indulge them.

Boone knew more about women than she realized. He understood her reaction to him, and was puzzled by it. "For a woman who's getting regular sex, you sure don't act as if your needs are being met," he commented.

She went as red as the book cover and her hand jerked under his.

He smiled, but not in a mean way. His fingers contracted more. "Tell me what's really going on, Keely."

His hand was comforting. She didn't fight the firm, caressing clasp. It felt so good. She wanted to climb into his lap and put her head on his shoulder and cry her eyes out. She wanted comfort, just a little comfort. But this wasn't the man, or the place or the time.

She took a deep breath. "Something's going on about my father," she confessed in a hushed tone. "I don't know what. Nobody will tell me anything. He's mixed up in something bad, and he has this friend…" Her soft features contracted and her eyes were full of pain at the memory.

"This friend," he prompted, squeezing her hand. He was very intent.

"Jock." The name tasted like poison in her mouth. "My mother thinks he has something to do with whatever's going on. I overheard her talking to Carly. She won't tell me anything."

"This man, Jock," he persisted. "You look frightened when you say his name."

"He…hit me," she confessed, fascinated by the expression on his face. "I was just barely thirteen. He'd been watching me while I was cooking. He made me nervous. He'd been in prison. He said he'd killed a woman. I let the biscuits burn." She bit her lip again. "He hit me so hard he knocked me down. My father heard him yelling and came into the kitchen and managed to get Jock out of the room." She wrapped her arms around her chest, cold with the memory. "It was just after that when Dad brought me back here to live with Mama."

"Good God." Boone's eyes were soft and quiet with sympathy. "No wonder you're uncomfortable around men." He was remembering. His jaw tautened. "That's why you were afraid of me in my office."

"I don't really know you," she confessed apologetically. "And you don't like me," she added uneasily. "You don't like me being friends with Winnie and you don't like me going around with Clark."

"No, I don't," he replied honestly. But he looked troubled.

"I understand," she said unexpectedly. "You know that I'm poor and you think I use Winnie and Clark..."

"The hell I do!" He lowered his voice quickly, looking around to make sure he hadn't drawn the attention of the librarian. He looked back at Keely, scowling. "You don't use people," he bit off. "You work like a soldier for your paycheck. Unpaid overtime, trips out to old Mrs. McKinnon's place to give her dog its diabetic injections because she can't do it, walking dogs at the shelter on weekends so the staff can handle adoptions..." He stopped, as if he hadn't wanted her to know that he was aware of her activities.

"Mrs. McKinnon loves her dog," she replied. "Maggie handles the shelter on Saturdays and feeds and waters the animals on Sunday. There's this tiny little budget. She already spends twice the hours she gets paid for to do all that. I just help a little."

His dark, quiet eyes studied her soft, oval face in its frame of thick blond hair, down to her pretty bow mouth. She wasn't a beauty, but she radiated a sort of loveliness that most women didn't.

"It's a pity," he said, almost to himself, "that you aren't older."

"I'll be twenty in December," she said, misunderstanding.

"Twenty whole years old." He looked down at her

hand. It was a useful hand, not an elegant one. Short nails, immaculately kept, no polish. No jewelry on those fingers, either. He frowned. "No rings?" he asked. He looked up at her ears where her hair was pushed back. "No earrings?"

She flushed. "I have little silver studs, but I forgot to put them on...."

"Clark hasn't given you anything?" he persisted. "He walked out tonight with a huge jewelry case."

"Oh, that was for—" She stopped at once, horrified.

His eyebrows arched and the corner of his mouth tugged up. "Not for you?"

She swallowed hard. "I don't like jewelry."

"Liar."

She flushed. "I don't have to be paid to give a man attention," she said curtly, and then realized how that sounded, and flushed even more. "I mean, I don't want expensive things from Clark."

He cocked his head to one side and watched her like a hawk. "In the past few weeks, he's gone through half the inventory of a jewelry store. I see the receipts, Keely, even if I don't pay the bills. I have an accountant to do that."

She was in a quandary now. She couldn't admit that Clark hadn't given that expensive jewelry to her, and if she denied it, she'd only get him in trouble.

"Your car is a piece of junk," he persisted. His practiced eye swept over the blouse and slacks she was wearing, the coat hung over the back of the chair beside her. "You've worn that same outfit to the house half a dozen times. You don't drive unless you have to, so you can save on gas money. And you won't let Clark give you a pair of earrings?"

Her teeth clamped down. She wasn't telling him anything else. She tugged at her hand.

He wouldn't let it go. "That waitress he brought to the house," he said softly, "was looking around between every bite, cataloging paintings and silver and furniture and putting mental price tags on the rugs and the chandelier."

She was horrified that she might react to that statement. Her eyes were almost bulging.

He pursed his lips and his dark eyes twinkled. "Clark thinks he's putting one over on me," he said in a hushed, soft tone. "He doesn't realize that Misty's father has a private detective agency that I can hire when I need to. Apparently, Nellie doesn't realize it, either, or she'd be more careful about going with Clark to motels."

She made a soft exclamation and her horror showed.

"You don't use people," he continued. "But Clark does. He's using you. And you're letting him."

"You don't know that," she protested weakly.

"I'm only surprised that your boss is so forgiving about it," he added, and his expression hardened. "Isn't he the jealous type?"

She sank down into her chair. She felt limp. She'd failed Clark. He'd never forgive her. "Dr. Rydel is thirty-two, Boone," she said gently, and didn't notice the reaction when she spoke his name. His eyes had flashed.

"Thirty-two." He parroted the words. He'd gone blank for an instant.

"Thirty-two," she repeated, looking up. "I'm nineteen. Even if I were a femme fatale, I'd have my work cut out. Dr. Rydel hates women. He only likes me because he thinks of me as a child. Like you do," she added in a different tone.

His eyes were unreadable. "There are times," he said softly, "when you seem older than you are." He frowned slightly. "Why don't you date, Keely?" he asked suddenly.

She was shocked by the question. "I…my job takes up so much time…" She'd walked right into the trap. She glared at him. "I date Clark," she said doggedly.

"Clark loves you," he replied unexpectedly. "Like a sister," he added almost at once. "He never touches you. He doesn't light up when you walk into a room. His hands don't shake when you're close to him. That doesn't add up to a romance."

What he was describing was exactly what happened with Keely when she saw Boone. She didn't dare admit it, of course. What had he been saying about Clark?

"When he brought the waitress home with him," he continued, "he spilled coffee all over the linen tablecloth trying to pour her a second cup. He actually fell out of his chair when he touched her hands as she passed him the salad bowl."

She grimaced.

"And I don't need a declaration to tell me who got that diamond necklace. It sure as hell wasn't you."

"You won't tell him?" she asked worriedly. "He's my friend, he and Winnie. I don't have many. I gave my word…"

His eyes glittered. "It bothers me that you didn't mind helping him get around me."

Her eyes were apologetic. "He said she was the most important thing in the world to him and that he'd die if he had to give her up. He thought it would make you so angry, seeing me with him, that you wouldn't think about Nellie."

He looked down at her hand. He caressed the back of it absently with his fingers. He didn't want to admit how angry it *had* made him. Uncharacteristically angry. Keely was a child. He couldn't afford to become involved with her. Just the same, he didn't want Clark taking advantage of her. Odd, how relieved he felt that she wasn't sleeping with Bentley Rydel. Her mother had been lying to him, trying to hurt him because he rejected her.

"Your mother is a piece of work," he muttered angrily.

She was puzzled, not having been privy to his complicated thoughts. "Why do you say that?"

He looked up. "What do you think of Nellie?" he asked, changing the subject.

She hesitated.

"Tell me," he prodded.

She sighed and met his eyes. "I think she's the worst sort of opportunist," she confessed. "She adds up presents and gives sex in return. Clark thinks that's love," she added cynically.

"You don't."

Her eyes were old. "Living with my father taught me some things. He was almost broke when he lost the game park because this woman played up to him and pretended to be awed at the way he handled the animals. She stroked his vanity and he bought her expensive things. Then there was a lawsuit, and we had absolutely nothing. Meanwhile," she added, "there was this sweet woman who kept the books for us, who took me to church and dated my father. She was shy and not beautiful, but he dropped her as soon as the other woman came along."

"What happened?"

"When he went bankrupt, his flashy girlfriend was suddenly interested in a local Realtor who'd just inherited a lot of property from his late father."

"I see."

"Clark is a sweet man," she said quietly. "He deserves better."

He leaned back, finally letting go of her hand. His eyes narrowed on her face. "She works for a living. So do you. I expected you to take her side."

"She's a snake," she returned. "And she doesn't exactly work that hard for a normal living. Her coworkers say she plays up to her male customers to get big tips. Clark told me. He thinks they're jealous because she's pretty."

He had a faraway look. "Beauty is subjective," he said oddly. "It isn't always manifested in surface details."

She smiled. Then she laughed. "Maybe I'm subjectively beautiful and nobody noticed," she said.

He realized, belatedly, that she'd made a joke. He laughed softly.

She looked around. The librarian was starting to close doors and turn out lights. She bit her lip. Clark was nowhere in sight.

"I don't think they'll let you stay the night," he pointed out.

She got up, grimacing. She picked up her coat and her purse. "At least there's a bench out front. I told Clark they closed at nine."

He got up, too, towering over her. "You haven't

learned yet that intimacy makes people lose track of time."

She couldn't meet his eyes. He sounded very worldly. She put her purse down and gingerly eased her left arm into the coat. He was behind her at once, easing the rest of the garment over her other arm and onto her shoulder.

"What happened to your arm?" he asked.

She felt his warm hands on her shoulders, the warm strength of his body behind her. She wanted to lean back and have him hold her. Insane thoughts.

"An accident," she said after a minute. "Nothing terrible," she lied. "But it left a weakness in that arm. I can't lift much."

There was a pause. His usually impassive face had a ragged look. "I have a similar problem with one of my legs," he said hesitantly. "If I overdo, I limp."

She turned and looked up at him. She'd noticed that. She'd never expected him to admit it to his enemy. "You were hurt overseas worse than you told Winnie and Clark," she said with keen insight. "Worse than you've told anyone. Except maybe Sheriff Carson."

His jaw firmed. "You see too much."

"In my own way, I've been through the wars, too," she replied quietly. "Scars don't go away, even if wounds heal. And they destroy people."

She wasn't looking at him as she said it. Her eyes had the same expression as his did. It was a moment of shared tragedy, shared pain. He moved a step closer to her. She looked up at him expectantly. It was as if the wall between them had lowered just a little, letting in new light. But even as he started to speak, a car drove up outside.

Boone tugged Keely back into the shadows of a

row of books. Outside the tinted glass windows, they saw Clark glance furtively at Boone's big Jaguar sitting next to Nellie's SUV. He bundled her out of his car and into the SUV and waved her out of the parking lot. He looked hunted. He stood at the front bumper of his car, looking toward the library and hesitating.

"The jig's up," Keely told Boone with twinkling eyes.

"No, it isn't. Come here." He took her hand and tugged her farther down the row of books, out of sight of the glass windows. "I hope you're a good actress."

"Excuse me?"

They heard the door open. Clark whispered something to the librarian. There was a returned whisper and muffled footsteps on carpet coming closer.

Boone let go of Keely's hand. "You won't tell me a damned thing," he said in a low voice, but one that carried at least to the end of the aisle. "I want to know where Clark is, why he isn't here with you." He nodded at her meaningfully.

She caught on at once. "I told you, he just went to get gas—"

Clark turned into the aisle where they were. His look of fear eclipsed when he overheard what Keely said. He seemed to relax.

"I'm back," he told her. "In the nick of time." He joined them and grinned at his brother. "What are you doing here?"

"I came in to get a book and found Keely," Boone muttered. "Why didn't you take her with you to get gas?" he asked suspiciously.

"I told him that I wanted to check out that canine anatomy book I was telling you about," she said to Clark.

"Oh. Right," he agreed quickly.

Boone gave them both a glare as the light overhead went out. "Now I won't have time to check on mine, no thanks to both of you." He turned on his heel and stalked out, pausing only long enough to speak to the librarian.

Keely rushed back to grab her own book and take it to the desk, telling the harassed librarian that she'd be back on Monday to check it out and apologizing for keeping her late.

The librarian smiled and said it was all right, but she followed them right out the door, locking up behind her.

"That was close!" Clark exclaimed when they were in the car heading back toward Keely's house. "How long had he been there?"

"Just a couple of minutes," she lied. "I thought we were in big trouble!"

"We would have been if he'd seen Nellie get out of my car and into hers," he said. "What a break that he was talking to you down an aisle instead of in front of the window!"

"Yes, wasn't it?" she agreed.

"I'll have to plan better next time," he said, almost to himself.

"Did she like the necklace?"

He chuckled. "She loved it! I ordered her a Gucci suit to go with it and had it sent to her apartment," he added. "She was very grateful."

She could imagine the form that gratitude took, but she wasn't saying anything. She was still wondering what Boone expected her to do now. She couldn't bear to tell Clark she'd sold him out. Not that she had, really. Boone wasn't stupid. Clark underestimated him, as usual. It was par for the course that Boone was always three steps ahead of everybody else.

"Nellie really is beautiful," she commented, for something to say.

"Absolutely." He grinned at Keely. "You didn't have any trouble before Boone showed up?"

"None at all. I was fine."

"I'll have to plan better next time," he repeated. "Boone's smart. I have to work hard to keep him in the dark."

"I'm sure you'll come up with something," she replied.

"We will," he replied. "We're in this together, remember."

This was likely to end in despair for Clark, either way, and she hated having agreed to being a party to it. Especially now that Boone was clued in. She wondered if she should tell Clark the truth. Probably she should, but she was wary of Boone's temper if he found out. She felt stifled.

"Don't look so worried," he said gently. "Everything will work out. Really it will."

"Did you know that Misty's father had a private detective agency in San Antonio?" she asked abruptly, and then could have bitten her tongue for the slip.

"Some agency," Clark muttered. "I had them check out a cowboy for us when we were hiring on a new horse wrangler. He had a rap sheet and their brilliant staff didn't find a thing."

She stared at him. "How did you find that out if they didn't tell you?"

"Boone found it out," he said. "He was suspicious of something the man did, so he asked Hayes to look into the man's background. He had a prior for burglary. A conviction, no less, and he'd served time. Boone fired him the same day."

"I thought even a bad detective could find out something like that," she replied.

He frowned. "That's what I thought. I mentioned it to Boone, too. He said that they hired a man with false credentials, but found it out only after they assigned him our background check. They thanked us for flushing him out."

She was curious about that. It seemed a little easily explained. But they were already pulling up in front of her house, and there was no more time for questions.

When Clark pulled up at the porch, Ella was standing just outside the screen door in just her slip with a full glass of whiskey.

"So there you are!" she raged as Keely opened her door. "Where have you been?"

"Why don't you come back home with me?" Clark suggested quickly, leaning over the passenger seat to look out at her.

Even her mother in that shape was preferable to being in the same house with Boone after their awkward conversation. She needed time to think over what he'd said. Not to mention her disquiet at having to listen to another long recital of Nellie's assets, which had lasted all the way home. She forced a smile. "I can handle her," she told him gently. "It's okay."

"If you say so." He sounded dubious. "You never did say what happened in Boone's office the last time you were at the house. We heard him close the door."

"He was just warning me off you," she prevaricated, and smiled again. "It didn't work."

He laughed, relieved. "Thank God. I couldn't handle having all my plans go south before we even get started good, and this is just the beginning for me and Nellie! You're positive you want to stay?" He gestured toward her mother.

She nodded. "Thanks for the ride. I'll see you soon."

"Sure. Take care." Keely closed the passenger door. He waved to her mother, who ignored him, almost dancing in her impatience to talk to her daughter. He drove away with a wave.

"What's wrong?" Keely asked when she got onto the porch, because this wasn't a simple case of a few drinks too many. Her mother's face was stark-white and she was visibly frightened.

Ella bit her lip. "Your father called again."

"Again? Where is he?" she asked. "Is he coming here?"

"I don't know." She took a big sip of her drink.

"What did he want?" Keely persisted.

She turned and looked at her daughter with wide, frightened eyes. The hand holding the drink was shaking. "He...he didn't say."

"Why did he call, then?"

Ella looked around nervously. "Let's go inside."

They did, and Ella locked the door. She was rattled, all right. She couldn't even find the right light switch to turn off the porch light.

"I'll get it," Keely volunteered.

Ella stood watching her, biting her lower lip. She was so pale that her skin looked like milk.

Keely stood quietly, waiting for the older woman to speak.

CHAPTER SEVEN

"I DON'T KNOW where to start," Ella said hesitantly. "I know your father didn't tell you anything about what happened here before he left with you."

"Nobody ever tells me anything," Keely replied bitterly. "I know that Dad's mixed up in something, that the police are interested in him for whatever it is and that Jock is involved somehow." She straightened. "And I know that you're broke and Dad is threatening you for money."

Ella bit her lower lip hard enough to draw blood. "You couldn't know that. Who told you that?" she demanded.

"Is it true?" Keely prevaricated.

Ella looked around wildly and brushed her untidy hair back from her thin face.

Keely moved forward a step. "Is it true?" she repeated softly.

Ella took a deep breath. For once, she really looked her age. "Yes," she said. "I thought the money would never run out. There was so much of it. Your grandparents invested in land when it was cheap. As the town grew, more people needed land, so they started renting it out for businesses. When they died, I continued the practice, raising the rents as the land prices increased."

"What happened?" Keely prodded.

Ella laughed hollowly. "I got greedy. My parents

would never buy me designer clothes or even a good car. They made me pay my own way, from the day I started working. They wanted me to go to college, but I thought I was smart enough. Your father thought I'd get all that money the minute I married, so he married me. But it didn't work out that way." She drew in a long breath, her eyes with a faraway look. "All I had was an allowance. Brent and I bought expensive cars and diamonds and ate in the best restaurants and took long trips overseas. We ran up a fortune in bills. My parents paid it, then they stopped my checks." She laughed again as she glanced at her daughter. "Brent got used to living high. He couldn't go back to wages. He found a way to make a lot of money quick." Her face tautened. "You were far too young to understand what was going on. My parents died in a plane crash and we inherited the estate, but there wasn't much left. Mostly just the land—we'd spent the rest. I wanted him out of my life. He wanted that game park, so I made a deal with him. I sold land and gave him the proceeds. I was free, still relatively young, and I wanted to celebrate. So I did. Then your father dumped you here and the luxury lifestyle was a thing of the past. I resented you for that. But it probably saved us from being tossed out into the street with the clothes we were wearing. I'd gone hog wild and didn't even realize it. By the time I did, it was too late."

She moved into the living room and sat down, heavily, in a chair. Keely sat down on the arm of the sofa across from her. It was unusual for her parent to speak to her like this, as an equal, without even sarcasm.

Ella brushed back her hair. "I managed to salvage a couple of the properties before they were foreclosed on for unpaid bills. But my renters found cheaper rents and moved out. I was left with empty buildings that I couldn't repair, and nobody wanted to use them. Within the past six months, it was suddenly all gone, except for the house and the land it sits on." She looked up at Keely. "Your father and Jock are broke and they need a grubstake. They want me to sell the house and property to fund it."

"But it's all you have left," Keely argued. "Tell them you won't do it. Sheriff Carson will look out for you."

Ella bit her lower lip. "It's more complicated than that, Keely," she replied quietly. "You see, your father and I did something…illegal, when you were very small. If he tells what he knows, I can go to prison."

Keely's mouth thinned. "If he uses it, he'll be incriminated, as well, and he can go there, too."

The older woman smiled sadly. "They'd have to catch him first, wouldn't they?" she asked. "He's been one jump ahead of the law all his life."

"What did you do?" Keely asked, reasoning that her mother would probably close up and say nothing else.

Ella took a sip of her drink. "I've lived with the guilt for years," she said, almost to herself. "I thought it wasn't going to bother me, what we did. I thought…" She took another sip of the drink. "A local boy saw Brent bringing in a shipment of cocaine and hiding it in our basement. He was going to tell the sheriff." She grimaced. "My father was dying and he'd already threatened to disinherit me because of Brent. If there had been a scandal, and Brent and I had been prosecuted, I'd have lost everything. They could have proved that I…paid for the shipment that Brent was going to cut and resell on the streets."

"What did you do?" Keely asked apprehensively.

"The boy liked to get high," Ella continued miserably. "He did it all the time, anyway. He had a supplier, one of Brent's dealers—she died and her sister married a local cattleman a few months ago. We promised him that we'd send the boy a kilo of coke, all for himself, if he wouldn't tell on us."

Keely was feeling sick. She already had an idea of who her mother was talking about. "And?"

"Oh, he agreed. In fact, we promised him a dime bag on the spot. That's a hundred dollars of cocaine in street talk. What we didn't tell him was that it was one-hundred-percent pure—it wasn't cut with anything to lessen the effect. We gave it to his supplier, and he had her inject him. And he died. Of course, she didn't know, either. But we had her in our pocket then, too, because she couldn't prove that she didn't know she was killing him."

Keely's eyes closed. "It was Sheriff Hayes Carson's younger brother, Bobby, wasn't it?" she asked huskily.

Ella sighed. "Yes. I've lived with the guilt and the fear all these years, terrified that Sheriff Hayes would find out. He wouldn't rest until he put me in prison. He's blamed others, and that took the heat off me. It was the only hope I had…"

"No wonder you paid for the game park for Dad," she said, seeing clearly the pattern of the past. "It's why you let him take me along."

Her mother nodded slowly. "After Bobby died, I couldn't bear to look at Brent anymore. He made me feel like a murderess. I was afraid, too, that he might get high one night and tell someone what we'd done. So he promised to leave town if I'd let him have the money for the game park. He even said he'd straighten up, give up drugs, try to get his life back together. He said he'd never wanted anything more than he wanted that game park."

Keely's eyes became tormented as she remembered what her mother had said; she'd had to pay her husband to take Keely with her.

"No," Ella said quickly, reading Keely's expression. "I wanted to hurt you that night. It wasn't true. Brent wanted you with him. He said that if I fought him, he'd go to the police with the truth. He had nothing to lose by then. He'd already been arrested for possession twice and gotten off with the help of a lawyer. But he'd never get away with murder, and neither would I. So I let him take you." She looked up. "I never even asked if Jock was the reason. You see, Jock had noticed you when he came by to see Brent and told him about the old game park that he was running. The owner wanted out. Brent said that Jock liked young girls. I didn't even connect it, at the time." She shivered. "I should be shot."

Keely felt sick all over. Perhaps that accident, as terrible as it was, had saved her from something much more terrible. Now she realized what had probably happened. Soon after her father had purchased the rickety old game park where Jock worked and started renovating it, Jock had been arrested. Apparently he'd served time in prison, too, because it was only two years later that he showed up at the park. That was when things started to go downhill, and only about a week before Keely's accident. After that, Jock couldn't bear to touch her. Probably it was his idea for Brent to dump Keely, so the two of them could pursue other illegal enterprises. Keely might have been part of the plan for those jobs, she thought with muted terror. She'd been saved from more than she knew at the time, even though she'd resented being deserted.

She hadn't known her father at all. She'd thought he loved her. In those two years when it was just the two of them, and Dina keeping books, her young life had been happy and secure. Her father had, twice, even given up drinking; although Keely hadn't known he was using drugs. But just before Jock had turned back up, Brent Welsh had involved himself with the flashy woman who took him for everything he'd saved; and there had been a good bit. Jock had been livid when he'd discovered that.

"What are you thinking?" Ella asked.

She looked up. "How happy we were for a couple of years. I guess it was while Jock was in prison, because he left when Dad and I settled into the game park and only came back a few days before Dad brought me here."

Ella looked relieved. "At least Jock didn't have much access to you, did he?"

"No," Keely replied. "I was afraid of him."

"I still am," Ella confessed. "Your father could be dangerous when he was drunk. But he said Jock was dangerous cold sober."

Keely smoothed her hands over her knees. "Thank you for telling me the truth."

Ella's eyes were troubled. "I was scared, Keely," she said abruptly. "I couldn't face the fact that I'd helped kill a man, even if nobody knew. I started drinking and I couldn't stop. It helped me forget." She bit her lip again. "I should never have said that I didn't want you, Keely. Or that your father was disappointed you weren't a boy. I wanted you so much. I would have given up anything rather than lose you. Carly was right. I should never have said such a thing."

It didn't mean that Ella loved her. But it was something. "Thanks," Keely replied.

Ella cocked her head. "Are you getting involved with the Sinclair boy?" she asked worriedly. "Brent would find a way to use you to his advantage if he could, you know. He's an addict. He can't stop. He's more dangerous now than he ever was when I lived with him, especially in his situation and with Jock egging him on."

Keely was trying to come to grips with the idea that her own parents had a hand in the death of Sheriff Hayes's young brother, and that her father was a drug dealer. She'd known about deals he'd made to acquire animals that weren't quite what she thought of as legal. But he'd hidden his worst side from her during those two years they were together. From her vantage point now, she'd been naive and stupid. Perhaps, she thought, it wasn't so much ignorance as denial. She hadn't wanted a larcenous parent. Even an alcoholic, which is what she thought her father was, didn't have the stigma of a thief. Then again, it was a matter of degree.

"You're remembering things, aren't you?" Ella asked. "Listen, Keely, I may not be a good parent. I may be the worst alcoholic in town. But I've never laid a hand on you in anger or put your life at risk, and you know it."

That was the truth. Keely might feel used by her mother, but she'd never been afraid of her. She nodded.

"I'd like to tell you that I'm going to start over. That I'll stop drinking and carping and seducing married men." She shrugged and made a self-mocking smile.

"But it would be a lie. I've been like this too long. I can't change. I don't want to change. I like getting drunk. I like men."

"I know that," Keely said in a resigned tone. "If you could just stop trying to make me feel inferior, that would be something. It hurts when you make fun of the way I am. Dad certainly isn't perfect, but he made me go to church every Sunday. He even said once that he was going to make sure I didn't end up like both of you."

Ella thought about that. She was still holding her drink. She took another sip. "Well, he was right to do that. Yes. He was. The best way to give up being an alcoholic is never to start drinking in the first place."

"I don't like the smell of it," Keely murmured.

Ella laughed. "Neither do I," she confessed. And she smiled, really smiled, at her daughter.

"Did either of your parents drink?" she asked out of the blue.

Ella's eyes darkened with pain. She took a big gulp of the drink. "My father did."

She waited, but no other confessions were forthcoming. She wondered at the hatred in Ella's eyes when she talked about her father. Keely remembered that she never had talked about him, or about her mother, either.

"More secrets," Keely murmured absently.

Ella only nodded. "Some are best kept forever." She got up. "Well, I'm going to bed. If the phone rings, do us both a favor and don't answer it."

"I wish I could," Keely confided, "but I still have a job that requires me to go out at all hours."

Ella frowned. "Do you have a cell phone?"

She flushed. "No." She couldn't afford even a cheap disposable one.

Ella went to her purse and dug out hers. "When you go out at night from now on, you take mine. I'll be with Carly if I go out." She waved away the instant objection. "We can use hers. You have to have a way to call for help. Your father and Jock might even try to kidnap you. Brent sounded desperate."

"Why don't they just rob a bank?" Keely asked, exasperated.

"Don't even joke about that," her mother said at once, and went pale.

"Sorry. I shouldn't have said it."

Ella turned toward the hall. "I'm going to bed. Be careful if you have to go out. Call the sheriff's office and have the deputies watch out for you."

"I will." She was thinking, though, of Sheriff Hayes's brother and how he'd grieved for him after he'd died of that so-called drug overdose. She couldn't bear the thought of being in any way involved, even if she'd had nothing to do with it. Her parents were responsible. Inevitably, one day it was going to come out. You never really knew people, she told herself. Not even your parents.

But despite everything, it made her feel warm inside, the unexpected concern from the one parent she'd thought hated her. She didn't go to bed at once. She savored the feeling of having a real mother for the first time in her life. Even if that mother was the next best thing to a killer.

CLARK PHONED HER two days later and asked her to the big charity dance at the local community center on Saturday. She wasn't on call for that one night, so she couldn't refuse.

"Is this desperate or what?" he asked miserably. "It's

the only thing going on in Jacobsville for the foresee-able future, unless you want me to sign us up for the summer square-dancing workshop," he added grump-ily. "I'll never get to see Nellie."

"I like dancing," she replied. "It's okay. You can sneak out and nobody will even miss you. Then you can say you had a stomach upset."

"You're a genius," he exclaimed.

No, she was just getting good at lying, she thought. She still was concerned about Boone's perception and Clark's headlong fling into disaster. And in the back of her mind was the thought of her father and Jock and their schemes.

THINGS WERE ROUTINE at work. She and her mother were getting along for the first time. Even Carly was kinder to Keely. And it seemed that the work she did around the house was slowly appreciated, right down to her cooking. She felt as if she had a new lease on life.

But on Saturday morning, while she was worrying over the one good dress she had that she was wearing to the dance, there was a phone call.

She answered the phone herself. Her mother was sleeping late—she and Carly had gone out on the town the night before—and she was expecting to hear from Clark. But it wasn't Clark.

"Has your mother put the house on the market yet?"

She knew that voice. It wasn't her father's. It was Jock's.

She hesitated, sick with fear.

"Answer me, damn you!"

"N-no," she stammered. "She hasn't…yet…"

"You tell her she'd better get moving. I know what she and your father did. He may not want to tell, but

I will. You hear me, Keely?" And he slammed the phone down.

Keely wouldn't have understood the threat even a week ago. She understood it now. She couldn't very well go to Hayes Carson and tell him that her mother had been accessory to a homicide. There could be no protection from that quarter, especially if Hayes found out who the homicide had been. Clark couldn't help her, either. She didn't dare involve Boone. She sat down, sick and frightened, and wondered what in the world they were going to do.

LATER, WHEN ELLA woke up, Keely had to tell her about the phone call.

Ella was hungover, but she sobered quickly. "Jock knows, then? I was afraid Brent would get high enough to tell him."

"What can we do?" Keely asked miserably.

Ella drew in a long breath. "I don't know. I'll have to think about this."

"You don't have the time!" Keely said. "What if he goes to the sheriff?"

Ella looked at her daughter and actually smiled. "Thanks," she said huskily. "It means a lot, after the way I've treated you, that you'd mind if I went to jail." She shrugged. "Maybe it would be just as well to get it out in the open, Keely. It's been so many years…if I had a good lawyer…"

"Yes," Keely was agreeing.

She glanced at the younger woman, so hopeful, so enthusiastic. Ella knew that no judge in Jacobs County would let her walk away from a homicide; not when the sheriff's brother was the victim, regardless of how much time had transpired between the death and the present. Keely was young and full of dreams. Ella was long past them. But she might be able to do something to save her daughter. She might be able to spare Keely, if she had the guts to do what was necessary.

"We'll work something out," she assured the younger woman. "You're going to that dance with Clark, aren't you? He's very nice. Maybe he'll marry you." Her eyes looked dreamy for a moment. "He's a good man. He'd take care of you, and you'd have everything you wanted."

"Clark and I are just friends," she said.

Ella glanced at her curiously. "It's his brother, isn't it? I didn't do you any favors with the lies I told him. I could call him up and tell him the truth."

"No," Keely said at once.

Ella stared at her. "You loved him, and I screwed it up for you. I'm sorry."

"He thinks I'm much too young for him," Keely said with a sad smile. She was remembering the way Boone had talked to her at the library and hating circumstances that had robbed her of even a chance with him. Now that she knew the truth about her parents, any sort of a relationship with him would be impossible. Boone Sinclair, with his sterling reputation and impeccable bloodlines, wouldn't stoop so low as to marry the daughter of drug users and murderers.

"You look so sad," Ella said. "I really am sorry."

"I know. It's all right," she replied.

Ella got up. "You'd better finish pressing your dress. I'd offer you one of mine," she added, "but you're much too slender."

"Thanks for offering," Keely said gently.

Ella smiled back, and something twisted deep inside her as she recalled how cruel she'd been to her child. She was sorry about it now. Maybe she could make amends. Maybe, just maybe, she could spare Keely any more heartbreak if she went about it right.

CLARK WAS RIGHT on time to pick up Keely. She was wearing a pretty green velvet dress that clung lovingly to her pretty figure all the way to her shapely ankles, with a fox stole that belonged to her mother. Ella had insisted that she take it. She also had high heels that were expensive and pretty, another loan from Ella, who wore the same shoe size. Keely had no evening shoes at all, never having had occasion to wear them. Her blond hair was clean and shiny, neatly combed, and her eyes were full of dreams.

"You look gorgeous," Clark said suddenly as he helped her into the car. "I mean it. You really do."

She smiled. "Thanks, Clark."

He got into the car, thoughtful. When he frowned like that, he reminded her of Boone.

"Is something wrong?" she asked.

He shrugged. "I was thinking that I've been using you and it's wrong."

"I don't mind."

"That's what makes it so bad," he replied. "I'm doing things I don't like just to keep Boone from asking questions about my girlfriend." He glanced at her. "If I really cared about her, I'd be doing things differently, wouldn't I, Keely?"

She was surprised by his attitude, and the question. "You're in love. It makes people do odd things."

"Am I? In love, I mean?" He accelerated around a curve. "I've invested in a king's ransom of jewelry and designer clothes for Nellie. She hasn't refused a thing. In fact, she's made suggestions about what I could buy her that she'd like best." He glanced at her. "I can't get you to accept a pair of inexpensive earrings."

She flushed. It sounded very much as if Boone had made some idle comment that had started his brother thinking about things.

"I don't like jewelry."

"Of course you like it, Keely. All women like jewelry," Clark replied. "But you won't accept it from me. You won't even tell me why."

She bit her lip. "It would be like accepting payment for helping you out."

"And that's wrong?"

"In my world, yes, it is. A small present at Christmas is one thing. But expensive jewelry, that's something else."

"That's what Boone says. His girlfriend was hinting that she'd like a diamond collar. He said she could whistle for it. He didn't have to pay women to go out with him. She was really mad. She stormed out without another word."

"I'll bet she came back," Keely said sadly.

"Of course she did. Boone's loaded, and he's a dish, and he's relentlessly chased by every spinster south of Dallas."

Keely's heart sank. Of course he was. Boone was every woman's dream. He was certainly Keely's.

"It started me thinking," Clark continued. "And not in a good way. If Nellie loved me, she'd be wanting to buy things for me."

"She couldn't afford your taste, Clark," she murmured dryly.

He thought for a minute and then laughed. "Well, no, she couldn't. But it's the point of the thing, Keely.

She hasn't bought me anything since we started dating. Not even a handkerchief or a music CD. Nothing."

"Some people aren't givers."

"Some people are gold diggers, though," he replied.

She leaned back against the seat with a little sigh. "I guess so. I've never understood why. I love working for what I get. My paychecks may be small compared to a lot of others, but every one thrills me. I worked with my own hands for what I have."

"Boone admires that."

"Does he?" She tried not to sound impressed.

"Not that he wants to. He does his best to ignore you."

"I noticed."

"Maybe he's right, Keely," he said solemnly. "You're very young, even to be going out with me."

She threw up her hands. "What is it about my age? For heaven's sake, I'll be twenty on Christmas Eve!"

He smiled. She made him feel good. She always had. She and Winnie were closer to him than any other two women on earth.

"You're the nicest friend I have," he said out of the blue. "I'm going to start treating you better."

"Are you, really? Then if you want to get me something..."

"Anything!" he interrupted. "I mean that."

"I'd love to have mats for my car."

He blinked. "What?"

"Mats. You know, those black ribbed things that go on the floorboard. Just for the driver's side," she added quickly. "It was used, so it didn't come with the original equipment, and Dr. Rydel's parking lot isn't paved. I have to walk through mud to get to my car when it rains."

Clark was still absorbing the shock. Nellie had asked, petulantly, for a diamond pendant she'd seen advertised in a slick magazine and here was Keely asking for a single mat for her damned car.

"Not anything expensive," she said quickly, fearing she'd overstepped. "I mean, for Christmas. I'm going to get you something, too, but it will be inexpensive."

He pulled up at the community center, feeling two inches high. He turned to her in the car. "You make me ashamed," he said quietly.

"Of what?" she asked.

He shook his head. "Never mind. We'd better go in. I think we're a little late."

"My fault," she said, smiling. "You had to wait while I found my purse." She held it up. "It was an old one of Mama's. She let me have it, and her cell phone, and she loaned me her fox fur—" she waved it at him "—and her shoes—" she held up one foot to show him.

He could have wept. She never asked for a thing. She wouldn't let Winnie loan her anything at all. He'd never felt so bad in all his life. He'd used her as a blind for his great love affair, put her in a position where Boone could savage her if he ever found out what she'd been doing and never even gave a thought to the consequences.

"Tonight is the last time I'm hiding Nellie behind you," he said suddenly. "I'll go off with her, this once. But from now on, I'm taking her right into the front door of my house."

"Have some catsup handy, won't you?" she teased. "Boone will have her for supper."

"I know that. Maybe it wouldn't be a bad thing to let him have a bite of her. For once, maybe she'd show her true colors."

She stopped smiling. "It might not be as bad as you think," she said softly. "I mean, she might care about you and still like jewelry."

"She might rather have just the jewelry," he returned cynically.

A big SUV pulled up into the parking lot. He grimaced. "She's early." He looked at Keely. "Want me to walk you in?"

She shook her head. "I can do it all by myself."

He handed her a ticket. "You're taking that, even if it's all you'll let me give you. I'll be back before you miss me."

She knew better than that. He might talk good, but he was still under Nellie's spell. She'd have him convinced by the end of the evening that he couldn't live without her. Poor man.

"Have fun," she said.

He harrumphed. "You have fun."

She got out of the car, closed the door and waved. She didn't look toward Nellie. She would have happily thrown rocks at her if it would have spared Clark.

MUSIC POURED OUT into the cold night air. They were playing a Latin number. She imagined all the town's excellent dancers, including Matt Caldwell and Cash Grier, were out on the dance floor dazzling the spectators. She was looking forward to watching them.

She gave her ticket at the door, tugged the fox fur closer and moved into the huge room where a live band was playing.

"I thought you'd be along when I heard Clark mention that he bought tickets," a deep, amused voice said behind her.

She turned and looked up into Boone Sinclair's dark, soft eyes.

CHAPTER EIGHT

KEELY COULDN'T MANAGE a single word. Boone caught her hand and tugged her into the community center with him.

"Should I ask where Clark is?"

She felt as if her feet weren't quite on the floor. "No need. I didn't see your car."

"That's because I didn't drive it here. I brought one of the trucks and parked it out back. I doubt Clark even noticed."

"He didn't." She looked around. "Is Winnie here?"

He hesitated. "No."

She stopped walking so that he had to stop, too.

He looked down at her appreciably, his dark eyes lingering on the way the emerald-green dress fit her slender, pretty body. "Green suits you," he mused.

"Winnie didn't come…?" she prompted.

"Kilraven said he wasn't coming," he replied. "She said it was useless to let men she didn't even like parade her around the dance floor."

She cocked her head and looked up at him. "Maybe she has a point."

He lifted an eyebrow and looked wicked. "Maybe she does."

She felt suddenly uneasy. She looked around again, for Misty this time.

"She's not here."

Flushed, she looked back up into his amused eyes.

"I came alone," he told her. "I mentioned that I wasn't buying diamonds for a casual date and she took offense."

"I heard."

"Oh? Was Clark impressed?"

"Yes. But don't count on it lasting any length of time," she added. "Once he's alone with her, he'll forget everything he said."

"No doubt." He pursed his lips. "Do you dance, Miss Welsh?"

Her heart skipped at the way he said it. He had no date, and he'd come anyway. And he was looking at her as if he could eat her. That was thrilling, even if she couldn't hope for anything more.

"I do," she replied. She sounded breathless.

He took the fox stole and her purse and laid them on a table next to where Cag Hart and his wife, Tess, were sitting. "Do you mind watching them?" he asked.

Tess grinned. "Not if I get to try on that stole."

"Help yourself," Keely invited with a big grin.

Tess wound it around her neck and struck a pose. She batted her eyelids at her husband. Her blue eyes twinkled in their frame of red hair.

"I'm not buying you a dead fox," Cag informed her haughtily.

Keely recalled that Cag had watched the "pig" movie and gave up eating pork. She wondered if he'd recently seen any other animated animal films.

Tess looked up and grinned. "There was this foxhound movie…"

"Will you stop?" Cag muttered, looking oddly flushed. "I like animals."

Tess bent over and kissed him. "So do I. But this

animal has probably been deceased for a number of years...."

He burst out laughing and kissed her back.

Boone tugged Keely toward the dance floor.

He slid one arm around her waist and pulled her closer, easing his fingers in between hers. She stumbled with nerves as he propelled her expertly into the slow rhythm, and he laughed, deep in his throat.

She felt like a fox, running for cover. Her heart was racing, her breath was stuck somewhere south of her windpipe. She barely noticed the music. She was too aware of Boone's powerful body against hers, the scent of his breath, the smell of his cologne. He made her feel weak and shaky all over.

His hand spread against her back over the soft velvet. "I like this dress," he murmured at her forehead.

"It's very pretty," she began.

"I like the way it feels," he corrected.

She laughed nervously. "Oh."

He nuzzled her cheek, so that she lifted her eyes to his. "Nineteen years old," he said quietly, studying her. He looked guilty.

She frowned. "You know, age isn't everything."

"If you trot out that tired old line about it being the mileage," he threatened softly.

"It's true, though," she replied.

He smoothed his fingers in between hers as they moved lazily to the music. "You've heard from your father, haven't you?" he asked suddenly.

She jerked in his arms.

He nodded. "I thought so. You've been jumpy since you walked in the door."

She felt miserable, when she remembered what her mother had said about Hayes Carson's brother. She would carry the guilt for her parents' actions until she died. And Hayes was trying to look out for her, not knowing the truth.

"Come here."

He stopped dancing, caught her hand and led her out the side door onto the dark patio, where only a strip of light from the room inside showed on the stones of the flooring.

"Tell me what's worrying you," he coaxed.

She leaned her forehead against his chest. If only she could. But Hayes was his friend. "It was Jock who called. He made threats. My father wants Mama to sell the house and give him the money," she said heavily. "He's got something on her, something he can use, if she doesn't do it. She's afraid of him."

"What does he have on her?"

She groaned softly. "I don't know."

He tilted her chin up. "Yes, you do, Keely," he argued, searching her eyes in the dim light from the patio windows inside.

Her eyes were tormented. "I can't tell you," she said sadly. "It isn't my secret."

His fingers caressed her chin. "You can tell me anything," he said, his voice deep and soft and seductive. "Anything."

He made her want to tell him. He was powerful and attractive. He made her blood run hot through her veins. She wanted to kiss him until the aching stopped. She couldn't tell him that, of course.

She didn't have to. Boone read the subtle signs of her body and her breathing and drew a conclusion. Slowly, so that he didn't frighten her, he bent toward her mouth. "I should be shot," he whispered.

His breath tasted of coffee. The exquisite feel of

flesh against flesh in such an intimate way made Keely's head spin. She'd rarely been kissed at all, and never like this. His skill was apparent.

But he seemed to lose control, just a little, as the kiss lengthened. His mouth grew quickly hungry. His arms contracted and riveted her to the length of his body, bending her into its hard contours. She stiffened helplessly at the intimacy, to which she was completely unaccustomed.

Boone lifted his head, surprised by her posture, by her reaction. She responded as if she'd never been held and kissed in her life; as if the demanding ardor of an adult man was unknown to her. And perhaps it was. He considered what he knew of her life from Winnie's vague comments.

He let her move back, just a step, but he didn't let her go. "It's all right," he said softly, smiling. He framed her face in his big hands and held it where he wanted it. His thumb gently pulled down her lower lip as he bent again. "All we have to fear," he quoted amusedly, "is fear itself…"

It was different this time. He didn't demand. He teased her lips, brushing them in brief little caresses that made her want more. His hands smoothed back her hair. They moved down her back, to the curve of her hips, and coaxed her closer. She shivered at the contact and for an instant his mouth became demanding. But when she stiffened, he relented at once.

It was like a silent duel, she thought, fascinated. He advanced, and when she hesitated, he withdrew. It was as if he knew the difficulty she felt, as if he was aware of how new and frightening these sensations were to her. He calmed her, coaxed her, until she began to relax and stop fighting the slow, steady crush of his mouth.

"That's it," he whispered when she sank gently against him. "Just don't fight it. Don't fight me. I won't hurt you."

She knew that. But it was still difficult to give herself over to someone who didn't know about her past. She was terrified not of his exploring hands, but of what he might find if he persisted.

So when she felt his fingertips teasing just around the edge of her breast, she jumped and pulled back.

She expected an explosion. Once, just once, she'd given in to temptation in her adult years and agreed to go out with a salesman who came through town. He'd grabbed her in the car and she'd jerked away from him. He'd been furious, snapping at her about girls who teased. And then he'd forcibly run his hand over her shoulder and her breast. She could never forget the look of utter horror in his face. He'd pushed her away from him. He took her home without a single word. He hadn't even looked at her when she got out of the car. It wasn't as bad as the date she'd had at the tender age of sixteen that had ended in such trauma. But it was bad enough. That was the last time she'd ever gone out with a man on a date.

But Boone wasn't angry. In fact, he looked pleased rather than offended at her lack of response.

He withdrew his hand and traced her swollen lips with it. "Well!" he exclaimed softly, and he smiled.

She was worried. "You aren't...mad?"

He shook his head. "Virgins need gentle handling," he whispered, and bent to kiss her, tenderly, when she blushed.

When he drew back, his expression was solemn and gentle. He smoothed over her hair, touched her cheek, her mouth, her chin. "When are you going to be twenty?" he asked after a minute.

"Chr-Christmas Eve," she stammered.

"Christmas Eve. In four months." He kissed her eyelids closed, smiling against them. "We'll have to do something very special for your birthday."

"We? Oh, you mean Winnie and Clark and you?"

He lifted his head and searched her eyes. "Why wouldn't you think I meant just you and me?" he queried.

"There's Misty," she reminded him.

He frowned, as if he didn't know who she was talking about. The magic seemed to seep away. He withdrew his hand and became aloof. "Misty," he repeated.

The magic drained out of the night. He became the distant stranger, the aloof man of the past. At that moment, he looked as if he'd never considered touching Keely.

She wrapped her arms around herself against a chill that didn't come from the night air. "It's getting cool," she said, trying to sound nonchalant.

"Yes, it is." He moved away from her, deep in thought. He paused to open the door for her.

She went through it without looking up. She said nothing. He said nothing. She went to the refreshment table and got a small cup of soda and sat down with it over against the wall.

She watched Boone stop at a group of cattlemen and stand talking to them. Her eyes darted around to see if Clark had returned. When she glanced toward the group of cattlemen again, Boone was gone. She didn't see him again.

CLARK PICKED HER up. He looked disheveled and out of sorts.

"The pearls were the wrong color," he said dejectedly. "She wanted pink ones. I got gray ones."

"I'm sorry."

He glanced at her and grimaced. "I hated leaving you there alone," he confessed. "I'm really sorry. I won't do it again."

"It was all right," she said. "I liked the music."

"You're the nicest friend I've ever had," he said after a minute. "But you shouldn't let me take advantage of you like this."

She laughed. "Okay."

He gave her a rakish grin. "Good girl."

"What's our next project?"

He sighed. "I really don't know. I'll let you know when she decides if she wants to see me again."

"She will," she said with conviction.

"We'll see."

DR. RYDEL WAS raising more hell than usual when Keely went in to work the next Monday.

"I told you to reorder that low-fat dog food last week," he was raging at their newest clerk, Antonia.

"But I did, Dr. Rydel," she said, near tears. "They had it on back order."

He made a rude sound. "And I suppose the urn containing Mrs. Randolph's old cat is also on back order?" he added sarcastically.

Antonia was red by this time. "No, sir, I forgot to check on it is all. I'm sorry," she added quickly.

It didn't make any difference. He stood in front of her and glared. She burst into tears and ran into the back.

"Oh, nice job, Doctor," his colleague, Dr. Patsy King, muttered. "She'll quit and we'll have to break in yet another clerk. How many is that so far this year? Let me think…six, isn't it?" she added with as much sarcasm as she could muster.

Bentley glared at her. "Four!"

"Oh. Only four." She rolled her eyes. "That makes me feel better."

"Don't you have a patient waiting, Dr. King?" he drawled, eyes flashing.

She sighed. "Yes, I do, thank God, but I came out here to get our clerk to schedule her next appointment. I suppose I'll be doing that myself!" She looked pointedly toward the back where Antonia was audibly sobbing.

He cursed.

She made a face. "Oh, like that's going to help!" she grumbled. She sat down in Antonia's chair and used the computer to schedule the next visit for her patient. While she was at it, she added up the charges and printed out a sheet listing them.

"I could help you do that," Keely offered.

"No, you could not," Dr. Rydel muttered. "I need you to help with examinations, not making appointments."

"Speaking of which, Keely, could you carry this dog out to Mrs. Reynolds's car for her?" Dr. King asked, and smiled gently.

"Of course," Keely answered at once, and walked off with Dr. King, leaving a fuming Dr. Rydel behind.

AFTER THAT MORNING, it was open war between the two senior veterinarians in the practice. Dr. King was three years younger than Dr. Rydel, married with two children, and she needed her job. But she threatened to leave if he didn't stop using the clerks for target practice. Keely and the senior vet tech and the other veterinarian, Dr. Dave Mercer, tried to keep out of Dr. Rydel's way until his temper improved. Nobody knew what had set him off, but he was like a prizefighter walking down the street wearing boxing gloves. He was spoiling for a fight.

It was a relief for Keely when the workweek was over and she could get away from the tension. She was still mooning over Boone and reliving the tender kisses he'd shared with her on the patio of the community center. She didn't understand his behavior at all. Everything had been fine until she'd mentioned Misty. Then he'd withdrawn as if he'd felt guilty about touching Keely. He'd left the dance rather than risk having to talk to her again.

Worse, people were gossiping about the two of them. Tess Hart had teased her about going out onto the patio with Boone and coming back inside flushed. She'd mentioned it to Cag. Probably he'd told his brothers and they'd told other people. So Keely got teased when she went to the grocery store, because one of the checkout girls had a boyfriend on the Hart Ranch properties. Then she got teased at the bank, because one of the tellers was married to Cag Hart's livestock foreman. That teller's married daughter worked at the 911 center with Winnie.

"You and Boone are the talk of the town, did you know?" Winnie teased her friend when they had lunch together at Barbara's Café that Saturday.

"Boone's going to kill me," Keely said miserably. "Clark's probably going to want to kill me, too, when he realizes that Boone knows what he's up to."

"Oh, Boone always knows," Winnie said easily. "Clark can never hide anything from him—or from me. But just between us two, I don't think this Nellie thing is going very much further. She got mad because Clark gave her the wrong color pearls. That, after he's given her most of a jewelry store!" She leaned forward. "And it turns out that she's married."

"What?" Keely exclaimed. "Does Clark know?"

"That, and more," Winnie said. "When I left home, Boone was presenting our brother with a thick file on Miss Nellie Summers. He said Clark wasn't leaving the house until he'd read every sordid detail."

"Poor Clark."

Winnie chuckled. "He was cussing mad after he read the first page," she said. "He wouldn't have believed it even two weeks ago, but apparently Boone picked just the right time to tell him the truth."

"I'm glad," she confessed. "It was putting me right in the middle, being used as Clark's cover."

"Clark shouldn't have done that. Boone was angry. He said Clark had no right to use you that way."

"Clark's my friend. I could have said no," Keely said softly.

"You never say no to anyone," Winnie replied, concerned. "You're too good to people, Keely. You won't stand up for yourself."

"I'm trying."

"Clark walks all over you. So does Boone. I'll bet Dr. Rydel does, too."

"Dr. Rydel walks all over everybody," Keely pointed out.

"Well, you do have a point there." She sipped coffee and then her eyes began to twinkle. "So what was going on with you and my brother at the dance?"

"Not you, too!" Keely wailed.

"I'm your best friend. You have to tell me."

Keely put on her best bland expression. "He wanted to talk to me about Clark without everybody eavesdropping."

Winnie's face fell. "Was that all?"

"What else would there be?" Keely replied. "You know Boone can't stand me. Usually he ignores me. But he knew Clark was up to something and that I was helping him. He got it out of me."

"He's good at that," Winnie had to admit. "They used to let him interrogate people when he was in the military." She toyed with her coffee cup. "He's changed so much since he came back from overseas. He used to be a happy sort of person. He's not happy now." She looked up. "He goes out with Misty, but he never touches her."

Keely's heart jumped. "How do you know?"

"He never picks up anything," she said with affection. "He just leaves his clothes lying around in his room. I gather them up and put them in the hamper for Mrs. Johnson. There are never any lipstick stains on his shirts." She paused, her lips pursed. "Well, that's not quite the truth. Last Saturday night, there were quite a few lipstick stains on his collar."

Keely's face flamed and Winnie laughed triumphantly. Keely knew that Winnie would go straight to Boone and tease him if she guessed what had happened. She couldn't let her friend know for sure. If Boone were teased about Keely at home, it would all be over before it had time to begin.

"No wonder he's been like a scalded snake all week," Winnie mused, watching Keely closely. "And he hasn't even called Misty. Odd, isn't it?"

"Just slow down, if you please. I danced with him,"
Keely muttered. "Of course I got lipstick on his collar."

Winnie's happy mood slowly drained away. She
frowned. "Are you sure that's all?"

Keely gave her friend a speaking look. "Boone can't
stand me. He was just trying to find out why Clark and
I had gone to a dance and Clark was missing."

"Oh, Fish and Chips!" Winnie muttered.

"Excuse me?"

Winnie shifted. "Good Lord, I'm catching Hayes
Carsonitis!" she exclaimed.

"What?"

"Hayes Carson doesn't cuss like a normal man. He
says things like 'Crackers and Milk!' and 'Fish and
Chips!' It rubs off when you're around him."

"What are you doing hobnobbing with Hayes Carson?" Keely asked.

"On the radio!"

"Oh. Right."

"He's not bad-looking," Winnie mused. "And he's
much friendlier than Kilraven. I should really set my
cap at him."

"You'd break Kilraven's heart," Keely teased.

Winnie wrinkled her nose. "Like he'd notice if I
flirted with another man," she said shortly. "He's trying Boone's tactics. He's ignoring me."

"He's probably just busy."

Winnie toyed with her napkin. "Men are not worth
the trouble they cause," she said irritably.

Keely laughed. "No," she agreed. "They aren't."

"And don't we both lie well?" Winnie retorted.

Keely nodded.

The little café was crowded for a Saturday, mostly
with tourists trying to enjoy the last fleeting days of

August. Jacobsville had an annual rodeo that drew crowds, because it attracted some of the stars of the circuit. The prize money wasn't bad, either.

"There are a lot of cars with out-of-state tags," Winnie murmured. "I guess it's the rodeo that draws them."

"I was just thinking about the rodeo." Keely chuckled. "Great minds running in the same direction."

"Exactly. I think—" Winnie's voice broke off. She was staring at the front door helplessly.

Keely glanced toward the entrance. Kilraven, still in uniform, was standing just inside the door. He really was hunky, Keely thought; tall, handsome and elegant with silver eyes and thick black hair. He was muscular without it being blatant.

"Excuse me," he called in his deep voice. "Is anyone here driving a red SUV with Oklahoma plates?"

A young man in jeans and chambray shirt raised his hand. "Yes. I am," he called. "Anything wrong, Officer?"

Kilraven walked to his table, spotted Winnie and Keely and nodded politely before he stood over the man. "Did you pick up a deer from the side of the road, sir?" he asked.

The young man laughed. "Yes, I did. It was just killed by a car, I think, because it was still warm and limp when I picked it up." The smile faded. "I was only going to take it home and cut it up for my freezer. Did I do something wrong?"

Kilraven cleared his throat. "You might want to call your insurance agent."

The young man looked blank. "Why?"

"The deer wasn't dead."

"Wasn't...dead?" He nodded.

"And it left the vehicle rather suddenly, through your windshield."

The young man was still nodding. "Through the windshield?" He stiffened. "Through my windshield? In my brand-new truck? Aaahhh!"

He jumped up, overbalancing his chair so that it fell. He almost trampled a couple getting out the door. His scream of dismay could be heard even with the door closed.

Kilraven shook his head as he paused beside Winnie. "The deer was just stunned," he said with faint amusement in his silver eyes. "We had a man make that same mistake about six months ago during hunting season. But fortunately for him, the deer came to before he could lift it into his truck."

Outside the café, the screams were getting louder.

Kilraven glanced outside and chuckled. "He'll want a report for his insurance agency. I'd better go write him up."

"Have they found Macreedy yet?" Winnie asked with a drawl and a grin.

Kilraven groaned. "He surfaced over in Bexar County about five yesterday afternoon trailing forty cars in a funeral procession. They were supposed to be headed for a cemetery in Comanche Wells, where they were due at three o'clock," he added, because Keely was looking puzzled. "He did finally get them to the right church...after several cars stopped to get gas."

"That's twice this month. They should never let Macreedy lead a funeral procession," Winnie pointed out.

Kilraven chuckled. "I told Hayes Carson the same thing, but he says Macreedy will never learn self-confidence if he pulls him off public service details now."

"Doesn't he have a map?" Keely wanted to know.

"If he does, he can't ever find it," Kilraven said with a sigh. "He led the last funeral procession down into a bog near the river and the hearse got stuck." He laughed. "It's funny now, but nobody was laughing at the time. They had to get tow trucks to haul everybody out."

"Hayes should cut his losses and put Macreedy on administrative duties," Winnie said.

"Big mistake. Hayes put him in charge of the jail month before last and he let a prisoner out to use the bathroom and forgot to lock him up again. The prisoner robbed a bank while he was temporarily liberated." He shook his head. "I don't think Macreedy's cut out for a career in law enforcement."

"Yes, but his father does," Winnie reminded him.

"His father was a career state trooper," Kilraven told Keely. "He insisted that his son was to follow in his footsteps."

"Hayes Carson is our sheriff," Keely said, confused. "Macreedy's a sheriff's deputy."

"Yes, well, Macreedy started out working as a state trooper," Winnie began.

Kilraven was chuckling again. "And then he pulled over an undercover drug unit in their van just as they were speeding up to stop a huge shipment of cocaine. They'd been working the case for weeks. The drug dealers got away while Macreedy was citing the drug agents for a burned-out taillight. Macreedy's dad did manage to save him from the guys in the drug unit, but he was invited to practice his craft somewhere else."

"So Hayes Carson got him," Winnie continued. "Hayes is his second cousin."

"Sheriff Carson could have said no," Keely replied.

"You don't say no to Macreedy's father," Kilraven retorted.

"At least he's learning all the back roads," Winnie said philosophically.

Kilraven grinned at her. The look lasted just a second too long to be conventional, and Winnie's delicate skin took on a pretty flush.

"Where's my rifle?" came a bellow from the parking lot. "Somebody stole my rifle!"

Kilraven glanced out the window. The young fellow who owned the red SUV was running down the street with a rifle, in the general direction that the escaped deer had gone. The gun's owner was jumping up and down in his rage and yelling threats after the deer hunter.

"I'd better go save the deer hunter," Kilraven remarked.

"I hope he has an understanding insurance agent," Keely mused.

"And a good lawyer. Stealing rifles is a felony." Kilraven nodded at them and went striding out the door.

"Well!" Keely teased softly. "And you don't think he likes you?"

Winnie's expression was so joyful that Keely envied her.

CHAPTER NINE

KEELY HAD LAUGHED at the predicament Hayes Carson was in with his cousin Macreedy, but it was impossible for her to talk about him or think about him without remembering her mother's pained confession about Hayes's brother, Robert.

She was feeling guilty about that when Clark phoned her.

"I'm sorry," she said as soon as she recognized his voice.

"You are?" He hesitated. "Oh. I guess you mean about Nellie. Boone knew all along, Keely," he added heavily. "I thought I was pulling the wool over his eyes. I always underestimate him. He'd hired his girlfriend's father's detective agency to investigate Nellie. I can't say I'm really surprised at what he found out. Well, I'm surprised that she was married and...fooling around with me, I mean."

"Boone is very intelligent," she said noncommittally.

"Yes, and he knows how to make people talk."

She grimaced. "I didn't mean to..."

"No! Not you. Me! He asked me what the hell I thought I was doing, leaving you at a dance alone all evening. He was furious."

"But I was all right."

"He knows that your father and his partner in crime

might make a grab for you, Keely. I knew it, or should have known it, and I put you at risk. Boone said anything could have happened. I'm really sorry, Keely. I was so crazy about Nellie that she was all I thought about. You're my friend. I should have been looking out for you."

It made her warm inside that Boone was worried for her safety. "It's okay, Clark," she said. "Honest, it is."

"He gets hot about you," he continued. "I'd almost say he's possessive of you, but that's ridiculous. He is fond of you, in his way, I think." He paused. "There was some talk about the two of you at the dance. You went outside together…"

"To talk about you," she countered. "He wanted to know where you were and what you were doing. He's very insistent."

There was a relieved sigh. "Yes, he is." He paused again. "Keely, you don't want to ever get mixed up with him," he said, in a stumbling sort of way that made her heart fill with disappointment. "Something happened to him overseas. He hated women for years after that she-cat dropped him when he was wounded. God knows why he's letting her lead him down the same path again. Maybe he wants revenge. He doesn't like women at all. He just uses them. Sort of like me," he added miserably.

Keely didn't know what to say, how to answer him. "He's not a bad person."

"I didn't say he was, just that he's hateful toward women. He's keeping Misty on a tight rein, and he doesn't watch his words when he talks to her. It's almost like he's keeping her around for some mysterious reason, but he doesn't really want to have anything to do with her. He couldn't care less if he's late for a date, or if he doesn't even show up. She spends most of their time together complaining about the way he treats her, and about you."

"Me?" she exclaimed. "But why? Boone doesn't give a hill of beans about me!"

"I don't really know. She's jealous of you."

"That's one for the books," she mumbled. "She's beautiful and rich. I'm plain and poor. I'm no competition at all."

"I could dispute that," Clark replied gently. "You have some wonderful qualities."

"I'm no beauty."

"Neither is she."

Keely laughed softly. "Of course she is."

"She's not a beauty inside," he said doggedly. "You are."

"Thanks, Clark. You're nice."

"Nice." He laughed. "Well, at least we're still friends. Aren't we?"

"Yes."

"Then you can go riding with me from time to time. At the ranch. When Boone isn't around," he added with a wicked chuckle.

"We both know you're not afraid of Boone," she chided.

"Not much, anyway."

"What did you tell Nellie, about not seeing her anymore?"

There was a long pause.

Her heart sank. "Clark, you're not still seeing her?"

There was a longer pause.

"Her husband might hurt you. Really hurt you," she warned.

He sighed. "You don't understand. It's complicated."

"I guess I don't," she replied. "Be careful. Okay?"

"I'll be careful. I know I have to break it off. But we had something special—on my side, at least. It takes a little time to adjust."

"You watch your back," she replied.

"I'll do that. See you."

"See you."

She hung up, but she was worried. Clark was playing with fire. If she and Boone were really friends, she'd tell him. But Boone hadn't called or come near her since the dance, when he'd kissed her so sweetly. She'd dreamed about him, ached to see him, but she hadn't had so much as a glimpse of him. Perhaps he'd just been leading her on, she thought sadly, to get information about Clark and Nellie. There was a miserable thought, and it kept her unhappy the rest of the day.

SHE AND HER mother were getting along better than they ever had, although Keely lived in terror that her father, or worse, Jock, might just show up at the door. Ella had talked to a Realtor about the house and land. She had to take Jock's threat seriously, she said, and she didn't want to go to jail. Keely was worried that the secret might come out anyway. She felt guilty just knowing about it.

Things got worse when Hayes showed up at the vet's office where she worked in the middle of the next week. He was somber and worried. He asked Keely out into the parking lot, away from the crowd in the waiting room, where they could talk undisturbed.

"What's wrong?" Keely asked him apprehensively.

"It's about your father," he began hesitantly. His face became hard. "I've heard something. A little gossip. It involves my brother…"

"Oh, heavens!" Keely ground out. "I'm so sorry!"

The expression on her face spoke volumes. She never could keep secrets, and this one had cost her many a night's sleep. If Hayes pushed, she'd have to tell him. She went pale.

"You know, don't you?" he asked quietly. "Tell me, Keely."

She wrapped her arms tight around herself. "If I do, my mother will go to jail," she said miserably.

"If you don't, your mother may die," he countered. "Your father was seen at a roadhouse over in Bexar County two days ago."

She actually gasped. "With Jock?"

"The person who saw him didn't know about the other man. Probably wouldn't recognize him. What does Brent have on your mother, Keely, and what has it got to do with my family?"

She leaned back against his patrol car, looking at him with dead eyes. "My father was apparently dealing cocaine before he left here with me, and he had some pure stuff. He made a deal with…" She stopped and bit her lip. She hadn't thought how it would sound.

Hayes seemed to know. He shifted his tall frame. "I know what my brother was," he said quietly. "You don't have to pull any punches on his account. He's long dead and buried."

She drew in a long breath. "Yes, but he was still your brother and you loved him," she said gently. "I loved my father. I never dreamed…" She stopped. "Your brother saw my father make a drug buy. My father offered him a small fortune in cocaine not to tell you."

"So that was it."

"My father gave it to your brother. He didn't tell

him that it was a hundred-percent pure. Your brother
had his supplier inject him with it. That's why he over-
dosed." She lowered her eyes. "I'm so ashamed!"

"No!" He moved forward and framed her face in
his big, warm hands. "No, Keely, it's not your shame
or your guilt! You're as much a victim as Bobby was.
Don't take that burden on your own shoulders. It's their
crime, not yours!"

Tears were rolling down her cheeks. Hayes felt for
a handkerchief, but he didn't have one. Keely laughed
as she tugged a paper towel out of her jeans pocket. "I
always carry them around," she explained, dragging at
her eyes. "We're constantly cleaning up messes. Some
dogs get sick when they're brought here."

"I can sympathize with them," Hayes said with a
forced smile. "I don't like going to doctors myself."

She blew her nose. "I wanted to tell you. I couldn't.
I haven't been close to my mother, until the last few
days, and I knew if I told, she could go to prison."

"What for?" he asked heavily. "There's no evidence.
Everybody directly connected with the case is dead.
The woman who gave Bobby the drugs was Ivy Con-
ley's sister, Rachel. She died of a drug overdose her-
self not long ago. She left a diary and confessed that
she'd given Bobby the overdose," he said surprisingly.
Actually Keely knew Ivy, who had just married Stuart
York, her best friend's brother.

Hayes looked thoughtful. "Your father and Rachel
handed Bobby the gun, but he pulled the trigger himself, figuratively speaking. Bobby was an addict from
the time he was twelve. I knew and tried to stop him.
I never could."

"You mean, Mama won't go to jail?" she worried.

"No." He hesitated. "But your father will, if I can

find one damned thing to pin on him," he added in the coldest tone she'd ever heard him use.

She felt sad, because her father had been kind to her. She hadn't known about his dark past, and she'd loved him. It was hard to know that he was one jump ahead of the law. She wondered why, what he'd done to get in so much trouble that he was running scared. "If he's running, and he needs money," she reasoned out loud, "he must be desperate to get away."

He pursed his lips. "You think like a detective," he mused.

"He's done something bad," she continued. "Or Jock has, and he helped." Her eyes were sad as they met Hayes's. "He was good to me, those two years I lived with him. If he'd never got mixed up with Jock again, he might have stayed changed."

"Bad men don't change, Keely," Hayes said in a resigned tone. "A lot of them are easily led. Others are just lazy, and they don't want to have to work for a living. Some have been so badly abused that they hate the world and want to get even. In between, there are good kids who use drugs or get drunk and do things that they regret for the rest of their lives." He shrugged. "I guess that's why God made lawmen." He smiled.

She smiled back.

"If you hear anything from him," he said, "you have to tell me right away."

"Mama's talking to Realtors," she volunteered. "She's really afraid of what he might do."

"So am I," he said. "I've got a friend up in San Antonio talking to the man who recognized your father. He's got a lead, and he's following it up. Maybe we'll get lucky."

"What should I tell Mama to do?"

He thought for a minute. "Tell her to go ahead and put the property on the market."

She opened her mouth to protest.

He held up a hand. "She doesn't have to sell it. She just has to appear as if she's selling it. It might buy us a little time. I'd bet money that your father or his partner is keeping an eye out around here."

"I'll tell her," she promised.

"And keep your doors and windows locked, just in case," he added grimly.

"We always do that."

"Keep a phone handy, too," he advised.

She nodded.

"I'm sorry you ever got involved in this," he said.

"We don't get to choose our families," Keely said philosophically.

"Isn't that the truth?"

SHE WENT HOME after work and told her mother what she'd learned from Sheriff Carson. Ella was obviously relieved.

"I was scared to death," she confessed to her daughter. "Sheriff Carson isn't going to arrest me? He told you that?"

"He told me," Keely replied. "But he does want you to put the house up for sale."

"I can do that." Ella smoothed her hands over her silk slacks. "Yes. I can do that." She looked her age. She hadn't even put on makeup. "I've only had one drink today," she said after a minute, and smiled at her daughter. "I'm shaky. But maybe I can give it up, if I try."

Keely felt the beginnings of a real relationship with her mother. "Really?" she asked, and smiled.

"Well, just don't expect too much." Ella laughed. "I've been a heavy drinker most of my life. It isn't easy to quit."

"I understand. I'll help. Any way I can."

Ella studied the younger woman quietly. "You're a good kid, Keely," she said. "I haven't been a good mother. I wish…" She shrugged. "Well, we don't get many second chances. But I'll try."

"That's all anyone can do," Keely replied. Impulsively she hugged her mother. Ella hesitated for a minute, but then she hugged her back. It was a moment out of time, when anything seemed possible. But it only seemed that way.

KEELY HAD HOPED that Boone might call her, or bring Bailey by the office for a checkup or even be at home when she went riding with Winnie on the occasional Saturday. But he stayed away.

She accepted an invitation to go riding at the Sinclairs', hoping for a glimpse of Boone. She knew it was pathetic, but she was hungry to see him, under any circumstances. Winnie led the way down a wooded path to the river that ran through the property. Keely started to get down off her horse.

"Don't," Winnie said quickly, indicating the tall grass. "Rattlers are crawling. One of the boys killed two of them near the river this week."

"It's really hot," Keely said, unnerved by the mention of snakes. She was terrified of them.

"Yes, and they like cool places," Winnie said. "We'd better get back," she added, checking her watch. "I have to go in this afternoon. One of our dispatchers had a death in the family and I promised to fill in for her."

"You're a nice person," Keely said. "I really mean that."

Winnie smiled. "Thanks, Keely. So are you. I mean it, too."

"How's Clark?" she asked on the way back.

"Heading for tragedy," Winnie said coolly. "He's still seeing that woman."

"How do you know?"

"He stuffed a jewelry box into his pocket when he thought I wasn't looking last night," she said.

"But she's married," Keely argued. "What if her husband finds out?"

"Clark will be very sorry," she replied. "That detective's report said that he was a truck driver who did long hauls, and he's got a prior for assault."

"Oh, boy," Keely muttered.

"One day we'll get a call for Clark at work, you wait and see," Winnie said grimly. "He won't listen. He thinks he can win her away from her husband. He's in love."

"That woman hasn't left her husband for a reason," Keely agreed. "She's probably afraid of him."

"That would be my guess."

They rode in silence until they were within sight of the barn.

"Boone's doing a stupid thing, too," Winnie said after a minute.

Keely's heart jumped. "What?"

"He's bringing that Misty person home for the weekend," she said tautly. "God knows why. He treats her badly, but she hangs on. I don't understand what's going on."

"Revenge," Keely guessed.

"That's what I thought, too. But Clark wasn't the

only one hiding jewelry from me. Boone had a jewelry box in his pocket, too, just like Clark," she said, glancing worriedly at Keely. "I saw it. A little square one, like a ring comes in. He was hiding it."

Keely's world was ending. She tried to smile. "I guess he discovered he really does care about her, huh?"

Winnie looked worried. "My brothers are both idiots," she muttered.

"Love doesn't make people rational," she said, glancing around at the parched pasture. "If we don't get some rain, even the animals are going to go loco," she added, trying to change the subject. "This drought is terrible."

"Worse for small ranchers than for us," Winnie replied. "We can afford to buy hay to feed our cattle. Now, this corn thing for fuel is pushing those prices even higher." She shook her head. "You try to fix one thing, and it damages another thing."

"That's life, I suppose."

"Don't look so glum," Winnie said gently. "Maybe it was a lapel pin or something that Boone bought for a friend. It might not even be a ring."

"Of course."

Winnie knew the other woman was hiding a big hurt. She changed the subject as they rode back toward the ranch.

They met a furious Clark at the barn. He was pacing, steaming. He saw the women ride up and went to meet them, along with a wrangler who took the horses to unsaddle and stable.

"What in the world is the matter with you?" Winnie asked her brother when the horses had been led away.

"That damned private detective who works for

Boone's girlfriend's father, that's what's the matter!" he raged. "Boone set me up!"

"Set you up? How?" Keely wanted to know.

"Nellie is *not* married," he ground out. "I was suspicious, because she lives in an apartment in town. None of her neighbors have ever mentioned that she had other men coming and going, much less that her so-called husband was parking his semi in an apartment parking lot. So I asked a friend of mine on the San Antonio police force to check her out for me, on the quiet. He found out that she's never even been married!"

Winnie was shocked. "Clark, I'm sure Boone didn't tell them to make up that report," she began.

"Boone hates Nellie," he shot back. "He'd do anything to break us up. And before you both say it, I know she has a mercenary streak. She likes pretty things, because she can't afford them. It's my business if I want to buy them for her...nobody's making me do it."

Winnie and Keely exchanged woeful glances.

"Anyway, she's furious because Boone checked her out and tried to break us up with lies," he added grimly. "She won't see me anymore."

Keely felt guilty. Although why she should was anybody's guess.

"I'm really sorry," Winnie said gently, kissing him on the cheek. "I wish I could stay and talk more about it, but I'll be late for work. We can talk later, can't we?" She frowned. "Oh, I forgot! I've got to drive Keely home...."

"I'll drive her," Clark volunteered. "She can console me."

Winnie hugged her brother, and then Keely. "I'll call you," she told her friend.

Keely nodded. She was disappointed that she didn't get to see Boone at all, and sad for Clark that he'd been lied to. It didn't seem at all like Boone to have people make up stories about Nellie.

Clark put her into his sports car and peeled out down the driveway. He was still furious, and it showed.

"What are you going to do?" she asked.

"I'm going to do what Boone wants me to do," he muttered. "I'm giving Nellie up before he finds a way to destroy her reputation."

She felt sad for him. "Boone is formidable," she said.

"He's too used to getting his own way. He's run things for so long that he thinks he can run people's lives, as well." He glanced at her. "Are you game for a little payback? After all, he's done his bit to hurt you, as well."

She felt a sense of dark foreboding. "What bit?"

"He told Misty that you were running after him at the charity dance," he said tautly. "I told you there was some gossip. She heard it and raised hell. Boone usually doesn't pay attention to her when she rants, but he did that time. He said you'd lured him onto the patio and flirted with him shamelessly."

She was so embarrassed and humiliated that she wanted to sink through the floor. That was an absolute lie, and Boone knew it. She bit her lip almost through.

Clark glanced at her stony expression and grimaced. "Sorry. I didn't mean to lay it on that thick."

"The truth is always best, Clark, even if it hurts."

"I couldn't believe it when I heard him," he said. "I know you don't chase men. And you never flirt. When she left, I gave him hell. He just walked away without a word. You can't argue with him. He ignores you!"

She felt very small. She'd gone running out to the Sinclair house to go riding with Winnie on the flimsiest excuse, hoping to see Boone. And he'd been telling lies about her to his girlfriend. It was the last straw. She felt sick to her stomach.

"Let's start going out together, for real," Clark said curtly.

"What good would that do?" she wanted to know.

"It would teach Boone a lesson about trying to run peoples' lives, that's what it would do," he gritted. "I'm sick of him leading me around like a kid. He can't stand Nellie because he says she's mercenary. But what is that gilt-edged gold digger he takes around with him, if she's not mercenary?"

"She isn't one of my favorite people."

"Or mine. And now he's talking about getting engaged," he muttered. "I heard him mention it to Hayes Carson on the phone. I couldn't hear everything he was saying, but he sounded furious. Then he mentioned that he was trying to get engaged. I couldn't believe it. But when I saw the rings sitting on his desk…"

Her heart fell the rest of the way into her shoes.

He sighed. "Well, I won't live in the house with that ratty woman, and Winnie says she won't, either. If she moves in, we're moving out. Boone can entertain her all by himself."

"I can't say I blame you," she said in a subdued tone. "She was willing to sacrifice poor old Bailey just to go to a concert."

"Something you'd never do in a lifetime," he replied and smiled across at her.

"I love animals."

"So do I."

"So what do you mean, that we'd pretend to go

around together, like we were doing before? Boone
saw right through it, Clark."

"He won't this time," he assured her.

She puzzled those words the rest of the way home
while she endured the pain of Boone's cruel taunts.
The man who'd kissed her so tenderly on the patio of
the community center hadn't seemed like someone
who would humiliate a woman who responded to him.
But she knew very little about men, and Boone had
certainly pegged her for a novice. Perhaps he was just
amusing himself. He'd moved away from her when
she mentioned Misty, and he'd been remote. Maybe he
felt guilty playing up to one woman when he was involved with another one. He had to explain the gossip
to Misty, so he'd made Keely the fall guy. Gal. Whatever. She could almost hate him for that. For certain,
it brought home the reality of her situation.

Boone was wealthy. Keely was poor. His girlfriend
was socially acceptable and pretty. Keely's father was
a criminal. That said it all.

Clark pulled up at her front door and cut off the engine. "We're going to San Antonio, to the ballet." He
held up a hand when she started to protest. "I'm going
to hire a bodyguard so Boone won't have the excuse
that I'm putting you in danger."

That was a new twist. She felt new respect for her
friend.

"And we're going shopping, whether you like it or
not," he added firmly. "You need some pretty evening
wear, something silky and off the shoulder," he added
with a smile.

Keely felt sick. "I don't wear those sorts of things,"
she said primly.

"I'm not asking you to wear your underwear," he

said gently. "Just something a little more feminine than what you usually go around in."

He couldn't know how he was hurting her pride. But it did show, and he noticed. He frowned.

"What's wrong?" he asked.

She clasped her hands together in her lap. "Clark, I can't wear clothes that don't button up to the neck, much less something off the shoulder," she said with grim pride. She raised her face. "I had an…an accident, just before Dad brought me back to Jacobsville. There are, well, scars…"

"God, I'm sorry!" he said at once. "I didn't know!"

"Nobody knows, not even my mother," she said, tight-lipped. "And you can't tell anyone, either." She lowered her eyes to her jeans. "It's something I've learned to live with, in my own way. But I have to dress within the limitations of my injury."

"That weakness in your arm," he recalled out loud. "That's part of it, isn't it?"

She nodded. Her face was flushed. "I'm sorry."

"No. I'm sorry," he replied quietly. He reached over and clasped her hand in his. "I won't tell anyone," he promised. "And we'll buy very conservative clothes. But pretty ones."

"I won't let you do that," she said proudly.

He pursed his lips. "Suppose I made you a loan?"

"I could never pay it back. You'll just have to make do with what I can afford to wear. My mother can loan me some of her more conservative things, and her fox fur. I'll look presentable. I promise."

He smiled gently. "Okay. If that's what you want."

"This bodyguard, you should probably ask Sheriff Carson about it," she said.

"I will. Go on in. I'll be in touch."

"Are you sure you want to do this?" she asked as she opened her door. "Nellie might come back to you."

"I don't know that I want her to," he replied. "We'll take it one day at a time. If you need anything, though, you let me know, okay?"

She wouldn't, and he knew it, but she smiled.

His dark eyes narrowed. "And I'm sorry that I told you what Boone said," he added solemnly. "It hurt you."

"Life hurts, Clark," she said quietly. "There's no getting around that."

"So they say." He leaned over to close the door, and powered the window open. "Next Friday night. The ballet."

She smiled. "I'll ask Dr. Rydel if I can leave work early."

"I'll ask him, too," he volunteered.

"You brave soul!"

"Yes, I've heard that he's making meals of the staff lately, but we get along," he chuckled. "I'll call you. So long."

"So long."

CHAPTER TEN

THE BODYGUARD WAS actually a Jacobsville police officer who worked odd jobs when he was off duty. He was powerfully built and never seemed to smile.

Instead of riding in the car with them, he drove his own private vehicle and followed behind them to San Antonio. Clark had paid for his gas and would have bought him a ballet ticket, as well, until he'd mentioned that he'd prefer being burned at the stake. So Clark had made other arrangements for when they were inside.

Keely was wearing the same green velvet dress she'd worn to the dance, and her mother's fox stole and high heels. She was nervous about mingling with the upper classes of San Antonio, but Clark held her hand and reassured her that they were just regular people like himself.

He recognized a friend of his and introduced Keely to him. The man was Jason Pendleton, who owned a truck farm in Jacobsville. He was usually with his stepsister, Gracie, but tonight he was with a redhead whom he introduced as his fiancée. The woman was brassy and not very polite. She dragged Jason away scant minutes later and led him to a local newspaper owner instead.

"I guess we aren't quite good enough company," Clark mused. "Old Peppernell over there does own a newspaper, but our family could buy most everything he owns out of petty cash. Jason will tell her that, at some point, and then she'll drag him back over here and gush and pretend that Peppernell is a cousin or something whom she had a duty to talk to. His sister, Gracie, isn't impressed by dollar signs. She has friends who don't have a penny. But Jason's fiancée apparently only associates with the ultrarich."

He was amused. Keely was mortified. "Is that the sort of people you know?" she asked uneasily. "They judge you by dollar signs?"

"Jason doesn't. His fiancée apparently does." He frowned. "I wonder where Gracie is? It's unusual not to see them together."

"Is it?" she countered, curious. "Brothers and sisters don't usually partner each other at social events, do they?"

"They're not related," he said carelessly. "Gracie's mother married Jason's father, and promptly died, leaving Jason to look after her. Gracie's mother is dead, but Gracie still lives with Jason. Until now, he hasn't been much for commitment. His fiancée is nice-looking, I guess, but she's grasping, too."

Keely had noticed that. She was watching the woman as Jason Pendleton bent his tall form to speak to her. The woman gaped at Clark and Keely and winced.

"She just got the bad news." Clark chuckled under his breath.

Keely laughed, too, but as she turned her head, her eyes collided with Boone Sinclair's. She shivered at the unexpected encounter. She averted her eyes at once and turned back to Clark, clinging to his hand. Her heart was racing again. Boone had accused her of chasing him shamelessly. She didn't want to have to speak to him at all.

Boone was with Misty. He tugged her over to where Keely and Clark were standing.

"Before you start," Clark told his brother belligerently, "I've got Jarrett from the Jacobsville Police Department acting as our bodyguard on the road, and Detective Rick Marquez has the seat on the other side of us at the ballet." He gave his brother a cold look. He was still smoldering about that private detective's report on Nellie. "I've covered all our bases."

Boone's dark eyes narrowed irritably. He looked at Keely until she was forced to meet that riveting stare, but she immediately turned her attention away from him. She couldn't forget what he'd said about her to his girlfriend.

"I still don't think it's a good idea," Boone said shortly.

"Boone, why don't we just enjoy our evening and let your brother and his…friend…enjoy theirs?" Misty asked haughtily. "He's over the age of consent, you know."

Boone gave Misty a look. He turned back to Clark. "Don't put her at risk," he said solemnly.

"I would never do that," Clark replied shortly. "And you know it."

Boone gave Keely a long look that she ignored. He was scowling when he escorted Misty to their seats.

"You invited Marquez?" Keely asked, for something to say.

"Yes. He loves the ballet, and he's our lookout inside, just in case your father and his friend decide to mount an attack in the audience," he added with pure sarcasm.

Keely laughed. "I don't think that's likely to happen."

"Neither do I. Boone's getting strange lately. He was giving Hayes Carson hell on his cell phone last night, God knows for what. Hayes is his best friend, but they're falling out."

"Are they?" she asked absently, still reeling from Boone's intense interest and not really hearing what Clark said. "Shouldn't we go in?"

"We probably..."

"Oh, *there* you are." Jason Pendleton's fiancée rushed up. "I'm so sorry we rushed away, but we had to speak to that friend of Jason's!"

Clark glanced at Keely and had to bite his tongue to keep from laughing.

Jason was giving his fiancée an odd sort of look, as if he hadn't noticed this social climbing penchant of hers. He wasn't conventionally handsome, but Keely could see why he drew women; and it wasn't because of his money.

She gave the couple a shy smile as Clark led her into the auditorium.

Detective Marquez grinned at them as they sat down.

"You're alone?" Clark asked, surprised.

"I can't get girls." Marquez shrugged. "Once they see the gun—" he indicated his shoulder holster "—and they realize that I carry it all the time, they usually leave skid marks getting out of my life. But it's okay," he said pleasantly. "I always wanted to spend my whole life alone with no kids or grandkids."

Clark and Keely burst out laughing.

He just grinned.

ALL THROUGH THE ballet, which was beautiful and riveting, Keely was aware of Boone's dark eyes watching her. She hated the feelings she couldn't help, because she knew what he really thought of her. It was humiliating that she couldn't wish them away.

When the performance was over, Boone stopped Clark, Keely and the bodyguard at the front door.

"We're stopping by Chaco's Bar and Grill for a nightcap. Why don't you join us? Your bodyguard is welcome to come in, too."

"I don't drink on the job," Jarrett said unapologetically. "But thanks."

"We should probably start toward home," Clark began, knowing Keely's reluctance to be around Boone.

"Just a nightcap," Boone said, and he had that expression that meant he was going to get his own way come hell or high water.

"Well, all right," Clark gave in, as he always did. He grimaced, because he'd had a glimpse of Keely's face when he agreed.

"We won't stay long," Boone promised.

He and Misty started toward his sports car. It was parked next to Clark's. Misty was complaining loudly about the intrusion on their privacy. Keely felt like doing the same. She didn't want a nightcap, especially with Boone.

But they ended up at the bar anyway. Keely ordered a soft drink. Misty glared at her while she ordered a whiskey sour with a smirk, as if she thought Keely was putting on some sort of Puritan act.

"Marquez would approve," Clark said gently when Keely was served. "You're not legal, yet."

"What?" Misty asked.

"You have to be twenty-one to have a drink in a bar," Clark said carelessly.

She frowned. "You're not even twenty-one?" she asked Keely.

"I'll be twenty on Christmas Eve, in four months," Keely said without looking at her.

Misty was irritable, and it showed. She sipped her drink and ignored Keely.

Boone didn't. He seemed restless. When Misty excused herself to go to the ladies' room—with obvious reluctance—and Clark decided to go, too, Keely was left alone with Boone.

She couldn't force herself to look at him. She sipped her soda with both hands wrapped around the glass and stared toward the bar.

"You haven't said a word to me all night," he said unexpectedly. "And you haven't looked at me once."

Keely did, then, and her eyes were blazing. "I didn't want it to seem as if I were chasing you," she told him coldly. "I understand that I threw myself at you at the charity dance and it offended you."

His jaw tautened. He looked away, as if the comment embarrassed him. "There are things going on that you don't know about. You shouldn't be wandering around the state with Clark."

"I'm as safe with him as I would be at home," she said. "Clark is a wonderful man. I'm very lucky that your private detective turned him off Nellie. Apparently," she added with a meaningful smile, "I'm more to his taste than she is."

His scowl was intimidating. But before he could speak, Misty was back. She swept into her chair and leaned against Boone's shoulder to distract him. Clark and Keely were stiff and uncomfortable, and they barely managed to remain civil for the time it took them to finish their drinks.

MISTY MADE A point of getting Keely momentarily alone on their way out to the cars.

"He's talked about nothing except you all night, God knows why! Well, you won't get him," she said icily. "I'm going to fix you!"

Keely didn't get a chance to ask her what she meant. Misty ran to Boone and almost tripped getting to their car. Misty was apparently jealous that Boone had mentioned Keely. She couldn't imagine why, but it thrilled her to think he might be regretting his bad behavior.

"WHAT THE HELL is wrong with Boone?" Clark asked on the way home. "I've never seen him so grim."

"I haven't the slightest idea," Keely said.

"I gave him the devil about that detective's report. He swore he hadn't put the man up to lying." He glanced at Keely. "It's hard for me to stay mad at him. But I'm sorry I couldn't get us out of that drink."

"It's okay, Clark," she replied. "He's a bulldozer. It's hard for anyone to say no to him."

"Especially me." He smiled. "When we were kids, Boone was always protecting me from the mean, older boys. He was never afraid of anything. I guess maybe he protected me too much. After our mom left, Dad was hell to live with. Boone took a lot of hits that were meant for me."

"He loves you."

"Yeah. I love him, too." He glanced at her. "Boone said that Sheriff Carson was out your way."

"Yes," she replied. "I had to tell him what Dad did."

"Excuse me?"

She bit her lower lip. Her father was a criminal. That was going to put Boone right out of her orbit forever. She was certain that Hayes Carson had already told him about Keely's parents. The two men had been best friends forever.

"My father was a drug dealer, Clark," she said quietly. "He supplied the cocaine that killed Sheriff Carson's brother Bobby."

"Oh, boy," Clark said heavily. "You poor kid."

"Now my dad's back and he and his partner want money, lots of it..."

"I could give them whatever they want," he said at once.

"No!" Her eyes were eloquent. "Don't you see, the only way to stop them is to keep them hanging around while Mama puts the house on the market. The police might have a chance to catch them before they can hurt anyone."

"Do you think your father would hurt you?" he asked.

Keely had never liked looking back. Her accident had hurt more than her body. When the little boy dropped into the lion pit, Keely's father had been standing on the other side. He hadn't made a move to help.

"Yes, he would, wouldn't he?" Clark asked perceptively.

Keely drew in a long breath. It had been just after the court case that Keely's father had brought her back to Jacobsville. He hadn't said much to her, and he hadn't met her eyes. She'd tried to tell herself that he'd only hesitated because he was shocked. But Keely hadn't hesitated.

"I've spent all these years trying to pretend that he

brought me back for my own good," she said. "But I think it was because I made him ashamed." She held up her hand when he started to ask a question. "I can't talk about it, not even now. It's so painful to think that my father was willing to stand by when a child's life was in danger. I loved him. But he was ready to sacrifice me to save himself." She looked up. "In the same situation, Boone wouldn't have hesitated a split second. Neither would you or Winnie."

Clark was solemn. "It's hard to lose faith in a parent. I know. When our mother ran off with our uncle, we were devastated. Three little kids, and she just left."

Keely was thinking that she would never have deserted her own flesh and blood. But she didn't say it.

Clark smiled. "You'll make a wonderful mother," he chuckled. "Your kids will be spoiled rotten."

She smoothed her right hand over her left arm. "No," she said absently. "I won't have children. I won't marry."

"A few little scars aren't going to matter," he told her.

She didn't reply. He had no idea. She couldn't tell him, either. She glanced at him. "I had a good time," she said. She smiled. "Mr. Pendleton's fiancée was a hoot." She chuckled. "Do you think he's really going to marry a woman who's that blatant about social climbing?"

"I think, like me, he got into a physical relationship that blinded him to a woman's true nature," he said after a minute. "I hope he's lucky enough to see the light in time."

She frowned. "That doesn't sound like you."

"I was watching Misty tonight," he replied. "She was all over Boone, her eyes like dollar signs. She likes going first-class. She pretends to have money, but I don't think she does. I think she's putting on an act, to try to get Boone back. I hope he's got better sense." He gestured with his hand. "I saw myself when I looked at him. I was just as enchanted by Nellie. But what I saw was an illusion." He glanced at her. "You won't even let me give you emerald earrings, and you love them," he said softly. "I've never known a woman like you."

"Actually there are lots of them, and they all live in Jacobsville and Comanche Wells," she teased. "Just plain unsophisticated little country girls who love animals and like to plant things and don't think marrying a rich man is the greatest of life ambitions."

He grimaced. "I'd never get one of those kind of girls past Boone," he said with resignation. "He always expects the worst when I date anybody outside our own circles."

That stung, but she didn't say so. Clark had been kind to her. "I have to go," she said. "I had a wonderful time tonight, Clark," she added. "Thanks."

"We'll do it again." He frowned. "I didn't mean that like it sounded—about dating girls outside my own circle," he added. "I always think of you as family."

She smiled. "That's the nicest thing you've said to me."

He looked sheepish. "I guess you'd rather I thought of you as an eligible young woman?"

She shook her head. "I like being your friend."

"I like being yours." He bent and kissed her cheek. "If you ever needed help, you know you could ask me."

She chuckled. "Of course I do. But I can take care of myself. Good night, Clark."

"Good night."

He watched her go into the house before he drove away.

HER MOTHER WAS unusually quiet. When Keely asked about the house, she only got evasive replies. Carly was nowhere in sight, and hadn't been for some time. She was out of town for a while, Ella said finally, and didn't refer to Carly again. There was also a disturbing phone call that Ella had answered with single syllable replies. She wouldn't tell her daughter what had been said or even who had called.

When a car pulled up at the front door on a rainy Saturday morning, Ella actually gasped. Keely ran to look out.

"It's Boone Sinclair," she stammered, shocked.

"Thank God," Ella said heavily. "Thank God." She walked back down the hall, went into her room and closed the door.

Surprised, Keely went out onto the porch as Boone exited the car and took the porch steps two at a time.

He was in working clothes, jeans and boots and white Stetson with a checked Western-cut long-sleeved shirt buttoned right up to the neck. He looked down at Keely, his eyes dark and stormy.

"Come for a drive," he said curtly.

She could have found a dozen reasons not to go. She wanted to come up with an excuse. Her mind agreed. But her body walked back into the house, grabbed her purse and a lightweight jacket and told her mother goodbye.

BOONE OPENED THE door of his car, helped her inside and went around to get in and start the engine. A minute later, they were speeding down the highway toward his ranch.

She was nervous, and it showed. Her hands played with her small purse while she listened to the rhythmic sound of the windshield wipers as they brushed away the pouring rain.

Despite all their recent turmoil, she felt safe with Boone. Safe, excited, hopeful, breathlessly in love. Her whole body ached to be held again as he'd held her at the charity dance. She hoped that didn't show.

It did. Boone was far too experienced to mistake her body language. He smiled softly to himself. If she'd been involved with his brother, as Clark claimed, she wouldn't be this nervous in Boone's company. That meant there was still time. If he could convince her that he hadn't meant to humiliate her.

He pulled out onto a pasture track that led to a closed gate, stopped the car and cut off the engine.

The rain flooded onto the windshield, making the outside world a gray blur. He unfastened his seat belt, settled himself crossways in his seat and stared at Keely.

The silence was a little unnerving. She glanced at him and found her eyes captured and held.

"Clark says the two of you are going steady," he said.

Now what did she say, she wondered frantically. It wasn't true, but Clark was using her as a tool of vengeance, apparently, for Nellie's loss. She bit her lower lip and tried to find a graceful way out of the dilemma.

"Did he say that?" she asked, playing for time to think.

His dark eyes narrowed. "Don't play games with me," he said curtly. "Are you or are you not getting mixed up with my brother?"

Sorry, Clark, she said silently, but no mere woman could have resisted that look in Boone's eyes.

"I'm not," she said, sounding breathless, as though she'd run a long way.

The tautness seemed to go out of him. "Well, thank God for one thing going right," he murmured. "I could have slugged Hayes Carson!"

While she was trying to work out that puzzle, he'd unfastened her seat belt and pulled her over the console into his arms.

"I thought this week would never end." His mouth ground down into hers as if he'd gone hungry for years and sought to satisfy the hunger in seconds. He crushed her up against him, mindless of her soft cry of protest. "I'm starving to death for you," he whispered into her mouth. "Dying for you—"

Had she really heard him say that? She gave up protesting. It didn't do any good, anyway. She curled up against him and ignored the pain in her shoulder and arm, going boneless as his ardor only increased at her response. Her head began to spin. It was the sweetest interlude of her life. Rain pounded on the roof, the hood, the trunk, the wind blew, but she heard nothing over the pounding of her own heart. She had no reserve left. Whatever he wanted, he could have.

Except when his hand searched under her blouse and up over her breast, inching toward the strap. She couldn't, didn't dare, let him feel her shoulder.

With a sharp little cry, she jerked away from him, her face flushed from his ardor, her eyes wild with passion and dread.

He misunderstood. His eyes grew cold. He pushed her away, dragging in harsh breaths, until he could control himself again. He'd taken her protests the first time he'd kissed her as virginal fears. But this wasn't. She'd rejected him. She'd lied about her feelings for

Clark. She couldn't hide the fact that she didn't want intimacy with Boone. His ego hurt, almost as badly as it had when Misty shied away from him in the military hospital.

"Boone," she began slowly, dreading what she had to tell him now.

"Forget it," he said, interrupting her. He put his seat belt back on and started the car. "Obviously you can't get past your feelings for Clark. No sweat."

He didn't say another word, or even look at her, until they were sitting in front of her house with the engine running.

"It isn't what you think," she bit off.

"The hell it isn't," he returned icily. "Goodbye, Keely."

The way he said it, she knew it wasn't simply a temporary farewell. He meant that he wouldn't see her alone again, ever. Her heart broke. He thought she'd rejected him and it wasn't true. She couldn't bear to see the look on his face if he got her shirt off. That would end any chance she had with him. Of course, she'd just done that, without the added trauma of what he didn't know.

She drew in a quiet breath. "Thanks for the ride," she managed in a polite tone. She opened the door and got out.

He still hadn't said a word. He was down the driveway before her foot was on the first step up to the house. She didn't look back. It wouldn't help.

HER MOTHER WAS still acting oddly. Almost a week had passed since Boone had taken Keely riding and kissed her. The rain had stopped and now the heat blazed. There were wildfires. Everyone was afraid to throw down a match or burn trash or even smoke a cigarette outdoors. It was almost time to harvest corn and hay and peanuts. The corn and hay would have to last the livestock through the winter; it was very important. Combines and tractors were sitting on ready, while the last days counted down to harvest.

On Saturday morning, the sounds of machinery could be heard everywhere. Winnie stopped by to pick up Keely for an impromptu lunch, assuring her first that Boone was out with the combines and wouldn't be in all day. He'd taken a cooler with him, bearing lunch and beer.

"I hope I have enough eggs to do the egg salad," Winnie murmured as they pulled up into her driveway past the huge posts that held the now-open gates that led to the house. "If I don't, I may have to run back to the store. Why didn't I think of it while I was in town?" she moaned. She glanced at Keely, who looked apprehensive. "Boone's really out with the combine," she promised. "I wouldn't lie."

Keely relaxed with a smile. "Okay. Sorry."

"Not your fault," Winnie replied, leading the way into the house. "Boone raged about you all week, in fact, not to mention Hayes Carson—God knows why. But this morning something came by express. He took it into the office, and got all quiet. He went out without a word, walking really slow." She grimaced. "God help the cowboys. Somebody will quit by sunset, you mark my words. He's seething!"

"You don't know why?" Keely had to ask. "It couldn't have been something about my father...?"

Winnie looked surprised. "What would Boone have to do with your father?"

Keely felt trapped. "You said he'd talked to Sheriff Hayes…"

Winnie scowled. "Keely, what's going on?"

She hesitated. "Did Clark say anything to you at all?"

"He said you had to take a bodyguard with you when you went to San Antonio," Winnie replied gently. "I'm not stupid. There's gossip about your father being in trouble and threatening you and your mother. But I don't think Boone would be mixed up with that."

"No. No, of course not," Keely said at once. She forced a smile. Winnie had no idea what was really going on with Boone and her best friend. It was probably better that she never did. Boone would never look twice at Keely again, anyway. She wondered how she was going to manage to draw back from her friendship with Winnie without making the other woman suspicious. She had to find a way. Just the thought of running into Boone again, after the way they'd parted Saturday, made her nervous.

They started lunch, but as Winnie had predicted, she should have bought eggs. She only had two.

"I can't make enough egg salad for us now and for the men later out of just two eggs," she laughed. She grabbed her car keys and her purse. "You finish the pasta salad and I'll run to the store. I'll only be fifteen minutes." She glanced at Keely's worried face. "He's over in the north pasture," she added ruefully. "Boone couldn't even *get* here in fifteen minutes. Feel better?"

"Yes," Keely said blatantly.

Winnie pursed her lips. "I do wonder what's going on between you and my big brother. But I won't ask. Yet."

She rushed out the back door and closed it behind her. Keely felt less secure.

She finished the pasta salad and put it into the refrigerator. She heard the front door open and close and felt a pang of relief. Winnie was back.

But the footsteps coming down the hall weren't soft and muffled. They were heavy and hard. Apprehensive, she turned.

And there was Boone, wearing stained jeans and boots, a shirt wet with sweat, his Stetson dangling from one hand. His eyes, as they met hers, were blazing with anger.

"Come into the office, Keely," he said tautly. "I've got something to show you." He turned and walked away, leaving her to follow.

She paused at the open door of the office, tugging at the buttons on her long-sleeved white shirt she was wearing over tan twill slacks. He was holding the envelope that Winnie said had come by express service this morning. He took out a photograph and held it out to her.

"Have a look," he said in a tone so threatening that it made the hair on the back of her neck stand up. "And then tell me you don't have anything going with Clark!"

CHAPTER ELEVEN

KEELY MOVED SLOWLY into the room and took the photograph Boone held out to her. She almost choked when she saw it. The picture showed two people in bed, in an intimate embrace. The man was Clark. The woman had Keely's face. But it certainly wasn't Keely's body. She almost laughed with relief at the very obvious attempt to frame her by putting her face on another woman's body.

She looked up with the amusement in her eyes, but Boone wasn't laughing. He was positively enraged, and he obviously believed the photograph was proof of her lies.

"This isn't me," she began.

"Like hell it isn't!" he raged. He tore the photograph from her fingers and ripped it to shreds, tossing it onto the carpet. "If you'd just told me the truth, I could have accepted it, Keely. You didn't have to lie!"

"But I didn't," she protested. "And I can prove it!"

Her hands went, reluctantly, to the buttons of her shirt. She didn't want to have to go to this extreme, but he wasn't going to be convinced easily.

He misunderstood the intent at once. "Spare yourself the embarrassment," he said curtly. "I don't care what you look like under that shirt. It was just a game on my part, Keely," he added with a cold smile. "A little flirting, a little teasing, a few kisses. I'm sure you didn't take it seriously. I only wanted to see how far you'd go. If you hadn't made it clear before, you certainly made it clear just now. Either of the Sinclair brothers will do, as long as you get enough to make it worth your while, is that right? And I thought you were so honest and upright and hardworking! It was just a sham. Like all the others, you're only after money!"

"That is not true!" she said defensively.

His eyes glittered again. "I don't want you here anymore. Ever. You get out of my house, Keely, and go home. And don't you come back again. I don't give a damn if Clark or Winnie invites you, don't come! Make an excuse, do whatever it takes. But don't come here again."

"You don't understand!" she began helplessly.

"I said, get out! Now! If you don't, so help me God I'll call one of Hayes's deputies and have you taken out in handcuffs!"

He was too angry to listen to reason, and he meant what he said. Keely couldn't bear the thought of being hauled off to jail for trespassing. It would be all over Comanche Wells and Jacobsville in no time, and she'd never live it down.

She sighed, feeling as if she'd been crushed. She loved him, and he could treat her so badly.

"I'm going," she said. "You don't have to make threats to get me to leave. Please tell Winnie something came up."

He didn't answer her. He swept back down the hall, out the door and into what sounded like a pickup truck. It roared away as Keely started down the long driveway. Boone didn't know that Winnie had driven her here. She didn't have a way home. But she was too wary of Boone to go down to the bunkhouse and ask for a ride. It would do no good, anyway—all the men were out in the pastures, bringing in the crops.

She was wearing a long-sleeved blouse, she had no water, she wasn't even wearing a hat. The sun was brutal. By the time she got out the gates and a quarter of a mile down the road, she was too sick and thirsty to go on. She'd sit in the shade by the highway, she thought. It was flat here. Winnie would come driving by sooner or later and spot her. Her white blouse would stand out in that grove of mesquite trees. She'd just have to be careful of the trees trailing limbs and long thorns, which were so dangerous that they could pierce a boot.

The big tree near the road afforded a little shade. There was a fallen limb next to it which seemed to have been there for a long time. She slumped down, exhausted by the heat, without looking first. That was a mistake. She heard the sound of frying bacon, which even her addled brain immediately connected with the source that would be making it this far away from a stove; a diamondback rattlesnake.

Before she could even turn her head to look for it, the snake struck. It bit her on the forearm and withdrew, still rattling.

Terrified, she jumped to her feet and ran backward before it could get her again. The bite mark was vivid, stained with blood. *Tourniquet,* she thought. *Stop the blood running to the heart. Get the bite lower than the heart...*

She dragged the handkerchief she always carried from her pocket and wrapped half of it around her forearm between the bite and her elbow. She grabbed up a stick and used it to tighten the handkerchief. *Only use it to keep the poison below the skin,* she recalled from

the first-aid book she'd read, *don't tighten it enough
to stop the circulation. Once tightened, don't loosen
it, get help.*

Help? She looked both ways. The road was deserted.
She'd been bitten by a poisonous snake. Her arm was
already swelling as the poison tried to make its way to
her heart. She kept her left arm down—it would be the
one that was already damaged!—and tried to breathe
slowly and shallowly. She'd need antivenin. Did they
have any at the Jacobsville hospital? She didn't have
her mother's cell phone. It was still on the counter in
Winnie's kitchen. The heat had already exhausted her
and her head was swimming. She was nauseated. The
bite hurt. It really hurt!

She closed her eyes, standing in the middle of the
highway. If somebody didn't come down that road
soon, it would be too late. She thought of Boone, the
way he'd been at the charity dance, holding her, kissing her so tenderly, almost as if he…loved her.

"Boone," she whispered. And she fainted.

WINNIE WAS CURSING her own bad luck as she drove
rapidly back to the ranch. Boone had called her, almost incoherent with fury, daring her to ever let Keely
back in the front door. He had photos, he said harshly,
of her with Clark that turned his stomach. He'd told
her to get out and he never wanted to see her on the
place again. He hung up before Winnie could tell him
that Keely had no way home. Now she was hoping she
could get back in time to save the poor girl a long and
uncomfortable walk.

As she approached the ranch road, she noticed a
bundle of rags in the road. But as she came closer, she
realized it wasn't rags—it was Keely!

She wheeled her car around and left it running, the door open, as she rushed to Keely's side.

"Keely! Keely!" she called, as she whipped out her cell phone and dialed the emergency services number without hesitation.

Keely's eyes opened groggily. "Winnie…snake… rattler…" She tried to lift her left arm. It was swollen and almost black already.

"Dear God," Winnie whispered reverently. A voice spoke in her ear. "This is Winnie Sinclair," she said. "Shirley, is that you? I thought it was. Listen, I've got Keely Welsh here in the middle of the highway with snakebite. It was a rattler, she said. I'm taking her to Jacobsville General myself, no time to dispatch an ambulance. Have them waiting at the door with anti-venin. Got that? Thanks, Shirley. No, I can't stay on the line, I have to get her in the car."

She hung up and managed to get Keely into the front seat and belted in, in a matter of seconds, with strength she didn't know she had. Her heart was pounding as she put the car in gear and left tire marks as she shifted into low gear.

A mile down the road she was met by flashing blue lights. She slowed. The car, Jacobsville Police, spun around in front of her. The door opened and Kilraven's head poked out. "Follow me!" he shouted.

She nodded, relieved to have help. He took off and she followed close on his bumper. Cars got out of the way. They went right through two red lights and turned into the emergency entrance to the hospital.

As soon as she stopped the car, Kilraven came running back to get Keely and carry her to her door where a gurney and Dr. Coltrain waited.

"Snakebite," Winnie panted. "Diamondback. She put on a tourniquet herself…"

"It's all right," Kilraven told her. "Shirley called them for you. Everything's ready, except the anti-venin," he added quietly. "They don't have enough, so they're having a state trooper run it down here to the county line. Hayes Carson's going himself to meet him and relay it back here." He put a big hand on Winnie's shoulder. "She'll be all right. You did good."

She bit her lower lip. Tears rained down her face. She turned it away from him and started up the steps.

He pulled her around and into his arms. "Don't ever be ashamed of tears," he said into her ear. "I've shed my share of them."

That was surprising and sort of nice. It meant he was human. "Thanks," she said huskily after a minute. She drew back and wiped at her eyes with the back of her hand. "I was scared stiff and I couldn't show it. She's my friend."

"I know. Come on. I'll walk you in. I had a call here, anyway. Remember old Ben Barkley? His son put a bullet through his leg when he started beating the boy's mother."

"Riley shot him?" she asked, surprised. The boy was sweet and helpful when he called emergency services to get help saving his mother from his habitually drunk father.

"Riley did," he asserted. He grinned, and bent low. "We're going to take him out to our firing range and help him improve his aim, in case he ever does it again."

She burst out laughing. It was such an outrageous thing to say.

"That's better," he said when he saw her face. "Stiff upper lip, now."

"I'm not British."

"You aren't?" he exclaimed. "Why, what a coincidence…neither am I!"

She punched his broad chest, laughing. They walked together to the emergency waiting room.

FURIOUS, HELPLESS TO do anything for her friend, Winnie took refuge in the only thing she could think of that might help—revenge. She phoned Boone and gave him hell.

"Slow down, slow down!" he complained. "I can't understand a word you're saying. Wait…" He cut off the engine on the tractor he was using to help with the harvest. "All right, what was that about Keely?"

"She was walking home, thanks to you, and she got bitten by a rattlesnake! She's at Jacobsville General… Boone? Hello? Hello? Damn!"

She hung up, even more furious now, because he wouldn't listen to her. She called Clark. "Where are you?" she asked when he didn't answer for almost a minute.

He sounded out of breath. "I'm, uh, I had to run to catch the phone," he said lamely. In the background, music was playing and there was a faint protest, which sounded as if it came from a feminine throat.

"Oh, hell, never mind," she muttered and hung up. She didn't need to ask where he was. He was almost certainly with that damned Nellie again. So much for restraint.

But he phoned her back ten minutes later, while she was waiting, hoping, for some sort of report about

Keely. She stopped nurses, who promised to go and check but never came back. She was getting frustrated.

"What did you want?" Clark asked.

"Never mind. Go back to Nellie," she muttered.

"Don't hang up!" he grumbled. "I'm not with Nellie. I'm over at Dave Harston's place helping him move a piano. His wife's making us lunch."

She felt her face go red. "Sorry."

He laughed. "I guess the sounds must be similar, but I swear I'm not doing anything I'd mind being seen doing. What's up?"

"Keely got bitten by a rattler," she said miserably. "I can't find out what's going on and I'm worried sick. Her arm was almost black, Clark. I'm scared—" Her voice broke.

"I'll be there in fifteen minutes. She'll be all right, sis. I know she will."

"Thanks," she said huskily, and hung up. She prayed that he was right.

A commotion at the desk caught her attention. Boone was bulldozing right past a nurse and a police officer—Kilraven—on his way back to the emergency room. Winnie almost cheered. If anybody could cut through red tape, it was her big brother. They could threaten, but they wouldn't stop him.

"Coltrain!" he bellowed.

"Over here," came a deep, resigned voice.

Boone hid it well, but he was terrified. Winnie's phone call made him feel guilty as hell, and he'd hardly managed to breathe as he rushed to the hospital. One of his cowboys had died from a rattler bite the year before. He was scared to death that Keely might not have reached help in time. If she died, he'd never forgive himself, never!

"Where is she?" Boone demanded, dark eyes flashing, face flushed. He'd come straight from work to the hospital in his work clothes, and never noticed how disheveled he was.

Coltrain nodded toward a cubicle where they were working on her. He knew better than to try to stop Boone. It would mean a brawl, where he could least afford one.

Boone walked into the cubicle and stopped dead. Everything seemed to go out of focus except for Keely's left arm. They'd bared her to the waist, pulling the sheet only over one breast, leaving the left one and her shoulder bare while they pumped antivenin into her in an attempt to save her life. She was unconscious. Her arm was almost black, swollen out of recognition. But it wasn't the swelling that Boone was fixated on. It was her shoulder. There were huge scars, which looked as if something with enormous teeth had taken a bite right out of her. The damage was staggering to look at. The pain she must have suffered—

He knew at once that his photographs had been faked, and later he was going to give somebody hell over that botched, so-called investigation. But right now, his whole focus was on this slip of a girl whom he'd misjudged, whom he'd almost killed with his outrage.

"What in hell happened to her?" Boone bit off.

"She was bitten…"

"Not the snakebite. That!" He pointed at her shoulder.

Coltrain wanted to tell him that he should ask Keely, but he knew it would do no good. "She jumped into a mountain lion pit at her father's game park to save a seven-year-old boy who sneaked under the rail when nobody was looking."

"Good God! And where was her father while all that was going down?" Boone demanded.

"Standing at the rail, watching," Coltrain said with utter disdain.

"Damn him," Boone said huskily.

"I couldn't agree more."

He held his breath as he looked at her. "Will she live?" he asked finally, having postponed the question as long as he could.

Coltrain looked at him. "I don't know, Boone," he said honestly. "The poison had a good bit of time to work before she was found…" He hesitated because of the torture in the other man's eyes.

Boone moved past the technicians to the head of the bed where Keely was lying, so white and still. He brushed back her sweaty hair with a hand that wasn't quite steady. He bent down to her ear.

"You have to live," he whispered, his voice forcibly steady. "You have to live. This is my fault, but I can't… live…if you don't, Keely…" He had to stop because his voice was breaking. She was blurring in his eyes. He never cried. His composure was absolute. But he was losing it. His thumb brushed her pale lips as he drew in an audible breath. "I'll kill that damned private detective," he whispered.

Keely stirred, just a heartbeat's movement, but he felt it. His forehead bent down to hers and his lips brushed against the pale, cold skin. "Don't die. Please…"

"You have to let us work," Coltrain said, catching the other man's arm. It was as rigid as metal. "Come on, Boone. Do what's best for her."

Boone hesitated just long enough to take one last look at her.

"Pity about those scars," one of the techs was saying.

"What scars?" Boone asked huskily.

Coltrain only smiled as he herded the rancher out of the cubicle and back out to the waiting room.

Winnie looked up as Boone was deposited in the waiting room. He paused, almost trembling with rage. He looked at his sister. "You call me if there's any change, any at all," he said heavily. "You hear?"

"Yes, of course," she replied. "Where are you going?"

"To kill a private detective," he said through his teeth. He'd added a few pithy adjectives to the sentence, which had Winnie's eyebrows arching toward her hairline.

He was gone in a flash. She connected the photos he'd mentioned to Keely's sudden departure and then to the private detective that Boone was going after. Clark walked in while she was mulling it over in her mind.

She turned to him. "Do we know any bail bondsmen?" she asked in an almost conversational tone.

KEELY HAD BEEN failing, but she rallied when they added the relayed antivenin to her drip catheter. She wasn't conscious, but she was groaning. Coltrain kept her under while they worked to stabilize her vital signs.

It was very late when he came out into the waiting room, smiling.

"She'll make it," he told them wearily. "But she'll be here for a few days."

"Thank God," they said almost in unison.

"We should send the boys out hunting rattlers," Clark suggested.

"Boone's already out after one of them, I'm afraid," Winnie said. She smiled at Coltrain. "Thanks."

"I like her, too," he replied. He smiled. "You'd both better get some rest. I'll have one of the nurses phone you if there's any change."

"Thanks," Winnie said again.

"It's why I'm a doctor," Coltrain said, grinning as he left them.

Winnie tried to phone Boone, but he didn't answer. She was about to try again when Sheriff Hayes Carson came into the room, his brown-streaked blond hair shining in the ceiling light. His dark eyes were turbulent.

"Have you been trying to reach your brother?" he asked Winnie. "Sorry, but they don't allow cell phones in detention."

Winnie groaned. "Oh, no."

"Oh, yes," Hayes replied. "Don't worry about calling anybody. I went and bailed him out myself while I was off duty." He put a hand to his ear. "I swear to God, the guards were writing down the words as he ripped them out. I've never heard such language in my life. At least the detective isn't pressing assault charges, however…"

"He isn't? Thank goodness," Winnie exclaimed. "But why?"

"He ran for his life. His employers weren't so fortunate." He actually smiled. "Detective Rick Marquez and I have been doing a little sleuthing of our own, after office hours, and with a little help from some friends. It turns out," he said in a low tone, wary of eavesdroppers, "that Boone's girlfriend, Misty, and her father are up to their necks in the regional drug traffic network. They ran for it when Marquez sent a DEA agent to their detective agency with a search warrant to have a look around. Last I heard," he added with a chuckle, "there was a statewide BOLO for them. I don't think we'll be seeing them again anytime soon."

Winnie was almost breathless. "Poor Boone. He and Misty were dating...."

"I asked him to do it," Hayes said quietly. "He was mad as hell, too. He said it was interfering with something very personal. I hated to strong-arm him into it, but he was the only person who had any sort of access to her."

Winnie's eyes lit up. "He didn't really care about her, then?"

"No. He couldn't stand her. He did it to help me cut off one of Jacobsville's top drug suppliers."

And Boone didn't want to because of something personal. Could it be Keely? She thought about the photos Misty's father's detective had dug up for him...

"They faked the photos," she burst out.

Hayes frowned. "What photos?"

"Never mind."

"How's Keely?" Hayes asked gently. "I heard about the snakebite from Boone."

"She's going to be fine. I still can't get him on the phone," she added worriedly.

"By now, he's made it to the nurse's station," he said. "He didn't stop cursing until we got to town. He's in the hospital somewhere. He'll turn up directly."

Even as they spoke, Boone walked in the door. He was disheveled, red-eyed and bruised.

"I know," Winnie said when he held up a bruised hand. "The other guy looks worse. Are you okay?"

He shrugged. "A little ragged, that's all. I called Coltrain. He says she'll be fine. The minute she can be moved, she's coming home with us," he added.

Winnie hesitated. "She's not going to want to do that."

"She's doing it, anyway. Has anybody called her mother?" he asked.

Clark came in from the soda machine with two Cokes. "Do you want something to drink?" he asked the two men. He frowned at Boone. "What in hell happened to you?"

"A slight altercation," Boone said nonchalantly. "I'd like a black coffee, if you're taking orders."

Clark grinned. "Anything for my big brother," he murmured, and left again.

"I'll drive by Keely's house and speak with her mother," Hayes said. "I'm going back in tonight because we've got a case pending, but I'm off tomorrow." He wagged his finger at Boone. "You go home and wash your mouth out with soap."

Boone put an affectionate arm around his shoulders. "You're the only man I know who thinks 'Crackers and Milk' is a curse."

"I give talks to little kids about drugs," he pointed out. "What if I slipped in front of a classroom of kids?"

"They probably know more bad words than you do," Winnie chipped in, grinning. "You should hear some of their parents talk on the phone when they call for the police to come."

Hayes winced. "I know. I have to hear them." He grinned at Winnie. "You know, you're pretty good on that radio. Kilraven likes having you on duty. He says you brighten up dark nights."

"He does?" Winnie's face became radiant.

"Cut that out," Boone said severely. "She's going to go back to college and get a degree and marry an educated man."

"I am not going back to college," Winnie said pleasantly. "I don't want a degree, and I'm not marrying any man, educated or otherwise, until it pleases me."

"So there." Hayes chuckled.

Boone glowered at her. She glowered back.

"I, uh, wouldn't get too hopeful about Kilraven," Hayes said gently, a little embarrassed. "He's had some tragedy in his life. He may act normal, but he hasn't gotten over the trauma."

Winnie moved closer to him. "Talk to me, Carson," she said quietly, using his last name, as she always did when she was really serious.

"A few years ago," he said quietly, "there was a violent murder up in San Antonio. Kilraven was working undercover there at the time, with the local police. It was a rainy Saturday night—when we always have dozens of wrecks—and he and his partner were closer than the patrol units, most of whom were tied up, so they volunteered to secure the crime scene. Kilraven recognized the address and ran in, before his partner could stop him." Hayes closed his eyes. "It was bad. Really bad." He paused. "What I'm telling you is that the man is an emotional trainwreck looking for a place to happen, regardless of his seeming composure. He's not going to put down roots in Jacobsville, Texas. He's put off dealing with his trauma too long. One day, he'll crash and burn."

"Did he know the murder victims?" Winnie asked hesitantly.

"He was related to them," Hayes said. "And that's all I'm saying about it."

Winnie wondered which relatives were involved. Poor man! "Did you speak to Dr. Coltrain about how soon we can take Keely home?" she asked her brother.

Boone shook his head. "No. But I will. I can guarantee it won't be tonight."

She managed a smile. Hayes had dashed her dreams to bits. She didn't want it to show. "I'm going home to get some sleep. You coming?" she asked Boone.

He hesitated. "I guess so." He looked at himself and grimaced. "I should have gone home and changed."

"Nobody will notice." She sighed. "A lot of people have been here all day and half the night, waiting for hope to make results." She indicated two families with white faces and red eyes. She smiled at them. They smiled back. Friends were made easily in emergency rooms. She said she was going home and asked if they needed anything that she could bring them. But they shook their heads. There were things they needed, but they didn't dare leave until they knew something. She understood.

WINNIE AND BOONE slept for a while and then drove back to the hospital. They ate breakfast in the cafeteria without tasting what they ate, and drank black coffee.

"What did you say to Keely?" she asked.

His eyes were tortured. "Too much," he bit off. He looked down into his empty coffee cup. "Those damned photos were so convincing!" He realized, too, that Keely hadn't been trying to seduce him when she started to unbutton her blouse. She was going to show him the scars. It was an act of bravery that he hadn't appreciated at the time. Now, it hurt him.

"She'll be all right," Winnie assured him. "You can make peace."

He laughed hollowly. "Think so?"

The cafeteria door opened and Hayes Carson came in. He wasn't smiling. He made a beeline for the Sinclairs.

"I need to talk to you," he said tersely, looking around to make sure he wasn't being overheard. "I just found Ella Welsh, dead in her living room!"

CHAPTER TWELVE

"DEAD?" BOONE EXCLAIMED, careful to keep his voice low. "Of what?"

"A gunshot wound," Hayes replied. He pulled out a chair and sat down. "I had the coroner out, along with a forensic team from the state crime lab and my own investigator. We found latent prints and a shell casing, but I don't need ESP to know who did it."

"Keely's father," Winnie guessed. "Or that partner of his, Jock."

"They were desperate for money, Keely said," Hayes replied. "I told Keely to tell Ella to put the house on the market, but not really sell it, to make Brent Welsh think she was complying. But the men must have gone to her and demanded immediate results. She either refused or infuriated them, I don't know." He sighed. "We don't dare let Keely see her body. It will have to be a closed casket."

"What?" Boone exclaimed.

Hayes's expression was eloquent. "They tortured her, probably to find out about any assets she hadn't produced."

"Good God!" Boone said heavily. "They'll come after Keely, won't they?" he asked coldly. "She'll be next, because she'll inherit what little Ella had to leave her."

"We haven't heard anything about sightings of them

since Misty and her father and the detective ran for the border," Hayes told him. "They may be spooked enough to keep running, if they were in the same network with the remnants of the Fuentes brothers' drug smuggling operation. Too, the murder may prompt them to keep running, since they know we'll be after them for it. On the other hand, if Ella left life insurance, Keely will get that. And Ella's savings accounts would mean ready cash. I talked to her banker already. He told me there is some money there."

"We'll need more men to protect the ranch," Winnie thought aloud.

"Several more, all ex-military, and I know where to find them," Boone said grimly. "I'll make the ranch into a fortress. Welsh will never get his hands on Keely!"

"I could make a comment here about vigilante justice," Hayes said with grim humor, "but I won't. Just don't step over the line. I can't afford any more bail money."

Boone chuckled. "You'll be paid back for that." The smile faded. "Poor Keely," he said heavily. "First the snake, now her mother."

"Someone will have to tell her." Hayes looked around him at the grim faces. "We could draw straws. Or we could ask Coltrain to do the dirty work."

"I'll tell her when the time comes," Boone said softly. "It's my responsibility now."

Winnie didn't say anything, but she looked thoughtful, and happy.

WHICH WAS A far cry from how Keely looked when she came out from under the effects of the medicines she'd been given.

Boone never left her bedside. She'd glared at him the first time she saw him there, when she was still too sick and weak to speak. By the third day, she was regaining some strength and she was furious.

"I know, I know," he said before she got started. "I got everything backward. I accused you of things you didn't do and threw you out of the house." He looked briefly tortured. "I know I caused this." He drew in a long breath, staring down at his boots. "God Almighty, I never meant for you to walk home with temperatures at the century mark! I must have been out of my head not to realize that you didn't even have a way to get home."

Keely wanted to rage at him, but she was still very sick and her arm hurt. She winced every time she moved. "It wasn't me…with Clark, in that picture you shoved in my face!"

He lifted his head and nodded. "I know," he said grimly.

That look, and the words, told her things she wouldn't have asked about. He knew. He knew about her shoulder. She closed her eyes and tears flowed out of them. She felt even worse now. She'd never wanted Boone, of all people, to know her secret. Her mind went back to the boy who'd thrown up when he saw her shoulder…

He moved close to the bed and bent over her, with one big hand beside her head on the pillow. "They'll kill me if I sit down here. I know you're still weak and you hurt like hell. But I want you to feel something." He drew her right hand up to his chest over the shirt and smoothed it down. He watched her eyes while she did it, saw the realization in her green eyes, and nodded.

She frowned as she met his eyes.

"There are more of them," he said stiffly, rising away from her. "A lot more—one that even took bone out of my thigh. When Misty saw me, in Germany, just after the bandages were removed, she ran out of the room. It's a little less messy now, after some plastic surgery, but the scars are too deep to be permanently erased, and it's noticeable. I don't go shirtless anymore," he added bitterly. "I haven't for years."

She felt the pain. She understood it. "I haven't worn anything short-sleeved since I was thirteen years old," she replied quietly. "When I was sixteen, a boy I liked asked me out on a date. He was just fumbling, you know, like boys will, but when he got my blouse half-off and saw the scars—they were fresh, then—he…" She closed her eyes. "He jerked the car door open and threw up. He was sorry, very sorry, but I was devastated. I knew, then, that I'd never have a normal life. I knew I'd never get married and have…have children…" Her voice broke and tears fell hotly onto her cheeks. She was weak and sick and in pain, or she'd never have let him see her devastation.

It affected him. He bent down again and drew his mouth over her eyes, her nose, her cheeks. "Don't," he whispered huskily. "You've been so brave, Keely. I can't bear to see you cry. Don't, honey. Don't."

Now she knew she was dreaming. Boone had never called her a pet name, and he didn't care if he hurt her. She closed her eyes, though, enjoying the dream. It was so sweet to have his breath on her lips, his mouth caressing her wet face, his deep voice murmuring sweet and impossible things.

The sound of the door opening stopped the dream, of course. Boone moved away and she was sure it had been her imagination. She'd been heavily sedated, after all, to compensate for the terrible pain. Boone's expression was taciturn, as usual, and he didn't look anything like a man who'd been whispering sweet endearments to her. Winnie and Clark came into the room, somber and worried, especially when they saw Keely's face.

"You didn't tell her?" Winnie asked angrily. "Coltrain said not to—"

"Tell me what?" Keely asked at once, dabbing her eyes with the sheet.

Winnie's face contorted. Boone glared at her. So did Clark.

"Tell me what?" Keely demanded, belligerent now, as she looked from one guilty face to the other.

"I said I'd tell her when it was time," Boone said shortly. "It's not time."

"Yes, but…" Winnie stopped, horrified, as the television, overhead, began with the lead story of the day's news. The first bit was a photo of Ella Welsh and news about her murder. That was what she and Clark had rushed back into Keely's room to tell him, because they knew the television had been on although turned down, so they could catch the evening news. They'd seen the beginning of this broadcast on the wall televisions as they passed through the waiting room. They hadn't thought about the murder story being broadcast so soon.

Keely burst into fresh tears, almost hysterical.

"Damn that thing! Shut it off!" Boone shot at Clark as he started toward the call button next to Keely's pillow. While Clark shut off the television, Boone pressed the button and asked the nurse to come in, before he bent to curl Keely's face into his shoulder. "It's all right, honey. It's all right. I'm so sorry. I never meant you to hear it like that!"

The nurse came in. Boone explained quietly what had just happened. The nurse grimaced and went to call Coltrain, who was, she explained, still making rounds.

The redheaded doctor was in the room scant minutes later. He ordered a sedative for Keely and waited until it took effect before he called the siblings out into the hall.

"It was the damned television," Boone said angrily. "Why do you have those things in every room in the first place?"

"It wasn't my idea, believe me," Coltrain replied at once. "Keely's going to have a hard recuperation if she has to go back to that house alone."

"She won't," Boone said at once. "She's coming home with us. I've already discussed it with Hayes Carson."

"Good thinking," Coltrain replied. He drew in a heavy breath. "I never expected that story to come out so soon. Hell, we don't even have a local television broadcasting station in the county."

"San Antonio is plenty close enough to pick the story up, especially on a slow news day," Winnie murmured. "There's nothing but political news, and everybody's sick of that."

"You'd better hire some bodyguards to protect you at home," Coltrain advised. "These guys are desperate enough to go after money any way they can get it."

"Everybody knows they killed Keely's mother— at least locally we know it," Winnie said. "They'd be stupid to stick around."

"These guys will never get work building spaceships," Coltrain said, tongue-in-cheek. "Otherwise, they wouldn't have risked coming here in the first place. Hayes Carson would love to get Brent Welsh in his sights on any pretext."

"So would I," Boone replied grimly. "He stood by and watched while Keely got mauled saving a kid from a mountain lion. Those scars are going to be permanent, aren't they?" he asked Coltrain.

Coltrain grimaced. "We might be able to get a plastic surgeon to clean them up, but they're very deep. She'd have half a dozen surgeries to anticipate, at least. And there's something else—the sutures weren't done well, either. She may face some real problems down the road. I'd recommend plastic surgery for that reason alone. But she has no insurance, you know."

"What the hell does that matter?" Boone asked blithely. "I'll take care of it. You talk her into it, and I'll pay the surgeon."

Coltrain grinned. "That's a deal."

Winnie didn't say anything, but she felt terrible that she and Keely had been friends for so many years, and Keely had never told her about the encounter with the mountain lion. She wondered if she'd said or done something that would make her best friend uncomfortable telling her about it.

"Is Keely asleep?" Boone asked Coltrain.

He nodded. "She'll be out for a while. It's just as well. That snakebite is still giving her hell. If Winnie hadn't found her when she did… Well, it doesn't bear thinking about," he added, cutting short the remark when he saw Boone's tortured eyes. "I'd better get back to work. If you need me, just tell the nurse on duty. They can always find me."

"Thanks," Boone said.

Coltrain shrugged and smiled. "I like Keely."

The siblings gathered around to discuss their plans. Boone decided that he'd better go and see Eb Scott in person. He was going to need specialized talent. Clark and Winnie would take turns staying with Keely. Nobody was going to get past them. They weren't armed, but they could certainly call for help.

IT WAS MORNING before Keely woke up again. The combination of all the drugs and the emotional upheaval of her mother's death had knocked her out for the night. She blinked sleepily, her mind clear and untroubled until she remembered quite suddenly what she'd seen on television the night before. It was like a rock on her heart. Tears stung her eyes, all over again.

"I'm so sorry, Keely," Winnie said gently, from her vigil in the chair beside the bed. "About your mother."

Keely glanced at her. She sighed. "I knew I'd lose her someday," she said, "and we were almost enemies for so long. But we were just getting to know each other again, and we were becoming friends..." She bit her lip, hard. "It's been a rotten week," she said after a minute.

"Yes, it has." She hesitated. "I wish you could have told me about your shoulder," she said. "I feel that I've failed you, because you couldn't trust me enough to tell me."

Keely grimaced. "I was afraid you'd tell Boone," she said softly. "Not that it would have mattered. He hated me..."

"No, he didn't," came the immediate reply. "You have no idea what's been going on, while you were out of it."

"He showed me a photograph of some woman with

my head on another body, in a compromising situation with Clark," Keely said heavily. "I knew it was a fake, but Boone didn't. He was furious. I was going to sink my pride and show him…and he thought I was trying to seduce him!" Her eyes smoldered. "I should have hit him with something! Then he tells me to get out of the house, and stalks off before I can say I haven't got a way home. When I get out of this bed," she added, building up steam as she spoke, "I'm going to turn him every which way but loose! That man has some lumps coming!"

Winnie had to fight a smile. Keely was such a gentle person, but she was really angry. "I'll help you thump him," she promised. "But he didn't know, Keely. And you don't know how he reacted when he found out, either."

"What do you mean?"

"When he saw you in the emergency room, he came out raving that he'd been conned by Misty's father's detective. He left and the next thing we knew, Hayes Carson was here, telling us he'd just had to bail Boone out of jail in San Antonio."

"What?" Keely exclaimed.

"He beat up the detective who faked that photograph." Winnie chuckled. "He was arrested and Hayes had to bail him out and bring him home."

"Will they prosecute him?" Keely asked, her anger forgotten in concern for Boone's future. "He isn't going to have to go to jail, is he?" she asked fearfully.

"Not likely. The detective, Misty and her father all ran for the border, and nobody's around to press charges," Winnie said smugly. "It so happens that they're involved with the Fuentes's outfit, can you believe it? Boone was only seeing Misty to feed Hayes

Carson information on her contacts. He was furious at Hayes for making him do it." She grinned. "I told you he wouldn't forgive her that easily after what she did to him."

"Boone got arrested." Keely said it, disbelievingly. "He never puts a foot wrong."

"He did this time. But there were extenuating circumstances. He was rather tipsy at the time."

"He was drinking?"

"From what we hear," Winnie agreed. She laughed. "My spotless big brother, drunk and beating up detectives." She shook her head. "What is the world coming to?" She grinned at Keely. "Apparently he thinks a little more of you than he let on, I'd say."

Keely was afraid to hope for much, especially after Boone had seen her wrecked shoulder. But his actions indicated more feeling for Keely than he'd expressed verbally. There was hope, she thought. He had scars, too. Perhaps he'd had worse experiences than she had, with people of the opposite sex who didn't understand or care about his scars.

BY THE TIME Boone came back to the hospital, Winnie and Clark had gone home for supper and to get a room ready for Keely when she was discharged. Coltrain had said she'd be ready to go the next day if she continued improving.

Keely didn't want to go home with them if Boone only offered out of guilt. But she didn't want to go to her home, either, with Ella's death so fresh on her mind. Nobody had told her where Ella died, but Keely suspected that it was at the house.

She had an unexpected visitor while she was worrying her choices to death in her mind. Ella's best friend, Carly, came in, dressed in black, red-eyed from crying.

"Did they tell you?" she asked gently, because she didn't want to upset Keely.

"Yes," Keely said huskily. "We were doing so well together…" Her voice broke.

Carly bent over the bed, and hugged her gently. "I've been out of town. There was a missed call on my cell phone, but when I tried to call Ella back, there was no answer. I got worried when I couldn't get you, either, so I cut my trip short and came home." She grimaced. "What a homecoming! Ella dead, and you in the hospital in serious condition. Are you going to be all right?"

"Yes," Keely said. "But I understand that the snake died."

It took a minute for Carly to get the dry humor. She smiled. "Poor snake."

"I expect his relatives are all sad." She dabbed at her eyes with the sheet. "I haven't had time to make any arrangements about the funeral."

"Do you want me to do that?" Carly asked solemnly. "Ella gave me a copy of her will and instructions for her funeral two years ago. I never really thought they'd be needed, but I humored her."

"Could you call Lunsford's and make the arrangements?" Keely asked gently. "She has a burial policy with them, which should cover everything. She paid it off a few years ago."

"I'll be glad to do that," Carly replied. Fresh tears rolled down her cheeks. "She was the only friend I had—the only real one."

Keely reached out her good hand and squeezed Carly's. "You were her only real friend," she replied. "I'm glad she had you."

Carly cried even harder. "I wish I could take back every mean thing I ever said to you, Keely," she sobbed. "I didn't really mean any of it. In the old days, I took care of you a lot when Ella couldn't. I lost sight of that. But I'll do anything to make it up to you now, if I can."

"Look after Mama's funeral arrangements," Keely said, "and we'll call it even."

Carly dried her eyes. "When do you want to have it?" she asked worriedly. "You don't look up to a funeral."

She wasn't. She hesitated. Boone came in the door, gave Carly a cold appraisal and moved to Keely's bed.

"I've arranged for some additional manpower at the ranch," he said without preamble. "What do you want to do about your mother?"

"Carly's going to take care of that," Keely said. "She knows where everything is, and she has copies of Mama's will and last wishes."

Boone glanced at the older woman. "If there are any outstanding accounts, I'll take care of them," he said.

Carly nodded. Her eyes were as red as Keely's. "Thanks." She hesitated. "You know," she said, staring meaningfully at Boone, "it might not be a bad idea to have her cremated, and the ashes buried in the family plot."

Boone knew then that Carly had seen Ella and wanted to spare Keely the trauma of it. His eyes narrowed. "I think that's a good idea. Keely?"

Keely wasn't sure. She hesitated.

"A Viking funeral," Boone said quietly. "Appropriate for a brave woman."

Keely burst out crying again. "Yes," she agreed, choking. "She was brave. Okay. That's okay."

Boone leaned over and gathered her as close as he could, kissing the tears away. "It passes," he said softly. "Everything passes. You'll be able to remember her with happiness one day."

"Yes, you will," Carly seconded. She went on the other side of the bed, and bent and kissed Keely's disheveled hair. "I'll go and get things started. The hospital and the funeral home may need your approval before they can proceed. I'll have them call you here."

"Do that," Boone said quietly. "But I don't think there will be a problem. You stuck by Ella when nobody else would go near her."

Carly took that for a compliment and smiled. "Thanks."

"If you can find that snake," Keely told Boone, trying to lighten the somber mood, "we can arrange the same sort of funeral for him. Of course, if he didn't die from biting me, we'll have to kill him first."

Boone managed a chuckle. "I'm glad to see that you're better."

She smiled weakly, grimacing as she moved her arm.

"Coltrain says she can go home tomorrow, so we'll have her with us," Boone told Carly. He pulled out his wallet, got out a business card and handed it to her. "If you need help with the arrangements, let me know."

"Okay. If we cremate her, we can schedule a memorial service when this is all over," Carly told him. She glanced at Keely worriedly. "You're not going to be able to manage a funeral in the condition you're in right now."

"I have to agree," Keely said. She caught her breath. "Oh, my gosh! My job! I didn't even call Dr. Rydel! He's going to fire me!"

"I phoned him," Boone said at once. "He's got a temp filling in for you. He and the staff send their best wishes. They sent you a big fruit basket. It just came, so the nurses gave it to me, but I took it out to the car. I'm taking it home. You can have it tomorrow."

"Thanks," she told him. "I was afraid of losing my job. I was too sick to call and tell them what was going on."

"Oh, everybody in Comanche Wells and Jacobsville knows everything that's going on already," Carly said. She glanced amusedly at Boone. "And I mean everything."

Boone's eyes actually twinkled, but Keely didn't see it.

Carly said her goodbyes and left Boone alone with Keely. He stuck his hands in his slacks' pockets and stood over her, his eyes soft and quiet.

"You look a little better," he commented.

"I wish I felt it. I'm still sick to my stomach and my arm throbs," she said huskily. She looked up at him. "I hate snakes."

"They don't like people sitting on them," he pointed out.

"I didn't. He was just all of a sudden there. I didn't even look at him sideways. He just rattled his head off and struck at me."

"Nervous."

She blinked. "Excuse me?"

"Rattlesnakes are nervous. They rattle to try to scare people into going away."

It had never occurred to her that a snake could be nervous. She said so.

He sighed. "Anyway, we got him."

"You got him? You did?" She was excited.

"The boys found him about twenty feet from where you were sitting when he bit you."

"What did they do with him?"

He pursed his lips. "Do you like cowboy hats?"

"I guess so. I don't wear them much, except when I go riding."

"You'll wear this one. It's just your size and it's got a nice new rattlesnake hatband. Or it will have, when the skin's tanned out."

"You didn't!"

"I did." He grinned down at her. "We'll go riding, when you're better."

"We will?"

One eye narrowed. "You go riding with Clark and Winnie all the time. You can go riding with me now," he said with faint belligerence.

"Okay," she said, fascinated. It almost sounded as if he were jealous of them. That was ridiculous, of course.

"I had a television put in your room. You can watch movies on pay-per-view. We've got satellite, too, so you can watch programs from all over the world." His eyes twinkled. "Then, there's the national news, with the presidential race on every channel, every hour, every day."

She sighed. "I haven't watched the national news for weeks. I can't stand the monotony. The only news they report is on the presidential election and every detail of the private lives of celebrities."

"The Spanish channel has the real news," he pointed out. "If you want to know what's going on in the world, that's where to find out."

She smiled. "I can't speak Spanish."

"I'll teach you," he said quietly, and his eyes were

insinuating that he had in mind teaching her other things, as well.

She flushed a little. Her life had been a closed, painful book, her future a dream that she never thought would be realized. Now, here was this dishy man with whom she'd been in love for years, looking at her with acquisitive eyes and smiling at her. It felt as if her heart might burst from joy.

He smiled. "Mrs. Johnston has an assistant cook, Melinda. She's from Guatemala. She's teaching us Mayan. You can learn, too."

"Mayan?" She caught her breath. "Their culture had astronomy and the concept of zero and raised beds for planting and irrigation while Europeans were knocking each other over the head with rocks."

"I know." He chuckled. "You spend your time off at the library reading books about them. Or so I hear from the head librarian."

She flushed. It flattered her that he'd learned things about her. "I'd love to go and see some of the Mayan ruins," she said. "I'd love to go to Peru and see the Inca ruins, too."

"So would I," he told her. "Maybe we can both go, one day."

For her, that was a pipe dream. She'd never save enough to pay for a plane ticket even to south Texas for a vacation. Her smile was wistful.

He saw that. "What else do you like?"

She smiled. "Ancient history."

"The Caesars, the philosophers, the politicians...?"

"Don't mention politicians!"

"What sort of history?" He chuckled. "And which historians do you read?"

"Tacitus. Thucydides. Strabo. Arrian. Plutarch. Those ones."

"Deep authors for a young mind," he commented.

"You listen here, I may be young, but I have an old mind," she told him. "I was pretty much on my own when my father took me out to west Texas to live in an animal park, and I was really on my own when I came back here, because Mama was drunk so much." Mama. The thought sobered her, made her aware of her recent tragedy. "I can't believe my own father would kill her," she said. "He was a little out of the bounds of law sometimes, but he never hurt anybody."

"He sold drugs," Boone reminded her. "That does hurt people."

"Yes, but you know what I mean," she replied. "He isn't a killer."

"Baby, all people are killers, given the right incentive," he said. "Anybody can kill."

She sighed. "I suppose so," she said sadly.

He bent and kissed her, gently, on her mouth. "I'm going to get a cup of decent coffee. What can I bring you?"

"A nice juicy steak with hash browns?" she asked hopefully.

"No chance I could get that past the nurses' station, unless they were all wearing nose plugs. Try again," he invited.

"I guess I'll wait for supper here," she said with resignation.

"When you're well again, I'll fly you up to Fort Worth and take you to this little steak place I know," he said.

Her heart jumped up into her throat. "You mean it?"

He drew in a long breath. "I had to date Misty to

feed information to Hayes, and I gave him hell twice a day about it. I was over her years ago. But I had to put on an act, to keep her from getting suspicious." His eyes darkened. "Hayes has a lot to answer for. She's vindictive. She set you up, and I was too angry to think straight when I saw those photographs."

Keely recalled that Misty had promised to get even with her. She'd done a good job of it. "She'll get her just deserts one day," Keely replied.

"We all do," he said philosophically. He glanced at his watch. "I have to make a few phone calls and get something to eat, then I'll be back."

Her eyes lit up. "Okay."

He smiled slowly. Disheveled, her hair uncombed, her face devoid of any makeup, she was beautiful to him. So easily, she could have been dead. He'd never have been able to live with that, knowing he caused her death.

He bent and kissed her again with breathless tenderness. "I'll be back soon," he whispered.

She smiled. "Okay. I'll wait."

He chuckled as he walked out.

Ten minutes later the phone rang. She answered it, thinking it must be Carly or Winnie or Clark.

"Keely, is that you?"

It was her father's voice.

CHAPTER THIRTEEN

"YOU KILLED MY mother!" Keely choked, overwhelmed with rage at just the sound of his voice. "How could you!"

"It wasn't me. I swear it wasn't!" he replied, and he sounded frightened. "Keely, I've never killed a person in my life. You have to believe me."

"You threatened her for money—"

"I had to! Listen, if I don't pay them, they'll...well, they'd already threatened to kill your mother, now they say they'll get you, too," he said nervously. "It's the Fuentes gang! I got mixed up with them because of Jock," he said bitterly. "He's been working for Fuentes for years. He even went to prison for him, just after you came to live with me. He said they paid better than any of the other distributors, and that he'd get me in because he had a cousin in the organization. But there was trouble right upfront because Jock double-crossed one of the bosses and pocketed some drug money. Then he hid out and left me holding the bag. They're after me, now." There was a sigh. "Your mother was right about Jock. She said he'd destroy me if I stuck with him, and he has. He keeps calling me, making threats toward you if you don't come up with enough money to help him to get out of town before the drug lords kill him. I don't know what to do!"

She had to clamp down hard on her feelings. He

was rationalizing his behavior, but she remembered that he'd stood by while the mountain lion dragged her away to what would have been her death.

"You go to Sheriff Carson," she told him. "Tell him what you've told me, and help him find Jock. That's what you have to do."

"Hell, Carson will lock me up and throw away the key!" he muttered. "I gave his brother the coke that killed him. No, I'm not going to the law."

"What else can you do?" she asked.

"Get enough money to pay Jock, so he'll get off my back. The Fuentes organization want Jock. They want to kill him, but they don't know where he is. They thought Ella did and they…" He was going to say they tortured her, but he couldn't make himself say that to his daughter, whom he'd failed in so many ways already. "Well, they killed her. Now, the only hope I have is to raise enough money to help Jock get out of the country before they catch up with him. He swore if I didn't, he'd tell them I was the one who double-crossed them. He'd give them back what he took and blame it on me!"

"If you give him money," she said in a weary tone, "he'll only want more."

"There's a chance he won't. He just wants to get out of the country before they do to him what they did to those drug agents they killed. He won't say so, but I think he's afraid of Fuentes's new partner. The partner is called Machado and he hates Jock. He'll kill him before Fuentes does if he gets the chance, and Jock knows it."

"Let him," Keely said coldly.

"Jock was the only friend I had, Keely," he said

heavily. "He stood by me when everybody else jumped ship."

Just as Carly had stood by Ella. But that had been because Carly genuinely loved Keely's mother. Jock had stood by Brent Welsh because he knew Ella had money, Keely thought, and he could use Brent to get some of it. But she didn't say that. He wouldn't have listened anyway.

"I don't have any money," Keely told him. "I work as a veterinarian technician and I make minimum wage. Mama—" Her voice broke. She composed herself. "Mama had some money in a savings account, but it's in her name and it's tied up in probate. I won't be able to get it for weeks." She didn't know if that was true, but it sounded convincing.

He cursed sharply. "There must be something you can sell!"

"She already sold it all," she said bitterly.

He muttered again, incoherent. "Then those friends of yours, the Sinclairs—they've got money. Ask them for it!"

"I won't."

"Your life is on the line, Keely!" he raged. "It's not a game! Jock's already said that he's got nothing to lose. He'll kill you if you don't help us."

She felt very old. Her mother was dead, she'd almost died herself. Boone knew her darkest secret and would surely not want her anymore, even if he was compassionate and understanding about her injury. He was scarred himself. But Keely saw no future for herself.

"I don't care," she said passively. "Let Jock do his worst. He might be doing me a favor," she said with black humor. "God knows, I'm never going to have a husband or a family, the way I look."

"I'm…sorry," he said slowly. "I'm very sorry, for what happened. I was so shocked that I couldn't even do anything. I feel bad about that. And I didn't think about how the scars might affect your life."

"Pity," she said, and felt hatred seethe through her. "Until that moment, I thought you cared about me."

"I do care, in my way," he said. "My parents were ice-cold with each other and with me. They never went out of their way to do one charitable thing for anyone else. I learned that you take care of number one."

"So did Mama," she replied. "Neither of you was fit to raise a child."

"Tell me about it." He laughed hollowly. "Once you came, our lives changed forever. She was too unstable emotionally to cope with a baby." He sounded bitter. "You spent a lot of time with Carly."

A light flashed in her mind as she recalled Carly's face. It was far more familiar to her than Ella's. No wonder the other woman had been so protective of her.

"But that's all in the past, and I've got bigger problems now. You have to try to get me some money. Jock says he won't wait much longer."

"Tell him to come see me. I can borrow a shotgun," she mused.

"It's not funny!"

"If you were in my position, it might be."

"Ask your friends if they'll help out. Even two thousand might be enough," her father persisted. "Take this number down, Keely. You can reach me here."

She grabbed a pencil and pad from inside the drawer by her bed. "Okay."

He gave her the number. "Do your best, honey," he

pleaded. "You lived against all the odds. I don't want you to die over a handful of money."

"I'll see what I can do," she said heavily, and hung up. It wasn't until then she realized that she was shaking.

WHEN BOONE CAME back, he found Keely quiet and preoccupied, staring into space.

"What's wrong?" he asked, because he knew at once that something was. He could feel it.

She frowned. "How do you know something is?"

He moved to the bed and dropped down lazily into the armchair by her bed. "I read minds. Come on. Tell me."

She sank back into the pillows wearily. "My father called. Jock's running from the drug lords and he wants money to get out of the country. He told my father that if I don't get it up for him somehow, he'll kill me. The drug dealers will probably send him back to wherever he came from in a shoe box."

He took off his hat and dropped it on the floor by his chair. He ran a big, lean hand through his black hair. "I'll turn Bailey loose on him, and when he gets through, Jock will fit in the shoe box. Or parts of him will."

"Is Bailey all right?" she asked.

He smiled. "Doing great, thanks to you." His smile faded. "I still can't believe I listened to that self-centered little cheater when you told me what was wrong with Bailey. I wish I could go back and live those few minutes over."

"It turned out all right."

He nodded. "Only because you had the guts to do what you knew was right. You've got grit, Keely."

"I'm just stubborn," she replied. "What am I going to do? I don't have anything I could sell that would bring enough money to buy Jock a plane ticket."

"We'll talk to Hayes," he told her. "He'll know what to do."

AND HAYES DID. They arranged for a sum of money that Boone would give her father to lure him into a trap. Keely had already given Hayes the number where her father could be reached when she got the money.

"You're not going," she told Boone when he and Hayes were discussing who was going to take the money to Jock.

"Excuse me?" Boone asked haughtily.

She flushed, but she wouldn't backtrack. "You're not going. Everybody around me is either dead or in danger, and you're not going to join my mother at the local funeral home. Let him do it." She pointed at Hayes. "He knows how to deal with criminals. He's good at it."

"Thanks," Hayes mused.

"I was with a Special Forces unit in the Middle East," Boone reminded Keely. "I came home."

She looked to Hayes for assistance.

He grimaced. "Okay, I'll work out the details once you get the money together. With any luck, we can nab both men."

"I'll call you," Boone promised.

When Hayes left, Boone watched Keely with faint amusement. "You're afraid I'll get hurt."

She shifted on her pillows. "My mother is dead because my father wanted money. I don't want to lose you…I mean, I don't want Clark and Winnie to have to lose you."

He pursed his lips. "I could have wrung your neck when I saw those photos," he said conversationally. "I could have wrung Clark's, too."

"I know you don't want him around me because I'm in another social class…"

"Stop that," he muttered. "I didn't want him around you because you're mine, Keely," he said curtly.

Warmth shot through her body like fire. Surely she was hearing things. Her expression said so.

"We'll have to do something about that self-image." He chuckled. "I don't know why you ever thought I didn't want you. Even Clark realized I was jealous as hell."

"You hated me," she exclaimed. "You ignored me when you came to bring Bailey to Dr. Rydel!"

"Camouflage," he replied. "I didn't know about your shoulder, then," he added, in a subdued tone. "All I could think about was my own defects. I'd already had evidence of how a woman would react to them. You're so young, Keely. I thought you were too young to cope."

"I'm older than I look," she replied.

"We both are." His dark eyes grew intent on her face. "I don't care about the obstacles anymore. We'll improvise."

She was tingling at the way he looked at her, but she was a little apprehensive. It was a modern world, in the circles Boone frequented. But Keely was living in the past. "I've never been…I've never had…I don't know how…" She gave up, exasperated.

"I know all that," he said gently. "We'll go slow. I won't rush you."

"Yes, but it won't matter," she said earnestly. "Don't you see? I was raised religiously, despite the bad role models my parents were. I don't believe people should sleep together if they aren't married."

"Funny," he returned with a smile, "that's exactly the way I feel, too."

She seemed to stop breathing. Her eyes were held by his. She felt funny. "It is?" she parroted.

"It is. So we'll get to know each other a lot better, then we'll make long-term decisions. Okay?"

She smiled. Her heart was soaring in her chest. "Okay."

He chuckled deep in his throat. It was the first time he'd felt happy since the ordeal began.

HE GOT THE money out of his bank, in cash, and phoned Hayes, who had Keely call her father and set up a time and place for the money to change hands.

"You got it!" her father exclaimed. "Keely, you're a wonder! This will save my life!"

"I thought it was going to save mine," she replied suspiciously.

"Of course, yours!" he said quickly. "I meant it will save us both! Where do you want me to meet you?"

"Dad, I'm still in the hospital," she pointed out.

"Oh! That's right. I guess I could meet you in the hospital, then," he said.

She repeated what he said, so that Boone and Hayes could hear him. Hayes nodded enthusiastically.

"Yes, that would be fine," Keely said. "When do you want to come?"

"Ten minutes," he said, and hung up.

She put the receiver back down. "He's on his way

here," she said. Her tone was bitter. "He said it would save his life. He wasn't ever concerned about mine."

"I'm sorry, Keely," Hayes told her. "But he never was concerned about the welfare of other people. If he had been, he'd never have sent Bobby that totally pure cocaine, knowing it would kill him."

Keely sighed. "I had hoped that—" She broke off, flushed. "Well, it would have been nice if he'd cared a little about me. But if he had, he'd have dived into that mountain-lion pit without thinking about the consequences when that little boy's life was at stake."

"Which you did," Boone replied.

She nodded. "I didn't think at all. I just reacted. Dad got sued by the parents because of it, but they called me to the stand and described the wounds I sustained trying to save the little boy. The family was shamefaced and asked their lawyer to withdraw the case. The little boy wasn't even frightened, and he didn't have a mark on him. But the judge wasn't so forgiving. He said that Dad should have had better fencing in place, and he named a figure for Dad to pay the family. But by then, Dad spent all his money on his pretty gold digger and had to borrow on the game park to pay off the little boy's family, and to take care of his legal fees. He lost everything. I guess he thinks I owe him for that."

"It seems to me that he owes you," Boone said coldly.

"Same here," Hayes agreed. He got to his feet. "I'd better get some backup over here. I'll talk to the security guard, too." He glanced at Boone. "You staying?"

"You bet I am," Boone replied doggedly. "I'm not

leaving her in here alone in case her father gets past you."

Hayes smiled. "I don't think he will, but better safe than sorry. Want a gun?"

Boone chuckled. "I never needed one. I still don't."

"Okay. Sing out if you need help. Thanks, Keely," he told her.

She nodded.

Hayes left and she stared curiously at Boone. "Why don't you need a gun?" she asked him.

"I had the highest score in my unit in hand-to-hand combat," he said simply. "I could even disarm my men when they came at me with weapons."

Her eyes sparkled. "Wow."

He shrugged. "It's a skill. We all have them." He smiled at her. "Yours is handling animals. I never told you that Bailey bites, did I?"

"He's never bitten me," she said, confused.

"You're the only person who knows him who can say that," he told her with a twinkle in his eyes. "Like I said. You have skills."

She smiled back.

He got to his feet and moved to the door, opened it and looked both ways. He came back into the room. He'd just turned toward the closet when the door opened suddenly and Brent Welsh came into the room.

"Quick, Keely, give me the money!" he told Keely abruptly. "Hayes Carson was downstairs—he got Jock the minute we walked in the door! Somebody tipped them off!"

"Then you should be safe," Keely told him. "If Sheriff Carson has Jock."

"I'll never have enough money to be safe," he said.

"But at least I can get away from the Fuentes bunch. Where's the—"

In a movement so fluid that Keely almost missed it, Boone caught Welsh's arm, swung him around and pinned him to the wall. He held him there with one big hand while he flipped open his cell phone and pushed a button.

"Let me go!" Brent pleaded with his captor. "I can't go to jail here, they'll kill me!"

"What a tragedy that would be," Boone drawled.

The door burst open and Hayes walked in, closing his cell phone. He put away the .40 caliber Glock he'd been holding even with his right temple, and grinned at Boone. "You don't forget that military training, do you?" He chuckled.

Boone grinned. "I get in some practice on stubborn bulls at roundup. Here." He propelled Welsh around so that Hayes could handcuff him.

"Keely, tell them to let me go!" Brent called to his daughter. "I'm innocent. It was Jock! He did it!"

Keely felt sick. She'd almost believed her father's false apology. "I can't help you," she said sadly. "Nobody can, now."

Brent's face darkened and he began to curse. Hayes grimaced as he pushed the man out of the room ahead of him and turned him over to a deputy.

"Sorry about that," he told Keely. "We had him, but he slipped away. We've got him now, thanks to you," he told Boone, "and his partner, as well. I'll talk to you later. Don't worry, Keely," he added. "These two are wanted for murder in Arizona. I imagine there'll be an extradition hearing very soon. Good job, Boone. If you ever want to work for me…?"

"I'd never fit in," Boone told him. "I use real curse words."

Hayes made a face at him. "'Crackers and Milk' is a perfectly good curse," he informed his friend.

"Ha!"

Hayes left with his dignity intact.

Boone moved to the bed and tugged Keely up into his arms, careful not to jar her sore arm. "And now we can concentrate on happier times," he said gently, smiling as he kissed her with breathless tenderness.

SHE HAD A room next to Winnie's upstairs, the most beautiful bedroom she'd ever seen in her life. She was afraid to walk on the carpet, which was pure white, dramatic against the blue curtains and bedspread and the blue tile in the bathroom.

"Gosh, the bathroom is bigger than my whole bedroom at home," she exclaimed when Boone carried her in and laid her on the bed.

"We like a lot of space," he told her, smiling. "Comfortable?"

She sank into fathoms of feathery softness. "Oh, yes!"

Winnie and Clark came in behind them, bearing flowers and fruit.

"The flowers came from the girls at your office," Winnie told her, "and the fruit's from Dr. Rydel."

"Does he often send you presents?" Boone asked darkly.

"Only when I get bitten by rattlesnakes and end up in the hospital," she told him solemnly.

Winnie and Clark burst out laughing.

Boone flushed a little. "Cut it out," he muttered.

He pulled his hat low over his eyes. "I've got to get the boys working out on the west pasture. I'll be back in time for supper." He grinned at Keely. "When you're better, you can make us some more yeast rolls."

She laughed, flattered that he'd liked them. "Okay."

"But not yet," he cautioned.

She saluted him. He laughed out loud, winked at his siblings, and left them with Keely.

"Imagine that." Winnie sighed, smiling. "You and Boone."

Keely flushed. "He's just being kind."

"Do you think so?" Clark mused. "I don't."

"Shoo," Winnie told her brother. "I'm going to settle Keely, then I have to go in and work for a few hours. I'm on a split shift this week."

"You're worth a fortune, and you're working for wages." Clark sighed.

Winnie made a face at him. "I like working for wages."

Clark's eyes twinkled. "You like working with Kilraven."

Winnie blushed. "He's just one of the guys I work with, now that I'm working dispatch full-time."

Clark wiggled both eyebrows and laughed as he walked out.

"Besides," Winnie told her best friend, "Kilraven doesn't like me."

Keely had doubts about that, but she didn't say a word. She just smiled.

Winnie helped her get into a flower-print ankle-length cotton gown with short puffy sleeves and a high neckline. She winced at the scars. "You poor thing," she said with genuine sympathy. "It must have been so painful!"

Keely lost her self-consciousness at that expression. "Most people would have said how horrible it looks. Yes, it was terrible. The first few days were the worst of my life. And then, even when it started healing, there were the scars." She shivered and leaned back into the pillows with a sigh. "But I guess it was really a blessing in disguise, because Jock had just gotten out of prison after two years, and he came on to me the day he got back. The scars were all that saved me from him. He thought I was repulsive." She looked at Winnie meaningfully. "I was thirteen years old," she said bitterly.

Winnie sat down on the bed beside her and squeezed her hand. "Some men are animals," she said gently. "Men used to come on to me when I went to parties because they knew who I was, who my family was. They didn't really want me, they wanted the wealth and power I had access to. Boone spent a lot of time making threats." She laughed. "That's why I like working for the emergency management center," she added. "Some of the newer people don't even know I come from a wealthy background. They treat me like everybody else. It's flattering."

Keely was curious. "Kilraven knows who you are."

Winnie nodded. She frowned. "It's odd, isn't it, that he doesn't seem to mind." She hesitated, looking down at her lap. "But most of the time he treats me just like he does the other dispatchers."

"I've always dreamed about Boone," Keely said. "I never thought he might feel the same way about me."

Winnie laughed. "I had a hunch about that when he

went off and beat up the private detective," she mused. "That's not like Boone. It wasn't just guilt, either. He may think you're too young, Keely, but he seems to have come to grips with your age."

Keely smiled. "I'm old for my age," she said drily. "And I'll say amen to that!"

CHAPTER FOURTEEN

BOONE CAME HOME dusty and worn-out, having helped move steers from summer pasture into the holding pens nearby, where they'd be held until they could be shipped to a feedlot for finishing as yearlings.

It was a long, arduous process, and somebody always got hurt. Fortunately, Keely noted, it wasn't Boone.

"You pay your foreman a fortune to do that job, and then you go out and work like you're him," Winnie fussed as he came into Keely's bedroom after he'd showered.

"I'm not cut out for the life of a gentleman of leisure," he pointed out, smiling. "How're you doing, sprout?" he asked Keely.

"Much better," she assured him. "Have you heard anything from Hayes Carson?"

He shook his head. "He'll get back in touch with us when he's got something to say. Meanwhile, stop worrying. You're safe here."

She smiled. "I know. It wasn't that. I just wondered."

"I'm starved," he told Winnie. "When are we eating?"

"Mrs. Johnston's outdone herself," Winnie replied with a grin. "Beef stew and Mexican corn bread."

"Worth working all day for," he said. "I'll bring yours up," he told Keely.

"I could come downstairs," she began.

"Not until Coltrain says you can," he replied firmly. "We don't want a relapse, now, do we?"

"I guess not. My arm's better, though," she said, moving it gingerly. "The swelling's gone down a lot."

"Damned snake," he muttered.

"That's exactly what I said when it happened," Keely assured him.

He grinned. "You do look better." His eyes slid over the flowered gown. They were bold and possessive.

THE MEMORY OF that look kept her occupied all through supper. He'd brought it himself, on a tray, to the amusement of Winnie, Clark and Mrs. Johnston, who added a flower in a vase to the tray.

After supper, Winnie went straight to her bedroom to change clothes. Clark went out. Boone changed into pajamas and a robe and came walking into Keely's bedroom with a file folder in his hand, reading glasses on and a pencil over one ear. He piled into bed with Keely, propping himself up on two of the mound of pillows Mrs. Johnston had brought her. He proceeded to open the folder and read.

Keely was fascinated. "What are you doing?"

"Working on printouts of the breeding program that our cow-and-calf foreman brought me," he told her. "We breed for certain traits, like low birth weight and lean conformation, and we use computers to make projections for us." He showed her the information on the pages.

"No. I mean…I mean, what are you doing in here, like that?" She indicated his pajamas and robe.

He gave her a conspiratorial grin. "I'm sleeping with you."

"You are not!" she gasped. "In the first place, I can't—"

"Sleeping," he emphasized. "You close your eyes and the next thing you know, it's morning."

She relaxed a little, but she was still wary.

"All the doors are open," he pointed out, nodding toward the hall. "They'll stay open. Nobody will notice that I'm in here."

Winnie walked past the doorway and smiled. She stopped suddenly, turned and stared.

Boone glowered at her. "What's the matter with you?" he asked his sister. "Haven't you ever seen a man in pajamas and a robe before?"

"You're in bed with Keely," she stated. "She's still fragile," she added worriedly.

"That's true, but her father's friend is something of an escape artist," he agreed. He reached into his pocket and pulled out a worn-looking Smith & Wesson .38 caliber police special. He put it up again. "Nobody's getting past me."

Winnie stopped looking shocked and began to grin. "I get it."

"Good. While you're getting things, how about getting Bailey and his bed out of my room and bringing them both in here?" he added. "He'll start howling if the light goes off and he's alone in there."

"He really does," Winnie told Keely. "He thinks Boone will die if he isn't there to protect him."

Keely smiled. "He's a sweet old boy."

"Who, me?" Boone drawled, peering at her wickedly over his reading glasses.

"The dog!" she emphasized.

"Oh." He went back to his spreadsheets, oblivious to the world.

Winnie chuckled. "I'll get Bailey."

SHE DID. SHE also got Clark and Mrs. Johnston. They all peered in from the hall, fascinated. Boone had never even brought a woman upstairs in living memory, and here he was in bed, in his pajamas, with Keely.

Clark started to speak. Boone lifted the gun, displayed it, put it back in his pocket without looking up from the spreadsheet.

"I haven't said anything!" Clark protested. "You shouldn't threaten people with guns just because they're curious!"

"It's for Keely's father's evil friend," Winnie told him.

"Oh. Oh!" Clark finally got it. "Okay."

Mrs. Johnston was grinning from ear to ear. Her white hair seemed to vibrate. She and Clark and Winnie just stood, staring and grinning. Boone reached in his other pocket and brought out a jeweler's box, just the size to contain a ring. He displayed it, still without looking up from the spreadsheet, and put it away again. Now Keely was looking breathless, too.

"Here's Bailey and his bed," Winnie said as she put the dog pallet on Boone's side of the bed. "We'll close the door on our way out."

"You'll do no such thing," Boone told her curtly. "This is a respectable household. No hanky-panky above stairs." He glared at Clark. "From anybody."

Clark threw up his hands. "I once, only once, sneaked a girl into my room for immoral purposes. He never forgets!"

"It was an act of charity," Winnie chided Boone. "He found her wandering all alone on a street corner and brought her home to get a blanket to put around her."

Everybody burst out laughing, even Clark.

"All right, that's enough. Everybody out. I've got work to do, then we're going to have a decent night's sleep." He glanced down at Keely, who was watching him with openly worshipful eyes. He smiled tenderly. "Some of us could use it more than others."

"I won't argue with that," Keely replied.

While they were looking at each other, their audience vanished.

Boone glanced at the doorway and chuckled deep in his throat as he looked down at his bedmate. "I do have evil purposes in mind," he confided in a low tone, "but they're probably all hiding ten feet from the door, waiting for developments. So we have to behave."

She sighed deeply. "Okay," she replied. Her hand, under the sheet, reached over to touch his muscular arm. She closed her eyes, comforted by the contact. "I've been afraid to sleep for days," she whispered. "Now I'm not."

He smoothed a hand over her blond hair. "Go to sleep," he said. "I'll keep you safe."

"I know that."

He went back to the spreadsheet. Seconds later, in the long silence that followed, three sets of eyes peered cautiously in the door.

"What?" Boone asked belligerently.

They scattered to the four winds. Bailey climbed into his bed, circled a few times, lay down and yawned and went back to sleep.

THE NEXT MORNING, Keely heard a car drive up. She opened her eyes slowly, disoriented. She was lying next to a warm, hard body that had her wrapped up gently against it. They were both under the covers.

Boone looked down at her warmly. "Ready for

breakfast?" he asked softly. "I hear movement from the general direction of the kitchen."

She curled closer. "I could eat."

They were both on her side of the bed and had apparently been close like that all night. Keely felt so safe and cozy that she was reluctant to move.

Voices murmured downstairs, and heavy, quick footsteps came up the staircase. Hayes Carson walked in, his uniform a little rumpled, like his blond, brown-streaked hair under his Stetson.

He stopped, lifting both eyebrows.

Boone yawned. "I've got a gun," he murmured.

"I haven't said anything yet," Hayes protested.

Boone glared at him. "To protect Keely with," he added.

"Oh."

Hayes marched over to the bed, threw his hat on the carpeted floor, climbed in next to Boone and lay back on the pillows. "God, I'm tired! I've been up all night helping interrogate Keely's father and his friend."

"Make yourself comfortable," Boone drawled sarcastically.

"Thanks, I will," Hayes replied. "This is the most comfortable bed I've ever been in," he added. He reached down, scooped up his hat and set it over his eyes. "I could sleep for a week!"

"Tell me what you're doing here first," Boone said.

"In order to save his skin, Keely's father made a plea deal. He gave us his friend Jock on a murder charge. It seems that Jock killed a woman in Arizona. He was the chief suspect, but they couldn't get the evidence to convict him. Keely's father has a watch that belonged to the dead woman, and he can put Jock there at the time of the murder." He smiled under the hat.

"What about my father?" Keely wanted to know.

"Three to five, on accessory charges. We talked to the assistant D.A. last night, too."

"Maybe it will teach him something," Keely said, but she didn't sound convinced.

"Don't look for miracles," Boone advised. "With lawbreakers, they rarely happen."

"Like you know," Hayes drawled from under the hat. He crossed his long legs.

There was the sound of another car arriving. A car door slammed. Voices murmured. Another sound of footsteps, but these were soft and quick and almost undetectable.

Kilraven poised in the doorway, staring. "Well, if that isn't just like county law enforcement," he muttered. "Walk out in the middle of an interrogation and leave the hard work to the local law!"

"Shut up, Kilraven," Hayes said pleasantly. "I haven't slept since night before last."

"Like I have!" Kilraven shot back. He scowled. He shrugged. "Hell, maybe you're right. A little rest might perk us all up. Hi, Keely," he greeted as he sank down onto the foot of the bed and sprawled across it at Hayes's booted feet. "Say, this is a really soft bed," he mused, closing his own eyes.

There were other footsteps. "Isn't anybody coming down for breakfast…?"

Winnie stood in the doorway, absolutely dumbstruck. There were four people in the bed. Two of them were in uniform.

"I'm not bringing trays up here," she announced. "Anybody who wants breakfast has to come downstairs and get it." She grinned. "There's enough for company, too."

"Are we company?" Hayes asked drowsily.

"Apparently," Kilraven replied.

"I suppose we all have to get up." Hayes sighed.

"It is my bed," Boone pointed out. "And Keely and I were here first."

Hayes sat up. He frowned. "What are you doing in bed with Keely?"

He produced the revolver from his pocket.

"Gun!" Kilraven exclaimed.

Boone just shook his head and laughed.

THE GUESTS STAYED for breakfast and then went on their way. Kilraven was giving Winnie an odd look. She was subdued with him now. It was as if all the joy and bubbly fun had gone out of her forever. She knew there was no chance that he'd ever care for her in any permanent way, and she wasn't the sort for temporary liaisons. It broke her heart.

Kilraven tried to catch her eye as he and Hayes headed out the front door, but she wouldn't look at him. She said goodbye in a perfectly natural, pleasant tone and went back to the table. Kilraven was frowning when he left.

"Don't you have a meeting with some visiting cattlemen today?" Winnie asked Boone.

"Yes, for a couple of hours. They want to see our artificial insemination labs."

"I have to get to work," Winnie said reluctantly. She glanced at Keely. "Clark's already gone up to Dallas for a meeting with some investors, and Mrs. Johnston's gone shopping."

"Bailey will protect me," she told them, reaching down to pet the old dog.

"You won't need protecting now," Boone said

gently. "Your father and Jock are safely behind bars at the detention center in San Antonio. They don't lose prisoners."

"So we hear," Winnie had to agree. "Make sure you keep the doors locked," she cautioned Keely.

"Of course I will," she said, smiling. "Don't worry. I survived a rattlesnake bite."

"You're tough all right," Winnie had to admit. "I'll be back as soon as I get off work. Take care."

"You, too," Keely said gently.

Winnie bent to kiss her and Boone before she left for her job. She managed to hide her heartbreak from them. She didn't want to spoil their joy in each other.

THE HOUSE WAS very quiet, with only the two of them in it, both still in their pajamas. Boone looked at Keely with an expression she'd never seen on his face before. He got up slowly, pulled out her chair, swung her up into his arms and started for the staircase.

"Time for dessert," he whispered, bending to her mouth.

"It was breakfast. You don't have dessert with breakfast."

"Yes, we do."

He kissed her hungrily. After a few seconds, Keely forgot her protests, wrapped her good arm around his neck and kissed him back with enthusiasm. He laughed softly at her innocent eagerness, and proceeded to teach her the proper technique. By the time they got back to his room, she was ready for promotion to the next level.

He put her down long enough to close and lock the door. His high cheekbones were faintly flushed with the force of his desire. "It's been years," he bit off, his dark eyes blazing down into hers. "I want you."

She was breathless, frightened, exhilarated, all at once. But those old scruples were grinding away at her.

"I know," he said softly. "You want to wait for a ceremony. That's weeks away." He pulled her to him, pushed her hips against the hard thrust of his body. "Don't make me wait," he whispered huskily.

"Boone…" She was torn, tortured.

He reached into his pocket and pulled out the jewelry box. He opened it. Inside were an emerald solitaire and an emerald-and-diamond-studded yellow-gold set of rings. "Everybody in this house knows that I intend to marry you. I've had this set of rings for weeks, waiting for Hayes to get enough evidence to put damned Misty and her father out of business! A piece of paper with a seal isn't going to make that much difference. With this ring," he said tenderly, sliding the emerald solitaire onto her ring finger, "I thee wed. The rest will come later. I love you, Keely," he added with reverence. "I'll love you until I die. Will you marry me?"

She could barely see the ring or him for the blur of tears. "Yes," she whispered.

He bent and drew his lips over hers, teasing them apart, coaxing them to admit the long, slow thrust of his tongue into her mouth.

She gasped as a charge of passion as powerful as a lightning strike shook her slender body. The shock was in her eyes when she met his.

"We begin here, now, Keely," he said solemnly. "The first day of the rest of our lives. Let me love you."

She was already too far gone to think of refusing him. His hands were under the gown, making non-sense of her fears about her scars. She closed her eyes, moaning softly, as his fingers smoothed expertly over the thrust of her breasts, followed in short order by his hungry mouth.

"Yes," she whispered unsteadily. And for long, passionate minutes, she said nothing more.

He paused just long enough to protect her. "It's too soon for babies," he whispered against her damp breasts. "We have a lot of living to do first. Then, when we're comfortable with each other, they'll come naturally."

"I love children," she said softly.

He smiled. "So do I."

Her arm protested when she reached up to him, but she ignored the pain. He pleasured her for a long time, until she was shivering all over with desire, pleading for an end to the anguish. At that moment, she felt him lose control. She arched up eagerly to meet the hard downward thrust of his body and tensed, crying out softly, as the barrier protested its invasion.

He hesitated, his whole body pulsing. "I hurt you," he ground out.

"Only a little," she whispered, because he looked as if it hurt him, too. "Don't stop."

"As if I could," he managed to say. He laughed as he moved again, and then he groaned and drove for fulfillment, helpless to stop himself.

She moved with him, blind with need, pulsating with delight that grew sharper and more pleasurable with every single second. She felt him in an intimacy that she'd never dreamed possible. Her last thought was that the culmination was going to kill her. The pleasure was so intense that, at the end, she cried out in a high-pitched, keening little tone that she'd never heard torn from her throat in her lifetime.

They clung together in the aftermath. He was spent. He could hardly breathe. Under him, Keely was holding tight, biting into his muscles with her short nails, still moving helplessly against him as the pleasure ebbed and flowed in her untried body. She was only just learning that the peak wasn't really the peak. She could feel the echoes of that intense, shattering climax happen over and over, just by moving in the right way.

He indulged her for a time, but then his lean hand caught her hip and stilled her. "No more," he whispered. "You're very new to this. It will be uncomfortable if we don't stop."

"Oh," she protested.

He kissed her tenderly. "Besides," he whispered, "we're tempting fate. These things are only good for one use. They can break."

Her eyes opened and looked up into his. They widened. "They can?"

She'd sounded almost hopeful. He chuckled. "It's rare, when that happens. We don't need a baby right now, at the beginning of our marriage."

"Are you sure we don't?" she asked.

He kissed her again. "I'm sure. And it isn't because I don't want one," he clarified. "I want time for us to travel and learn about each other."

"Travel."

He chuckled. "Anywhere you want to go."

"You mean, we could go to Wyoming and see Old Faithful?" she asked excitedly.

He propped up on one elbow. "I was thinking of someplace more exotic."

"Oh. Like Florida." She nodded.

He scowled. "The pyramids. Chichén Itzá. Sacsayhuamán. Zimbabwe. Those sorts of places."

"You mean, go overseas?" she exclaimed. "We could do that?"

He studied her rapt, pretty little face, and he smiled again. "Yes. We could do that."

"Wow."

He kissed her once more and withdrew, wincing when she winced. "I told you," he mused. "It takes time and practice to avoid these little pitfalls."

"I suppose so." She looked at his broad chest, where deep scars cut across it. There were more on his belly, and one, much worse, on his broad thigh. She reached out and touched them, testing the hard ridges with her fingertips, exploring. "Badges of honor," she murmured aloud.

He was watching her watching him, his dark eyes keen and alert. He smiled. "I've been self-conscious about these for years."

"They aren't that bad," she replied.

His own eyes were on her shoulder, her scars equally as deep as his and less cared for. "If you want to have plastic surgery, you can," he told her. "But I'd love you if you were missing an arm or a leg. Nothing will ever change the way I feel. And I don't mind your scars."

"I don't mind yours." She reached over and kissed his chest, where the thickest, hardest ridge ran right across it, diagonally. "I'm so glad that stupid woman ran from you," she murmured.

He laughed. "So am I, now."

She cuddled close to him, more secure and less embarrassed. It seemed to be a natural thing, this combining of bodies. It was certainly fulfilling.

He wrapped her up in his arms, careful not to jar the sore one any more than he already had. He closed his eyes. He'd never been so happy in all his life.

HE'D PLANNED TO have a big wedding, but his conscience got the better of him, so the next day he drove
Keely over to the probate judge's office in Jacobsville
and married her.

"You really are a prude, you know," Keely teased
him when they were back on the street wearing wedding bands, with the license in Keely's handbag.

He shrugged. "Pot calling the kettle black," he replied, smiling tenderly.

She pressed close against him, still a little weak and
shaky from the snakebite, but so happy that she felt
like bursting. "There's one thing left that we have to
do," she said reluctantly.

"Yes. Do you want to call Carly, or shall I?"

She linked her fingers into his. "I'll call her."

THEY HAD THE funeral a week later, a small memorial
service at the cemetery, where Ella Welsh was buried
next to her parents. It was a sad interlude in a happy
whirl, because Winnie had insisted on a society wedding. Boone and Keely reluctantly gave in. Winnie's
enthusiasm was contagious.

So they were married in the autumn, with the ma-
ples wearing glorious red-and-gold coats, and chry-
santhemums for Keely's bouquet. She tossed it outside
the church and watched with amusement as her bridesmaids scrambled for it. But it was the best man, Hayes
Carson, who caught the bouquet. He grinned widely
and gave a courtly bow when everyone stared at him.
A glowering Dr. Bentley Rydel had also attended the
wedding, along with Keely's coworkers, and Carly,
who cried buckets and said that Keely was the most
beautiful bride she'd ever seen.

Boone and Keely went away for a month, touring

Spain and Africa and much of Europe. They came home weary of travel, but with beautiful memories.

"You're not going to be happy giving morning teas for brides and hostessing dinner parties, are you?" Boone asked when they'd finished supper and were sitting in front of the fireplace in the living room.

"I'm not cut out for it," she replied worriedly.

He grinned and pulled her close. "Then do what you please."

"I'd like to go back to work for Dr. Rydel," she said slowly. "I guess you wouldn't like that?"

He looked down into her wide, soft green eyes. "We've already agreed that you have skills, and they apply to animals. I think it would be a good idea. I'll have days when I have to be out of town on business, and I'll have workshops and conferences to go to. You can come to some of them, but you won't like being on the road so much. Work for Rydel." He kissed her. "Just don't forget where you live and who loves you."

She grinned and kissed him back. "I could never forget that."

He stretched and yawned. "Clark's got a new girl, Winnie says," he murmured after a peaceful silence. "A nice one, this time. She works in a library."

Keely smiled. "Good for Clark. How about Winnie?"

He hesitated. "I don't know. She's changed. She's gone all silent lately. Probably mooning over Kilraven." He shook his head. "That bird isn't going to settle down in some small town. He's got *big city* written all over him."

Keely promised herself that she'd make time to talk to her best friend and let her cry it all out.

"Sleepy?" he asked.

She nuzzled against his shoulder. "Not really. Why? Did you have something in mind?" she teased.

"In fact, I did." He leaned closer, brushed his mouth over hers in a whisper of contact. "Yeast rolls."

Unprepared, she burst out laughing. "Yeast rolls?"

"I haven't had a decent roll since before we married," he pointed out, "and you're all healed now. Besides, nobody makes bread like you do."

"Well, if that's how you feel, I'd love to bake you some yeast rolls!" she replied. Her eyes shimmered with amusement. "But I'd need a little encouragement, first."

He pursed his lips. "What sort of encouragement?"

"Be inventive," she coaxed.

He got to his feet, swung her up into his arms and started for the staircase. "Inventive," he assured her with a chuckle, "is my middle name."

She tucked her face under his chin and listened to the heavy, hard beat of his heart and smiled with anticipation. She felt as if she were being reimbursed for all the long years of loneliness and sorrow that she'd endured. Her scars, she decided, didn't matter so much after all. And the happiness she'd found with Boone was worth every one.

* * * * *

YOU HAVE JUST READ A
HARLEQUIN
SPECIAL EDITION
BOOK

If you **enjoyed** reading this **page-turning romance,** be sure to look for all six Harlequin Special Edition books every month.

REQUEST YOUR FREE BOOKS!

2 FREE NOVELS
FROM THE ROMANCE COLLECTION
PLUS 2 FREE GIFTS!

YES! Please send me 2 FREE novels from the Romance Collection and my 2 FREE gifts (gifts are worth about $10). After receiving them, if I don't wish to receive any more books, I can return the shipping statement marked "cancel." If I don't cancel, I will receive 4 brand-new novels every month and be billed just $5.99 per book in the U.S. or $6.49 per book in Canada. That's a saving of at least 25% off the cover price. It's quite a bargain! Shipping and handling is just 50¢ per book in the U.S. and 75¢ per book in Canada.* I understand that accepting the 2 free books and gifts places me under no obligation to buy anything. I can always return a shipment and cancel at any time. Even if I never buy another book, the two free books and gifts are mine to keep forever.

194/394 MDN FELQ

Name	(PLEASE PRINT)	

Address		Apt. #

City	State/Prov.	Zip/Postal Code

Signature (if under 18, a parent or guardian must sign)

Mail to the **Reader Service:**
IN U.S.A.: P.O. Box 1867, Buffalo, NY 14240-1867
IN CANADA: P.O. Box 609, Fort Erie, Ontario L2A 5X3

Not valid for current subscribers to the Romance Collection
or the Romance/Suspense Collection.

Want to try two free books from another line?
Call 1-800-873-8635 or visit www.ReaderService.com.

* Terms and prices subject to change without notice. Prices do not include applicable taxes. Sales tax applicable in N.Y. Canadian residents will be charged applicable taxes. Offer not valid in Quebec. This offer is limited to one order per household. All orders subject to credit approval. Credit or debit balances in a customer's account(s) may be offset by any other outstanding balance owed by or to the customer. Please allow 4 to 6 weeks for delivery. Offer available while quantities last.

Your Privacy—The Reader Service is committed to protecting your privacy. Our Privacy Policy is available online at www.ReaderService.com or upon request from the Reader Service.

We make a portion of our mailing list available to reputable third parties that offer products we believe may interest you. If you prefer that we not exchange your name with third parties, or if you wish to clarify or modify your communication preferences, please visit us at www.ReaderService.com/consumerschoice or write to us at Reader Service Preference Service, P.O. Box 9062, Buffalo, NY 14269. Include your complete name and address.

DIVE INTO OTHER GREAT

HARLEQUIN
SPECIAL EDITION

BOOKS

Ever dream about meeting that **perfect someone** even if he's a single dad who happens to be a Texas tycoon or the **mysterious** new man in town? Harlequin Special Edition will take you there.

Take a break from the everyday and **dive into** an **amazing journey** through the ups and downs of finding **love** while juggling family, second chances and more! Six new books every month.

If thrilling romances and heart-racing action is what you're after, then check out Harlequin Romantic Suspense!

NEW LOOK COMING DEC 18!

Featuring bold women, unforgettable men and the life-and-death situations that bring them together, these stories deliver!

Dial up the passion to Red-Hot with the Harlequin Blaze series!

Harlequin Blaze stories sizzle with strong heroines and irresistible heroes playing the game of modern love and lust. They're fun, sexy and always steamy.

Red-Hot Reads

www.Harlequin.com

HBPOS

It all starts with a kiss

Check out the brand-new series

HARLEQUIN KISS

Fun, flirty and sensual romances.
ON SALE JANUARY 22!